MYSTERY FOLLOWS HER

A COZY MYSTERY MULTI-AUTHOR COLLECTION

DIANNE ASCROFT   ELLEN JACOBSON
TAMARA WOODS   SARAH BIGLOW
AUBREY ELLE   BEATE BOEKER
ADRIANA LICIO   VIKKI WALTON
ANGELA K. RYAN

MYSTERY FOLLOWS HER

A Cozy Mystery Multi-Author Collection

Edition I

Cover Designer: DLR Cover Designs

CONTENTS

THANKSGIVING AND THEFT

DIANNE ASCROFT

1

"It's so good to be back here. I'm glad you invited me." Lois Stone smiled at the motherly black-haired woman beside her as they walked along the quiet residential street.

Lois was surprised by how good it felt to be back in her old Toronto neighbourhood. She had only left the city early in the summer, barely three months ago, and the time had flown since then. Fenwater was so different from the big city and she had been fully occupied discovering everything about her new hometown.

In recent years she had become increasingly worried about the dangers of city life and an incident in the spring had been the final straw, spurring her to leave the city and move to the small town of Fenwater. But she had missed her old neighbourhood and her friends. How could she not? Until her husband's untimely death three years ago, she had shared more than twenty years with him in a house across the road from where she was standing. They had always been involved in their community and enjoyed the company of their neighbours. Her neighbours were especially good to her after James's death.

Maria Rizzo smiled back at Lois. "Angelo and I are so happy you spend Thanksgiving with us. We miss you and your cats."

"I've missed both of you too. You'll be glad to hear that the cats have completely settled into our new home."

"Good. You won't worry about them while you're away. Just enjoy the weekend. We have a big Italian-Canadian Thanksgiving with all our family and friends at the restaurant on Monday."

"That sounds wonderful! No one cooks like you do, Maria."

Lois knew this very well as Maria had often brought her meals in the weeks after her husband's death when Lois could barely motivate herself to do anything. Maria's kindness was one of the things that had got her through her first months alone.

"We walk too far? You tired after such a long drive?" Maria asked.

Lois glanced at her powder blue Volkswagen Beetle parked at the curb in front of the Rizzos' house. "No, I'm fine. It's only an hour and a half from Fenwater to here and we've only walked around a few streets. I'm not tired at all."

Lois was delighted to wander the streets that comprised her old neighbourhood. Situated in a small valley in the west end of Toronto, the neighbourhood was about fifteen streets long and four streets wide. A central road ran through the length of the valley and a park, which flanked the Humber River, nestled into one side, parallel to the road. Steep hills at either end of the valley separated it from the chaos of the city.

"Good. We will walk in the park then come home for coffee. I baked Savoiardi biscuits this morning." In answer to Lois's puzzled frown, Maria explained, "Ladies fingers. That's what you call them."

"Oh, I know the ones you mean. Your ladyfingers are

delicious. That's something I've missed. And, like I said, I really missed you too."

Lois felt the lump in her throat as she spoke. Despite her growing unease about the safety of life in the city earlier this year, she hadn't wanted to leave her friends.

Maria smiled. "Angelo and I missed you too. It's good you come for Thanksgiving."

Maria linked her arm through Lois's and the two women continued walking, past the Rizzos' white clapboard house to the end of the street. They crossed the road and passed a sand-coloured brick bungalow, the former home of Lois's best friend Marge Kirkwood. Images of summer evenings on their way to the park to watch the sunset, when Lois and her husband had stopped to chat with Marge as she sat on her tiny porch, popped into Lois's head. Marge had sold her bungalow a little over a year ago and moved to Fenwater to be near her aging mother. When Lois's fear of the city had become unbearable this spring, Marge had persuaded Lois to follow her to the quiet town.

Next to Marge's former home was the narrow pedestrian entrance to the park. Lois took a deep breath and tried to quell the anxiety that suddenly swelled in her chest as they approached it. There was nothing to worry about. They were going for a walk in a lovely park where she had spent many happy hours when she lived in this neighbourhood. On this sunny October afternoon, the clusters of trees that stood along the riverbank, and also the outer perimeter of the park, separating the neighbourhood streets from the grassy expanse within, would be adorned with brightly coloured leaves. Some of them would flit on the breeze and drift to the ground, creating brittle, rustling piles for children to scatter. A few cyclists and joggers would pass them on the paved path that ran through the park, curving to match the course of the river. The Humber River flowed the length of the park from somewhere north of Toronto to Lake Ontario at its southern end, dropping over a series of small waterfalls, set out at intervals along the route. Often parents, with baby carriages parked beside them, sat on the bank near the waterfalls, letting the sound of the steady rushing water soothe their infants.

During Toronto summers, Lois had never tired of watching the rippling water flow past her, and the antics of the birds and other wildlife. In the fall she followed the progress of the squirrels frantically hoarding acorns for winter. She smiled at the thought of the busy creatures. They were sure to see some of them scurrying up and down tree trunks today.

As they entered the park, Lois slowly let out the deep breath she had taken and surveyed the grassy area in front of her. There was a cyclist in the distance but other than that the park was deserted. It felt calm and peaceful in the way she remembered before fear had become the emotion she associated with this place. As she gazed up the path, she imagined for a moment that James was walking toward them. She blinked and looked again. No one was there. She had known there wouldn't be. James was gone forever. She made an effort to push away the sadness that followed, determined to enjoy her time here with Maria.

The two women strolled, arm in arm, along the path. Lois took slow, deep breaths and tried to let her peaceful surroundings calm her. She would only think of the happy times here, not about the one that had changed everything.

When the breeze stilled, the fall sun warmed Lois's face. She spotted a black squirrel scurrying across the grass to the nearest tree, its cheeks bulging with provisions for the coming lean season.

She squeezed Maria's arm and nodded toward the squirrel. "Isn't he cute?"

Maria laughed and nodded. "And a hard worker. He will live well this winter."

They continued along the curving path as it meandered toward the river. The water flowed noisily over one of the small waterfalls and Lois thought of the place that had been her favourite spot, not far ahead along the river bank, where several tall oak trees shaded the small clearing they formed. For years she had loved to sit there with her back against one of the trees, gazing at the river or reading a book. She and James had often stopped there to watch the sunset. It had been a happy spot until the evening that Lois found James collapsed against one of the trees in the clearing. The night he died. But she wouldn't remember that night. She would think of all the other times she had spent there.

Lois decided that when they reached the spot, they would stop and watch the river, and she would remember only the happy times there. She drew in a shaky breath.

Maria turned to her, smiled and patted her arm. Her friend knew how painful some of Lois's memories of this place were. "You okay? We can just go home for coffee."

Lois made herself smile. "I'm okay. Let's keep walking."

The stand of oak trees and its clearing was not far ahead. Lois gazed at it as they approached. In the light breeze, golden leaves rippled on the oak trees and a few of them drifted to the ground. It looked just as Lois remembered. When the women stepped into the clearing beyond the oak trees, they would be in a quiet enclosure removed from city life.

But, as they came closer, the peace was shattered by a high-pitched cry. Lois turned to Maria and the women looked at each other, wide-eyed. They stopped walking, listening intently. Another sound, more like a grunt, followed. Then a longer, low groan. The sounds came from behind the oak trees.

Lois pulled her arm free from Maria's and ran toward the

sounds. Images of James slumped against a tree in that clearing flashed through her mind. She had to help him and stop his attackers. Before her rational mind could catch up with her memories, and make sense of the sounds, she reached the oak trees and looked into the space beyond them. She stiffened, horrified by what she saw.

2

In the clearing, a white-haired woman cowered on her knees, gripping her purse. A man in grey fleece track pants and a dark blue jacket with the hood pulled up loomed over her hunched form, wrestling with her for the purse. The woman clung fiercely to it. Before Lois could move, the attacker slapped the woman's face and punched her arm hard, tugging at the purse.

The man's actions galvanised Lois into motion. She barrelled toward the struggling pair and launched herself at the attacker from behind. Wrapping one arm around his chest, she gripped his upper arm on his opposite side with her free hand.

Panting, she grunted, "Let go of her!"

The attacker thrust the white-haired woman away from him, pulling the purse from her grip as she fell. He shook himself, as if trying to shake off a pesky terrier, but Lois clung on, grunting as she wrestled with him. She felt something push against her shoulder and glanced to her right. She hadn't noticed Maria follow her into the clearing but her friend was now clinging to the attacker's shoulder. Despite the two women behind him, the man continued to struggle.

He shook his upper body from side to side, trying to loosen the women's hold on him.

Dropping the purse, the man swivelled abruptly to grab Maria's arm, taking her by surprise. He wrenched her grip free from him and pushed her away. She fell heavily against one of the trees. Lois's first impulse was to run to her friend to make sure she was okay but she wouldn't let the attacker get away. Not like the ones who had pounced on James when he was alone in this clearing with no one to help him. She held grimly to him.

With a low growl, the man half turned toward Lois and stuck one leg between hers. Kicking her right calf, he knocked her foot off the ground. Lois tightened her left arm around his chest but she lost her grip on his other side and her right hand flailed in the air, trying to grab his arm again. Her hand came down on his collarbone and her nails raked his neck as she tried to grip his shoulder, but she couldn't hold on as he twisted from side to side beneath her.

Lois felt the moment she lost her balance and began to fall backwards. Instinctively she reached behind her to break her fall, letting go of the man. She grunted her frustration. She couldn't let him get away, not like James's attackers had. She landed on the ground with a thud, her hands helping to break her fall while her legs spun in the air as if she were riding a bicycle upside down. As she hit the ground, she looked up and glimpsed the side of the attacker's face. It was a young face, narrow with longish sandy hair that stuck out of his hood and fell forward, hiding his eyes. He seemed familiar somehow.

Lois glanced sideways and saw Maria struggling to her feet. The man darted forward and pushed her friend's shoulder so that she fell to the ground again. Lois's forearms ached from the impact of the fall but she pushed herself upright, trembling as she shifted into a sitting position and pulled her legs under her. But before she could stand, the attacker turned from Maria to the purse lying near Lois. He scooped it up then ran from the clearing.

Lois scrambled to her feet in time to watch his lanky form barrelling across the park. She knew she wasn't fast enough to catch him and he had too much of a head start anyway. Pointing at his retreating figure, she shouted, "Help! Stop him!"

She darted glances back and forth as she shouted, searching the park for someone who could help, but no one was in sight to respond to her plea. As she watched helplessly, the attacker disappeared through the nearest exit, which led onto a street in the middle of the valley. He would be gone before Lois could get to the street. She turned and looked at the other two women.

Maria was on her feet and bent over the white-haired woman sitting on the ground.

Lois moved toward them. "Are you two okay?"

Maria nodded. "But I worry about this lady."

Lois bent over the white-haired woman. "Are you hurt, ma'am?"

The woman turned her agonised gaze toward Lois. "How can it be gone?"

"Your purse?"

The woman nodded. "I never go anywhere without it. What will I do?"

Lois rubbed the woman's shoulder. "Don't worry. We'll report it to the police. I'm sure they'll find him." She suppressed a sigh. *I know it's a long shot but I have to give her some hope.*

"But I can't replace it."

Lois frowned. "Did you have a lot of money in it?"

"My brooch."

"Did he steal your brooch too?"

"It was in the purse. I always bring it when I come here."

The woman continued as if she were talking to herself. "I meant to wear it today. Like every year."

Lois gently rubbed the woman's shoulder again. "Let's check whether you're hurt and then we'll get you off the ground. Do you have any pain anywhere?"

"Just my knees." The woman didn't resist when Lois examined her arms and legs then helped her to her feet. She hunched forward, pressing her arms tight against her body as if doing so would ease her mental pain.

"What's your name?" Lois asked.

"Sally. Sally Hayes."

"I'm Lois Stone and this is my friend, Maria Rizzo." Lois nodded toward her companion.

Sally nodded absently at the women. A frown wrinkled her face. "I guess I shouldn't carry it with me. I should have known it was safer at home."

"Your brooch?"

Sally nodded.

"What about money? Did you have much in your purse?" Lois asked.

"What's left of my pension cheque that I cashed at the bank last week."

"We'd better report this to the police as soon as possible. Maybe they can find him before he goes very far." Lois looked at Maria. "Would you go back to your house and phone the police?"

"Of course. I go right now. And you bring Mrs Hayes. It's too cold for her to stay here. I will have coffee and cookies waiting." Maria hurried away.

Lois gently slipped her hand under Sally's arm and led her toward the path. "My friend Maria lives just down the street from the park entrance. It's not far. Are you okay to walk?"

Sally nodded. "Oh, if only I'd worn it today like I do every year, my lovely leaf wouldn't be gone now."

"Your brooch?" Lois asked.

"Yes. It's a silver leaf with three white pearls on it. Vince gave it to me for my birthday." Sally's eyes had a faraway look, and she slowed her pace. "He said a leaf was a perfect present for a fall birthday."

Lois murmured soothingly. "Yes, it is. I see why it's so special to you."

"Oh yes, I treasure it. His last birthday gift to me. My birthday was Thanksgiving weekend that year. Nineteen fifty-four."

Lois kept a firm grip on Sally's arm and tried to urge her along the path. The breeze was getting chilly again and she wanted to get the older woman into the warmth of Maria's house. It would be better for her to wait for the police inside after the shock she had just had. "Oh, you've certainly had it a long time."

Sally nodded and her eyes filled with tears. "His last gift to me. I never imagined how soon everything would change after that Thanksgiving."

Lois felt herself choking up. She knew what it felt like to lose your life partner, especially when you weren't expecting it. She murmured soothingly but didn't speak.

Sally continued, "Hurricane Hazel hit the next weekend." She looked at Lois. "Were you here then?"

"No, my husband and I didn't come to the valley until about ten years later. But I've heard what a bad storm it was."

"You have no idea. We were hit hard here along the Humber River. Vince was on afternoon shift that day. John Inglis plant down on Queen West. His car got swept to the side of the road by the rising water several times, but he managed to get home. Then he went out again to check on a couple of our older neighbours on the street. That's when it hit our house."

Lois nodded but didn't interrupt Sally.

"The wind – it blew down an old beech tree in the

13

backyard. It came down right on the roof and smashed the kitchen window too. The water just poured in. From the attic into one of the bedrooms. I couldn't do anything to stop it. There was water everywhere. Vince boarded up the kitchen window when he got home. But it took a few days before we could do anything with the roof."

"Oh, that's terrible. It must have been so frightening for you alone in the house."

Sally nodded. "It was. But the worst thing was seeing how hard Vince had to work afterwards. We didn't have insurance so he was working lots of extra hours to pay for the repairs. We'd been in that house since we got married and Vince had done so much work to improve it over the years. We finally had it finished. And then the hurricane did so much damage. It was heartbreaking to have to do all that again."

"Oh dear. It must have been a hard time for you both."

"It was. The children helped us as much as they could but they were busy with their own young families. Vince did all the work he could as well as working extra hours to pay for the rest."

Lois smiled sympathetically. "He sounds like he was a wonderful husband."

"He was. There wasn't anything he wouldn't do for his family. That's why I lost him. I tried to tell him we didn't have to fix everything at once but he was determined. He wanted it back to normal as soon as possible for me. He worked himself to death the next few months till his heart just gave out. He had a heart attack at work and that was it."

"Oh, I'm so sorry." Lois felt her throat clog with unshed tears. She understood Sally's pain better than most would since James had come to this park for an evening run and was attacked by a group of teenagers. He collapsed due to the shock. No one knew he had a heart condition.

"That Thanksgiving. My birthday. Those were the last really happy, worry-free times we had together before the storm hit and Vince had to break his back to repair our home. So I come to the park every year around this weekend to think about him. I don't like cemeteries. I like to remember him here, near where our house was. Where we were happy. I always bring that brooch with me. Usually I wear it." Sally took a shuddering breath. "And today I didn't. Now it's gone."

Lois squeezed Sally's arm as they reached the entrance to the park. "Well, we're not far from Maria's house and the police should be there soon. The sooner we tell them what happened, the sooner they can start looking for the mugger and get it back for you."

"Do you think they can?"

"I really hope so."

3

S itting on the worn sofa at Beth Darrow's house that evening, Lois wrapped her hands around her mug of coffee and earnestly regarded her friend. "My heart just went out to her. The poor woman. Not only was she mugged but she lost a brooch that her late husband gave her." Her voice rose. "I'd string up that guy if I got hold of him."

"I don't know how anyone could do that to an old woman. It's terrible. I was scared last spring when I was threatened by someone I knew. It must be even more scary to be attacked by a complete stranger. You have no idea what they'll do." Beth shook her head slowly. "What a start to your visit to Toronto. Not what you expected, I'm sure."

Lois nodded emphatically. "Yes, you can say that again."

Beth regarded Lois, a smile lighting up her face. "I'm so glad you're here though. I've missed working with you on projects for the historical society and meeting you for lunch. And I've really missed you! It's so strange to walk into Annette Library and not see you sitting behind the reception desk."

"I've missed you too." Lois felt her throating tightening with emotion. She took a deep breath. "I don't miss the frightening things about the city that made me want to move but I do miss my friends. It's great to have Marge in Fenwater. She's introduced me to so many people and helped me settle in. But I wish I could have all my friends there with me."

Beth set her mug on the coffee table that was set between them. "Well, you're here this weekend so let's enjoy it. Have you got any plans?"

"I'll drop by the library tomorrow morning and see my friends on the staff. I'm sure I'll see some of the regular patrons too. I don't have any plans for Sunday. On Monday the Rizzos are hosting a private Thanksgiving dinner at their restaurant for family and friends. They asked me to invite you and your niece if she's not busy."

"Thanks. I'd love to come. When I phone Amy later, I'll invite her too."

"Good." Lois turned her gaze to look out of the front window at the veranda and the front yard beyond.

Beth followed her gaze. "This time of year I miss the flowerbed that borders the front path. It looks kind of bare out there with winter coming."

"Hmm, yes." Lois continued to stare out of the window.

"You always liked the pansies in that flowerbed."

Lois turned her gaze to her friend, her brow furrowed. "Mmm?"

"Every summer you always raved about the pansies," Beth repeated.

"Oh, yes, I did." Lois shook her head and set her mug on the coffee table. "Sorry, I'm a little distracted. I can't get what happened to poor Sally out of my mind. It makes me think of James too."

Beth raised her eyebrows. "Because she was also attacked in the park?"

Lois sighed. "Partly. And I guess it's knowing we both feel the same pain. She was robbed of the last gift her husband gave her. That must feel like losing him all over again. It's been more than three years now but I haven't stopped missing James. After seeing how upset Sally was, I think maybe you never do."

"I know you won't forget him, but I'm sure the pain will lessen as time goes on. And haven't you got a gentleman friend now in Fenwater?"

Lois's cheeks coloured. "Bruce? Yes, he's been a good friend to me since Marge introduced us. I like him. But he hasn't asked me out or anything. If he does, it will be difficult to try to move on when I still miss James so much. I'd feel a bit guilty."

Beth nodded, sympathetically. "Well, don't make any rash decisions. Take it slow and see what happens."

"I will." Lois stared out the front window again, sighing. "I wish the police officer had been more reassuring to Sally."

"The one that took her statement after the attack?"

Lois nodded. "Yes. He took statements from Sally, Maria and I, and he asked Sally to go to the police station next week to help them put together a composite of the attacker's face. But before he left, he said that they rarely get purses back in these types of robberies. Unless the thief takes the money out and drops it somewhere nearby it's not very likely."

"Aw, that wouldn't be what she'd want to hear."

"No, it wasn't. Sally was so upset when he said that. The money doesn't matter as much to her as the brooch. After her daughter came and picked her up, Maria and I walked around the neighbourhood, looking for the purse. In case the mugger threw it on someone's lawn or in a hedge or something after he got the money out of it. But no luck."

"That's a shame."

Suddenly Lois's eyes widened and she sat up straighter. "Hey, I know. When I'm at the library tomorrow morning I'll ask one of the staff to type up a notice and photocopy it for me. I'll put it up at the shops in the neighbourhood. I'm sure

Maria would let me give her contact details in case someone finds the purse."

"What about the police? If someone finds it, they should call them."

Lois frowned. "Sometimes people don't like to speak to the police. But they might let Maria know if they find the purse or the brooch."

Beth nodded. "Okay, I see. How come you and Maria weren't asked to help with the face composite too?"

"We only saw the guy for a short time." Lois smiled ruefully. "And most of that time we were wrapped around his back trying to hold him or lying on the ground after he threw us off. Neither of us got a good look at him. I only saw his face for a few seconds." Lois pursed her lips, thinking. "But there was something about it that was familiar."

"What?"

"I'm not sure. I only really saw the side of his face."

"Was it his eyes? The shape of his nose?"

Lois scrunched up her eyes as she tried to remember the man's face. "I didn't see his eyes. His hair hid them. His hair's a similar colour to Bruce's but his face is narrower."

"Maybe it was just that his hair reminded you a bit of Bruce. Maybe that's why he seemed familiar to you."

Lois thought for a moment. "No, I don't think that's it. There *was* something familiar about the guy. If I could just think what it was." She stared at the wood grain pattern in the pine coffee table and tried to remember the attacker in detail.

Beth regarded Lois steadily. "I've got an idea. Close your eyes. Picture the guy."

Lois closed her eyes. "Okay."

"Now think about the places you used to go in Toronto. Can you picture him in any of them?"

Lois let her mind wander. After a few moments she spoke. "I can't picture him in the park. I don't remember passing him when James and I walked there. And I knew most of the people I saw on the streets of the neighbourhood. Even if I didn't know their names, I knew them to see. I don't remember many strangers there – and I did really notice strangers after James died." Lois tried to suppress a shudder as she remembered how frightened she became of walking alone in her neighbourhood after James was mugged and died.

"Where else did you regularly go?" Beth prompted her.

Lois opened her eyes and looked at her friend. "Grocery shopping."

Beth looked at her expectantly.

Lois frowned in concentration. "Mmm, besides the Dominion supermarket there were lots of little shops along Annette and Jane Streets that I went to." She paused. "I can't picture him in any of them or on the streets near them either."

"You met me for lunch sometimes. Was he in the diner we went to?"

Lois squinted one eye until it was half-closed as she tried to remember. "No, it was mostly regulars that went to that diner. He wasn't there."

"What about the library? You spent lots of time at work."

"Yes. So many people came in and out of the library every day. But we knew many of them."

Lois leaned back on the sofa and stared at the opposite wall. A hazy memory was niggling at her. She tried to relax and let it form in her mind. Beth raised one eyebrow as she watched her, waiting.

Lois leaned forward suddenly and said urgently, "I think I know. It *is* the library! I can picture him on the front steps coming into the building."

"Good. You remember his whole face then."

"No. Not his face. I can see him with his head down as he came up the stairs. I can't picture him in the library and I don't know if I ever spoke to him when he was there. But I have this memory of him on the front steps."

"How can you be sure it's the same guy?"

"I don't know. But I just have this feeling it is. If only I could remember more about him." Lois pursed her lips then let out a groan. "Ugh, I have to remember! The police have to catch this guy."

Beth smiled, sympathetically. "Don't worry. Now you know where you saw him before. Give yourself time to remember more. It might be in your subconscious. You just have to let it surface."

"But I need it now!"

"Try to be patient. It'll come if you don't push it. Maybe if you talk to some of the staff at the library it might jog your memory."

"That's a good idea. Maybe one of them might even remember him too. I can ask them when I'm there tomorrow morning."

Lois rolled her shoulders to loosen the muscles in her neck then leaned back against the sofa again. She felt more optimistic now. Someone at the library was bound to remember the guy. She would find out who he was and give the information to the police. Maybe then Sally would get her brooch back.

Beth stood up. "Good. Now try to put it out of your mind for the rest of the evening. I'll get us more coffee and you can tell me what Fenwater's like."

4

S miling, Lois leaned back in the swivel chair and gazed through the doorway into the next room. Even just sitting at one end of the horseshoe-shaped main reception desk, chatting with the librarian on duty, she felt like she was home again. She had spent so many hours over the years working behind this desk.

Through the doorway leading to the Adult section of Annette Library, she saw Mrs Rose engrossed in a novel at one of the reading tables. It was probably a mystery that the library had recently acquired. Ben Weston was at another table taking notes from a book. She was sure it was a history book. Several members of the local historical society were seated at a third table, probably discussing the latest project they were working on. Beth's friend, Shelley Carter, and also Alice Harle, the society's treasurer, were among them.

"Things are much the same, I see," Lois commented to Roberta Becker, her former colleague and the librarian on duty this morning.

"Yes, pretty much."

She smiled at Roberta. "Thanks for typing and

photocopying that notice for me. Hopefully it will help get the purse back."

As Lois spoke, she noticed Shelley glance up from her conversation with Alice. Shelley waved at Lois then quickly rose from the table and walked to the reception desk.

"Hi, Lois! I phoned Beth this morning and she said you were back. It's great to see you."

"Thanks. It's good to be back."

"Beth told me you had a terrible start yesterday to your first time back in the city."

Lois raised her eyebrows and nodded. "Uh-huh, my friend Maria and I frightened a mugger away from an old lady in the park near where I used to live."

"That must have been really scary."

"Yeah, it was. But the worst thing was that the guy got away." Lois paused and looked from Roberta to Shelley. "Actually, maybe you two can help me. I thought the mugger looked familiar and I've realised that I recognised him from here. I distinctly remember him coming up to the front door of the library. And I think it was more than once, maybe even regularly. I have no idea who he is but maybe if I describe him, one of you might know."

"Sure, I'll try," Shelley said.

"Me too," agreed Roberta.

Lois took a deep breath and tried to compose her thoughts. "Okay, I didn't get a good look at him but this is what I remember. He was taller than me but only by a few inches – maybe five eight. And he was thin but strong. He got free from Maria and I when we were both holding on to him. He had grey track pants and a blue jacket with a hood. The hood was up so I didn't get a good look at his face but I could see that it was thin. And from what I could see of his hair, it was sandy-coloured. It would have come down below his collar if he was wearing a proper shirt."

"What colour were his eyes?" Roberta asked.

"His hair was hanging over his face so I didn't see them."

"What about his nose? What was it like? Big? Small?" Shelley asked.

"Like the rest of him – narrow, thin. I guess it was kind of pointed, sort of sharp at the tip." Lois scrunched up her face. "That's all I can tell you about him. I haven't a clue who he is but I can picture him coming up those front steps into the foyer. I know I've seen him here."

"Well, that's a few things to go on." Roberta gazed through the glass in the double front doors to the flight of steps beyond. "I think I know a young guy who might fit your description. He's a university student. Comes in mostly on Fridays. Maybe he doesn't have classes that day."

"Was he here yesterday then?" Lois asked.

Roberta thought for a moment. "No, I didn't see him." She frowned. "I'd hate to think he might have anything to do with that mugging but he fits your description. He's pretty quiet. Keeps to himself. He comes to study. I think it's law he's studying."

"You have to watch those loners. Never know what they're thinking," Shelley said.

"But he's at university. He's not a rough type," Roberta argued. "And he'll be a lawyer one day."

"Yeah, but students are always short of money. And law textbooks aren't cheap. Maybe he was desperate," Shelley said.

Roberta and Lois nodded, thoughtfully.

"I've seen him waiting tables in the Good Ole TO sports bar beside the Odeon Humber Cinema. I think he works there weekends," Roberta said.

"I wonder if he'll be there tonight?" Lois asked.

From the corner of her eye, Lois saw someone approaching the reception desk. A white-haired, slightly stooped woman, with an armful of mystery novels, stopped in front of the desk. "Will who be there? Is there a fellow you've got your eye on?" the woman asked Lois.

Lois smiled fondly at the older woman. "Definitely not, Mrs Rose. I'm not in town to see a man but it's good to see you again. I was telling the girls about a mugger I encountered in the park yesterday."

"Oh, my goodness! You certainly don't want to see him again. You weren't hurt, were you?"

"No, I'm fine." Lois explained again what had happened and described the mugger to Mrs Rose. "Since I think I recognise him, I want to figure out who he is so I can tell the police."

Mrs Rose was quiet for a moment. "I think I've seen someone around here that fits that description."

"Is it the university student who sits in the far corner there?" Roberta pointed to the opposite side of the Adult reading room. "The one studying law?"

"No, not him. I don't think he'd ever do such a thing. He seems a nice young fellow. Quiet and polite. I'm sure he wouldn't do such a terrible thing."

"But money troubles can make people desperate," Shelley said.

"That may be, but I don't think so in this case. Not that young man. I was thinking of a young fellow who comes in here a couple afternoons every week. But not Saturdays. I've never seen him borrow any books. He seems to come in to read that day's newspaper – the *Toronto Star*. He's not a *Globe and Mail* type, if you get my meaning. Not a professional person. He seems to mostly read the sports section. And he always wears a blue jacket and jeans."

"What days does he come in?" Lois asked.

"It varies. I've only seen him afternoons but it could be any weekday."

Lois pursed her lips. "Oh, I won't get to see him then. I'm

going back to Fenwater on Tuesday and the library will be closed for the holiday on Monday."

"If you head over to Arnie's, the family hardware and household goods store on Annette Street, near Runnymede Road, you'll probably see him. He works there."

Lois nodded thoughtfully. "It wouldn't hurt to get a look at him. If it's the right guy, I could get the police there before he finishes his shift. Thanks, Mrs Rose. I'll head over there now."

"Don't go on your own," Roberta said. "If he is the mugger, what if he recognises you? If you corner him, who knows what might happen."

"I could go with you. I've a couple errands to do near there," Shelley said.

"Thanks, Shelley. Why don't we go now then we can meet up with Roberta afterwards for a coffee on her lunch break?" Lois turned to Mrs Rose. "Why don't you join us too? It would be good to catch up with you."

Mrs Rose smiled self-consciously. "Oh, there's no need to invite me along with you girls."

"Mrs Rose! We're hardly girls anymore. And you're not that much older than me. You've been a regular patron of this library and a friend of mine for years. Of course, you've got to join us. Just give Shelley and I time to go to the hardware store first." She smiled. "I'm sure you can find a book to occupy you until we get back."

Mrs Rose smiled shyly and her face turned pink with pleasure. "I'd love to then. See you in a little while."

5

Lois peered through the glass into the window display crowded with power tools, rakes, paint tins, toasters, and blenders. Arnie's Hardware was a typical family-owned store that sold a wide variety of hardware and household goods. Lois was relieved to see that they didn't stock only items of hardware. She had never really felt comfortable around tools and such. James had been the handyman at their house. "What should we pretend we're looking for, in case any of the staff ask us?"

"We can just say we're having a look around. We don't have to buy anything."

"I hope that doesn't annoy them."

"Don't worry. Let's just go in and walk up and down the aisles. Keep an eye out for the guy Mrs Rose described."

Lois nodded, took a deep breath and opened the door. She tried to appear relaxed as she passed the cashier behind the counter while avoiding the woman's gaze. She had to force herself to walk sedately as she wanted to dash into the nearest aisle, out of sight. When she was halfway down the aisle she stopped and stared at the detergents and cleaning products stocked on the shelf, without seeing them.

"Can I help you?"

Lois turned toward the chirpy voice. A young woman wearing a navy blue T-shirt with the name Arnie's Hardware on it smiled at her. The sales clerk's chestnut hair, tied back into a ponytail, bobbed as she spoke.

"Ah, oh no. I was just looking." Lois squinted at the products on the shelf. "At the fabric softeners," she added.

"There's some great new ones. They make such a difference to how comfortable your clothes feel," the young clerk said.

Lois's gaze slid across the shelf from Snuggle to Bounce and on to an innocent child's face on a blue bottle. She forced a smile. "Downy. That's what I wanted."

Under the clerk's gaze, she lifted the bottle off the shelf.

"Would you like me to ring that up for you?"

Lois stiffened and tried to think of a reply to avoid following the clerk to the cashier's desk.

"Not yet. We wanted to look at a couple other things first," Shelley said.

Lois tried not to sigh audibly with relief when Shelley replied. She shouldn't have let the sales clerk fluster her like that. "Yes, that's right. We do. Thanks for your help."

As soon as the clerk left, Shelley grasped Lois's upper arm and steered her further down the aisle, squeezing past a woman with a large shopping basket dangling from her forearm. The women rounded the corner and walked up the next aisle. The shelves they passed were stocked with paint tins and rows and rows of small cardboard boxes containing a vast assortment of nails and screws. Lois was out of her depth in this section of the store and she hoped the sales clerk wouldn't appear again to offer her assistance.

Ahead of them, halfway up the aisle, a young man with sandy hair was piling more boxes of nails onto the shelf. Lois hesitated when she spotted him and swallowed hard, gripping the bottle of Downy to her chest. He must be the man they were looking for. Would he recognise her? What would he do if he did? She tried to keep calm and study him without appearing to do so.

The male sales clerk was slim and his hair reached the collar of his Arnie's Hardware T-shirt. The T-shirt was a similar colour to the jacket the mugger had worn. As she regarded the clerk, Lois tried to imagine him wearing a jacket rather than the T-shirt. There was definitely a resemblance to the man she had seen in the park. Mrs Rose might have found the mugger for them.

From behind, Shelley nudged her forward. Lois wondered whether her friend had spotted the clerk, who quietly continued stocking the shelf. Lois reached back and tapped Shelley's arm. Before she could pull her hand away, Shelley squeezed it then let go, acknowledging that she had seen him too.

Lois tried not to hurry up the aisle or to stare at the young man as she approached him. When she was almost close enough to reach out and touch him, he lifted a small box of nails out of a large brown cardboard box on the floor and glanced at her as he straightened up. Lois held her breath but tried to keep her expression neutral, resisting the urge to yelp when their gazes met. The clerk smiled at her then moved closer to the shelf to give the women room to pass him. He obviously didn't think they were looking for hardware items.

"T-Thanks," Lois managed to stutter as a clear image of him at the library formed in her mind. She thought they would never reach the end of the aisle.

When they emerged from it, she spotted the cashier looking at her. "If you need help finding anything, there's a couple staff around. I can call one of them if you like. Tina looks after the household goods and Mark's in the hardware section."

Lois felt her cheeks heating up. She felt like she was being watched at every turn. She usually liked good customer service but she would prefer the staff in this store not to be so helpful.

"Thanks, but I'm okay," she called to the cashier, hoping the woman didn't notice that she was blushing. *What will that woman think if she notices how flustered I am? Maybe she'll assume I'm here to shoplift.*

Lois glanced into the third aisle. A couple of male customers were perusing the shelves. The last aisle was empty and she walked to the end of it then turned to face Shelley.

Before Lois even had time to gather her thoughts, Shelley said, "He must be the guy Mrs Rose was talking about."

"Unless there's any other staff working today."

"The cashier only mentioned two names and we've seen both of them. It has to be him." Shelley watched her intently. "So, do you recognise him?"

Lois nodded slowly. "Mrs Rose is right. He comes to the library to read the newspaper. He never asks the staff for help or talks to anyone. He just reads the paper. He's done that for ages."

"And is he the same guy who attacked that woman in the park?"

"Shh!" Lois hissed. "Keep your voice down."

Shelley looked embarrassed. "Sorry, I got carried away. But he's two aisles away. I'm sure he didn't hear me."

Lois glanced toward the front of the store and noticed that a man had entered the aisle. He was standing a few yards from them, reading the label on a metal tin on the shelf. Lois inclined her head toward the customer and Shelley nodded her understanding.

"Well, is he?" Shelley whispered.

Lois pursed her lips then spoke quietly. "He's the right height and build. But his face doesn't look right. It's not as narrow. And he has a wide nose. A rounded one. The mugger had a pointy sort of nose."

"So, it's not him?"

"No, I don't think so."

"Are you sure?"

Lois pulled up one side of her mouth. "Yes, pretty much."

"That's a shame. Wouldn't it have been great if we had caught the mugger here?" Shelley's voice rose again and Lois frowned at her. "Sorry," she whispered.

Lois glanced toward the end of the aisle. The customer who had been peering at the shelf a moment ago turned his head away from them to look back at the shelf. He wore a Blue Jays baseball cap pulled down over his face, hiding his expression from view. The cap had a dark streak across the white front section like someone had dabbed paint on it. Lois hoped the man hadn't heard their conversation.

Lois sighed. "I guess I should buy this Downy and we can head back to the library to meet Roberta and Mrs Rose."

Shelley laughed. "You don't have to buy the Downy."

"Well, I don't want to put it back in the aisle where I got it and run into the clerk again."

Shelley took the bottle of Downy that Lois was clutching to her and shoved it onto the bottom shelf, behind a stack of workmen's gloves, then led the way toward the front of the store.

"Too bad he wasn't the right one." Shelley spoke to Lois over her shoulder. "So when will you go to the Good Ole TO sports bar to check out the other guy?"

"I'm meeting Beth for dinner tonight so I'll suggest we go there. It's about halfway between her house and the Rizzos', so it will be convenient for both of us."

"Well, I hope you're luckier tonight. It would be great if you found the guy this weekend and then the police could lock him up."

Lois didn't reply, hoping to stop Shelley from saying any more about it before they left the store.

"Excuse me," Lois said, apologetically, as she squeezed

past the man at the end of the aisle. He stepped closer to the shelf to let them pass him, without speaking. Glancing at the shelf, Lois looked at the metal tin with the red nozzle on it and wondered what the man could find so interesting about the tin of three-in-one oil that he had spent several minutes studying.

6

Lois sat back in the booth and surveyed the walls of the Good Ole TO sports bar. Not a sports fan, she was amazed to see the diverse array of memorabilia from Toronto's professional teams covering the walls. Blue and white hockey and football jerseys were interspersed with powder blue baseball shirts. A Maple Leafs hockey jersey hung on the opposite wall above a pair of crossed hockey sticks that had players' signatures scrawled in black ink along their lengths. Baseball pennants and caps with the distinctive Blue Jays logo on them were mounted on a side wall. Several large, autographed team photos were prominently displayed. Players gazed out of their black frames, proudly displaying large silver cups. Although her knowledge of sports was limited, Lois knew that the trophies were either the Stanley Cup or the Grey Cup, the championship trophies for the hockey and football leagues.

Beth looked up from the menu she was reading. "You've probably heard that their burgers are legendary."

"No, I hadn't. I have to admit this is my first time here. James and I never thought of this place to eat."

"Shelley and I come here for dinner once in a while."

Lois nodded. "That makes sense. It's close to home for both of you."

"And it's just outside West Toronto Junction, in a municipality that doesn't have a ban on serving alcohol like the Junction does. We come here when we fancy a glass of wine with our meal." Beth set her menu on the table. "Are you ready? After we order you can tell me how it went at the library this morning."

A blonde waitress with a bushy perm, wearing a form-fitting powder blue baseball shirt and faded blue jeans, stopped beside their table. "Hi! What can I get you ladies?" She reached into the black cloth money belt riding loosely on her hips, pulled out an order pad and looked expectantly from Lois to Beth.

As Lois was about to answer, the waitress shifted sideways to allow two young men to slide into the next booth. Lois glanced at the newcomers. The pair were slim with longish light-coloured hair covered by Blue Jays baseball caps. The one nearest Lois had his slanted down over his eyes. Lois smiled to herself. It seemed that it was the fashion now to wear baseball caps everywhere. It didn't seem that long ago when men took off their hats as they entered a building, but not anymore.

Lois turned back to the waitress and realised she was waiting for her order. "I'll have a cheeseburger with just tomatoes. No mustard."

"Regular or jumbo?"

"Oh, not too big. I guess, that's regular."

The waitress nodded as she wrote on her order pad.

"Same for me but give me mustard and onions as well." Beth looked from the waitress to Lois, a question in her expression. "And we'll share a carafe of red wine."

Lois nodded her agreement.

"Thanks. It'll just be a few minutes." The waitress smiled at the women as she closed the order pad and left the table.

Beth eagerly leaned across the table toward Lois. "So, did you have any luck at the library this morning?"

Lois raised her eyebrows. "Um, maybe. We'll see tonight."

In response to Beth's puzzled frown, Lois filled her in on what Roberta and the library regulars had told her, and the unfruitful visit she and Shelley had paid to Arnie's Hardware. When she finished recounting the events at the hardware store Beth was laughing.

"I'd have loved to see you two skulking around the aisles. You'll probably be banned from there now."

Lois shrugged. "I guess we were a bit clumsy about it. We must have looked shifty."

Beth grinned. "Mmm, as long as they didn't call the cops because they thought the two of you were shoplifters!"

Lois quirked one corner of her mouth upwards. "Never! We don't look the type. But I'm not going to worry about what they thought of us in the hardware store. I'm more concerned about following up on the information I got this morning. I've ruled out the sales clerk at Arnie's Hardware. He definitely wasn't the right guy."

"So now it's down to you and I to check out the other guy here tonight." Beth surreptitiously scanned the room. She lowered her voice. "What's the plan?"

"Keep an eye out for a sandy-haired waiter. I need to get a good look at him."

"We'll see all the waiting staff coming and going here in the middle of the bar. We can't miss him if he's working tonight."

"Let's divide the room in half. You take the half of the room that you're facing and I'll take the other side. If you see any waiters that fit the description I gave you, let me know so I can take a look at him."

Beth nodded as their waitress appeared and set a carafe of red wine and two wine glasses on the table between the women then left. Beth poured each of them a glass of wine and they began chatting about other topics, surveying the room as they talked.

"Did I tell you—" Beth was midway through the sentence when she pulled her gaze away from the space behind Lois and looked at her friend. "I think it's him."

Lois tensed. "I don't want to turn around and give away that I'm watching him. Where is he?"

"He just went into the kitchen."

Lois felt her heart beat faster and tried to take slow breaths to keep calm. "I think I saw the sign for the ladies' restroom beside the kitchen."

"Yeah, next to the kitchen door there's a hallway that leads to the stairs down to the restrooms."

Lois nodded. "Okay, let me know when he comes out of the kitchen and I'll head for the restroom so I can get a look at him as we pass each other."

Lois slid to the outer edge of the seat as Beth watched the kitchen door. Tensed as she waited for Beth's signal, she thought her back might go into a spasm before it came.

Suddenly Beth's gaze shifted from the space behind Lois to her friend's face. She whispered, "Now."

Lois slid out of the booth and spun around to face the kitchen door. As she straightened up, she saw almost too late that their waitress was nearly on top of her, her arms loaded with plates piled with food and a glass bottle of ketchup in one hand. The waitress jumped and the ketchup bottle flew out of her hand and clattered onto the next table.

"Oh, sorry! I didn't see you there." Lois gasped as she swerved away from the booths to avoid the waitress.

Not stopping, Lois walked briskly toward the back of the room. She spotted a thin, sandy-haired waiter carrying four plates balanced on his arms. He was wearing the same powder blue baseball shirt and jeans uniform as their waitress. His shirt hung looser on his lanky frame than hers did on her curvy body. The waiter threaded his way around tables and passed Lois on the opposite side of an empty one.

Lois tried to get a good look at his face without appearing to stare. After he passed her she continued toward the back of the room. She would have to go to the restroom and back to avoid drawing attention to herself. As she descended the stairs, she thought about the waiter's face. It was thin and his sandy hair was around the same length as the mugger's. His nose was thinner than the guy in the hardware store. He definitely looked more like the mugger. But she had been surprised by his intense blue eyes; she wasn't sure whether she could imagine eyes like that on the mugger.

In the restroom she washed her hands and stared into the mirror at her own reflection. She wished she could study the waiter's face as carefully. His features were similar to the mugger's but she wasn't certain that he was the same person she had seen in the park.

She climbed the stairs and headed back to her table. The two young men seated at the table behind hers briefly looked up as she neared their table and her face reddened. She hoped the ketchup bottle the waitress dropped hadn't shattered and made a mess of their table but she couldn't face apologising to them. How could she explain her abrupt departure from the table without even stopping to apologise for her clumsiness? She straightened her shoulders and pretended not to see their glances as she passed them. The Blue Jays baseball cap worn by the young man sitting nearest their booth briefly caught her attention. In the white front section sporting the Blue Jay logo, there was a streak of navy that wasn't part of the design. Lois wondered why the young man would wear a dirty cap to a restaurant; he should have kept it for painting or doing odd jobs.

The delicious smell of the cheeseburger greeted her before she even sat down. She was glad to see that the chips on the plate beside it were golden brown. She hated greasy chips. "Mmm, smells good," she said as she reclaimed her seat.

"Sure does." Beth lifted her burger and paused. "Well, is it?" She inclined her head toward the kitchen. "Is it him?"

Lois pursed her lips, stabbing a chip with her fork. "He looks more like the guy than the one in the hardware store but I can't be sure."

"Why not?"

"Well, the waiter's eyes are really blue. I'm not sure I can imagine them on the mugger."

Beth frowned. "But you didn't see the mugger's eyes, did you?" In response to Lois shaking her head, she continued. "That might be his eye colour. Just concentrate on the features you did see at the park."

Lois forked the chip into her mouth, chewed and swallowed it, then sighed. "Maybe I could be sure if I saw him in the same kind of clothes the mugger wore. It might be the staff uniform that's throwing me off."

The women ate in silence for several minutes. As Lois ate, she tried to imagine the waiter's and the mugger's faces side by side. She could almost see both of them in her mind but it was hard to draw the details into focus.

Laughter at the bar near the front door interrupted her thoughts. As she turned in that direction, she noticed the young man sitting in the next booth glance at her then look away as if he didn't want to make eye contact with her. He turned his attention to the bar.

Their waitress was leaning against the bar and talking to the sandy-haired waiter. This was the opportunity Lois had hoped for to study the waiter without him noticing. It was an added bonus that she didn't have to strain to hear the conversation between the two staff members either.

"Are you staying for a drink after your shift tonight?" the waitress asked.

"Nah, I can't," the waiter replied.

"Why not?"

"Gotta jog in the morning and study in the afternoon."

"But everyone's going to hang out. It'll be fun." The waitress gave him a wistful smile. "I'll miss you if you can't make it."

"You could come jogging tomorrow. At the park in the Humber Valley. About ten o'clock."

The waitress smiled and shook her head. "Bit early on a Sunday morning. Maybe another time."

The two staff members set the drinks the bartender had poured for their customers on their trays and went their separate ways.

Lois leaned toward Beth, excitedly. "Now I can be sure whether it's him."

Beth raised her eyebrows, still chewing.

"Since he's going jogging in the park tomorrow morning, I can get a look at him in a track suit again. Then I'll know."

"Be careful. Don't take any risks and don't let him see you. I should come with you."

"Thanks, but you don't have to. Maria and I will go. She's always up early."

Beth's eyebrows pulled down into a frown. "Are you sure? You're too good a friend for me to let anything happen to you. And I owe you after you rescued me from my kidnapper last spring."

Lois glanced away from Beth to hide the tears welling up in her eyes, touched by her friend's concern. As she turned her head, she was aware that the young man at the next table slid down in his seat. She hoped she wasn't disturbing him. It was bad enough that she had caused the waitress to drop the ketchup bottle on their table.

She turned back to Beth. "It'll be fine. Thanks for the offer though."

"No problem. But if you change your mind, phone me in the morning."

7

Lois tried not to look at the cluster of oak trees as she and Maria passed them. Now she had two upsetting memories of the clearing behind those trees. She never would have imagined when James was attacked three years ago that she would encounter another mugging in the same spot. But she had and it only happened two days ago. She tensed as the memory replayed in her mind.

"You okay?" A concerned expression on her face, Maria patted Lois's arm.

Lois nodded. "Yes, just letting memories run away with me for a minute. But that's enough of that."

As the two women walked, arm in arm, along the paved path toward the opening where they had entered the park, Lois made a conscious effort to push the disturbing memories out of her mind. They shouldn't be her focus this morning. When she had returned to the Rizzos' house last night after dinner with Beth, the couple were keen to hear about her search for the mugger. She wasn't surprised when they both volunteered to come with her to the park this morning. While she appreciated their support, she thought that two women would blend in easier than the three of them. Besides, Maria had also seen the mugger and might recognise him.

The two women had arrived at the park at quarter to ten and walked slowly down the path past where they had encountered the mugger on Friday. They continued a short distance further then turned and headed back in the direction they had come from. Lois hoped that this section of the path was on the waiter's regular jogging route.

Lois led Maria off the path to the concrete reinforcement wall, which jutted out for several yards from the manmade waterfall onto the river bank. The wall supported the river bank when the water level rose during storms. Lois stopped in the middle of the wall and leaned back against the waist-high, rounded-top structure. Maria leaned on the wall beside her. From this spot they could appear to be gazing at the waterfall but they were close enough to the path to observe passersby.

Lois wrapped her arms around her waist. The sun was bright but it was still chilly in the morning air. She hoped they wouldn't have long to wait. At this time on a Sunday morning the park was quiet. Some people would be at church, others not out of bed yet. This was the time for joggers and cyclists to enjoy the path without having to dodge rambunctious children, mothers pushing baby carriages and couples strolling arm in arm.

Lois watched two young women chatting as they breezed along the path, standing on their bicycle pedals as they cycled toward the southern end of the park. A young man in faded jeans and a worn jean jacket, with the collar turned up, plodded in their wake. His Toronto Blue Jays baseball cap sat low on his forehead; an out-of-place blue streak across the white front section drew Lois's eye. *Those caps must be handy for painters*, she thought. *That's the third one I've seen covered with paint streaks.*

The young man looked straight ahead, paying no attention

to the two women as he walked. At the cluster of oak trees not far from the women, he stepped off the path and walked to the edge of the river. A middle-aged man in a track suit puffed as he jogged toward them. He slowed to a walk and waved as he passed. The women returned his wave. It reminded Lois that, before the attack on James, she had enjoyed the camaraderie she shared with people she met in the park.

Glancing from the path to the river, Lois listened to the water flowing steadily over the miniature waterfall. Sunlight glinted on it as it dropped to the next section of the river and splashed upwards in a white spray. The sound of feet pounding on the paved path drew Lois's gaze back to the path.

A young man in grey track pants and a green and white baseball shirt was running toward them. He glanced at the river as he approached, and Lois saw the deep blue of his eyes.

Lois squeezed Maria's hand. Without looking at her friend, she said, "This is the guy."

The women sat in silence as the jogger approached. Lois flicked her gaze between the river and the path then looked past the path to the grassy expanse beyond, keeping the jogger in the corner of her eye. She hoped it wasn't obvious that she was observing him. When the young man was almost level with them, she couldn't resist looking directly at him. He was puffing but running at a brisk, steady pace, his arms pumping in time with his legs. He noticed her gaze and Lois felt her heart start to pound. Before she could look away, he raised his hand briefly in greeting as he passed them. Lois stared after him, too unsettled to notice that she hadn't returned his greeting.

She turned to Maria. "Did you get a look at him?"

Maria nodded. "That's the one from the restaurant?"

"Yes, definitely. Do you think he's the mugger we saw?"

Maria grimaced with one side of her face and rubbed her cheek. "He looks sort of like him – the hair, the size, the track pants. I only saw the mugger for a minute. I was behind him, then on the ground where he pushed me. Before I got up, he was gone."

"What's your gut feeling? Is it the same guy?"

"Maybe, he sort of looks like him. But I couldn't say for sure. What do you think?"

Lois frowned. "Like you, I can't be sure. And I remember him in his waiter's uniform last night. So the two images sort of blur together. It's hard to decide whether I also saw him in the park on Friday." She grunted in annoyance. "I thought I'd know for sure if I saw him in his running clothes." She pursed her lips. "And his eyes. They're such a deep blue. I just don't remember that about the mugger." She looked earnestly at Maria. "Do you?"

Maria shook her head. "No, I don't think so." She frowned at Lois. "What do we do now?"

"I don't want to wrongly accuse anyone, but I think I'd better tell the police about him. They can find out where he was on Friday. If he's innocent, they'll be able to rule him out." Lois sighed. "I really don't like pointing a finger at someone without being sure, but if I say nothing and he is guilty, someone else might get hurt. When we get back to the house, I'll phone the police, okay?"

"Sure, of course. We'll go now?"

Lois glanced around her. Maybe it was the cheerful sunlight or the peaceful silence in the almost deserted park, but this morning the park didn't seem as threatening as it had ever since James was mugged. Lois had never even considered being in it on her own since that night. But she wasn't afraid this morning.

Lois smiled. "I think I'd like to spend a short while here before I go back to your house. I'll phone the police as soon as I get back."

Maria patted her arm. "I stay with you?"

"Thanks, but I'll be okay on my own."

Maria regarded her for a moment. "If you're sure. We'll have coffee and Savoiardi biscuits when you get back."

"Sounds good."

For a few seconds, Lois watched Maria walk along the path toward the entrance then she turned and surveyed the park. How many times had she sat here or walked along the path with James? Sometimes she had come to the park on her own to walk and think or to sit in their favourite clearing.

The sunlight dappled the branches of the trees that stood in clusters throughout the park. Graceful and solid, they surrounded the central grassy expanse. Squirrels scurried up and down their trunks. Birds that hadn't left before the coming winter chirped in their branches.

She turned her head to gaze at the river. The noisy rush of water tumbling over the waterfall beside her was invigorating and she loved the way the sun glistened on the water's surface like shiny beads bobbing in the current.

Her senses awoken by the beauty around her, Lois was glad she had faced coming back to the park. She had loved this place until the evening that James was mugged and died. The images that remained of that evening had marred all her other memories of the park for three years. Until now. She took a deep breath and smiled. It felt good to be comfortable and happy here again. Even though she had encountered a second assault this weekend, it hadn't erased her love for this place. Maybe it was the act of confronting the mugger this time. Doing something instead of feeling like a victim. Whatever had caused her change of heart, she knew that she would leave Toronto after this weekend with all the memories she treasured restored. She wouldn't forget what had happened to James and Sally here but she would remember all the good times too.

Lois turned her gaze from the river to the path again. The

young man in the jean jacket was walking from the water's edge back to the path, his hands stuffed in his front pockets and his lanky form bent forward as he walked. The park certainly didn't seem to lift his mood. Once again as he passed her, he ignored her. Although his face was partly hidden by his cap, she noticed he wore an enigmatic smile and she wondered what he was thinking. He wasn't at all friendly like most people she encountered in the park; he seemed rather a loner.

Oh well, Lois thought, *it's none of my business. He can enjoy the park on his own if that's what he wants.*

Lois turned back to watch the river for several more minutes. When she looked back at the path it was empty. The young man had disappeared.

She stood up and headed toward the path. *I'd better get back to the Rizzos'. Maria will be wondering what's happened to me.* She smiled. *And after I phone the police, there's coffee and ladyfinger cookies waiting.*

8

_____

"Hi, Beth. Come in." Lois ushered her friend into the Rizzos' diner. "Where's Amy?"

"Sorry, I meant to tell you Saturday night. She can't make it. She's at my brother's."

Lois frowned. "Oh, I hope I haven't dragged you away from your family Thanksgiving."

"Don't worry. We have lots of family dinners together. I wanted to see you again today before you head back to the boonies."

Lois laughed. "Fenwater is not the boonies! You'll have to come visit me and see for yourself."

Beth grinned. "I might just do that."

"Let's get something to drink. I think there's just a few more guests expected, then we'll be eating."

The two women threaded their way through the diner to the beverages table set up at the back of the room and Lois poured drinks for them. On their return journey, she pointed out the array of dishes set along the Formica and chrome counter that ran nearly the length of one side of the room. No one was seated on the red padded stools as the counter was being used as the serving table.

"It smells delicious," Beth said.

"Yes, it does. Maria and Angelo have been cooking since early this morning. They are both fantastic cooks. I don't know how we'll ever eat all of it."

Beth laughed. "I'm willing to give it a try." She peered at the counter. "It looks like there's just about anything you could ever want."

Lois nodded. "You could say that. It's a combination of a Canadian Thanksgiving dinner and an Italian family meal." She pointed out several of the dishes on the counter. "There's a huge turkey and ham, and all the vegetables and trimmings. Then there's Italian dishes too: meatballs in a spicy tomato sauce, potato gnocchi with a garlic butter and mushroom sauce, and lamb chops and ragu. I don't even know what you call some of the pasta they've made to go with them. We'll be stuffed before we even get to the desserts."

Beth raised her eyebrows and grinned. "Did you say desserts? As in more than one? This just gets better."

"Uh-huh, it does and…"

Lois's voice trailed off as she noticed a young couple ahead of them. In her early twenties, the woman was petite and stylishly dressed in a white blouse with a ruffle front and puffy sleeves, and black wool trousers. Her silver hoop earrings jiggling, she patted her curly red hair as she spoke to the young man beside her. In contrast to the well-dressed woman, her fair-haired companion was dressed in a long-sleeve white shirt with the collar open and sleeves rolled up, and faded jeans. His hands stuffed into the front pockets of his jeans, the young man hunched forward, listening to his companion.

There was something familiar about the man but Lois wasn't sure what it was.

"What were you saying?" Beth asked.

"I, uh, sorry, I've lost my train of thought." Lois paused and looked at the young couple again then back at Beth. "Do you know that couple? The short girl in the white blouse and the guy in the white shirt and jeans beside her?"

Beth looked at them for a moment. "I don't think so. Why?"

"I just have a feeling I've seen the guy before but I can't place where. Never mind. It's not important. Why don't we look for seats up at the front of the room? I think we'll be eating soon."

"Sure. Sounds good."

Lois continued up the aisle toward the couple, trying not to stare at the man as she approached them. She still thought that she recognised his face but couldn't figure out why. This often happened to her in Fenwater as her friend Marge introduced her to so many people that she couldn't keep track of them all. She had resigned herself to that. But today it was annoying her. If she recognised someone in her old neighbourhood, she should know them.

As Lois pulled her gaze away from the man, she accidentally caught the eye of his female companion. The woman surprised Lois by giving her a huge smile.

"Isn't this fabulous?" the young woman gushed as Lois continued walking toward the couple.

Lois wondered whether the woman had noticed that she had been staring at her companion. If she had, it didn't seem to bother her. "Yes, it is. The Rizzos have done a wonderful job."

"Anna said it would be amazing. My friend Anna is Mr and Mrs Rizzo's daughter."

"She is." Lois nodded agreement.

Lois had known Anna since she was a young child and had watched her grow up. She'd finished university last spring and returned to Toronto. Lois knew that Maria still could barely believe her daughter was a grown woman and had her own apartment now.

"Are you friends of Mr and Mrs Rizzo?" the young woman asked.

"Yes, I lived on the same street as them for many years."

"Oh, that's nice. By the way, I'm Debbie." She glanced beside her. "And this is Leo."

"Hi, I'm Lois." She motioned to her friend. "This is Beth."

Lois noticed that Leo only glanced briefly at the older women and shot them a grimace that she supposed was meant to pass for a smile. What a strange couple. Debbie was so bubbly and gregarious and Leo seemed to be her complete opposite. She imagined that Debbie's chatty manner might irritate Leo sometimes.

Leo turned away from the group and looked toward the front door. Lois wondered if he was looking for something else to occupy his attention so he didn't have to talk to the women. Maybe he hadn't wanted to come today. *Oh well, it doesn't really matter. It isn't any of my business,* Lois thought.

Viewing Leo in profile, Lois noticed something sticking out of his back pocket. She smiled to herself when she realised what it was. He had stuffed a Blue Jays baseball cap into his pocket. Lois wondered whether Debbie had made him take it off. A dark streak across the white section of the fabric caught her attention.

Lois squinted at the mark on the cap. Now she knew why she thought Leo looked familiar. She *had* seen him before. Saturday night in the Good Ole TO sports bar. He was one of the young men sitting at the booth behind her. Debbie hadn't been with Leo that evening to make him take his cap off indoors. Lois grinned at the thought but her grin quickly disappeared when she remembered that it was her fault that a bottle of ketchup had landed on his table when she had jumped out of her booth to get a look at the waiter.

As the young man turned back to the group, Lois felt her cheeks heating up. She hadn't said anything to either of the young men when she returned to the table on Saturday night. She would have to apologise now.

Lois looked at Leo. "I thought I recognised you—"

Leo glanced at her then looked away. He said gruffly, "I don't think so. I've never been to this diner before."

"No, not from here. I think you and one of your friends were sitting in the next booth to Beth and I on Saturday night at the Good Ole TO bar." Lois paused. "I'm afraid I didn't see the waitress when I got out of my booth and she dropped a ketchup bottle on your table. I hope she didn't get any of it on you."

Leo shook his head. "Nah, she didn't."

"Well, I'm really sorry I was so clumsy. I should have apologised at the time."

Debbie's forehead puckered. "Leo couldn't take me out on Saturday night. He'd already promised to meet his friend, Alec." She raised her eyebrows, took a deep breath and made an effort to smile. "But he did drop by my apartment yesterday. It was my birthday. So he said he'd come with me today too."

"Oh, that's nice." Lois wasn't sure what else to say. She had only met this young woman and didn't want to hear personal details of her relationship with Leo. Now that she had apologised for the accident she had almost caused in the sports bar, she would like to find a graceful way to end this conversation.

Getting ready to make her excuses and move past the couple, Lois said, "It's nice meeting you. I hope the wonderful meal this afternoon helps to make up for not celebrating your birthday on Saturday."

Debbie beamed. "Oh, it will. And Leo gave me a gorgeous present. I don't know why he doesn't want me to wear it today. It would go great with my earrings."

Without any encouragement from Lois, Debbie opened her large turquoise purse and pulled something out of it. She opened her hand to reveal a dainty silver brooch in the shape of a leaf. Three pearls adorned the exquisite piece of jewellery.

Lois murmured her admiration for the brooch then stifled a gasp as an idea entered her head. She looked at Debbie and stuttered, "Oh y-yess, it's very pretty."

"I think it would suit my outfit today, don't you?" Debbie held the brooch against the shoulder of her blouse. Before Lois could answer, she continued, "But Leo said he'd take me somewhere special next weekend and I should save the brooch till then." She pursed her lips into a pout. "I'd really like to wear it today though."

Debbie's bubbly openness convinced Lois that the young woman had no idea where Leo likely got the brooch. From the corner of her eye, Lois looked at Leo again. His sandy hair was a similar length to the mugger and his body shape matched. She made a conscious effort to keep her expression neutral, wondering whether Leo recognised her from the park as well as the sports bar. Hopefully he would just associate her with the Good Ole TO sports bar.

"That's a good idea to keep it for your special outing next weekend." Lois made herself smile. "Now I hope you'll excuse us. I think Beth and I are going to grab seats. Enjoy the meal."

Before Debbie could engage them in further conversation, Lois hurried to the front of the diner and slid into a booth next to the window, facing the room. She waited impatiently for Beth to sit down opposite her.

Leaning forward, Lois spoke quietly, trying to appear relaxed. "That was the guy. The mugger."

"Leo?"

"Yes."

"How can you be sure? What about either of the guys you checked out on Saturday?"

"That brooch Debbie has – it's exactly like the one that Sally Hayes described to the police. And Leo does resemble the mugger – same hair colour and roughly the same height and build."

Beth nodded. "Okay. So, what now?"

"I've got to contact the police."

"How are you going to do that here?"

"The Rizzos have a phone in the kitchen. I'll go call them. Be right back."

Lois slid out of the booth and walked to the back of the restaurant. She glanced at Debbie and Leo as she passed them. She was glad to see that they were engrossed in a conversation with Anna Rizzo and her boyfriend and didn't notice her pass their table.

9

L ois heard a noise outside but she resisted the urge to turn around again and look out of the window. Facing Lois, Beth didn't seem perturbed by whatever had caused it.

"This dinner really is delicious," her friend said.

Lois nodded absently, swallowing a bite of turkey breast. She looked at her friend. "What was that noise?"

"Just some kids going past bouncing a ball." Beth smiled at her. "Try to enjoy your meal. There's nothing you can do now except wait until they arrive."

Lois nodded agreement, but until the police arrived, she knew she wouldn't be able to relax. All the guests were seated and enjoying their meals. Leo was unlikely to leave in the middle of Thanksgiving dinner, but she still wished the police would hurry. She continued to eat, half-listening to Beth chatter about friends they had in common.

Leo and Debbie were sitting several booths away and she was glad that Leo had his back to her. Although she tried not to stare at them, she couldn't help glancing in that direction frequently. So far, she had managed to avoid catching Debbie's eye.

As Lois anxiously waited for the police to arrive, an image of Leo's baseball cap flashed into her mind. That paint streak across the front of it made it easy to recognise. Now that she thought about it, she had seen it somewhere besides the sports bar on Saturday night. While she and Maria were waiting to catch sight of the waiter jogging yesterday morning, a young man wearing a cap with a paint streak on it had walked past them. Lois had seen him again leaving the park just before she went back to Maria's house. His face had been mostly hidden by the cap and the collar of his jacket but it must have been Leo. Had he heard Lois tell Beth in the sports bar on Saturday evening that she would be there Sunday morning? But if he was the mugger, why wasn't he worried that Lois might recognise him? She remembered that, although the man didn't appear to pay any attention to her and Maria, he seemed to be smirking. Was he laughing at Lois for suspecting the waiter?

Lois's thoughts were interrupted by Beth. Her friend glanced up at the window then spoke quietly. "Don't turn around but a police cruiser just parked outside and an officer is getting out of the car."

Lois tensed but heeded her friend's caution. The door buzzer rang and Angelo Rizzo walked down the aisle to unlock the front door. When she called the police, she had had a chance to tell Maria her suspicions about Leo. Opening the kitchen door a crack, she had pointed him out to her friend. So, the Rizzos were expecting the visit from the police officer.

Every pair of eyes in the restaurant turned toward the police officer as he followed Angelo through the diner. Lois recognised the officer as the one who had interviewed Sally, Maria and her after the mugging. Angelo and the officer stopped beside the table where Debbie and Leo sat with Anna and her boyfriend. Lois heard Angelo apologise for interrupting their meal before the police officer asked Leo to accompany him outside. Lois couldn't see Leo's face and she wished she knew how he had reacted to the police officer's request. Whatever he was thinking, Leo didn't object to the request. He left the table and walked in front of the police officer toward the front door.

Lois wondered whether Leo had figured out why the officer wanted to speak to him. Was the mugging on Friday the first time he had committed such a crime or had he been involved in any others? When Leo was a couple of booths away from where Lois was sitting, he looked directly at her and she shivered. His angry glare left her in no doubt that he knew she had contacted the police. Lois shifted her gaze away from his.

She glanced back at Leo's face and saw his gaze flick to the front door, which Angelo had left unlocked when he let the officer in. Almost imperceptibly Leo tensed then spun around. He shoved the police officer toward the nearest booth, where the officer landed in the middle of the table amidst the guests' half-finished meals. Then he sprinted toward the front door with the same agility he had shown when he escaped from Lois and Maria during the mugging.

Lois's eyes widened in disbelief. Leo couldn't get away. Sally Hayes deserved to get her brooch back and have justice for the frightening attack she had endured. Without thinking about what she was doing, Lois jumped out of her booth as Leo drew level with it and shoved him sideways as hard as she could. Although he was stronger than her, she caught him off guard and he sprawled across the desserts set out on the chrome counter.

Lois threw herself on top of him and a moment later she felt Beth leaning on top of her and Leo as if they were tackling an opposing player on a football field. Between the two women, they held on to Leo despite him thrashing and kicking beneath them.

"Lock the front door," the police officer called to Angelo a moment before he appeared beside the trio wrestling over the counter. Angelo hurried past them to obey the officer.

"Thank you, ladies. You can let go of him now." The officer spoke with authority despite the comical sight he presented in his uniform shirt streaked with tomato sauce.

Lois and Beth let go of Leo and straightened up. Leo silently followed suit, making no attempt to bolt. Maria appeared beside the group with a roll of paper towels and handed sheets to each of them.

As Lois wiped tiramisu and apple pie off her sleeve, she looked at Leo. "I'm afraid I'm not going to apologise for the mess this time like I did about the ketchup. If you were the one who attacked Sally then it's the least you deserve."

Leo's only response was to glare at Lois. As he turned his head toward her, his open collared shirt shifted slightly on his shoulder, revealing three thin red marks on his neck just above his collarbone in the same spot where Lois's nails had caught the mugger.

The police officer wiped the tomato sauce off his shirt, leaving a large wet stain in the middle of it. He looked at Leo. "I have some questions for you in regard to stolen property."

Leo glared at the officer. "I don't know nothing about no stolen stuff."

"Then you shouldn't mind answering my questions," the officer said.

"Should I get the brooch for you, officer?" Lois asked.

"Where is it?"

Lois indicated the booth where Leo had been sitting. "Leo's girlfriend has it."

"Would you ask her for it? But if she refuses, let me deal with it."

Lois nodded and walked down the aisle to Debbie. The young woman was sitting open-mouthed, watching the scene at the front of the room.

Lois smiled kindly at her. "I'm afraid the police officer needs to see the brooch that you showed me."

Debbie frowned. "Why? Leo gave that to me for my birthday."

"I know, but it might be stolen, so the officer needs to check that."

Reluctantly Debbie fished in her purse. She handed the dainty silver brooch to Lois. Her voice quivered. "I know Leo doesn't have a lot of money. He just works for himself as a handyman. But he wouldn't steal to get me a birthday present."

"We better let the police officer ask him about it."

Considering the evidence, Lois thought that the bubbly woman was about to be proven wrong. It was a shame Debbie would be hurt by her boyfriend's actions but there was nothing Lois could do to soften the blow. She returned to the group at the front of the room and handed the brooch to the officer then watched as Angelo accompanied the officer and Leo to the police cruiser.

As the cruiser drove away, Angelo returned to the restaurant. He headed straight to the booth where Leo had pushed the police officer over the table and began clearing up the mess, apologising profusely to the guests sitting there. Further down the room she saw Anna leading Debbie toward the restrooms.

Lois looked at Maria and Beth then at the mess on the counter. Despite being relieved that Leo hadn't got away, Lois was embarrassed by the chaos his capture had caused.

Beth gave her a fake pout. "Darn it. I was really looking forward to that dessert."

Lois grimaced and turned to Maria. "I'm really sorry about ruining your desserts. Look at the mess we made."

Maria shook her head. "Don't worry. It was better you caught him. Besides, you must know, I always make lots. There's more tiramisu and apple pie in the kitchen."

Lois smiled with relief. "Well then I'll help you clear up this mess before you serve dessert."

"I'll help too," Beth said. "I can't wait to taste that tiramisu."

10

_____

L ois wrapped her arms around her waist, hugging herself against the chilly air as she and Beth stepped into the park. Her lips quirked into a smile as she realised that her visit to Toronto had started in this park on Friday and she was here again as it drew to a close.

Lois surveyed the expanse of grass and trees ahead. "It's hard to believe that what started as a quiet walk in this park with Maria turned the whole weekend upside down. Even after what happened to James, I never expected to run into another mugger here."

Beth smiled sympathetically. "I guess your weekend didn't go exactly how you expected."

Lois nodded. "You can say that again. But I did get to see everyone I wanted to." She looked at her friend and smiled. "And we've had a couple good chats. But I still haven't asked you how you're doing after your kidnapping ordeal. I got caught up in my move last summer and I wasn't much help to you in the months afterwards."

"Don't worry about that. Without *you*, I'd still be held captive. I can't tell you how glad I am that that's over and done with, and I'm fine now. Have you heard how that lady who got mugged is doing?"

Lois stuffed her cold hands in the front pockets of her jeans. "Sally phoned Maria's house yesterday evening after that very eventful Thanksgiving dinner." She quirked one eyebrow up. "So I had a chance to speak to her. The mugger roughed her up and she has a few bruises but they're healing. The police phoned her after Leo was arrested to ask her to come to the police station this morning. They want her to identify him in a line-up."

"Don't the police already have enough evidence against Leo without asking her to do that? After all, he had her brooch," Beth said.

"He did, and Maria and I sort of recognised him after I saw the brooch. His girlfriend also let it slip after the police officer took him away yesterday that he's been charged a couple times for breaking and entering but was never convicted. I phoned the police station to tell them that I gave him the scratches on his neck. It also doesn't look good for him that he tried to run when the officer wanted to question him. But if Sally can identify him, that should definitely secure his conviction."

The women strolled along the path that ran parallel to the river and, as they neared the waterfall, the cheery gurgling of the water running over it gave Lois a rush of pleasure.

"What about Sally's belongings? Will she get them back?" Beth asked.

"When the police are finished with the brooch, she'll get it back. I don't know whether they've found her purse and the money. She might never get that back. But at least she'll get the brooch. That's what is most important to her." Lois felt tears clog her throat. "You can't replace a gift from your husband after he's gone."

Beth patted her arm. "No, you can't. I'm glad she'll get it

back." She paused. "By the way, were you right that you remembered the mugger at the library?"

"With how crazy things were at the Rizzos' diner after I realised Leo was the mugger, I've barely given that any thought but, yes, I do remember him there a few times. He kept to himself. I don't know what books he was looking for."

Beth grinned. "Did you stock any for apprentice thieves?"

"Definitely not." Lois paused, thinking. "Oh, I meant to tell you yesterday that I remembered seeing Leo in the park Sunday morning as well as in the sports bar Saturday night. And I've since realised that he was in the hardware shop on Saturday too."

Beth's eyebrows shot upwards. "Has he been following you ever since he mugged Sally?"

Lois shook her head, emphatically. "No, I think it was just a coincidence that he was in the hardware shop, but he must have recognised me from when Maria and I interrupted the mugging. Then he heard me tell Shelley that I was going to the Good Ole TO bar that evening to get a look at the waiter. I should have watched what I was saying. We walked past him as I was telling her that. So then he showed up at the restaurant and sat in the next booth. At the bar he must have overhead me tell you I was going to the park Sunday morning to get another look at the waiter. So then he went to the park."

"But why?"

"I'm not sure. Maybe he wanted to know for sure I'd pinned the mugging on the wrong person. He must have been feeling confident on Sunday morning when he saw that I didn't recognise him at all. That's why he was smirking as he passed me. He must have felt sure then that he was going to get away with the mugging and I'd identify the wrong guy. I feel bad now that I made that call and reported the waiter to the police. I'm sure he's not too happy with me."

"You did what you thought was right. But, if it really bothers you, you could call him at the bar and apologise."

"That's a great idea. I think I'll do that."

"So did Leo follow you to the Thanksgiving dinner too?"

"No, that was just coincidence. He couldn't have known I'd be there. And I probably wouldn't have put all the pieces together then either if Debbie hadn't showed us her birthday gift from him. That's what tripped him up in the end."

Lois glanced toward the river as they walked. They were almost at the cluster of trees where she and Maria had rescued Sally from the mugger on Friday. She stepped off the paved path, and walked into the clearing behind the trees and stood at the water's edge. Beth stopped beside her. For several minutes they listened to the water flowing past. Whenever Lois stood here, she felt a mixture of peace and sadness. But, even though she had twice encountered violent crimes here, she still loved this spot.

She turned her head to look at Beth. "It's funny that a place as lovely as this could have such bad things happen at it. But, at least they've caught the guy who mugged Sally. I really wish they had caught the boys who attacked James too. If only there was some clue to who they were."

Beth nodded. "I know. It must be terrible not to at least know they were punished for their crime, even though it won't bring James back. But try not to dwell on it. You can't change anything."

Lois smiled sadly. "I know. I won't ever forget what happened but I try not to let it consume my thoughts. My life's different now than I ever expected but I'm content. I have my lovely stone cottage, and Raggs and Ribbons, and good friends."

Beth laughed. "Do those cats still keep you on your toes?"

"They do. And sometimes I think they know more than you would expect from a cat. The way they look at me…"

"Cats always have a way of looking at you so you don't know whether it's wisdom or distain."

"My two are quite affectionate, especially if they want something. I think it's wisdom I see in their eyes."

Lois smiled and shook her head. She wouldn't mention that Ribbons had helped her more than once to decide whether or not to trust new acquaintances, and to figure out clues that helped to solve crimes. She also wouldn't tell Beth about her cottage's resident animal ghost, Beldie. It might be a bit much to expect her friend to believe such a tale. If Beth came to visit, she would find out whether or not her friend could sense Beldie's presence.

"It's great that you've got Marge just down the street from you in Fenwater. That's much like when you lived here in Toronto." Beth winked. "And not to mention your new man Bruce."

"He's not 'my man'! I've told you, we're only friends. He's never even asked me out on a date." Lois stopped speaking, pursing her lips. "I don't know whether I'd be ready for that."

"James has been gone more than three years now," Beth said, gently. "If you like Bruce, there's no harm accepting an invitation if he asks you out."

Lois nodded. "I know. For now, we're friends and I enjoy his company. That's enough. We'll wait and see what the future brings."

"Fair enough. When are you heading home?"

Lois gave Beth a startled look. Home? This valley nestled in the middle of the bustling city of Toronto was her home. She frowned as she considered this. No, it wasn't anymore. She still felt at home here but it wasn't her home. Fenwater was. It seemed strange to say that about the small, friendly town. This neighbourhood had been her home for so many years and she had so many good memories of her life here. But her life had changed and moved on. She *was* going home this afternoon.

Lois shrugged off her moment of melancholy. "Well, you know Maria! She won't let me leave until after lunch.

Angelo's working at the restaurant today but she stayed home to make lunch. She said I should ask you to join us. I know she'll have made enough to feed an army." Lois grinned at her friend. "And there's some tiramisu left from Thanksgiving dinner yesterday."

"You don't need to ask me twice!"

Laughing, Beth tugged Lois's arm and moved them toward the path. As they walked, Lois took a last look over her shoulder at the water glinting in the sunlight. She couldn't help loving this park and this spot. She was glad that she no longer feared it.

Lois quickened her step to a brisk walk and pulled Beth along with her. They had better work up an appetite on the way back to the house if they were going to do justice to one of Maria's fabulous meals.

∾

CONTINUE READING THE *CENTURY COTTAGE COZY MYSTERIES* series with Book One, *A Timeless Celebration*.

DIANNE ASCROFT IS THE AUTHOR OF THE *CENTURY COTTAGE Cozy Mysteries* series and the Second World War historical saga series, The Yankee Years. She is a Canadian who has a passion for Canada and Ireland, past and present. Dianne enjoys walks in the countryside, evenings in front of her open fireplace, and folk and traditional music. She lives on a small farm in Northern Ireland with her husband and an assortment of strong-willed animals.

Read more from Dianne Ascroft
www.dianneascroft.com

BURIED BY THE BEACH

ELLEN JACOBSON

1

———

"I can't believe you convinced me to wear this ridiculous outfit," I said to my friend, Ben Moretti, as I pulled up to the waterfront park. "I'm a middle-aged woman, not some kid going to a costume party."

"You look great, Mollie," he said. "That pirate wench look really suits you."

I scowled, inspecting the ludicrous get-up I was wearing—an off-the-shoulder white blouse, a red corset, and a dark purple full skirt over a petticoat. Even though the temperatures aren't as high during May in Florida as they are during the height of summer, my feet were still going to sweat to death in the black boots I had on to complete the look.

Ben was in heaven, dressed in full pirate regalia. The young man had always wished to have been born in earlier times, fancying himself as some sort of Jack Sparrow, sailing the high seas in search of plunder, rum, and women. Instead, he had to settle for living on his rundown sailboat at the Palm Tree Marina, eking out a meager existence repairing boats, and searching for the perfect woman to share his dream of sailing around the world.

My husband and I also live on a sailboat at the marina, which is where we had met Ben. Thankfully, Scooter was out of town on business. If he had seen me dressed up like this, I'm sure he would have come up with a new pirate-themed pet name for me, like Barnacle Babe or Fish Face McGhie.

Ben flipped down the visor and inspected his appearance in the mirror. "What do you think? Should I wear the patch on my right eye or my left? Which do you think the ladies would prefer?"

"Definitely the left," I said. "It makes you look more mysterious."

He switched the patch to his left eye, then adjusted the stuffed parrot perched on his shoulder. "There, that should do it. Do you mind popping the trunk so that I can get my sword out?"

After rummaging through the back, he tapped on the car. "Hurry up, Mollie. We're going to be late."

I rolled down the window. "I'm not getting out looking like this. Tell you what, I'll run back to the boat, change into something less flamboyant and meet you back here."

Before I could lock the car door, Ben opened it and pulled me out. "No way. You look the part. Besides, it's for a good cause. All the proceeds from the Pirate Day Treasure Hunt are going to the animal shelter. Mrs. Moto would even approve of what you're doing."

I smiled, thinking about our Japanese bobtail cat and how she had won first prize at the pet costume competition earlier in the year. "Mrs. Moto would look cute dressed as a pirate." I shook my head. "But I don't."

"Smile," Ben said as he whipped his phone out.

"Wait a minute, did you just take a picture of me?"

"Uh-huh. I promised Scooter I would."

I lunged at Ben, trying unsuccessfully to grab the phone. "Please, don't."

He grinned. "Too late."

"Fine. But I'd watch your back if I were you."

"Me? You should be the one to watch your back with all the dead bodies you keep finding around town."

"That's not fair. It's not like I go out searching for dead bodies. I just happen to ..." My voice trailed off as I recalled all the investigations that I had become embroiled in since I moved to Coconut Cove.

"Stumble across them?" Ben suggested.

"Stumble." I nodded. "Yes, that's it exactly. Finding them is merely accidental."

Ben swung his sword from side-to-side. "If there are any murderers out and about today, I'll protect you."

"Thanks, but I don't need—"

A shrill voice interrupted. "Stop goofing around, Ben. Put that thing away before you end up hurting yourself."

I turned and saw Nancy Schneider, who owned the Palm Tree Marina along with her husband, Ned. Her arms were folded across her chest and her lips pressed firmly together.

"It's made of plastic," I said to the older woman. "And before you say anything, no, we're not late."

She looked at her watch. "Yes, actually you are."

I held up my phone and pointed at the time on it. "No, we're not."

"That's not the correct time. It must be broken."

"No, it's not. Ben, show her your phone." He reluctantly pulled it out of his pocket. "See, his has the same time as mine. Your watch is running slow."

Her eyes narrowed as she peered at me over her reading glasses. "You're mistaken."

Before I could respond, Ben grabbed my elbow. "It's not worth it," he whispered to me. Then he turned to Nancy. "Do you want me to make her walk the plank for getting us here late?"

"Suck-up," I said under my breath.

She ignored both of us, pointing instead at a cardboard

box on the table behind her. "Take that and go man your booth. The treasure hunt is going to start soon."

"What's inside?" I asked.

Ben scratched his head. "What are we supposed to do again?"

"Didn't either of you read the instructions I emailed last week?" Nancy asked. "It clearly stated the rules for the event, and what your roles and responsibilities are."

Fortunately, I was wearing sunglasses so Nancy couldn't see me roll my eyes. There's nothing she loves more than bureaucratic rules and regulations, instruction manuals, and overly complicated spreadsheets. I wouldn't be surprised if she had a three-ring binder in her kitchen detailing the health and safety protocol for operating her toaster. So, when I received Nancy's email, I did what I had always done— deleted it and feigned ignorance.

"Email? Um, I don't think so," I said. "Maybe you could summarize the key points for us."

"Humph." She yanked the lid off the box, pulled out a rolled-up piece of parchment paper with burnt edges, and thrust it into my hands. "Start with this."

Ben peered over my shoulders while I unfurled the document and laid it on the table. "Cool," he said. "That looks just like a treasure map. It's got a pirate ship, and a skull with crossbones on it."

"That's because it is a treasure map," Nancy snapped. "You're here for the treasure hunt, aren't you?" She pointed at the bottom of the map. "See this star here? It marks the starting point. The kids register here. We hand them a copy of this map, then they follow the trail through the park. At each of the stations, they have to complete a pirate-themed challenge. For each challenge they complete, they get a clue."

Ben grinned. "And the clues lead them to the treasure, right?"

"Correct." Nancy indicated a large red 'X' on the map.

"The trail takes them through the waterfront park. There will be a treasure chest set up in the gazebo. If they've solved the clues, they can exchange them for treasure."

"What's the treasure?" I asked.

"Melvin's Marine Emporium has donated these." Nancy reached into the box and pulled out a black t-shirt featuring an image of a pirate with the words, "To err is human, to arr is pirate," underneath it.

"Ooh, these are cool," Ben said. "I want one."

Nancy glared at Ben. "If you had read my email ..." She looked off into the distance as her voice trailed off, her mouth agape. "Oh, my word ... is that who I think it is? What in the world is she doing back here?"

I peered in the direction Nancy was looking. "Who are you talking about?"

She pointed at a woman pushing a walker across the parking lot. "That's Cora Goodwin."

"That name sounds familiar," Ben said.

"Well it should," Nancy replied. "She's Coconut Cove's most illustrious criminal."

"You mean it's *the* Cora Goodwin?" Ben furrowed his brow. "But I thought she was dead."

"She doesn't look dead to me," Nancy said. After a beat, she added, "But I bet there are some people who wish she was."

"Who's Cora Goodwin?" I asked, watching as the woman in question slowly made her way toward a bench.

Nancy pursed her lips. "Oh, that's right. You and Scooter are recent transplants to Coconut Cove. This happened long before your time. Cora was Ambrose Hazelton's private secretary."

"Hazelton as in the Hazelton Estate? That big place on the outskirts of town?"

"Yes, that's the one. Ambrose made his money manufacturing vegetable peelers."

Ben nudged me. "Word is that he was also involved in smuggling Cuban cigars. He stole them off of ships bound for Europe and sneaked them into Florida. Kind of like a modern-day pirate."

"Ben, don't speak ill of the dead. Those are just rumors," Nancy said. "Ambrose was a respected member of the community. Besides, he never smelled like smoke."

"So, what does Cora have to do with Ambrose other than having been his secretary?" I asked.

"Well, back in the eighties, there was a robbery at the Hazelton Estate. The family's prize jewels were stolen, including the 'Calico Jack Emerald' necklace."

"That's a strange name," I said.

"You've heard of Calico Jack, haven't you?" Ben asked. "He was a famous pirate."

"Nope. The only pirate I'm familiar with is Coconut Carl."

Nancy glowered. "Do you want to stand around here all day talking about pirates, or do you want to know what happened?"

"I'm all ears," I said.

Placated, she continued. "The night of the robbery, Ambrose heard a noise around midnight. He went downstairs and discovered that someone had broken into the safe in his office. The same safe that only two people knew the combination to—Ambrose and Cora. And since Ambrose certainly wouldn't have stolen his own jewels, it had to have been ..."

When Nancy paused for dramatic effect, Ben eagerly said, "Cora."

She gave him an approving nod. "Correct. Cora lived on the estate—Ambrose liked to have his secretary available at all hours—but when the police knocked on her door to question her, she didn't answer. They broke down the door and discovered that Cora had ..."

This time, I answered. "She had disappeared."

Instead of the approving nod I was expecting, all I got from Nancy was a scowl. "Who's telling this story?"

"You are," I said, holding my hands up meekly.

"They searched everywhere for her but couldn't find her. She had hightailed it out of town. The necklace and Cora were both gone."

"So you think she did it?" I glanced over at Cora, who was now seated on the bench. She pulled the walker toward her and opened a bag that was attached to the front of it. She pulled out a large manila envelope and stared at it thoughtfully.

"Of course she did," Nancy said. "She knew the combination to the safe and fled town."

I shrugged. "Well, in my experience. Things aren't always as cut and dry as that."

"Things are usually black and white, in my opinion," Nancy said.

"If she is guilty, why do you think she showed up now?" I asked.

"That is a mystery, dear," Nancy said.

Ben rubbed the stubble on his chin. "Uh oh, looks like trouble."

A middle-aged man wearing an olive green t-shirt and camouflage pants was standing over Cora, gesturing angrily at her. "You," he yelled in a voice that sent shivers down my spine. "How dare you show your face here after all these years."

Cora shrunk back. "Everett? Is that you?"

Instead of answering, he yanked her off the bench. "What did you do with the necklace?"

~

A CROWD HAD GATHERED AROUND CORA AND EVERETT, watching the drama unfold. From what I overheard, it seemed apparent that the entire town believed she was guilty.

Cora squirmed in Everett's grasp, but he held on tight, continuing to demand what she had done with the stolen loot.

"You're hurting me," she said.

Ben put his hand on the hilt of his plastic sword and took a step forward. Before he could intervene though, a burly man wearing a police uniform pushed his way through the crowd. "Move aside, folks," he said in a commanding voice.

Everett sneered at Cora. "Good, Chief Dalton is here. He's going to take you to jail."

"What's going on here?" the chief asked.

"It's Cora Goodwin. Arrest her." Everett released the frightened woman, causing her to lurch into the chief's arms.

She looked up at him, her eyes wide. "Please, you have to help me."

"Why don't you sit down, ma'am?" After he lowered her onto the bench, he asked, "Are you really Cora Goodwin?" She nodded. "Why are you back in Coconut Cove?"

She looked sideways at Everett, then said, "I'm here to clear my name."

"Clear your name?" Everett jabbed his finger at her. "You should have tried that forty years ago."

"But I have proof now," she said weakly.

"Proof? Ridiculous." Everett said through clenched teeth. "Well, Chief, what are you waiting for? Arrest her."

"I can't. The statute of limitations has expired."

"But she stole our family's most prized possession."

The chief arched one of his bushy eyebrows. "Maybe, maybe not."

Everett gaze turned steely. "I guess you don't like your job

74

much. I'm going to see that you're fired as a result of this insubordination."

"Maybe, maybe not," the chief said, arching his other eyebrow. "Now, I suggest you go about your business and leave this woman alone." He turned to the crowd. "All of you."

"You haven't heard the last of this," Everett said before storming off.

The chief stared at his retreating back impassively, then turned to Cora. "How about I buy you a cup of coffee? And you can tell me what's going on."

She nodded. He helped her with her walker, then escorted her to his squad car.

"Well, that sure was some excitement," Ben said after they left.

Nancy looked at her watch. "We're going to be late starting the treasure hunt." She pointed at the cardboard box. "Grab that, Ben. The two of you need to hurry and get set up."

As Ben and I started to walk toward our station, I noticed a manila envelope lying on the ground next to the bench where Cora had been seated. I bent down and picked it up, then looked at Ben, my eyes wide. "It's addressed to me."

2

"**W**hat's inside?" Ben asked as he shifted the box in his arms.

"Why don't we head to our station first? It will be a bit quieter there." I said, eyeing the crowd that was still milling about. I tucked the envelope in my purse. "You know how nosy folks in Coconut Cove can be."

"What's that expression ... the pot calling the kettle black?"

"I am not nosy." I stamped my foot, which I instantly regretted when my heel struck something hard buried under the sand. I tumbled backward, my skirt flying up. Thankfully, the petticoat stayed in place. Maybe that's why ladies wore those undergarments back in the day, to save themselves from embarrassing moments like these.

"You okay, Mollie?" Ben asked.

"I think so," I said, doing a quick self-examination "Well, there is one casualty. The heel is broken off my boot. Darn. I'll have to put flip-flops on instead."

"If I didn't know better," Ben said as he helped me over to the bench, "I'd think you fell on purpose to get out of wearing them."

"Listen, if pirate wenches had known about flip-flops, they would have worn them instead of these stupid boots. And yoga pants. They would have worn those too," I said as I brushed sand off my skirt. Reaching into my purse, I pulled out a pair of emergency flip-flops that I always carry—along with emergency chocolate—and exchanged them for the boots. "There, much better. Shall we?"

"Aye, aye, lassie," Ben said.

When we got to our stand, we quickly set up. Then I opened the envelope and slid the contents onto the table. There were three pieces of paper. I turned the first one over. "This looks like a picture of an old treasure map."

"Pass that here," Ben said. "Hmm ... that looks familiar. I feel like I've seen it before."

"What's that in the corner there? See, next to that palm tree."

"It looks like a man standing next to a coconut." Ben held the paper up and peered at it more closely, then he grinned. "It says Coconut Carl underneath it."

"Really? Let me see." Coconut Carl was a bit of a legend in these parts. A pirate who loved women, plunder, and booze. There was a statue of him in the local bar, the Tipsy Pirate. Legend said that if you rubbed his belly three times while drinking a shot of rum, you'd have good luck. "If that's Coconut Carl, then that must mean this is a map of Coconut Cove."

Ben pointed to a depiction of an island. "Yep, I think you're right. That's Destiny Key."

I furrowed my brow. "I wonder why Cora had a copy of this map."

"Better question is why did she want you to have it," Ben said. "What else was in there?"

"It looks like some sort of math problem," I said, picking up the next piece of paper.

"Math?"

"Yep. It's a series of numbers—twenty-five, forty-two, and twenty-nine—with 2,132 underneath. But that doesn't add up," I said, pointing at the paper.

"Add up?"

"Well, the way it's written, it looks like it's supposed to be addition. But twenty-five, forty-two, and twenty-nine add up to ..." I scratched my head. "I'm not sure exactly what it adds up to, but it's a lot less than 2,132."

"Maybe it's supposed to be a subtraction problem," Ben suggested.

Before we could figure it out, two young boys bounded up to our stand, their harried parents trailing behind. Both boys sported eye patches and tricorne hats just like Ben.

"Whoa, look at his sword," the older boy said.

The younger one bounced up and down. "He has a parrot on his shoulder. I want a parrot too." He spun around and tugged on his mom's hand. "Can I have a parrot?"

She shook her head. "For the last time, no parrots."

The boy ignored her, instead twirling around in circles screaming 'parrot' at the top of his lungs. The other boy ran back and forth brandishing an imaginary sword.

The dad looked apologetically at us. "Sorry, they've got a bit of a sugar high going on."

"Boys, that's enough," the mom said.

When they ignored her, Ben stood, put his hands on his hips, and said, "Avast, mateys!" He turned and whispered to me, "That's pirate talk for pay attention."

"Do you want to walk the plank?"

The boys stood still, their eyes wide. They shook their heads.

"Do you want me to keelhaul you instead?"

"No, captain," they both said in unison.

Ben grinned. "Good, then come here and let's see if you know any pirate riddles."

While Ben handed an answer sheet and markers to each of them, I moved Cora's papers to the side of the table.

The mom helped the younger boy with his marker. "What do they need to do?"

"If they can solve the riddles, then they'll get a clue stamp on their cards," I explained.

"Why don't I read them out loud, and you write down your answers?" Ben said. "Okay, here's the first one. 'It sits on a pirate's shoulder and never flies away. The silliest thing about it is that it repeats what you say.'"

The older boy smiled, then scribbled on his answer sheet. The younger boy looked perplexed until I pointed at Ben's shoulder.

He jumped up and down. "It's a parrot."

"Very good," the mom said, ruffling his hair. Ben continued asking riddles while the dad snapped pictures.

After the boys successfully answered all the riddles, I stamped their cards. While they showed them to their mom, the dad asked if we had seen the commotion earlier.

"You mean with Cora Goodwin?" Ben asked.

"Yes. Can you believe she had the audacity to show her face in town?"

"Everett didn't look very pleased about it," Ben said.

"Who exactly is Everett?" I asked.

The man raised his eyebrows. "You don't know Everett Hazelton? Everyone knows the Hazeltons."

"Mollie's new to town," Ben explained before turning to me. "Everett is Ambrose's son."

I cocked my head to one side. "So was he at home when the robbery took place?"

"No, he was out of town. He was devastated when he heard what had happened," Ben said. "The 'Calico Jack Emerald' had belonged to his mother and his grandmother long before that. When he got married, the necklace would have gone to his wife."

I toyed with the pendant on my necklace. "Sure, I can see how his wife would have been disappointed. Emeralds are nice, although personally I prefer diamonds."

The man laughed. "If you had ever seen the size of this emerald, you might change your mind. Anyway, Everett never married."

"Is that because he's in the Army?" I asked. Both men looked confused. "Well, isn't that why he was wearing camouflage?"

"No, that's for hunting. Everett hunts wild pigs." Ben motioned with his hands. "They're all around these parts."

"Everett never got married, because, well, he's Everett," the dad said. "Ornery, like a wild pig."

His wife tapped him on the arm. "Honey, we better get going. The sugar high is starting to wear off, and they're getting cranky."

As they walked off toward the next station, I dug in my purse and pulled out a bag of M&M'S. "Speaking of sugar highs, mine's starting to wear off too."

BEN AND I WERE BUSY THE REST OF THE MORNING, ASKING KIDS pirate riddles and stamping their clue cards. I tried to call Chief Dalton several times to see if he had Cora's contact information. I wanted to speak with her about the envelope she had dropped and why it had been addressed to me. Although, as usual, he didn't answer my calls or return my messages.

After trying to reach him for the tenth time, I sighed. "I could really use some more chocolate."

"What happened to the M&M'S?" Ben asked.

"They're all gone."

"And the Snickers bars?"

"Gone too." I chewed on my lip, then emptied my purse onto the table. "There's gotta be something in here." After digging through the contents, I raised my arms in victory. "I found a Hershey Kiss!"

Ben stared at the silver-wrapped treat and licked his lips. "Just one?"

"Um, yeah. They're kind of hard to divide into two, even with a knife."

Fortunately, Ben was distracted by a young woman approaching our booth. While he greeted her with a cheerful "Ahoy, matey," I quickly unwrapped the Kiss and popped it into my mouth.

The woman tilted her head to one side. "Ahoy?"

"Shiver me timbers, lassie," Ben said. "Don't you know the basic pirate greeting?"

"Uh … no." She looked at him dubiously. "Is that what you're supposed to be dressed up as—a pirate?"

I smothered a laugh while Ben squirmed in his chair.

"What can we do for you?" I asked. "It doesn't seem like you're here for the Pirate Day Treasure Hunt."

She fixed her gaze on me. "Are you Mollie McGhie?"

"I am."

"Good. I've been looking everywhere for you." She rubbed her hands together. "Did Cora Goodwin give you an envelope?"

Ben leaned forward. "Yes, she—"

I kicked him under the table to silence him. "Cora Goodwin? Was she the lady who got into an altercation with Everett Hazelton earlier today?" I asked innocently.

"I don't know anything about that," she said. "I just need the envelope back."

"Who exactly are you?" I asked.

"Oh, sorry. I had thought I said." She toyed with the lid on her coffee cup. "Anyway, about that envelope?"

"Sorry, I still didn't catch your name."

"It's Antoinette," she said sharply. "I'm Cora's caregiver."

"Caregiver?" Ben asked. "What's wrong with her?"

"She has dementia. She's always doing crazy things like putting her alarm clock in the fridge and giving envelopes to people." Antoinette gave us an ingratiating smile. "She realized that she made a mistake giving you that envelope and wants it back, so she sent me here to get it."

I cocked my head to one side. "Do you have her phone number? Maybe I can give her a call and clear things up."

Antoinette shook her head. "No, that wouldn't be a good idea. Talking on the phone gets her agitated. Look, the best thing is to give me the envelope, and I can take it back to her."

I shrugged. "Well, I don't know what to say. Cora never gave me an envelope."

"Are you sure?"

"Positive."

Ben looked at me quizzically. "But—".

I kicked him under the table again, then smiled brightly at the young woman. "I can say with a hundred percent certainty that she didn't give me anything."

"Huh," she said.

I handed her one of the answer sheets. "Do you want to try your hand at a pirate riddle?"

"No, thanks." She crumpled the paper up and tossed it on the table, then turned and strode off.

"Why did you lie to her?" Ben asked as he rubbed his shin.

"I didn't lie to her. Cora didn't give me anything."

"You really do need some chocolate," he said. "The sugar withdrawal is doing something funny to your memory."

"Cora didn't *give* me an envelope. She *dropped* an envelope, and I picked it up. There's a big difference." I wrinkled my nose. "Didn't you think that there was something a bit off about Antoinette?"

"Well, yeah," Ben said. "She didn't know what 'ahoy' meant or what a pirate looks like."

"Besides that. There's something I don't trust about that girl. There was no way I was going to give that envelope back to her. I really need to track Cora down myself and find out exactly what's going on."

3
_____

While Ben went to get us coffee, I tried calling the chief again. This time, he answered. Probably because I used Ben's phone instead of mine and he didn't recognize the number.

"Chief, don't hang up," I said quickly.

"Mrs. McGhie, is that you?" he asked gruffly.

"Yes, listen, it's about—"

"For the millionth time, Mrs. McGhie, you do not need to phone the police station every time you think you've spotted a UFO."

"But this isn't about extraterrestrial sightings," I spluttered. "It's about—"

"And you don't need to call every time you suspect an alien abduction has occurred."

"No, you don't understand. I'm calling about ..." I slammed the phone down on the table. "I can't believe he hung up on me," I muttered.

"Who hung up?" Ben asked, handing me a coffee cup.

"The chief."

"Well, that isn't really a surprise, is it? You've been a thorn in his side since you moved to Coconut Cove."

"If by 'thorn in his side,' you mean that I solve cases. Then, yes, by all means, I'm a thorn in his side." I took a sip of my drink. "Oh, this is so good."

"I had them put extra chocolate in your mocha."

"Thanks," I said with a smile. "You know me so well."

"What did you do with that envelope from Cora, anyway?"

"Oh, I tucked it in that cardboard box earlier. There were so many kids running around, I didn't want anything to happen to it. Want to hand it to me? We never did finish looking at what was inside."

I spread the three pieces of paper out on the table. "Okay, so let's recap. We have a photo of an old treasure map and some sort of math problem."

"I wish I could remember where I've seen that treasure map before," Ben said.

"Finish your coffee," I suggested. "Maybe the caffeine will jolt those memory cells of yours."

He drained the contents of his cup. "Nope, didn't help."

"What about these numbers—can you make heads or tails of them?" He shook his head. "Neither can I. Let's set it aside for a while with the map."

"What's on the last piece of paper?" Ben asked.

"It looks like part of a letter." I examined the torn-off piece of cream-colored bond paper. "It seems to end mid-sentence. Can you check the envelope and see if the rest of the letter is in there?"

Ben looked inside the envelope. "Nothing else in there."

"Okay, well let's read it and see if we can figure out what it's about."

I furrowed my brow as I read the passage.

'I never meant for this to happen. I had hoped things would die down in a few years and you could return to Coconut Cove. But now that I know I don't have much time left, I want to make amends. Enclosed you'll find the information you need to ...'

I started to hand the paper to Ben when my phone buzzed. "Hang on, let me check my texts."

"Anything interesting?" Ben asked.

"There sure is. It's from the chief. He says that Cora Goodwin is in the hospital and she's asking to see me."

~

AFTER CHECKING TO MAKE SURE BEN WOULD BE OKAY MANNING our station by himself, I rushed to the hospital. When I got there, Chief Dalton was pacing back and forth, talking on his phone. He held up his hand, motioning for me to wait. While he continued with a very boring conversation about speeding tickets, I searched online for information about the Hazelton family.

The first thing to pop up was an article about Everett in a hunting magazine. There was a picture of him dressed in camouflage, grinning as he stood proudly behind a dead pig. The article went onto say that wild pigs can weigh up to two hundred pounds and that, while they're not usually dangerous, they can become aggressive when cornered or injured. I shuddered at the thought of a wild pig coming after me and impaling me with its tusks.

The next link took me to photos of the Hazelton Estate posted on Instagram. The house and gardens were absolutely gorgeous. Looking at them made me wish that I still lived in our cute little beach cottage rather than a rundown sailboat at a marina.

When I had finished drooling over the pictures of the estate, I clicked on Ambrose Hazelton's obituary. It mentioned how he had made his fortune from vegetable peelers but didn't say anything about the rumors of him smuggling Cuban cigars into Florida. Everett was listed as his sole surviving family member, Ambrose's siblings and wife having predeceased him.

While I was reading about how Ambrose loved puzzles and model airplanes, I felt someone tap me on my shoulder. I turned and nodded at the chief. After I tucked my phone in my purse, I asked him what room Cora was in.

"You're too late," he said.

I gasped. "You mean she's dead?"

"Dead? Why would she be dead?" he asked.

"After the way Everett accosted her at the park, I thought he might have ..." I looked around to make sure no one was listening in, then lowered my voice. "I thought he might have, you know, murdered her."

The chief closed his eyes and rubbed his temples. "Mrs. McGhie, you have an overactive imagination. No one has been murdered in Coconut Cove."

"You mean recently, right?" I said.

He narrowed his eyes. "As I was saying, you're too late to see Miss Goodwin today. The doctor gave her a sedative. She'll be out for hours."

"Why was she sedated?"

"I can't say."

"You can't say, or you won't say?"

"Yes."

"That's not an answer." When he didn't reply, I folded my arms across my chest and stared at him. "Well, can you at least tell me why she wanted to see me?"

"She said she needed your ..." the chief paused and shuddered as though he had just swallowed something bitter. After exhaling slowly, he continued, "She said she needed your investigative expertise."

"She really said that?" I grinned. "Word must have gotten out about all the murders I've solved."

"Hmm. More likely, she heard how you investigate UFO sightings."

Ignoring his jibe, I said, "This would be a lot simpler if you had just told me exactly what you and she talked about.

When you left the park, you said that you were going to take her for a cup of coffee. How did you end up here at the hospital?"

"We didn't get coffee. We ended up coming directly here."

"That's awful. Did it have to do with her dementia? Her caregiver had mentioned that she gets agitated easily."

"Dementia? As far as I know, she doesn't have dementia or a caregiver. When she got into my squad car, she started having severe hip pain. You saw how she uses a walker."

I mentally patted myself on the back. It felt good that my hunch about Antoinette had been right. Though if she wasn't her caregiver, who was she and why did she want Cora's envelope?

The chief looked at his watch. "Now, unless you have anything of importance to tell me, I need to be someplace."

"An urgent speeding ticket meeting?"

He pointed to the nurses' station. "If you have any further questions about Miss Goodwin, you can check with them."

As I scowled at the chief's retreating back, my phone buzzed. I grinned when I read Ben's text. He had figured out the mystery of the treasure map and wanted me to meet him at the Coconut Cove Historical Museum.

I AVOIDED ALL THE KNOWN SPEED TRAPS ON MY WAY TO THE museum and still managed to get there in under fifteen minutes. Ben was sitting outside, polishing his sword with a napkin. When he saw me, he stood and adjusted his eye patch.

"Ahoy there, lassie."

"Ahoy there, yourself. Sorry I left you by yourself at the treasure hunt."

"It was fine. There were only a few stragglers after you

left. Besides, you were on a much more important mission. What did Cora say?"

"Nothing." After I explained about Cora's condition, I asked Ben why we were at the museum.

"Come on inside, and I'll show you."

We walked through displays on the founding of the town, the geology of the local area, and underwater archaeology before reaching our destination—an exhibit on the pirates of Coconut Cove.

"I visited here a couple of years ago," Ben said as he escorted me to the back of the room. "There was a girl volunteering here at the time who was really cute."

"Any luck?"

He frowned. "No, she had a boyfriend."

I patted his arm. "The right girl is out there for you, I know it." Then I pointed at the wall. "Is that what I think it is?"

"Yep, it's the original treasure map."

I pulled Cora's envelope out of my purse and compared the picture that was in it with the original.

"They're not exactly alike," I said as I raised myself on my toes and squinted at the map hanging on the wall. "Do those look like numbers to you? Right there, next to the right-hand corner of the frame."

"I think so, but it's hard to tell from here," Ben said.

I looked around the exhibit room. "It looks like it's just us. Why don't you take it down so we can have a closer look?"

Ben shoved his hands in his pockets. "I don't know about that, Mollie."

"You're a pirate, right? I mean, look at how you're dressed. All dapper with your eye patch and your parrot."

"You think I look dapper?"

"Not just dapper. You look dashing." His face reddened. "And pirates are the ultimate rule-breakers, right?"

"I guess so."

"Well, then what do you say we get a closer look at that map?"

After reassuring Ben that I didn't see any security cameras, he removed the map from the wall and set it down on a display case.

"That looks similar to the math problem in Cora's envelope," Ben said. "The numbers are different though."

"You're right," I said, examining the numbers which appeared to be written in pencil. "Let me get a shot of that." After checking my phone to make sure the photo came out okay, I gave Ben the all clear to hang the map back up.

He started to lift it up, then paused. "I think I feel something attached to the back," he said, flipping the map around so I could see.

"You're not going to believe this," I said. "It's another manila envelope."

"Quick, grab it. This is awkward to hold."

I snatched it off the back, but before I could open it, someone cleared their throat behind us.

"Ahem, can I help you?" A man wearing a volunteer badge on his vest looked back and forth at us warily.

"Oh, the map was crooked," I said, quickly tucking the envelope behind my back. "My friend was adjusting it."

"You should have reported that to the front desk. Visitors aren't supposed to touch the exhibits."

"You're absolutely right, sir," I said, holding my hands up. "We'll just be on our way."

As we scurried out of the museum, Ben said, "I hope whatever you found was worth it."

4

Later that evening, I was in the marina office, killing time while I waited for Ben to arrive. We had made plans to rendezvous after his band rehearsal so that we could try to figure out Cora's mystery.

While I looked at the books on display, I reflected on the clues we had found so far. First, there were the three pieces of paper in the envelope Cora had addressed to me—a math problem, a photo of the treasure map from the historical museum, and a letter fragment. At the museum, we had discovered two additional clues—a different math problem written in pencil on the original treasure map and an old key hidden in an envelope on the back of the map.

Just thinking about the math problems gave me a headache, so I pushed that to one side of my brain and concentrated on the letter. The line that said, "I hoped things would die down in a few years and you could return to Coconut Cove," made me think that it had been written to Cora. She had fled town after the jewelry theft. Did the writer think that Cora would no longer be under suspicion in a few years? And if that was the case, who had written the letter? Who believed her name would have been cleared?

Nancy's shrill voice interrupted my thoughts. "Are you just going to stand there all day or are you going to buy something?"

"I'm just browsing."

"We don't browse in here, dear."

"Well, you can't expect me to buy something without checking it out first." I picked up a book about sailing in the Bahamas and started leafing through it. "Just give me a few moments so I can see if this will meet our needs."

She leaned against the counter while I examined the book. "Did you hear about Everett Hazelton and Cora Goodwin?"

"I was right there next to you when it happened."

She frowned. "No, not at the waterfront park. Later this afternoon at the hospital."

I looked up from the book. "What happened?"

"Everett stormed into her room, demanding to know what she did with the jewelry. When she didn't answer, he held up a pillow and threatened to smother her with it."

I put my hand to my chest. "She must have been terrified."

"She was. She started screaming, and one of the nurses ran into the room. They called the police and hauled Everett out of there, but Cora was still so upset that they eventually had to sedate her." Then, her gossip session finished, she pointed at the book in my hand. "Time's up. Are you buying the book or not?"

"I'm not sure. Scooter has been talking about sailing to the Bahamas one of these days." I flipped through the pages, then tapped my finger on one of the nautical charts at the back. "I think Mrs. Moto might enjoy going to this island given its feline name."

"Let me see that." Nancy grabbed the book, adjusted her reading glasses, and peered at the map. "Oh, Cat Island. Ned and I sailed there several years ago. There's a fascinating monastery there." Then she snorted as she handed the book back to me. "In any case, I doubt that boat of yours would make it that far. The two of you have a lot of work to do to make her seaworthy."

I frowned. The list of boat projects Scooter and I had to do was overwhelming. The older woman was right. There was no way we'd ever get to the Bahamas on our boat.

As I started to replace the book on the shelf, Nancy shook her head. "Looks like you bent the cover, so you'll have to buy it now."

I gritted my teeth. "It wasn't bent until you grabbed it from me."

"Rules are rules, dear."

After she rang the book up, I glanced at the map of Cat Island again. Then it hit me. I knew what the numbers meant, and they didn't have anything to do with math.

～

I SENT BEN A QUICK TEXT, TELLING HIM I'D MEET HIM BACK AT the marina later and sped to the waterfront park, slowing down when I neared a known speed trap.

After parking the car, I pulled up an app on my phone and double-checked where exactly I needed to go. After entering the set of numbers on the paper in Cora's envelope and the set of numbers written on the map, I was rewarded with an 'X' on the app.

I grabbed a flashlight out of my purse and walked down the beach until I reached a trailhead. As I made my way along the path that cut through the dense brush, loud snorting sounds sent shivers up my spine. When I shined my flashlight back and forth, glowing eyes looked back at me. I saw furrows on the side of the path too. They looked like someone had plowed the sandy soil, but after reading the article about Everett in the hunting magazine, I knew better. They were signs that wild pigs had been rutting in the area.

I considered turning back, but my curiosity got the better

of me—I needed to know if I was right about the mysterious numbers. The article had also said that wild pigs rarely attacked humans. The odds were on my side, or at least that's how I convinced myself.

Cautiously advancing, I reached the end of the path. I double-checked my phone. The site appeared to be about twenty feet away from my current position. I trudged through the brush, wincing as tree branches snapped back and hit me in the face. When I reached a small clearing, I paused, sweeping the flashlight back and forth.

Then I gasped—there were more glowing eyes, except this time, they weren't wild pig eyes; they were human eyes.

"What are you doing here?" A man's voice demanded. He walked toward me, brandishing a shovel in his hands.

As I turned to run back to my car, I tripped on a root and tumbled onto the ground. The man continued to advance toward me. I groped through the decaying leaves around me, trying to find my flashlight. Once I secured it, I got to my feet and shined it in his direction, hoping to blind him with the light.

"Hey, I know you," I said when his face was fully illuminated. "You were at the treasure hunt earlier with your wife and two boys."

He put his hand over his eyes to shield them. "I didn't think you'd be smart enough to figure it out. When you were at the museum, you couldn't even figure out what the numbers meant."

My eyes widened. "You were there?"

"I was," he said, swinging the shovel back and forth in his hands. "Now what do you say we forget that you ever saw me here."

"I'm fine with that. I'll just be on my way," I said, slowly creeping backward. Then I jumped when I heard a loud crashing noise to the right of me. Two wild pigs ran into the clearing, startling the man. He shrieked, dropped the shovel, and tore past me.

My heart thumped in my chest as the pigs looked at me. Then they turned and ran in the other direction, clearly more frightened of me than I was of them.

Once my breathing had returned to normal, I rushed over to the hole the man had dug, grabbed the object inside, and thanked the wild pigs for scaring him off before he could retrieve it.

WHEN I GOT BACK TO THE MARINA, BEN WAS WAITING FOR ME ON the patio. When he saw what I was carrying, he whistled. "That is so cool. It looks like a miniature treasure chest. Where did you get it?"

"Remember those numbers?" He nodded. "They weren't math problems. Turns out they were longitudes and latitudes. Once I figured that out, I was able to pinpoint the location of this treasure chest."

He cocked his head to one side. "They didn't look anything like longitudes and latitudes."

"I know. That's what threw us off. But I remembered something my mom did once. She was going to let me use her credit card for something. She's a little paranoid about people hacking her computer and reading her emails, so rather than send me the number all written out like it is on the card, she broke it up into chunks to make it look like a math problem."

"That's smart," Ben said.

"Kind of. But if someone is smart enough to hack her computer, they're probably smart enough to figure out her little code." I set the small dark wooden box on the table and brushed dirt off it. A metal band wrapped around it and was secured with a rusty padlock. Reaching into my purse, I pulled out the key that we had found taped to the back of the treasure map in the museum. "Want to bet this unlocks it?"

"Hurry up," Ben said as I tried to insert the key into the lock. "I want to see what's inside."

"It's jammed," I said.

"Let me try." While he jiggled the key back and forth, I told him about the man I had encountered.

Ben raised his eyebrows. "You mean it was the same guy that brought his kids to our treasure hunt station?"

"Uh-huh."

"But how did he know where to dig? He didn't have the numbers."

"He said that he saw us in the museum. I think he followed us there and hid somewhere. Once we left, it was easy enough for him to check out the treasure map."

Ben furrowed his brow. "Okay, that explains how he got one set of numbers. How did he get the other?"

"It's my own fault, really," I said. "When they came up to our stand, I set the papers in Cora's envelope to the side. The piece of paper with the numbers was on the top. I remember him taking pictures of his boys. I'm guessing he also snapped a shot of the numbers at the same time. He had all the information he needed."

"But he didn't have this." Ben held up the key.

"Did you get it unlocked?"

"I did. But I think you should have the honor of opening it."

I bit my lip as I slowly lifted the lid, then I gasped when I saw what was inside. "Is that what I think it is?" I asked.

He peered over my shoulder. "Yep. It looks like you found the 'Calico Jack Emerald.'"

5
———

The next morning, Ben and I met at the hospital. I chuckled when I saw how he was dressed. "You're still in your pirate outfit."

"You better believe it, lassie. I don't have to return it to the costume rental shop until tomorrow. I'm going to wear it until then and get my money's worth."

"Did you sleep in it?"

"No comment," he said sheepishly.

"What time is it? Chief Dalton should be here by now."

"There he is," Ben said, pointing at the burly man walking toward us.

"What was so urgent that I had to meet the two of you here?" the chief asked.

I looked down at the treasure chest I was holding. "This."

"What is that? A child's toy?"

"Hardly," I said. "I didn't sleep a wink last night, keeping an eye on it."

"Your problems with insomnia do not constitute official police business," the chief said.

"Well, okay, if you don't want to know what's inside,

that's fine with me," I said with a shrug. "We'll just go ahead and show it to Cora without you then."

"This has to do with Miss Goodwin?" The chief grabbed the box from me. "We'll see about that."

Ben and I trailed behind him as he strode to Cora's room. He knocked gently at the door and a faint voice called out for us to enter.

"Miss Goodwin," the chief said as he removed his hat. "How are you feeling today?"

"Much better," she said. "I understand from the nurse that Everett is still in jail?"

"That's correct, ma'am. He's facing very serious charges." The chief looked sideways at Ben and me. "Mrs. McGhie and Mr. Moretti have something they want to show you."

The woman leaned forward in her bed and smiled brightly at me. "Are you Mollie McGhie?"

"I am," I said, smiling back.

Her smile faded. "There was something I wanted to give you, but I don't know what happened to it."

"The envelope?" I asked. She nodded. "I found it."

"You did," Cora said, clapping her hands together. "That's wonderful. I was hoping to get your help with a little mystery."

The chief cleared his throat. "Is this something the police should help you with instead, ma'am?"

"Oh, I'm sure you're far too busy to worry about something like this," Cora said gently.

"Like speeding tickets," I muttered under my breath.

"What was that, Mrs. McGhie?" the chief asked sharply.

"I was just saying that we should probably show Cora what's inside the chest you're holding."

"Fine," he said, setting it down on the hospital tray over the older woman's bed. "But if this is one of your tricks—"

"I promise. No tricks." I nodded at Ben. "Can you unlock it?"

After Ben inserted the key and lifted the lid, he turned it toward Cora. Tears streamed down her face when she saw the necklace and other jewelry inside. "You did it. You found the treasure Ambrose hid."

"Ambrose?" Ben and I asked in unison.

"Yes, Ambrose." She leaned back against her pillow and wiped her face with a tissue. "Ambrose always did love puzzles. Right before he died, he sent me a letter including a sheet with numbers on it and a picture of an old treasure map. I couldn't figure out what they meant. I even showed it to this young woman who was helping me out with cleaning and light housekeeping, but she didn't have a clue. I've had a hard time keeping on top of things since I broke my hip."

"A young woman? What does she look like?" I asked.

After she described her, Ben and I looked at each other. "That sounds like Antoinette."

"You know Antoinette?" Cora asked.

"We met her yesterday. She said you sent her to find me and retrieve the envelope."

Cora shook her head. "No, that's not true. She actually quit working for me last week. I haven't seen her since then."

"Did she quit right after she saw what Ambrose sent you?"

"Now that you mention it, she did."

"Huh. I wonder if she was working in cahoots with that guy?" I mused.

The chief fixed his gaze on me. "Mrs. McGhie, perhaps you could explain."

"Why don't we discuss it later? I think there's a couple of people you're going to want to talk to about this. First, I want to hear more about Ambrose."

Cora nodded. "I remembered reading an article about you, Mollie, and how you had solved murders here in Coconut Cove."

The chief straightened his shoulders. "That isn't exactly true, Miss Goodwin."

"Shush," I said. "Don't interrupt this nice lady."

Cora patted my hand. "I decided to come back to Coconut Cove and see if you could help me. And you did."

"How exactly did you help, Mrs. McGhie?" the chief asked reluctantly.

I tapped the side of my head. "Good old-fashioned detective work. Ambrose wrote down the latitude and longitude to where the treasure chest was located. He put one of them on the piece of paper he mailed to Cora and wrote the other one down on an old treasure map." I looked at Cora. "I assume he thought you'd recognize the treasure map and go to the museum to check it out where you would discover the other set of numbers."

She shook her head. "I would have never figured that out."

"I would have never figured it out either if it hadn't been for Ben. We were lucky he remembered seeing the map at the museum."

"Thank you, young man," Cora said. "Mollie is lucky to have you helping her."

Ben beamed at the praise, then asked Cora about Ambrose's involvement in the theft.

"Poor Ambrose. There was a lawsuit about his vegetable peelers after someone nearly cut their finger off. He ended up losing most of his fortune. He was at his wit's end, so he decided to ..." she paused and looked at the three of us. "Can you promise to keep this between us?"

Ben and I said yes; the chief said no. "Ma'am, this involves a criminal matter," he explained.

"Don't you think Ambrose wanted the truth to come out? Otherwise, he wouldn't have sent you that letter."

She nodded slowly. "I suppose you're right. Well, you see, Ambrose couldn't bear the thought of losing the Hazelton

Estate. So, he faked the robbery to collect the insurance money."

"But why did he let you take the blame?" I asked.

"I wanted to," she said. "I couldn't bear to see him so distraught. We agreed that I would leave Coconut Cove for a while and that we'd let everyone believe I stole the jewelry. I thought that eventually things would die down and I could return." She pressed her fingers against the bridge of her nose and sniffled. "I realize now how foolish that was. There was no way I could ever come back to Coconut Cove. Ambrose kept sending me checks and telling me to wait just a little longer, but the years kept stretching on."

I squeezed Cora's hand. "You loved him, didn't you?"

"I did. I think in his own way he loved me too. He said as much in the letter he sent me." She squeezed my hand back. "That's why I only put part of the letter in the envelope for you. The rest of it was just too personal to share."

I glanced over at the chief. "Are you getting teary-eyed?"

"No, just allergies," he said gruffly. "You look like you could use some rest, Miss Goodwin. I'll take the jewelry with me and process it, then come back and ask you a few more questions later." The chief looked at me sideways. "Someone should have called me the minute they found this jewelry in the first place."

"Maybe you should start returning my calls," I muttered.

"What was that, Mrs. McGhie?"

"I said that there's one more thing we should do before you take the treasure chest away." I smiled and held the 'Calico Jack Emerald' necklace up to Cora. "Want to try it on first?"

∽

START THE *MOLLIE MCGHIE COZY SAILING MYSTERY* SERIES with Book One, *Murder at the Marina*

. . .

ELLEN JACOBSON IS A CHOCOLATE OBSESSED CAT LOVER WHO writes cozy mysteries and romantic comedies. After living on a sailboat for many years, she now travels around in a teeny-tiny camper with her husband and an imaginary cat named Simon.

Read more from Ellen Jacobson
www.ellenjacobsonauthor.com

CLOSED OUT

TAMARA WOODS

1

_____

Fraya Taylor thought the phrase, "The silence was deafening," was a dramatic exaggeration until she walked into the front room of the Mystic Eye Bookshop, and everybody stopped talking. She could hear the ticking of the clock behind the register.

Fraya was the official conversation killer of Whisper Valley.

The weight of their stares; their disapproval pressed down on her. She didn't bother trying to smile reassuringly or even meet anyone in the eye. She kept her eyes on her feet as she rushed through shelving the books at her aunt's bookshop and then scurried away.

She felt like such a coward.

With her head down, Fraya barreled past the metaphysical shelves, and displays full of crystal balls, athames, crystals, sage bundles, candles, and other occult items that would be perfect for any witch or people who were into that sort of thing. Fraya thought it was all bunk, but plenty of people kept buying it. Today she didn't take in the deep mauves and purples in the Mystic Eye Bookshop, and she barely registered the soft sounds of New Age music playing in the background or the gentle incense burning. Fraya walked past the area she thought would be perfect for seating and a little tea set-up. She'd even been telling her aunt for months that she should hook it up.

Before everything had gone south.

She sneezed as she settled into the backroom. Aunt Maybel's backroom was as bad as her office — full of chaotic mess. Boxes overflowed with inventory or stacked on bookshelves that were in no sort of order. One naked light bulb hung from a chain in the middle of the room, its light swinging cast little shadows against the wall that made Fraya uneasy.

Beyond that, there wasn't a whole lot to do back there, so cleaning was it. Fraya looked down at the vintage velvet dress her cousin Isa had given her for her birthday last year. Dust would be such a pain to clean off. She unearthed an apron with a silhouette of a witch reading a book on it and tugged it on. She liked to dress up for work, even though now, she was sporting something less colorful than normal. A dark blue dress with matching gloves and shoes made her look like she was in mourning.

I guess I sort of am, she thought.

She had managed to organize a box of the books when a head peeked into the room. "How you doing, my favorite niece?"

Aunt Maybel's bright lavender and yellow dress with matching headwrap seemed to light up the room. Fraya could use some of that light. Logically, she knew her aunt had to tend to her customers, but sometimes she wished she fell higher on that priority list.

"I'm fine," she said with the mere wisp of a smile. That's all she could muster up at the moment.

"You sure?" Aunt Maybel looked her over, and Fraya could sense her aunt noting her messy hair, how her dress hung on her frame, how the bags under her eyes looked like a set of matching luggage.

Fraya just nodded. Opening her mouth right then ran the risk of her crying, and she didn't want that. She needed to show that she could be strong.

Everything was fine, and she wasn't at all dying inside.

"Why don't you go home? Take the rest of the day off." Maybel hugged her close. Her special blend of bergamot, honeysuckle, and a scent that she could never place soothed Fraya's heavy heart.

"Maybe go on down to the diner and grab you a snack. Have you been eating?" Again Fraya answered with a nod, but this time it was more hesitant. When was the last time that she'd had something to eat? She couldn't remember. The days were fading and falling into nights, and she couldn't seem to make heads or tails of them. She gently pulled away from her aunt.

Maybel pulled out a few bills from her headscarf and pressed them into her niece's hand. "Get you some food, girl. We'll be all right without you."

Even this tiny bit of kindness that was expected from her aunt filled Fraya's eyes with tears. She couldn't even control her trembling lip. Her aunt smoothed down her hair.

"You're going to be just fine. I read your cards today. Some big changes are coming, but you're going to be fine." Aunt Maybel said, her voice strong and confident in her beliefs. At her words, Fraya stifled the instinct to roll her eyes.

She could feel her aunt's blunt fingers pulling her hair this way and that. "Those nappy roots is showing. You got you some good hair. You should just let it flow free and wild instead of putting all those chemicals in there, wrecking those curls. Chop the rest of that stuff clean off."

Fraya quickly backed up, embarrassed that someone had seen her hair up close in its current state. She hadn't felt like going through straightening her kinky curls lately. Why bother?

"Auntie, ain't nobody seen your hair since the 60s," Fraya pointed out defensively. She couldn't remember a time when her aunt hadn't worn headwraps with matching dresses. Today she looked more like an exotic peacock than the owner of a witchy bookshop.

The older woman patted her scarf. "And that's how it's going to stay too. I look good." She struck an old Hollywood pose with her hand on her hip and her head thrown back. A real smile peeked on Fraya's face, a tiny one.

Her aunt's eyes twinkled in satisfaction, then she switched back to caregiver mode. She made a shooing motion at Fraya. "Go on now, git. You get you something for lunch. And later on, you can come back by the house for dinner."

"Maybe."

Fraya settled her purse on her shoulder and was out the backdoor before her well-meaning but so very pushy aunt could say more. Fraya loved her, but she was a lot. Rushing as she was, Fraya didn't give herself a chance to steel herself, before setting foot outside.

Whisper Valley was a small town in West Virginia nestled in the Appalachian Mountains. It sported a few stoplights, beautiful foliage, and a robust gossip community. It was the kind of town where memories were long and grudges were longer. There also wasn't a taxi service and driving definitely made things easier.

Her heart panged for her missing car. It hadn't been much, but she'd bought it with her own money. She'd had to sell it so she could continue to pay their mortgage.

But surprise, they'd lost the house anyway. She'd lost it, not him. He was long gone.

She hated to go down this road. There was nothing at the end of it, but depression and a bad time. *Is this a good time?* a part of her asked. She ignored the question. She was trying to make it through day to day.

"Heard from your thief of a husband?"

Fraya's head snapped up as she almost ran straight into Richard. She didn't bother hiding her grimace. *This guy.* He was the guy who flirted with her over and over again in high school. And she'd turned him down over and over again. He took great joy in how bad her life had turned out.

"No, I haven't, and I'm pretty sure I won't, but thanks for asking, Dick," she said.

He wiggled his caterpillar brows at her. "If you missing some company, you know where I live."

She looked at him like he'd lost his mind and kept it moving.

It was almost time for their five-year high school reunion, and he still hadn't gotten the hint. Whenever she looked at him, she could still see the Juggalo face paint that he favored when they were tweens.

Walking down Main Street used to be comforting. She liked passing by the people she had known all of her life and feeling like she was around her extended family. The buildings didn't change too much, except during all the major holidays. Each business had its own little spin on spiffing up the windows. That was always her cousin Neilina's favorite thing when they were growing up.

But things weren't like that now. Not anymore. Losing thousands of dollars and almost destroying an entire city's economy did something very sour to an extended family.

2

The taller she'd grown, the more her childhood home seemed to shrink. When she was growing up, the two-bedroom apartment had felt huge. It was the place where she'd planned her outfits and spent as much time on the phone as humanly possible, where she'd plotted to beat Isa at doing stuff first, even though she was doomed to failure. Moving back to her mama's after her marriage had crumbled felt like failure too.

I got married first, she admitted. *And I'll get divorced first, too.*

At that thought, Fraya lost her taste for the pepperoni roll, but she kept chewing anyway. Her aunt was right; she hadn't been eating much at all. Buying food was a chore she put off most of the time. Today was no different. She'd run to the Pothole Diner, grabbed two pepperoni rolls fully loaded and fries, and hurried home.

This was how she'd been living for over a year, and the streams of judgment were never-ending.

How was she supposed to know that Jackson would betray her like that? The crystal balls were her aunt's thing, not hers. Fraya's tender heart remembered how cute he looked in high school, working on being the biggest, baddest football player in the school.

She'd thought he was so cute even before she'd met him. He'd been one of the town heroes. When they'd first met, he'd hit her with a door when she was walking around a corner. It had been an accident, but he'd still had to work to convince her to give him a chance after that. Where had she gone wrong? Where were the signs that he was really the villain of her story?

Her phone vibrated in her pocket, breaking into her thoughts. She looked down at the number and frowned.

Another unknown call.

Probably Jackson. He'd been calling her from different numbers trying to get her to accept his lame apology. How many was it up to this week? Five? Seven? Might as well take it now and get it over with.

"Hello? This better not be you, Jackson."

"Baby, I'm glad you answered."

Fraya huffed in annoyance. "I'm not. And don't call me baby. I needed to make sure it wasn't another bill collector coming for my neck."

His pause felt heavy. "I'll make this up to you someday." If she could still believe in his words, those would've affected her.

But they were empty now.

"That's one of those things that you really can't do. You've got nothing for me anymore, Jackson. Just accept it and move on."

"I'll always love you."

She clicked the phone off and threw it onto the couch. Her cigarettes were right there. She knew she should quit, but Fraya grabbed her case, tapped one out, and lit it. She'd started smoking when she learned Jackson had broken the entire town's trust in them and — what's worst — her trust in him.

It had started a year ago with a booming knock on the door. Jackson was sacked out on the couch, watching a Sanford & Son rerun telling her about his miserable day. She'd been making their lunch. Fraya liked to cook simple meals for them. He was always so appreciative, and it made her smile every time.

Hoagies were his favorite.

She'd just pulled out the fixings for a salad when that knock came. They weren't expecting anybody.

That insufferable Deputy Watson, with the biggest smirk on his face, filled her doorway.

"Looks like your luck has finally run out," he said. "I've been waiting for this for years." His mustache had almost wiggled in happiness.

"What are you talking about? Though it's good to see you admit that you've treated my family like trash for years."

"Hey, honey, maybe I should take care of this," Jackson said as he rose from the couch. He knew about how the sheriff never missed a chance to provoke the Cofindager cousins. "Is there a problem?"

"You know the problem. But your time has come." Deputy Watson pushed up against Fraya until she was forced backward, allowing a couple of other cops inside with them.

Deputy Watson pushed through the doorway spouting off their Miranda Rights while his deputies cuffed them.

"What is this? Why am I being arrested?" she asked repeatedly, even when her arms were twisted behind her back and her wrists zip-tied.

Their grandfather clock bonged, announcing it was Noon. The sound reverberated through her, shaking her. She threw that clock away later. That sound was too much for her after that day.

Watson had finally snapped. "Oh, like you don't know? All that money you two done taken offa these poor people around here? You oughta be ashamed of yourself."

She'd looked at her husband with tears in his eyes. "Jackson? What's going on?"

"Don't worry baby. I'm going to get you out of this," he'd said. "Don't say anything else until we talk to our lawyer."

His eyes remained locked forward.

He never could look her in the eye when he was lying.

It had felt like a waking nightmare.

She hadn't learned her charges were embezzlement and wire fraud until she'd gotten to the station. That had begun some of the most brutally draining months of her life, and they hadn't stopped yet. The charges against her were dropped quickly, when it was clear that Jackson had funneled all of that money through secret channels that she hadn't known existed.

He'd discouraged her from coming to visit him in jail. He didn't want her to see him like that. He'd said that everything would be dismissed, and everything would be fine — just a big misunderstanding.

They had never been poor, but they definitely weren't drinking Cristal while using gold-plated toilets. The lawyer argued that Jackson was a frugal thief, trying to set up his future, one that may not have even included his wife. After that day in court, she hadn't returned to support him. She couldn't stomach it.

And now he was out, but not back in Whisper Valley. Thank God. She had no idea where he was, and she wanted to keep it that way. His calls were bad enough. Even though she had been cleared of charges, the small-town mindset hadn't changed. People like that jerk Richard, who wanted Fraya knocked down a peg or two, gleefully hung onto the rumors and suspicions. Even the folks she thought would be on her side had been curiously absent.

She'd never felt so alone.

Fraya sipped her pop, her mouth feeling as dry as a desert thinking about it all. This was the first and last time. She refused to go out like this again. She'd been a pair of clown shoes.

A fool.

How could something like this have been happening with her totally clueless? That part at least she and the town agreed on.

There had been rumors about Kilster Factory for a long time, but that's how the town gossips rolled. If they weren't talking about somebody, they weren't happy. The factory rumor mill muttered about mob affiliations and folks getting whacked. She'd tried to dismiss it and press forward.

She wanted peace and a family where everybody was actually together. Her mom being on the road so much had left her as a latchkey kid, always fending for herself unless Aunt Maybel was saddled with her. She and Jackson had talked about having kids. And she'd wanted that so much, her own little family. Her heart wrenched thinking about the baby names that she'd hidden away in her diary, ready to use at a moment's notice. She'd wanted a baby boy with his daddy's eyes and his mama's smile.

Now it was all over.

Three quick knocks in succession sounded at the door, startling her out of her memories.

Isa.

Fraya slowly rose, not really in the mood to have visitors, but realizing there wasn't going to be a way around this. Isa had a quietly stubborn way about her. She was immovable once she dug in her heels.

Fraya eased the door open.

"Hey cuz, what's up?" Isa was an inch or two shorter than Fraya, wearing a basic pair of shorts and a red t-shirt, but her head was topped by a cute wide-brimmed straw hat with matching shoes, which sported a thick red ribbon tied around her ankles.

Isa grabbed her close for a hug. Fraya stiffened for a moment and then relaxed into her cousin's embrace. Her top was incredibly soft. Probably some vintage designer clothing that she'd found at a thrift store over the summer.

"That's enough of that. C'mon in," Fraya said, stepping out of the way. And then she let the door swing closed behind her.

"Do you want to go on a walk or something? I know you haven't been spending much time outside."

Fraya shook her head. That sounded like the absolute worst idea ever.

"Aunt Maybel sent me by."

Fraya rolled her eyes. "Aunt Maybel needs a hobby."

"She's right. You can't stay cooped up in here forever." Isa put her hand on her cousin's arm. "I'll be with you. And Clare is going to meet up with us."

Clarebel was Isa's childhood best friend and usually joined them for ensuing shenanigans. But Fraya wasn't in the mood.

Isa crossed her arms. "You gotta stop acting like you're guilty of something."

"I am guilty."

"Of what?"

"I chose him."

Isa sputtered. "Oh please! Now you're guilty of embezzlement because a man fooled you? Get out of here with that bull."

"What are you trying to say?"

"I thought what I said was *real* clear. Get your head out of your butt and rejoin the living."

Fraya's eyes narrowed. "You know what? I think I'd rather be alone. Thanks for stopping by, cuz. Tell Clarebel I said hi."

"She's actually on her way over here," Isa admitted.

"Welp, you can go ahead and meet up with her on your way to wherever you were trying to drag me."

"Don't get mad, Fraya." Isa put her hands on her hips and heaved a sigh. "This apartment hasn't been your home since you were a kid. Your marriage was good until it wasn't. But you're still a good person, regardless of whatever else has happened. You know in your heart you need to move on."

Fraya's chin wobbled a bit, but she stayed stubbornly silent. Who was Isa to tell her what she should do? Had she ever been through this before? This was Fraya's cross to bear, not her cousin's.

"I just wanted you to come hang out. They're playing music down at the waterfront tonight. Come with." Isa leaned forward and dropped her voice. "Don't let those a-holes think they've got you."

Fraya's eyebrows raised. "A-holes" was strong language for her cousin, who never swore. But she couldn't get out of her feelings to put herself in front of the judgmental firing squad.

"You know I love you, even when you get on my nerves, right?" Fraya pulled her cousin in for a hug and held her close.

"You're still stupid, but I love you, too." Her laugh had a bit of a watery edge that Fraya ignored.

"I hate to see you like this, Fray."

"I'll be all right. You know me." Fraya could hear that her bravado didn't quite make it.

Isa gave her an extra squeeze and then walked out the door.

THE NEXT DAY, FRAYA WENT TO AUNT MAYBEL'S HOUSE. SHE needed some mothering. Her own mother was out of state, doing her truck-driving thing, like she had since Fraya was little. And Aunt Dinetta, Neilina's mother, was gone as much as NayNay was. She was always on the move.

Fraya took the back stairs two at a time, wanting to get into the house as quickly as possible so she could avoid the stares. The door opened into the kitchen, where it felt like a time capsule. Her aunt hadn't changed things up since she moved there. Everything had that pea green color that used to be so popular in the 60s and the walls were covered in daisy chain wallpaper. It was tacky by today's standards, but it was a second home for Fraya.

She'd decided to take up her aunt's dinner offer. She just didn't have it in herself to make another meal for just one.

"C'mon in, baby. Could you grab the phone?" her aunt hollered from the backroom.

"The phone? It's not..."

The jangling phone interrupted Fraya's sentence.

She nodded. Of course. The living room was on the other side of the house, and the phone was in the most unfortunate position right beside the television. The TV wasn't on, thank goodness. Usually Auntie would have her stories or Wheel of Fortune on so loud it would make your brain dive-bomb looking for an exit.

"Hello, this is the Cofindager residence, how may I help you?"

"Are you and your family fully covered by your insurance policy?" Telemarketer. After letting her run her spiel for a few minutes, Fraya politely made her way out of the conversation. What a terrible job to have.

A flyer stuck underneath the phone caught her eye. Her name was on the top in Aunt Maybel's curly script. She tugged it loose. Hawaii? She frowned. What in the world?

"I'm glad you found that," Aunt Maybel said from behind her.

"Is this for me?" Fraya asked.

Her aunt nodded. "It looks to me like you can use an out."

"What do you mean?"

"Your home is gone. Your marriage is in shambles. No one is talking to you the way they used to. I noticed it even at the shop."

"Is my being at the shop affecting your bottom line?" she asked, her throat tight.

"I wouldn't say that..." her aunt hesitated.

But you wouldn't not say it either, Fraya thought. This felt like the last betrayal. It was like her aunt had driven a hot poker right through her heart.

"I don't want to be a burden to you or anybody else, Auntie," she said, her voice so quiet that Maybel had to lean in to catch her words. "I'm going to go now."

"Now, Fraya..."

She just shook her head and headed out the door.

Fraya ran all the way home. She was not a runner like Isa and didn't possess NayNay's natural ability to move. But she wanted to get away from everything as quickly as possible. The pounding of her feet hit with her heartbeat, and she concentrated on the rhythm, ignoring any side-eyes or glares thrown her way. She was just a body in motion.

When she reached her mama's house, she unlocked the door and threw herself inside. She slid down the door, panting on the floor, tired of all these emotions. Exhausted with feeling like a villain when she hadn't auditioned for the role.

She was just tired.

Her flip phone rang from her purse. She hunted down the tinny sound and flipped it out.

"Hello?"

"Hey, baby girl, how are you doing?"

"I'm fine, Mama. Where you at these days?" Her mother had been a truck driver ever since the factory had shut down the first time.

"I'm in Alabama right now, about to put this pop out at this store. I wanted to check in with you."

"I'm alright, Mama."

"Are you? Are you sure?"

Fraya paused. "What are you getting at?"

"I've been talking to your Aunt Maybel."

Does that woman never sleep? Fraya muttered.

"You've been moping for months, honey. You can't go on like this."

"Mama, you have no idea what it's been like for me."

"You're right, I don't," her mama admitted. "And for that, I'm sorry. And you know I love you and love you being there..." She hesitated.

"But?" Fraya prompted, her heart thudding in her chest again.

"But... I can only let you stay at the house until the beginning of the month. I've met a special someone, and she's moving in. Three women in one house is too much."

"Are you serious right now?"

"Don't I deserve some happiness?" Her mom's voice snapped at her eardrums. She sighed heavily. "I'm sorry, baby girl."

Fraya closed the phone and threw it. It bounced off the back of the couch and landed near her feet. She leaned her head back and felt the pain spread through her heart. But it had changed... the flame streaming through her was anger.

Her aunt wasn't there for her. Her extended "family" of the town was against her. Isa wasn't there for it. Who knew where NayNay was? Even her own mother, the woman who had given birth to her, wasn't in her corner.

Where does that leave me?

She looked down at her hand and looked at the flyer again. She had the money to pay for the flight. Why not do this? Her pulse quickened, and she couldn't tell if she was excited, afraid, or a strange brew of both.

Am I really doing this?

3

I guess I really am, she thought as she walked through the Honolulu airport. She yawned widely. The red-eye flight had taken something out of her.

With the difference in locale, time zones, and the lack of sleep, she felt like she was Alice, and Hawaii was Wonderland. Everything felt so foreign. The plants she saw were tropical and gorgeous; their sweet scents lingered in the air. Even the air felt different; it was hotter and heavier, more humid than back home. Like being in the South, but different.

She followed the bulk of people heading out of the plane into the terminal. The connecting throughway was open on the sides, with greenery everywhere. She even spotted a fountain. It was the feeling of the tropics before she'd even stepped foot on the soil.

It was much different from the airports she'd visited on her way. The terminal felt like it hadn't been remodeled in a while, and ukulele songs played over the loudspeaker. There were even hula-dancing ladies. She saw folks receiving leis, but it looked like a service offered by hotels rather than something she'd just receive when she left the building.

So, this was the tropics. She found her luggage and walked out to the bus and cab stands. She sat on a bench as an idea dawned on her. Her decision to move to the islands was so impulsive: a whirlwind of buying airline tickets, getting rid of her stuff, getting a ride to the airport, and shedding her former life in a matter of days. And she'd forgotten one valuable thing.

Probably the most vital thing ever.

"Where am I going to live?" she mumbled to herself. A woman walking past tugged her child a little closer to protect her from the strange woman talking to herself. Fraya tried to smile reassuringly at the child, but only succeeded in making her cry.

This is why I don't act on impulse, she thought. *And why I don't have kids*.

When she'd done a bit of research on the area, she found that Waikiki Beach was *the* tourist destination location. Might as well go there.

Fraya assumed a bus or van would be cheaper than a taxi. She waited to hear one of the drivers mention Waikiki. This one didn't have the name of a hotel on the side, so she clambered on. She had her wallet ready to pay on her way out.

An early morning fog hung low over the city. She watched as the town grew closer outside of the window. Palm trees, so many palm trees dotted between a smorgasbord of architecture. Shorter buildings had a beachy vibe with soft pinks and blues that felt like a throwback to the 50s, starkly contrasting newer ones of imposing metal and glass. *Back home it's just old*, she thought.

Fraya wondered what her family really thought of this abrupt move. She'd call them once she was settled. Somewhere. She didn't want to make them worry. Her family would freak out when she told them she hadn't prepared a place to stay beforehand. Maybe there's a hostel available? Or she'd have to look to see if there was somewhere else she could stay.

I guess I could stay on the beach?

She gulped, not entirely comfortable with the idea. If she lived on the beach, what would she do with her stuff? At the moment she had a book bag, her purse, and one suitcase.

And no place to live.

An older woman with a pleasant smile sat down beside her. She had a flower in her hair and wore a brightly colored muumuu that reminded Fraya of her Aunt Maybel.

"Aloha, sweetie. Is this your first time here?" Her voice had a lyrical lilt to it that made Fraya think of rainbows and gentle waves.

Fraya nodded. "I didn't realize how long this journey would be."

She chuckled. "Oh yes, it doesn't look the same on the maps, does it?"

"No ma'am, not at all!" Fraya joined in with the other woman's laughter.

"I think you'll find it's worth the trouble," she said.

I hope so, Fraya thought.

"I'm visiting my grandkids. I suppose my children, too." She winked at Fraya and pulled out her cell phone. "Would you like to see their photos?"

"Of course."

She opened her photo gallery, telling Fraya all of their names and their favorite things. It made her miss her Aunt Maybel. She was the one in the family most likely to show off photos of her favorite nieces. (They were all her favorite nieces.)

Before she knew it, the bus driver announced over the loudspeaker that they were now in Waikiki. Fraya's eyes widened. She couldn't believe that people were out and about so early.

But these folks are on vacation or getting to work tending to the tourists, she reminded herself.

Fraya turned to her new friend and asked where the best place was to get off for the beach.

"You can get off anywhere, really. The beach is minutes away."

She thanked the woman for her advice and departed at the next stop.

Fraya tugged her suitcase behind her, strapped her bag to her back, and shoved her purse inside. The water beckoned her from where she stood. She could smell it! She felt a burst of energy and made her way through the leisurely strolling people to Waikiki Beach. She found a freestanding lanai where there were many stone tables and benches. There weren't many unoccupied spots, even though it was early in the morning. She claimed one where she could sit and put her suitcase down. She didn't want to roll it through the sand.

Where am I going to put my stuff?

The water was gorgeous. She had to stifle the urge to leave her belongings behind and rush into the ocean. *Maybe it could wash away the last year*, she thought wistfully. Even at this early hour, there were people already in the water. Some people had their blankets out, claiming their spots on the sand. A few folks jogged past.

The longer she watched, the more one thing stood out. Families were together; couples held hands. She felt awkward being alone. In Whisper Valley, she may have felt alone, but her family was just a phone call away. This was different. She was on an island five thousand miles away from home. She couldn't help wishing that her husband accompanied her instead of being alone. They'd always talked about visiting Hawaii one day.

And then she remembered his betrayal and shook off that wanting. This was no time for wishes and feeling sorry for herself. She needed to find some place to put her bags so she could explore unencumbered.

She was happy her luggage was on wheels as she pulled it behind herself, heading toward the hotels. Some advertised their prices outside and were completely out of her range. There was no way she could stay here. Maybe it was cheaper elsewhere. She wasn't sure.

Fraya found someone who was handing out maps of Waikiki for a few bucks. She was right beside the beach, but the entire area seemed to be beside the beach. Up the street, there was a zoo and an aquarium. There was a place for shopping in the middle that looked kind of cool called the Marketplace.

The area was much smaller than she'd realized.

I guess the place feels huge on foot, she thought. The map also showed the shops and the hotels that were definitely out of her price range. But then she honed in on the only hostel in the area. She hoped it wasn't like that one movie. She shuddered.

NayNay was the horror buff. Isa preferred romcoms, while Fraya liked funny horror movies.

She cut up through an alleyway and down another street, pulling her suitcase behind her. She would be so glad when she could park that damn thing somewhere. The hostel was a compact building connected to a shop where she could rent a scooter if she wanted.

"Maybe I'll do that," she murmured to herself as she stared through the window. A sparkly blue one tempted her until the daily rental fee caught her eye, and she swallowed thickly. Maybe finding a place to stay first was more important than the scooter. But it was definitely going on her bucket list.

On the outside of the hostel, there was a tiny handwritten scene with the Aloha Sun spelled out in pretty script. She entered the building to find light wood furniture and kitschy decor. The woman at the front desk had long black wavy hair and a welcoming smile. Her name tag had palm trees on it and declared her name to be Toni. Fraya wanted to ask her where she got her hair done. It must've taken work to tame the black woman's kinky coils.

"I'm sorry, we don't have any openings right now. Our next opening isn't for another month."

"A MONTH?!" Fraya swallowed audibly. A day or two she could handle, but how would she deal with living on the streets for so long while she tried to find a home? What if she couldn't find a place immediately?

The younger woman clicked her tongue in sympathy. "I'm so sorry. Do you have anywhere that you can go?"

Fraya shook her head.

The woman became all business. Apparently, this wasn't her first rodeo. "Well, there are a few homeless shelters on the island, and a couple are nearby." Another map was added to Fraya's growing pile.

"We do have more lockers than beds here. You can rent a locker. It should be fine, but I'd take out any of your valuables, just in case."

Fraya smiled gratefully, and signed the paperwork and paid for a locker. Toni handed her a piece of paper with the code on it and the locker number. They were on the opposite end of the wall and were fairly large. Her suitcase fit easily inside. Her mama had always taught her to hide cash in different spots for just this kind of emergency. She grabbed a few bills and put them in her sports bra. They weren't going anywhere in there.

As she shut the door with a snap, her actual reality sunk in. She was living in a nightmare. She'd moved halfway across the world. She had enough money for the first and last month's rent, as well as a deposit. She had a little extra for food, but not much at all. She was going to need to find a job and shelter.

Fast.

4

It sprinkled just enough for a rainbow to shine across the sky over Waikiki Beach. The colors were so saturated, Fraya felt like she could touch them. She was trying to concentrate on the moment, instead of worrying about her messy past and even messier present.

Let go and let God, right?

Fraya stood near the edge of the ocean, her toes digging in the sand. The waves seemed to kiss her feet, soothing and welcoming. She wanted to jump in but she held herself back. Her sandals dangled from her fingers.

Two people paddle-boarded past. This new side of her, this bold Hawaii-living person, wished she was a yoga devotee so she could do some sort of sun/moon crouching-dragon hidden-tiger pose and get in touch with her inner strength. And calm. She could use some of that too.

"Beautiful day."

Fraya started. A guy stood next to her in a pair of board shorts and nothing else. His hair was long and wild. She could tell he had been in the ocean. His skin was tanned, and he had his arms crossed against his chest. He was the epitome of who she pictured as a surfer.

"It really is lovely," she agreed. The calls of seagulls punctuated their silence as the ocean worked its magic.

"My name's Jeff, by the way." He held out his hand to shake hers.

She took it, and when he lingered a little too long, she pulled back. "Fraya."

"New to town?"

She nodded. "I'm pretty fresh off the boat."

"Have you gone out yet?"

"Naw, I don't even know where to go."

He handed her a flyer. "This is a pretty chill spot. Not a lot of people know about it. Not a lot of tourists. And they don't water down their drinks."

"Okay…"

"Maybe come down tonight?"

"Maybe I will."

They soon said their goodbyes.

"You should have a dip in the water," he said over his shoulder. "Let Mother Earth cleanse your spirit."

She mulled over his words as she stood there: how she'd obeyed the rules all these years, living up to everybody's expectations. With what had it left her?

Nothing.

Fraya wore a sports bra and boy shorts under her dress. She dropped her shoes beside her Outkast book bag that she'd been carrying forever. She pulled her dress over her head, tossed it down beside her gear.

Before she could talk herself out of it, she ran into the ocean.

Her breath caught in her throat. The water was much chillier than she'd expected but refreshing. She felt more alive than she had in her whole life.

Water definitely wasn't her first language, but she could kick around a bit. This was her first step into experiencing what life had to offer. And here on the island of O'ahu, life seemed to come from the ocean. Maybe if she spent more time in the ocean, more life would come to her.

None of the creatures though, she thought. *They can stay far away.* She looked around cautiously for a minute and then splashed in the water once more.

Once her treading water felt like she was pushing through a quicksand, Fraya pulled herself out of the ocean. Her water-logged legs were wobbly, and the ocean salt was harsh on her skin. She grabbed her dress and pulled it back on, grimacing at the way it clung to her salty skin.

Where's my book bag? I left it right here.

Her sandals were where she'd left them with something shiny to which she didn't pay attention.

Her bag was gone.

Her wallet was in there. Her money. Her phone. What was she going to do? She looked around in a panic, trying to calm her breathing. She could hear her pulse in her ears.

Her eyes scanned the area, and she saw one person who wore a dark blue jacket and a hat in this heat, walking away from the beach. Andre 3000 and Big Boi were clearly displayed on the bag on their back.

Fraya dropped her shoes and ran as fast as she could with the sand shifting under her feet and her legs feeling clumsy. They must've sensed that she'd seen them, because they started running too. Unfortunately, they were on the sidewalk and wore actual shoes.

"Hey! Stop! He's got my bag! Somebody stop him!" Fraya called out, pointing her finger in the man's direction, looking around for help.

When she turned back to him, he was gone. She stood there panting, looking around her. Her most important worldly possessions had been stolen. She had no friends and no one who could help her.

She'd never felt so alone.

~

FRAYA SHIFTED FROM ONE FOOT TO THE OTHER AS SHE STOOD IN front of the one officer who seemed to have the Waikiki Beach beat. Her skin felt itchy from the drying salt water, and she wanted to put on the sandals she'd rescued before the ocean had washed them away.

"And you left your bag on the beach with nobody around ya?"

His tone held an implication that made Fraya immediately bristle. "I don't exactly have an entourage."

"And you expect somebody to keep track of your things for you? Like the police?" He looked down at his notepad while he pretended to take notes.

"Are you serious right now?"

A blonde woman rushed over, her eyes wide. Her arms flailed about her. "Officer, I'm so glad you're here! Somebody stole my bag!"

Fraya said, her tone bitter, "Sorry, he doesn't care. You should've taken it into the ocean so the fish could play with it."

"Excuse me?" the woman asked, her tone more confused than anything else.

The cop shot Fraya a look that she ignored. "Don't let this woman concern you, ma'am. What happened?"

"This is my first day of vacation. And now somebody stole my bag while I had a quick swim." She started crying.

Fraya squelched the urge to roll her eyes. *If you don't stop with the dramatics.*

"I'm so sorry, ma'am." The same police officer, who had treated Fraya like a joke, handed this new woman a handkerchief.

Fraya snorted. *Typical.*

As they stood there, two other women came up with the same complaints.

With her lips pursed and her arms crossed over her chest, Fraya gave him a pointed look. "What's next, officer?"

He looked up from his notepad and scanned everyone. "Unfortunately, it's hard to track down thieves — especially people who are on their feet. The only thing we have to go on is Miss --" He checked his notes. "-- Taylor's description of a person in a hat and a blue jacket. I'll write up a report, and hopefully, we'll be able to find the perpetrator."

"That's it?" The woman, who'd been crying before, suddenly dried up and looked furious. "That's the best you can do?"

"I'm sorry, ma'am."

"'Sorry' doesn't find my stuff."

"And my stuff was stolen last week. Has it been found?"

The other women started to chime in. The women surrounding him were each demanding a definitive answer of their own.

Fraya's eyes narrowed in determination. There was no way she was going to lose everything that meant the most all in one fell swoop. She had to get her things back and maybe the things for the other women she was talking to as well.

She assumed the person must've been a local. A tourist wouldn't know how to get away so easily. And that person couldn't have run with all of their bags at once. Maybe there was more than one person involved. Was this some kind of coordinated effort? Fraya looked at the group of victims again. All of them were women. All of them had the "fresh off the plane" look to them. The robbers had targeted tourists. *That's why they're in Waikiki,* she thought.

"Ladies, ladies, please!" The officer's voice cut through the angry rabble. "Of course I'll do my best to find the thief, but I'm not entirely sure I'll be able to do so."

Way to invite confidence. Fraya shook her head.

He held up his hand when their voices got louder. "Please,

ladies. Give me your contact information, and we'll move on from there."

"Contact information?! My phone was in my purse!" snapped the one who'd been crying those crocodile tears. Her blue eyes were narrowed, and her button nose was pink.

"Then your hotel information will work fine."

"How about you give me your card?" Fraya finally said. She had zero confidence in this man's ability, and he'd clearly shown that this was not a priority for him. And she had no hotel number to share.

He cut his eyes at her and reached into a pocket and handed her one.

"Ayden Mahelona," she read out loud. "I'll be in touch."

Fraya slipped on her sandals and headed toward the hostel to see if she could gain access to her suitcase, even though she didn't have her code. Hopefully, the same girl who'd been working before would be there now.

"Ma'am, are you going to leave your — never mind," Officer Mahelona called after her.

5

With assured steps, Fraya walked quickly from the beach to the hostel. She eyed those scooters again.

As she walked into the hostel, the air was much cooler, much to her relief. She hoped she'd get used to the humidity soon. She smiled. The same woman who'd checked in her bags was working at the front desk.

"Aloha, Fraya. Back so soon? Is there anything else I can help you with?" Toni asked with a welcoming smile.

"Aloha, Toni, I really hope you can help me. Today's been a rough one," Fraya said in a rush.

The receptionist's face looked vaguely concerned, but she kept a professional smile. "I'll help however I can. What's going on?"

Fraya explained the robbery, her lack of clothing, and the lock combination.

"And I'm not sure if the police officer cares too much about it."

"Why not?"

"I think the thief targeted tourists, and he didn't seem to care."

Toni nodded knowingly. "I think a lot of times, since folks aren't staying a long time, they're not top priority."

"I'm going to be here for a long while," Fraya said. *For better or worse.*

Toni looked Fraya over for a minute and seemed to decide. She grabbed two sets of keys off of the wall and led Fraya to the locker set. She reset the combination.

"Set it to something you'll remember," she advised with a smile.

Fraya set it for her mother's birthday. Even if the thief somehow knew what the random numbers were on her planner, they'd have a hard time guessing her mother's birthday.

While she was yanking some clothing out of her suitcase, Toni looked around and then leaned closer.

"Listen ...you need a shower? We have a communal bathroom upstairs. Usually it's just for guests, but I can help you out."

Fraya cleared her throat to push back the tears. "Thank you so much."

Everything had been so hard since she'd arrived in paradise. The anxiety was high, and her stomach was in the tightest of knots. At least right now, she could wash off her exhaustion, as well as the sand that had crept its way into places where it had no business.

The other black woman directed her to walk up the stairs and to the shared bathroom. She handed Fraya the spare key. "Just give it back to me when you're done. I can't do this too many times, but girl, you need a break."

"You have no idea," Fraya's smile was weary around the edges. She thanked Toni again and quickly made her way up the stairs. Everything in the building was more about service than fashion. The stairs were metal and were wide enough for three people to walk side by side. *At least there's no rust*, she thought as her sandals squished underneath her. She was glad she'd packed two spare sets of shoes in her suitcase.

The hallway was pretty basic, white walls, and a cheap tile floor. Wet sand had collected in some areas. The bathroom was at the end of the hallway, and she pushed on the door. They'd forgotten to lock it.

Inside there were two separate sides. The right side had a few toilets and stalls. The left side had a few showers with cloth curtains. Directly in front of her was a mirror, and her mouth dropped in horror. No wonder that woman wanted to help her so badly.

"I look like a train wreck," she said under her breath.

"Don't worry about it; we're on vacation. We all look a little crazy, sister!"

Fraya turned in surprise. One of the women who'd taken umbrage with that cop was standing there. How'd she gotten here so quickly? Fraya wondered. She had clearly been sipping on some morning margaritas, which were treating her mighty fine.

Was she drunk when she was talking to that cop? Fraya marveled at the idea of being anything but sober as a judge talking to a police officer. *We live much different lives.*

She pushed her blonde hair back with her sunglasses on top of her head. "Hey, you look familiar. Were you that girl talking to the cop today?"

Fraya nodded. That wasn't how she wanted to see herself, but that was neither here nor there.

"We've got to stick together, girlfriend," she said with a knowing wink. "That cop ain't gonna do nothing."

Fraya was a little taken aback. Earlier, she'd sounded like she was a continental traveler and now she was more like Erma from the sticks. She couldn't get a handle on this person, and that made her feel nervous.

"I'm Fraya," she said with a smile.

"I'm Kandy with a K," she said, giggling a little.

That name sounds like she hangs out on poles, but that's none of my business.

"I need to take a shower, but are you serious about figuring this thing out?" Fraya asked.

Kandy nodded, and she seemed to lose her giggle. "I have to get my stuff back. They have my passport, and we fly out in two days."

Fraya grimaced in sympathy. Getting a replacement for a passport would take way more time than two days. Maybe she could help this girl while she helped herself. "Then we've got two days to get this thing figured out. Where can I find you?"

Kandy said she was in 6-B, and they agreed to meet up after Fraya's shower. Fraya shuffled off with renewed vigor. There wasn't a lot of time to waste. She had her clothes in a plastic bag, and she left it at her feet just outside of the curtain. The showerhead was fixed to the wall at an awkward angle. When she leaned too far back, the curtain touched her backside, which made her inwardly squeal every time. Too far forward, and she could barely feel the spray. But the water was warmer than the ocean, at least, and she cleaned out her sandy crevices and conditioned her poor hair. As soon as she was able, she was going to deep condition it and really give it some extra care.

Fraya made quick order of her shower and dressing. Her outfit was a maxi dress. It was bright and loose-fitting and honestly reminded her of Aunt Maybel. Hopefully, the bright colors would enrich her mood. She felt like a dark cloud was following her everywhere, and she was tired of it.

I'm in the tropics. Sure, my wallet's gone, I can't call my family, and I'm a pariah in my hometown, but I can live my best life out here. Right? Right.

Her pep talk done, Fraya took a moment in front of the mirror to moisturize her hair and put it up in a bun, with a dab of gloss to top it off so she felt put together. She rushed out of the bathroom. The left side of the hall featured the A rooms. The right side listed the Bs. She found 6-B and knocked. A tall, bronzed guy opened the door with a grin.

"They have room service here? I would've definitely ordered you up if I'd known that," he said.

Fraya blinked rapidly. Was that a compliment?

"Dude, get out of the way. That's my homegirl, Fraya. She doesn't need your crap." Kandy shoved him away with her hip. "C'mon in, girlfriend."

Fraya raised her eyebrows expectantly at "Dude" until he moved out of the way.

"My bad," he said.

He posed a little at the door, trying to get Fraya's attention, which she absolutely ignored. He may not have meant to sound like a douche canoe, but he totally had.

The room was set up dormitory-style with a couple twin-size bunk beds on either side of the room. There were two matching dresser drawers and not many decorations on the walls. But everything was spotless and Fraya didn't feel awkward sitting anywhere.

Kandy led her into the shared living space where there was a large couch and a few unoccupied chairs. None of them matched, but they all shared the shabby chic beach bum look with seafoam green, blues, and mauves abounding.

Through a doorway, she saw a compact kitchen that they shared.

"Are you thirsty?" Kandy named off drinks including beers, a pitcher of margaritas, and some water.

"No, I'm good, thanks."

"I've been working on this buzz too hard to let it go to waste," Kandy said. "Dude, hook me up with another margarita?"

"Solid."

Fraya covered her eyes for a minute. It was always

awkward when people tried too hard to be "down" with her. Who said "solid" other than a dancer on Soul Train?

"Okay, let's get down to it," Fraya said. She pulled out her spare notepad and a pen from her shower bag. "When was your stuff stolen?"

Kandy's face turned serious. "Yesterday morning. I reported it then, but just like you saw, nothing. So I came back down there today. When I heard you talking to him and getting that same run-around, I thought maybe the waterworks would help."

Fraya nodded. The crocodile tears had definitely been flowing. "They didn't work, though."

"No, he seemed immune to them," she said. "Which I didn't appreciate at all," she added, sucking her teeth.

Of course not. "You said your bag was stolen yesterday?" Fraya thought for sure she'd said it was the first day of her vacation to that cop. Maybe she'd misheard her.

The other girl nodded. "Yup, yesterday morning. About the same time in the morning that they got you, actually."

That's interesting. "They? Did you see more than one person?"

Dude handed Kandy her drink. She took a sip, staring down at her feet. "I've been thinking about it all night. I was body surfing in the waves."

"The waves were so gnarly, dude! Remember when I hit that close out? And I was all... whoa! And you were all 'Dude, look out!' And I was---"

"Dude." Kandy lifted her hand to stop him. "Later. We're trying to sort some stuff out."

"Oh, sorry." His head hung low for a second, and Fraya looked at the two of them.

"Are you brother and sister?"

His head shot up, and his eyes brightened. "We're twins, bro!"

Kandy rolled her eyes. "Don't tell anybody. I don't even want them to know we're related."

"Whatever," he said, shrugging nonchalantly.

"Whatever your face," she shot back.

I don't have time for this, Fraya thought. "Okay, okay, let's get back to what happened. You were in the ocean, right?"

Kandy with a K nodded. "Yeah, and we were having an awesome time. We'd just gotten here. And I looked at the beach and I saw someone getting close to our stuff, and they reached down and casually put the bag on one shoulder like no big deal, right?"

Fraya nodded, scribbling away.

"And then they started moving real fast. And then someone pulled up in a car, picked them up, and they were gone."

Fraya paused in her note-taking. *When they grabbed my bag, they didn't bring the car to the beach.*

"Could you see what kind of car it was?" she asked instead.

Kandy took a sip while she was thinking.

"It was a green car and the license plate said GNARLY," Dude said with a grin.

"How do you know what the car's license plate said? Weren't you surfing?"

"When I saw they'd gotten our stuff, I brought in my board and ran after them. I'm pretty fast, bro."

"Yeah, and they had to stop because there were a bunch of people crossing the road," Kandy quickly added.

"That too."

Fraya frowned thoughtfully. "Were you able to see anybody in the car?"

"The person on the passenger side took off their hat, and they had long blonde hair and flipped it around like this." Dude mimicked what would look like an average shampoo commercial.

It tugged a bit at Fraya's memory, but she hadn't been there for long enough to see many people doing things.

"Do y'all remember anybody specifically being on the beach?" Fraya asked.

"Just that one guy with the flyers," Kandy said. "You remember. You all were talking by the ocean."

Why were you watching me? Fraya wondered. She hadn't seen them at all. "Oh yeah, I remember him," she said.

Dude nodded knowingly. "Yeah, that guy looked super shifty."

They soon finished up talking, and Fraya left feeling like she had more questions than answers. But things were getting tough, and the day was getting shorter. Soon, she'd have to face not having a place to stay that night.

"Maybe it won't be cold on the beach," she whispered as she walked through a group of obvious tourists, who gave her a wide berth.

Great, now I'm acting like a homeless stereotype, she thought, keeping her thoughts inward. She didn't have a lot of options, so she chose to hit up the library. That was free, at least.

6

F raya made her way to the Waikiki Public Library. It was only a few streets up from the hostel at the end of Kapahulu beside the Ala Wai Canal and a golf course. The waterway smelled kind of funny that day, but it looked pretty. The library itself wasn't that remarkable, but palm trees standing in the garden and beautiful flowers growing nearby really sold it to her. *I'm at a library in Hawaii,* she grinned. Now she felt like she was living the life.

As she walked inside, the vestibule had signs up for library events this month and the next. And local events as well. She noted the bathroom was in that hallway. As she entered, the reference desk and computer area were to the left. To the right was the kids' section. There weren't many people there now, which was perfect. She didn't want to socialize.

I wish I had my phone. I could totally charge it in here. Then she realized she could send an email home at least so her family could get an update.

Fraya approached the front desk where an Asian woman was scanning books into the system.

"Excuse me, is there a way for me to get a pass to use a computer for an hour or so?" she asked.

The librarian returned her smile. "Aloha! Of course, do you have your license?"

Fraya's stomach dropped as she remembered her license was in the wallet that had been snaked from her. Her face reflected her disappointment as she shook her head.

The librarian took out a form and asked Fraya to fill it out. Since she didn't have an apartment to list yet, she scribbled down her last address.

"*Mahalo*," she said as she took back the clipboard. She input the data into her computer and then gave Fraya a piece of paper with a code on it.

"You can log onto the computer with this code. It only lasts for one hour. If you need more time, let me know and I'll give you another code."

Fraya thanked her and quickly made her way to the computer. Logging in was a breeze, and she shot off a vague message to her cousins letting them know she had safely arrived, but was having phone issues. They would spread the word to the aunts. She looked up the local newspaper, the *Honolulu Star-Advertiser*, to see what was happening in the area. She scanned a story about some politics with the local community's anger about a new tax for downtown businesses, and another about the potential barge of some sort that people seemed really split on. Then she ran across an article that gave her pause.

This one detailed the rash of robberies on Waikiki Beach, where the tourists were the clear targets. The thief's M.O. varied in terms of time period. Some were in the morning, and others occurred later in the evening. They seemed to aim for people who appeared alone. There had been at least a dozen incidents over the last week. Fraya's eyes widened. Granted, she wasn't from the big city or anything, but that seemed like a lot of people robbed in a short period of time.

No wonder that cop was there. The thefts seemed to only

happen one at a time, which was odd. She wondered why the robber changed it up with her and Kandy.

She noticed other inconsistencies as she kept reading. One person thought there was a guy, and another thought it was a girl. *Different people, or one person who sometimes looked more masculine or more feminine?* Fraya wondered.

She remembered the shiny thing she'd found alongside her sandals. She inspected the ring she pulled out of her pocket. It was a typical clunky class ring with a yellow square-cut gemstone on its face. A name was etched on the inside. Could this be the thief's, or did the ring belong to someone else?

"Oh! That's a nice ring. Are you a Tiger?" asked the guy beside her on his computer.

"Excuse me?" Fraya frowned in confusion.

"A Tiger! You go to Kaimuki High School?" He nodded down at the ring. "That's the school colors, yeah?"

Realization dawned on her. "Oh! No, I found this ring. I hope I can find who owns it."

"Maybe they got the classes online?"

"Thank you so much, you've been a great help."

He gave her a shaka and returned to his computer.

He hadn't even realized it, but he'd given her something extra to go on. She looked up the class of 2008, like the ring said. As she scrolled through the online directory of that class, she couldn't say she was surprised when she saw a familiar face.

7

After her computer time was over, Fraya stayed in the library until it closed in the early evening. She felt like a ship without a dock, and the library was her only safe harbor. She pulled the flyer out of her pocket and examined it. *The Blue Finn, huh? Flyers are running my life these days.*

She consulted her map, and then made her way down Kalakaua past the aquarium and the zoo. She made a note to at least go see the fish at some point. Ever since she'd argued about animals being locked up in cages with her cousin NayNay, she wasn't sure how she felt about zoos.

Families and couples were all around her. Bikes drove by in the lanes, and a city bus drove past her, its motor rumbling. At first, she tried to keep herself out of everybody's way, ducking and dodging like she had back in Whisper Valley. Feeling like a criminal. But then it dawned on her.

These people don't know me.

The freedom in that one thought was invigorating like a sip of ice-cold sweet tea on a summer's day. She smiled to herself. She could be herself here. She could be anybody or anything that she wanted to be. No one could stop her. For a moment, it felt like everything would be okay.

I need to get an actual home, she thought. *To speak to my family.* Which led back to retrieving her bag. The longer it was gone, the more likely it would be thrown in the trash or parceled out to people. *If it hadn't been already.* The thing she needed the most was her phone. She could get reissued cards and everything like that if she could call and figure things out. Though there were other things that were irreplaceable. Like her wedding ring.

Fraya looked up the address on the flyer on her map. She was only a few blocks away from The Blue Finn. The night was balmy with the ocean breeze playing in her hair. *Will I ever get used to the smell of the ocean?* she wondered. *Or the palm trees.* In front of the beach, there was a statue of King Kamehameha. She stopped and read the plaque. There were leis draped on his arms, his neck, and at his feet on the ground. A few tiki torches were lit beside him. As someone strummed a ukulele, she turned to watch a *halu* perform a hula on the green space nearby. Their movements were seamless and flowed like the waves behind them. *Can a West Virginia girl learn all them moves?*

As she listened to the music and watched the dancing, she noted the surrounding people. Couples held hands, walking around the shops. Families packed up and left the beach as the sun went down. Everyone seemed to be in a group of some sort, except for her. She fought back the sadness that wanted to take her down.

Instead of dwelling on that, she considered the ring that had fallen beside her sandals. It had definitely been a "man" cut. She could assume it was there when she got there. But the way the light caught it and made it all shiny, she was sure she would've seen it when she'd looked for a spot for her stuff. Maybe someone else had walked by her things, but she had noticed no one. And she'd been vigilant, which was why she'd caught sight of the guy running off with her bag.

And then there were those inconsistencies with the

newspaper accounts, Kandy's account, and her own experience. How did those fit? What she knew: the person took her stuff and then ran off. She hadn't seen them pass it off to another person or a getaway car.

But they faded into the crowd on the sideway when Officer Body-ody had stopped her.

He'd looked so good, but she'd learned a long time ago, police weren't part of her scene. And look how much he was out there doing. He could've turned and tried to stop that thief, but he stopped her instead.

She jerked when someone ran into her. "Excuse me, Miss," a man said with a grin that bordered on a leer.

Fraya didn't make eye contact and made her way around him quickly. It was time to go to the bar and get off these streets.

She didn't notice the exterior of the bar until she was right in front of it. *No wonder they pay that guy to hand out flyers,* she thought. The curb appeal didn't exist. Nothing there screamed aloha, Hawaii, or anything tropical. There wasn't anybody at the door when she walked in. Jeff was sitting at the bar.

She leaned in toward him so he could hear her above onslaughts of a rumbling snare and bass of old school hip-hop playing in the background.

"Thanks for inviting me here. This spot looks fun," she said with a smile.

"I'm glad you came. Recruiting people for this bar is a new gig, but I like it."

She looked around and noticed that many of the people were holding the same flyer that she was. He must've been walking up and down Waikiki all day.

"It looks like you brought in a pretty good crowd. I hope you get a good commission for that," she said. She wondered if she could do a job like that. She needed extra money, and she could be engaging if she put her mind to it.

"It's not too bad. I still don't have enough people in here to get the numbers that I need to pay some bills off. But the night's still young!"

His voice took on a weird edge when he looked around and caught eyes with someone else. A short white girl with a bad bleach job and what looked like an even worse attitude stomped over and got her finger in Fraya's face.

"Hey! Back off. He's *my* man. Why don't you find your own?" She took a step forward, and her stank sour beer breath had Fraya leaning away.

What the heck? He's kind of cute, but definitely not worth all of this, Fraya thought. She put her hands up to show that she wasn't touching him. The last thing she needed was some jealous girlfriend going off on her.

"I'm not doing anything. He recruited me to come to the bar, and that's all. Just like the rest of these people here."

"Hey, babe, I thought we talked about this. That's not cool." His voice was disappointed. "This is my job now. You can't go to the customers and freak them out."

She ignored him and poked Fraya in the middle of her chest. "That's all it better be, or you don't want to know what will happen to you."

Her mama had always told Fraya not to start any mess, but if she needed to, to finish it. She put her hands down. "I suggest you get your hands off me."

The girl smirked and emphasized each word with a poke.

"What?" Poke.

"You?" Poke.

"Gonna" Poke.

"Do?" The last poke had enough weight behind it to force Fraya to stumble back a step.

Fraya's entire body stiffened. She didn't want or need any of this. But the insecure mess in front of her was a drunken bully, and she would not take it. She stood up to her full height since she had a few inches on the girl. She smacked the girl's finger away.

She leaned in and then raised her voice. "What you're not fixing to do today is lay your hands on me. I don't care who you're dating or not dating. Your boyfriend ain't that fine, anyway."

"Hey!" he protested.

"And if you are that worried about him talking to random strangers, that's more of a *you* problem than a *me* problem. Get yourself together."

Before it could go any further, Jeff the flyer guy stepped in-between them. The punch the girlfriend let fly glanced off of his arm. He looked down at it and shook his head.

"Get out of my way!"

He shook his head again. "You gotta calm yourself down, before you get me fired."

"You're getting yourself fired. Fired from this relationship!" She threw her hair over her shoulder and crossed her arms.

His face changed, and he cocked his head to the side. "You know what? Okay then. You go on, grab your things, get out of the apartment, and then you try to find a place you can afford around here on what you make."

The girl's eyes widened, and just like that, she changed tactics. "Baby, you know I love you."

Her voice was so sticky sweet, Fraya wondered if she kept listening to her, would she come down with the diabeetus.

"I just get jealous when these hoes get all up on you. I'm sorry I hit you." She tried to rub his arm, but he shrugged it off.

"That's not cool. She didn't do anything wrong and you're trying to start fistfights." He threw his hands up in the air. "I can't handle that. We gotta go and discuss all this."

They walked off, the girl gesturing madly and the guy with his head down and his hands in his pockets. Fraya was clearly forgotten. *He seemed like an all right person, maybe he just needed a better choice of ladies.*

She shrugged philosophically. Oh well. According to the

flyer, she could have one free drink. Fraya approached the bartender, and he gave her a nod.

"What do you need tonight?"

That list is way too long for us to get into, she thought. She said out loud, "What comes free with the flyer?"

He looked at her assessing. "I think you might like a Mai Tai." Before she could weigh in, he was off.

At least he hadn't asked for I.D.

He returned a few minutes later with an orange drink that had a healthy slice of pineapple on top. Her stomach grumbled in response, reminding her that she needed to take it easy on the drinks. She'd skipped dinner earlier.

"Here you go." He slid it over to her on a coaster. "It's supposed to be a cheap drink but after that girl tried to start a fight, I gave you an upgrade."

Fraya took a sip under his watchful eye and gave him a thumbs-up. It was delicious, frosty, and sweet. She took a couple of her bra dollars and put it in his tip jar. He gave another nod, but this time with a hint of a smile and went back to wiping the counter.

Taking another drink from the straw, Fraya turned toward the rest of the bar. The outside may have been boring, but inside they had gone full tourist trap. Against the wall, some booths had cartoony hula dancers tacked up on the wall. Other booths had privacy screens that looked like palm trees. Even the small dance floor had been fashioned from bamboo.

To her left, the tables didn't have the privacy screens. The seats were mostly full. Fraya spotted a cute dark-haired guy seated alone at one. He wrote in a notepad with a furrow on his brow, which she found intriguing. *Should I go talk to him? That's crazy; I would never do that at home.*

This isn't home, she reminded herself. She took another sip for courage and approached his table.

"Is this seat taken?" she asked.

He didn't respond. She raised her voice and asked again

right when there was a pause between songs. He jerked up in surprise, his hand scrawling across the page.

"Can you hear me now?" she asked with a grimace.

"Loud and clear." He grinned at her wince..."I'm just teasing. Have a seat."

She sank onto the chair. "I'm sorry that I made you streak ink everywhere."

He shrugged. "No worries. I'm Keith."

"Fraya."

They exchanged pleasantries for a moment until Fraya couldn't hold back her curiosity. "What are you working on?"

"This is the follow-up to my debut novel. Action-adventure stories."

"It's so noisy, and there are nosey people like me. How can you concentrate with all of this?"

He seemed to consider her words. "If I'm being honest, I'm not sure. I was feeling stuck in this scene and sometimes the loud sounds, the energy, makes it easier for me to focus. Does that make sense?"

She shook her head. "Not to me, but I think it doesn't matter. As long as it works for you."

"Are you a writer?" Even in the dim lights, his eyes had an intensity that she hadn't experienced in a long time.

It was as flattering as it was uncomfortable. "I... I mean…" She reminded herself that she could be whoever she wanted to be. But this was a stretch. She settled on the truth. "I have a hard time calling myself a writer."

He grinned. "Then you must be one."

From then on, the conversation flowed smoothly, and Fraya thoroughly enjoyed herself. Keith was the most relaxed person she'd ever met. His vibe was so chill that she felt more at ease than she had in a while. After she finished her drink, he offered to buy her another.

And another.

"It's getting late, do you want to grab a slice from this

street vendor?" Keith asked. "He's a cool guy, and he stays open extra late when I'm in town."

"Sure, let's do this. Pizza sounds amazing." Fraya stood, and the world shifted under her feet. She stumbled a little.

"When's the last time you ate?" he asked.

"Why are people all the time asking me that?" she grumbled, finding her balance again. "I'm fine. I haven't stood up in a while, that's all."

He gave her a side-eye, skepticism written all over his face.

"I'm fine. Really. Watch." She tried to close her eyes and touch her nose. She ended up stabbing herself in the eye.

"You're doing great," he said, his tone wry. He held out his arm to her, and she took it, stumbling into him.

Keep it together. And why didn't you get something to eat earlier?

The Blue Finn had started heating up as more people piled in. It was a relief to step outside into the balmy air. They walked past the curious mix of high-end fashion and locally-owned shops. Partygoers were definitely out and about that night, laughing and grinning, and probably drinking way too much.

Like me.

Before she knew it, she was spilling all the tea about her living situation and her stolen bag.

"You can't sleep out on the beach, Fraya," he cautioned. "You can definitely be arrested for that."

Wouldn't be my first arrest, she thought. "Three hots and a cot. What more can I ask for?" she said, instead.

They headed toward a white food truck near a bus stop, a couple streets up from the hostel. Petey's Pizzas was emblazoned in red on the side with an enormous pizza slice drawing. A few people were in line, but Fraya assumed folks would really show up after all the bars closed.

"We can at least get your bag back."

"How?" she asked. "I don't know ---"

Keith interrupted her. "Aloha, Petey! Howzit, brah?"

Petey took off his glove to shake Keith's hand. Fraya couldn't guess his height, but he was a wide round man with a moon pie face. His hair was underneath a net. His smile was so bright and contagious. Fraya grinned at him as Keith introduced them.

He got Fraya two pepperoni slices and himself a slice that had the most toppings.

"I can't eat all of that!" The slices were the biggest she'd ever seen. They were served on a stack of three paper plates instead of two.

"Then you'll have one for later," he said, matter-of-factly.

And how could she argue with that? They took them to a nearby bench and ate in companionable silence.

"Let me help you with this." Keith crumpled up his paper plate and tossed it into the garbage can nearby.

"With what? This slice?" Fraya had found the room somewhere for that second slice. It was an after-bar miracle.

He shook his head. "No, with where you stay tonight."

Fraya turned toward him and raised her eyebrows. "I've been drinking, but I'm not that drunk. If you think I'm --"

"No, it's not like that!" He laughed a little. "That was a full-on jump with your conclusions. I'm only a little insulted."

She was glad he couldn't see her blush in the streetlight. "What's your suggestion?"

"One lady in my writing group has been living in Waikiki since the 70s. I'm sure she'd give you a couch for the night."

"I don't want to keep an elderly lady up for the night."

"I wouldn't call Norma a lady. Or elderly. She would probably cuss you out."

Fraya's eyebrows raised. This was going to get interesting.

8

D ry. If the Sahara Desert had taken up residence in her mouth, she wouldn't have been surprised. She needed water — all of it.

Fraya swallowed reluctantly. She didn't remember a bench feeling so soft and comfy. And she couldn't smell the ocean or feel the sunshine on her face. In fact, where was she?

She reluctantly opened her eyes and immediately startled. A large glass was far too close to her face.

"After all that snoring, I knew you'd be thirsty." On the other end of the large glass was an older woman with a wide-brim hat that had flowers that matched the couch.

Another lady with black spikey hair wearing a shirt that read *An apple a day keeps anyone away if you throw it hard enough,* said, "I told you to leave the girl alone. She's not even awake yet. She's my houseguest."

"She's my guest, too. You're not the only one who lives here, you know," hat lady shot back.

"I wish I was," apple t-shirt woman grumbled.

"Ladies, give the girl some room so she can sit up. She needs some air, honey." The last woman was a little younger than the others. Her feather boa matched her silk dressing gown, pink and fluffy.

Fraya smiled gratefully as she tried to hide her confusion. She'd had a couple nights of drinking too much in her past, but that had usually resulted in Jackson hauling her home, not her waking up on a couch covered in large pink roses with a trio of geriatric ladies fighting over whose guest she was.

The lady with spiky black hair said, "Mine is the name that's on the lease. You two are just freeloaders."

"Oh, *pshaw*." The woman threw the pink boa over her shoulder, and a few pink feathers floated to the ground.

"Sweetie, you're shedding like a peacock. If we needed that, we could bring one down from the North Shore." She adjusted her hat and then handed the drink to Fraya. "I figured you'd need a little pick-me-up. You sure tied one on last night."

"Thank you. I don't normally do that."

"Oh, you told us, dear," the boa lady said, checking her lipstick in her pocket mirror.

"Several times," spiky hair added.

Fraya sputtered as she tried to drink her tea. She felt like a jerk, but she was glad she wasn't on the street last night. *Speaking of last night…*The place seemed more familiar to her now. It had an open floor plan, though she guessed it probably hadn't always been that way. The walls were white with blown-up concert photos dotting the walls. Except for the couch that she sat on, all the furniture in the living area was covered in buttery brown leather with matching throws. In the middle was a coffee table with a runner down the center.

"He went to get you something to eat," the boa lady said.

Fraya stopped trying to look around inconspicuously.

"That's really nice of him. I'm not even sure why he's doing this."

Norma snorted. "I bet you don't."

Fraya stiffened. "What's that supposed to mean?"

"She's saying that you're a lovely girl, stranded on the island. Of course, Keith wants to help you," Boa-lady said, her voice rolling like a fog.

"This would be insulting if I didn't feel awful." She took another sip and tried to remember the women's names.

"Rose?" she asked, pointing at sassy t-shirt.

"Heck no!"

"Oh sorry, you're Rose." Fraya said, pointing at the lady with the boa. She nodded and waved the end of her boa.

"And you're Norma," she said, turning back to sassy t-shirt.

The lady who'd handed her the iced tea was sitting on the chair, crocheting what looked like a blanket. "I'm sorry, I don't remember your name."

"No one ever does. It's Winnie." Her smile was genuine but held such a sadness that Fraya felt a pang of guilt.

I won't forget it again.

The door on the side swung open as Keith walked in. He had a bag of donuts in one hand and a to-go box of coffee in the other. He immediately turned to the couch and flashed a smile with an adorable dimple at Fraya.

"Good," Norma nodded with approval. "We can't talk shop on empty stomachs."

"Talk shop?" Freya asked dumbly, a little blindsided by that dimple. *How much did I drink to not see that dimple last night?*

"We're helping you to blow this case wide open." Norma's voice was matter-of-fact.

"We actually made a plan last night…" Winnie started.

"But we know you were in no shape to remember," Rose finished. "I'm surprised you remembered our names."

Me too. "I don't want y'all to overextend yourselves. Letting me stay here last night was help enough." She turned to smile at Keith as he settled beside her on the floral monstrosity. "Do you know about this?"

He shrugged and offered her a smaller bag that had a breakfast sandwich in it. "You might as well sit back and let them go. They're not to be stopped."

Norma grabbed a donut and started talking. "Fact: the thief likes to steal from unaccompanied women."

Rose poured coffee into a blinged-up reusable coffee mug. "Fact: from what you say, they prefer attractive women to ugly ones. Not sure what that's about." She took a sip and seemed to moan or something. "This coffee is exactly what I need."

"Fact: the thief does it in the morning when people don't expect crazy things to happen." Winnie nibbled on a donut.

"Okay, what's the plan?" Fraya asked.

"We're setting up a sting," Norma smacked in satisfaction. "Good donuts, kiddo."

Keith grinned back at her. As Fraya looked around at this group of aging Charlie's Angels, she wondered what she'd gotten herself into.

AFTER THE PLANNING HAD CONCLUDED, WHICH CONSISTED OF the older woman hammering out details and Fraya and Keith listening, Fraya made a break for it. She needed to at least change clothes and freshen up, even if she couldn't take a shower at the hostel.

"I'll walk with you," Keith said, flashing that lethal dimple.

She held up a hand. "I appreciate that, but I think I need some time to myself. I'll see y'all in the morning."

He nodded. "I can respect that."

"Well, you shouldn't. You should just go on with her anyway," Norma snorted, chocolate sauce from the donut smeared across her face. "You new kids don't know nothing about nothing."

"Consent's a thing, honey," Rose said, sipping her coffee. "And your voice getting on people's nerves is another."

"I'll have you know, my voice is melodic," Nora boomed, and it felt like each word exploded in the back of Fraya's skull.

She stood and made her apologies before she left. Rose gave her a pair of sunglasses to wear because she had "such a delicate constitution today."

These sunglasses are saving my life, Fraya thought as she looked for a street sign. She checked her map and found she wasn't too far from the hostel. She walked down the street, trying to pretend like she wasn't wearing last night's clothes. It was early morning, but the sun was already high in the sky. She hoped she could get into her suitcase with no issues.

Not many people were milling about, but the traffic was picking up. She found the charm in Waikiki's older architecture with modern conveniences thrown in. And all the restaurants. Fraya couldn't wait until she was able to try some local cuisine.

An ABC convenience store was tucked away by a Korean BBQ spot that wasn't open yet. She walked into the convenience store so she could get a bottle of water. The coffee had been great and all, but if she didn't drink water, she was going to dry out and blow into the ocean. She grabbed the biggest bottle of water and a bowl with pineapples. She'd never had fresh pineapple before.

"Sorry about that." Fraya grimaced, passing over her bra money. She should've gotten that out before going to checkout.

"No worries, *mahalo*."

Near the store, a tree offered shade to a bench underneath,

and Fraya quickly took a seat. She ate a piece of pineapple, and it was like her taste buds were singing. She sat in last night's clothes, hair probably looking a mess, homeless, eating pineapples like she didn't have a care in the world. *What a strange turn of events,* she mused.

And she hadn't even thought about smoking in the last couple of days, she realized. She figured if she had one in this heat, she'd be coughing and hacking all the time. Didn't really go with the island vibes.

She quickly finished up her fruit and water, and then tossed her trash in the nearby bin. With renewed energy, Fraya picked up the pace and made it to the hostel in a few minutes. The front desk was empty, which was fine. She didn't want to have a conversation. She had a mission. She pulled an outfit and her bath products out of her suitcase.

Looking around, she still didn't see the front desk person. She darted up the stairs and snuck into the shower. She figured she didn't have much time to clean up before she got caught. No sooner than she'd entered a stall, she heard two sets of footsteps walk in. She made quick work of her shower and hoped they would be finished by the time she left.

As she turned off the shower, the two voices she heard were familiar, and they were on the other side of the bathroom. She couldn't hear them that well.

"You think she knows?" *Was that Toni from the front desk?*

"Brah, she's not paying attention. We're still good." *And Kandy's brother, Dude? He sounds different -- more like an islander than some guy from California.*

"C'mon gimme some of that sugar."

"You're a wild one."

And then what sounded like passionate kissing. What's going on here?

9

"**M**iss, you can't sleep here. Miss, you need to wake up."

Someone was tapping the bottom of her sandals with something hard. Fraya groaned and tried to snuggle deeper into bed. Until she realized she wasn't on her bed. She was on the bench in Waikiki Beach. She sat up abruptly, wiping the sleep from her eyes.

"Oh, it's you," she said when she finally opened her eyes. It was Officer Mahelona, and he'd been tapping her foot with his flashlight. That was probably better than shaking the mess out of her, but couldn't he have just kept speaking to her?

But she had to admit, he looked fine in those civilian clothes.

"Sorry, I haven't been able to find a place yet," she said. Yesterday, she'd gone back to the library to check on the emails she'd sent to respective landlords. Nothing. Emailing, going to the library, waiting for a response, and then doing it all over again felt like a waste of time. She needed her phone.

He snapped at her, "Are you blaming me for that?"

Fraya frowned. "Are you alright? I didn't say anything

about you." She cleared her throat. Sleeping outside sure did make waking up a chore. She needed water and a mint.

He had the decency to look embarrassed. "Sorry, I'm facing a lot of heat from the department. I'm still new to this beat, and I can't seem to figure out what's going on with these robberies."

She scooted over and patted the bench beside her. He sank down, looking at his hands.

"I'm glad I caught up with you. I wanted to apologize for the other day. I know it seems like I wasn't listening and considering your situation. I was."

He looked down at his feet, "It's all I've been thinking about."

Yeah, because your boss called you out, the petty side of Fraya thought. But when she looked at his miserable face, when she *really* looked at him, she felt a connection. He was just trying to make it too. Maybe he needed some kindness.

"Wanna know a secret?" Fraya asked. He looked back at her with a raised brow.

"We've got a little sting operation going on here."

His jaw tightened. *Uh-oh, was he going to make this a thing?*

"Who is 'we'?" he asked.

"Don't worry about it," she said with a cocky smile.

"How is it that you just got on the island, and you're already making moves? And I've been working here for two weeks and still haven't figured this out?"

"You need to think outside the box," she said. "I'm so new, I don't even know what the box looks like."

He laughed and shook his head. "Tell me more about this sting."

He reached into his pocket and pulled out a pack of gum. He grabbed a stick and started chewing it and offered her one. She took one, thinking of her nasty morning breath, and blushed. They chewed in silence until she felt like her breath wasn't too nasty.

She leaned closer to him and whispered about the events that were going to be taking place. "But the thing is, if you're sitting here and they remember you in your uniform, they might not come through."

"So we need to stay away from the action," she continued. "But someplace where we can still see what's good."

He pointed to the seating area behind them, and she nodded. She felt awkward wearing yesterday's clothes again, but at least it was shorts and a t-shirt, not a dress or something awkward.

I'll never take being able to wash clothes for granted again, she thought.

The place had quite a few stone tables with accompanying benches. She snagged a table while the cop grabbed some food from a seller. He came back with two large cups and spoons sticking out of them.

"What's this?" Fraya asked curiously. It seemed like a strange choice for breakfast.

"Shave ice. It's good. I got you the taro flavor. It got ice cream and some other stuffs in there. You'll like it."

"What flavor you got?" she asked, looking in his cup.

"Lilikoi."

"Thank you so much," she said. "Huh, well, those are two things that I know nothing about. When in Rome, right?" She took a cautious bite and was pleasantly surprised. Taro must've been the purple slushy bits mixed in with the vanilla ice cream. It was incredible, savory and sweet. She felt like a whole different person. Sleeping on a beach. Eating ice cream for breakfast. Who even was she?

They ate their shave ice, chatting quietly. This was the most comfortable she'd ever felt around a cop. She still didn't trust him, but she'd eat his shave ice. Some birds flew around, picking up scraps left from other people. A baby girl babbled happily while her mama and papa looked on. Fraya kept scanning until she saw the familiar face. Then she tapped

Officer Mahelona's shoulder and tried to point discreetly when she saw Norma.

The older lady walked like she wasn't used to being on the sand, like Fraya, now that she thought about it. She wore a shirt that said, "Something spicy." Her big straw hat with the Hawaii flag on it marked her as a tourist.

As far as Fraya could tell, Norma was the only person getting into the water alone. The woman stopped a safe distance away from the water to fling off her clothes and set them beside her big red book bag and her sandals. She tip-toed into the water and made a show of shivering as she did.

"Oh, she's good," Officer Mahelona said. Fraya agreed.

Nothing happened at first. She played in the water, and no one seemed to pay any attention. And then Fraya saw him. A guy was casually jogging down the beach, but he had on clothing that was a little suspicious. *It's too hot here to wear a tracksuit,* she thought. But it made it hard to see his body. And his hat was pulled down over his face. Couldn't see his hair.

He headed toward Keith's friend's stuff, trying to be inconspicuous as they watched him pick up the bag and take a turn picking up speed to go toward the street.

That was when Officer Mahelona made his move.

He stood swiftly, but silently. He made his way around the people milling around in their leisurely pursuits. He knocked into someone without apologizing. And then he picked up the pace rapidly to the point of running down the sidewalk.

"Police!" Officer Mahelona yelled while he was in pursuit. He kicked it up and ran full-on after the thief. Fraya held her own end of the bargain. She rushed to intercept the other person involved in the robbery. She had broken off from the crowd and was making her way behind the benches and people.

Fraya grabbed her by the book bag that her brother had handed off to her. "Hold up for a second, Kandy. We need to talk."

10

———

L   ater that day, Fraya sat at the L&L Drive Inn a few streets down from where she'd stopped Kandy in her tracks. She had thought it was a drive-in like the old-fashioned one that they went to sometimes as kids where they could pile into her mama's truck and watch three movies all in one night. But no, it was a restaurant.

"How did you know they were the ones?" Keith asked, taking a bite of his chicken.

"Their information didn't actually mesh with anybody else's account of the robbery. And once I found the ring that Dude had dropped and looked it up, I realized they were locals who were trying to prey on tourists."

HIS PHOTO HAD BEEN VERY CLEARLY ON THE KAIMUKI WEBSITE along with his real name: David Aarons. Oddly enough, Kandy's name really was Kandy with a K.

"They didn't realize who they were dealing with," Norma said with a satisfied nod. Keith and his writing group had invited Fraya out for dinner. They were seated at a back table. Miss Rose wore white linen that somehow hugged her curves,

Norma sported a t-shirt and shorts with an attitude of the righteous, and Winnie with her wide-brim hat and her crochet square. They were all good-naturedly teasing each other and having fun. Oddly enough, Fraya didn't feel like a third wheel. They treated her like a niece.

The L&L served local meals -- plate lunches, they called it. Fraya was digging into the moco loco, a couple hamburgers smothered in gravy over a bed of rice topped with two eggs over easy. It was such a weird pairing of foods, but once she had that first bite, she was all in.

She had just shoved another bite into her mouth when a shadow loomed over her. She turned to look up, and it was Officer Mahelona. "Here you go," he said, handing Fraya her beloved Outkast bag.

She thanked him profusely before frowning. "How did you know where I was?"

He nodded at Keith. "I wanted to make sure you got your gear so you could take care of what you need to take care of."

Keith grinned at her, and she grinned back. The day was definitely looking brighter.

"A big strong police officer like you, you probably have a really big ... appetite. Would you like to join us for a snack?" Miss Rose asked, her eyes drinking him in like she was in the Sahara, and he was iced water.

"I … uh … I have to go ahead and get out of here. Enjoy your dinner." The officer gave a quick nod to everyone and was on his way.

"Another one that you chased off," Norma snorted.

Rose's chin took on an upward tilt. "I didn't chase off anything."

"If that boy would've moved any faster, he would've left skid marks." Norma thunked her drink down in emphasis.

"You're just upset because he couldn't see you past my womanly attributes." Rose gave a pout.

"Nobody is out here trying to get with an aging trollop."

"Trollop!"

"Ladies, we're leaving Fraya with a terrible first impression," Miss Winnie said, putting down her blanket to pat Fraya's hand. "Don't mind them. They were born in a barn. Besides, Rose dear, you know he was out of here like greased lightning, sweetie."

Fraya laughed, enjoying herself for the first time in a long time.

Her phone started ringing in her bag, startling her. "I haven't heard that sweet sound in so long," she said with a grin.

"Is this Fraya?" The woman's voice had that musical quality to it that Fraya was starting to associate with folks who had lived on the island.

"Yes? Can I help you?"

The woman went on to explain that her cousin was Officer Mahelona and he had told her about Fraya. And she knew of an older couple in Kailua with a small cottage for rent.

"It's right on their property, right near the water. Sometimes they go out of town, so they ask that the tenant be willing to care for the pups, get rid of rubbish, those things, yeah?"

Fraya gave a sound of approval. "Where is Kailua?"

"That's up North Shore," Norma butted in. "That's the best part of the island, in my opinion."

"Hush now," Winnie admonished. "She was not talking to us."

"Well, she asked a question. And I had an answer." Norma took a bite of her burger with unapologetic vigor.

Fraya suppressed her giggle and finished up the call with Leilani, Officer Mahelona's cousin.

"I guess I'll be going to see my potential new place tonight," she said with a grin.

In less than a week, she'd gone from moping and hiding back home to finding her bag and her freedom in the islands, new friends, and potential a new home, too. Maybe there was something to her aunt and her tarot cards.

Probably not. She took another bit of loco moco and laughed at something Norma said. For the first time in a long while, Fraya felt like things were going to be okay.

~

THANK YOU FOR READING *CLOSED OUT*, WHICH IS THE PREQUEL to *Wiped Out* the first book in the *Beach Bound Cozy Mystery* series. Join the rest of Fraya's tropical adventures!

TAMARA WOODS IS A COZY MYSTERY-WRITING HILLBILLY LIVING in Hawaii with her mathmagician. She loves taking a closer look at small-town living, which may be why her stories move at a slower pace with good people and good food. She'll never turn down pics of your kitties and puppies. She's here for writing, binge reading, tacos, and wine, not necessarily in that order.

Read more from Tamara Woods

Join her newsletter and find out all her news first:

bit.ly/TamaraGazette

And visit her website:

www.tamarawoodsauthor.com

TREASURES IN HEAVEN

SARAH BIGLOW

1

Nine days, only nine more days until Chaplain Margot Quade finished her tour of duty and returned home to Port Marie, Vermont. She wasn't sure what awaited her back home, although she had faith that whatever plan God lay out for her it would become obvious once her boots struck American soil. Life in the desert changed with the trauma her unit had suffered. They were now down two men, both had returned stateside. One fully draped in funeral honors, while the other wrapped himself in the guilt and weight of grief.

Margot sat in the chapel, where she'd spent many of her days recently, enjoying the solitude. The door behind her opened, though, disrupting the quiet. Her attention immediately shifted to the Private standing there in the doorway, one foot in the room and one foot out.

"Everything alright, Private McPherson?" She asked. Henry McPherson had been a recent transfer to base. He was lanky with the pale complexion of someone not prone to spending time outside.

"I … uh, it's nothing. Sorry to disturb you, Ma'am," he muttered, pivoting on his heel to leave the room.

She stood and closed the distance between them in

seconds. "You're not disturbing me, if that's what you're concerned with. I'm here to talk if you need it." She gestured to the empty seats around them. "Besides, I'm more than happy to just sit and share the space in silent worship, if you'd prefer."

Private McPherson paused a moment longer and nodded, pulling the door shut behind him and joining Margot in one of the padded seats. "I'm not really religious," he mumbled.

"That's okay, too." Margot returned to her seat and closed her eyes. *Please Lord, show me what the path ahead holds.* She exhaled and felt the warm air around her stir. She believed in God working in simple and subtle ways to guide her actions. She chose to believe this moment was such a time.

"Chaplain, can I ask you something?" Private McPherson's voice drew her attention from her thoughts.

"Sure."

"I'm new here. I know that I'm just the bottom of the food chain. However, if something happened that I didn't agree with, I should tell someone, right?"

"Of course. You should report it to a superior officer." Since she technically outranked him she turned and gestured for him to speak. "Is there something you need to get off your chest?"

His pale cheeks turned pink, and he ducked his head. "No. Just thinking out loud. I'm sure it's nothing. I probably misread the situation."

She silently questioned his reluctance to share whatever was weighing him down. There were plenty of people she could see being apprehensive about reporting incidents to their commanders, right or wrong. Still, she didn't peg McPherson as being one of those individuals. "I'm happy to talk through it with you, to put your mind at ease," Margot offered.

Private McPherson shook his head and got to his feet. "Thanks for the chat, Chaplain. I'll see you around base."

He darted out of the room. Margot was left wondering what had drawn him to this place and kept him from making any sort of confession. She didn't hold his lack of religion against him. She served everyone on base, regardless of faith, athough she could see whatever McPherson carried was weighing heavy on his heart. If Private Derek Nesbit had been around, she would have confided in him, but she was alone here. She didn't mind the others in her unit, but she didn't share the same kinship with any of them like she did with Derek.

The door to the chapel opened again, and she turned. "Change your mind, Private?"

Commander Jackson Flannery stood in the doorway, his girth filling the space with his broad shoulders and solid torso. "I'm assuming that wasn't meant for me."

Margot stood and saluted. "No, Sir."

He waved his hand at her. "At ease." He looked around the room without entering. "I heard you'd been spending a lot of time in here."

Margot shrugged. "Seems the right place to be, especially to sort out one's grief."

"It's never easy to lose a fellow soldier," he agreed.

Margot took a step towards her superior. "Can I help you with something specific, Sir?"

"I know you're the one providing guidance to the troops around here. Still, I wanted you to know that I have your back if you need a sounding board."

She smiled. "I appreciate that."

"You know where to find me if you need to unload." He gave the chapel one last look before he left her.

Everyone seems off today.

Maybe it was in her mind, tinged with grief, but she couldn't shake the feeling that Private McPherson needed her. She set out to find him, checking the barracks, but coming up empty.

"You look lost," a gruff bass tone said when Margot stepped out in the blinding late afternoon sun. Heat and light rippled off the sand stretching out all around them.

She spun to see Lieutenant Zachary Banks standing there with his uniform shirt untucked and an unlit cigarette tucked behind his left ear. He'd transferred to base not long after Derek's departure. Margot didn't like to judge, but she always found Lieutenant Banks to be a little too cocky for her taste.

"Just looking for someone," she answered.

"Maybe I can help?" He offered, giving her a smile that telegraphed he thought she couldn't handle the task in front of her simply because of her sex.

"I appreciate the offer, Lieutenant, but I'm fine," Margot replied and turned toward central command.

"Who's your little lost sheep? Maybe I've seen them," he continued, falling into step beside her.

She bristled at his obvious dig at her profession and her sex. He was part of the problem with the armed forces men who believed women weren't fit to serve. However, she knew that every job came with its fair share of difficult co-workers, so she kept her opinion of him to herself. Still, that didn't mean she wanted him tagging along on her search.

"Chaplain, there you are," Private William Parnell called, stepping into view a few paces ahead of them. "Been looking for you."

Parnell had been part of her unit since she'd arrived in the desert. Until recently, he'd been a loner, not really showing much interest in spending time with his brothers and sisters-in-arms. Perhaps Banks' reputation made even the lone wolf stick close to the pack at times.

"No need for your assistance, Lieutenant," Margot lied. She didn't like not being truthful, but it was better for him to think she'd accomplished her task and made him go away. "I've found who I was looking for."

Banks glowered at Parnell, but pivoted on his heel and

stalked back to the barracks. Parnell stared after him until Margot cleared her throat. "Thank you for the save."

"Banks is a misogynistic creep. Were you actually looking for me?" His dark grey-blue eyes narrowed at her below pale blond brows.

"I'm afraid that was a bit of a fib. I'm looking for Private Henry McPherson. Have you seen him recently?"

"I think I saw him heading out toward the village. He tried to catch a ride on a Humvee headed out. Why? What's he done?"

"Nothing...nothing at all. I just wanted to finish our conversation that got interrupted."

"I'm sure he'll be back," Parnell answered.

Margot couldn't shake the feeling that he was wrong. Icy dread trickled down her neck, making her shiver despite the hot and arid climate. "It's really important I find him," she insisted.

"Then we look for him," Parnell said and gestured for Margot to lead on.

She wasn't sure what would have drawn McPherson to the nearby village. Still, if Parnell had seen him head that way, then that was the direction they would follow. She led Parnell out into the desert. They made it half a mile before a body-like form up ahead drew Margot's focus. Taking off at a jog, she closed the distance quickly. Her boots kicked up dust and sand in her wake as she fell to her knees beside Private McPherson.

2

"What happened?" Her throat was raw as she took in the blood covering his desert fatigues. The entry wound in his chest was small, likely a bullet. The fact he was still breathing gave her a kernel of hope.

"I ..." he gurgled and then coughed, blood staining his hands as he tried to stem the flow from the wound.

Margot turned to Parnell. "Help me get him up."

"I don't know that moving him is the best option," Parnell replied, but joined them on the roadside. "Let me take a look."

A protestation died on Margot's lips as she remembered Parnell had field medic training. He pulled on McPherson's shirt, the buttons popping loose so he could assess the damage. He probed the edges of the wound, forcing McPherson to twist away from his touch, a grimace of pain contorting his facial features.

"You can't treat him out here," she insisted.

"We're half a mile from base; I don't think he's got that long."

Margot maneuvered herself to heft McPherson's weight onto her shoulders. "We have to try. Now help me."

Parnell moved to support the man's other shoulder. Together they staggered back toward base moving as quickly as they possibly could. While they made their way through desert dunes, she tried to keep one hand on his back, partly to steady him and to staunch the bleeding.

"I'm … sorry," Henry gurgled as the edge of base finally came into view.

"Save your breath, soldier," Parnell ordered and picked up the pace.

Margot's vision tunneled, focusing on the entry to base. In her mind, she plotted their course directly to the medical facilities. They crossed back onto what was considered American soil. She expected to be surrounded by soldiers offering aid or demanding to know what had happened to McPherson. The soldiers who'd seen their approach didn't move though.

"Why are they just standing there?" Margot's voice was two octaves too high as they veered right.

"They're doing their job, Chaplain," Parnell answered and backed through the entry to the medical facility.

The smell of antiseptic clogged Margot's nose, pulling painful memories to the forefront. They laid McPherson on a gurney, and Parnell began stripping his clothes to get a better look at the damage. Margot studied the young soldier's face. For a moment, he was Peter Abrams, laying in her lap in the desert, begging for home as the life left him.

"I … I need …" McPherson rasped, pulling Margot from her memory.

She bent down and clasped both of her hands around his. "Tell me. Let me help you."

"Confess," he continued, his skin ashen even covered in grime and sweat.

"Now's not the time," Margot insisted, even though her visual assessment of the man told her that he was, in fact, short on time and right now might be all he had left.

"I need to get him into surgery if I have any chance of saving him," Parnell said, shoving Margot aside and wheeling the gurney out of view.

She sunk back against the wall and took several slow breaths to steady her racing heart. *What had he wanted to confess?* When he'd come to the chapel earlier, he'd asked if his duty required him to report things he knew to be wrong. Had he done something he feared would get him dishonorably discharged or even court martialed? All she could do was wait and pray that he pulled through surgery.

~

"CHAPLAIN?" A SOFT VOICE DREW MARGOT BACK TO THE present. "Everything alright, Ma'am?" A female soldier stood over Margot.

When had she sat down? She blinked up at the woman. "Yes, sorry. How long have I been sitting here?"

"A while. You need some help?" The soldier gestured to Margot's hands. "I could take a look at that for you."

Margot looked down. "No, it's not my blood. Private Henry McPherson ... how is he?" Margot used the wall to push herself back to a standing position.

"I'm not sure, Ma'am," the soldier answered.

She needed to find Parnell. He may be a loner, but he was a good man and she knew he wouldn't lie to her if things had gone south. "Excuse me. I'm going to clean up."

She side-stepped the young woman and searched for a restroom to get cleaned up. The sounds of the facility fell away as she scrubbed her hands until they were raw. Although small, it was something she could control in a situation that felt so beyond her grasp. As she stood there, staring at her reflection in the mirror, she vowed to find out what had been weighing on Henry and what had drawn him to the desert.

"There you are," Parnell said, catching Margot as she stepped out of the restroom.

"How is he? Can I see him?" The words fell out of her mouth before she could stop them.

"He made it through surgery, but for the time being he's in a medically-induced coma to let him heal."

"But I need to know what he was trying to say before you took him away."

"It will have to wait until he's conscious. I'm more worried about the bullet I dug out of his spine being one of our own."

"Are you sure? Could one of the locals have gotten hold of one of our weapons?"

"Anything's possible, but he wasn't carrying. Which, come to think of it, seems odd, too." Parnell's blond brow furrowed, and Margot could almost hear the wheels in his mind turning the problem over and over.

"Just let me know when he can have visitors." She leaned in closer. "Maybe keep what happened quiet. If you're right, and he was hit by friendly fire, we don't want to spread any misinformation."

"Roger that, Chaplain," Parnell said.

If Henry couldn't tell Margot what was on his mind, she'd have to go looking for answers on her own.

3

_____

Margot had never felt so out of place in a location, even though she had every right to be there. As she moved about the barracks, searching for Henry's room, she could sense every pair of eyes on her. When she finally found his room, she heaved a sigh of relief to find it empty. His bunkmates were nowhere to be seen.

"What were you trying to tell me?" She wondered aloud, studying his bunk.

At first glance, nothing obvious jumped out at her from being amiss. The bed was meticulously made like all the others in the room. An extra pair of fatigues and boots were set neatly at the foot of the bed. A picture of a smiling young woman showing off a diamond engagement ring hung on his bed. Her heart skipped a beat as she realized his fiancée had no idea that he'd been so badly injured. She detached the photo and looked at the back. Someone had scribbled 'Mr. & Mrs. McPherson soon to be three." She'd assumed the woman's ring had just been the reminder of what awaited him back home, but he had a baby on the way, too. A child could change a great many things. It could motivate a person to do things that they might not otherwise have done.

Though he wasn't that kind of person. *Was he?*

In truth, Margot didn't know very much about Henry's personal life or his character. Their conversation earlier that day had been the longest interaction she'd had with him. However, if anyone knew him, it would be his unit mates and his commanding officer. Which meant she needed to have another conversation with Commander Flannery.

∿

MARGOT FOUND HER COMMANDING OFFICER IN THE CHOW LINE. She picked up a tray and fell in line behind him, studying the food in front of her with only mild interest at best. "Sir, do you have a minute?"

Flannery turned to face her. "Something I can help you with, Chaplain?'

"Possibly."

He nodded and hitched one thumb over his shoulder. "Join me."

After passing through the rest of the line, she followed him to a secluded table. She settled with her back to the wall, surveying the other soldiers eating their food in small clusters. It almost reminded her of high school cliques except at a moment's notice, every man and woman in the room would have everyone else's back.

"What's on your mind? Is it Abrams?" Flannery took a long swig from his glass.

"Not exactly, Sir. I was wondering what you could tell me about Private Henry McPherson."

"McPherson? The new kid?"

Margot nodded and took a bite of soupy green beans. "He stopped by the chapel earlier, and it looked like he needed help. Although he didn't stay long enough for me to really speak with him, I was hoping you might be able to give me a little background. See if I can figure out what might have been weighing on him."

"Well, I think he mentioned that he's got a wife back home. Seems he married right out of high school. Kid can't even drink."

"I think I'd heard that, too," Margot replied. "How is he getting along with other people here on base? I know when soldiers are that young, sometimes they have trouble fitting in out here."

Flannery looked around, as if he didn't want to be overheard, then said, "Now, I'm not one to talk badly about those under my command, but I think Banks took the kid under his wing. To be honest, I'm not so sure that was a good thing."

Is that why Banks was so eager to help? "I see." She contemplated the rest of the food on her plate, her appetite souring. She must have failed to mask her discomfort, because Flannery cleared his throat, drawing her gaze.

"Why are you really asking about this kid, Chaplain?"

Did she tell him the truth? She had to believe that word of an injured soldier had made its way up the ranks, even if she'd asked Parnell to keep things quiet from their fellow soldiers. "You didn't hear?" Time to gauge what he knew.

"It's a big base, with lots going on. Something I should know?"

He'd always been a good man with solid judgment, even when his decisions had resulted in unfortunate consequences. Besides, if she was going to figure out what Henry had been up to, she needed allies. "I found Private McPherson in the desert, about half a mile from base. He'd been wounded."

"Off base? You're certain?"

"Absolutely. I don't know what he was doing there. Somehow, he did manage to say that he was sorry before passing out. Parnell and I were able to get him to medical."

"He shouldn't have been off base. He wasn't on assignment."

"I can't shake the feeling that something is going on that made him feel uncomfortable. Something he wanted to share with me before his injury."

Flannery's brows narrowed. "Your words say injury, but your face says it's something worse."

"He's in a medically-induced coma. So, we can't ask him for the details."

"Anything else I should know?"

Margot swallowed the lump in her throat. "It may have been friendly fire. Or at the very least, it was one of our weapons that was used."

He nodded, pushing his tray aside, before standing up and tugging his uniform jacket down. She stood out of respect and habit. "Whatever is going on, let the MPs take it from here, Chaplain."

"Yes, Sir." Watching him walk away, she had no intention of letting this go. She was a firm believer that God put circumstances in her path for a reason. It's how she'd ended up serving her country. A young man came to her seeking counsel, and she wasn't going to let him down.

4

———

A small window remained before Margot would be
called in to give a statement to the MPs about what
happened. She hadn't mentioned anything about Private
Parnell to them, but she owed him a heads-up before he got
dragged before them without warning.

She didn't have to look hard to find him. He sat in the
medical facility, flipping through a book that she suspected he
had no real interest in reading. He looked up at her approach,
and his shoulders relaxed a fraction of an inch.

"Everything okay?" She took a seat beside him.

"Just a bit tense. I don't like the idea of someone trying to
take out this kid."

Margot turned to see Henry's unmoving figure through a
tiny window in the door next to them. "How long have you
been sitting here?"

"Since you left, actually. Didn't feel right leaving him
alone. Got a bad feeling and couldn't shake it."

"You're not alone. I wanted to let you know that the MPs
may be asking to speak with you. I let Commander Flannery
know some of what happened."

"What'd he say?"

"To let the professionals handle it."

Parnell snorted, the lines around his eyes crinkling for the very first time since she'd known him. She hadn't been certain he could express positive emotions. "You're not going to do that, right?"

"Like you, I can't shake a bad feeling either. Flannery said that Lieutenant Banks had taken Henry under his wing."

"That guy is an asshole. Um … Sorry for the swearing," he said, his cheeks flushing in embarrassment.

"He's not my favorite person either," she agreed.

"If you're looking for an explanation of what happened, I'd start looking there." Parnell muttered. "There's something off about that guy. He's the kind of guy who gets joy from kicking puppies."

Margot didn't think Banks was that cruel, although he did have a high opinion of himself. Also, if Henry thought he was doing something untoward and was going to report it, she had no doubt Banks would take matters into his own hands. "How long do you think he'd been out in the desert like that before we found him?"

Parnell shrugged one shoulder. "Ten minutes. Maybe twenty. Probably felt like an eternity to him, though."

Was that enough time for Banks to get back to base before Margot ran into him? Henry must have gone out there immediately after leaving the chapel. She was going to need to speak to Banks, even though she really disliked that idea.

"Chaplain Quade?" A caramel-skinned officer called from down the hall.

Margot stood at attention as the MP approached. "Mind coming with me?"

"Yes, Sir," Margot replied and left Parnell to keep watch over Henry.

"So, you found Private McPherson?" the officer questioned her from across a small table in the officer's lounge.

"I did. He'd stopped by the chapel in some sort of distress and I wanted to ensure he was okay," Margot replied, beginning to feel like a broken record.

"What was he upset about?" The officer probed.

"I wish I knew. He didn't say anything, and he was in bad shape when I found him."

"Did you find him by yourself?"

"No. Private Parnell assisted me. He has medical training. You'd have to speak with him about Private McPherson's condition and prognosis."

"We'll be doing that. Now, the report we got said he was hit by friendly fire. Is that true?"

"I don't know. What I do know is that Private Parnell told me the bullet he retrieved was one of ours. Who shot it is a mystery to me as much as you."

"I see." He wet his lips and leaned in close. "Anyone you think could have done it?"

"Again, Officer, I wish I knew. He has a wife at home. He seemed like a nice, young man, but I don't really know him intimately. I've given you all the information I have."

"I appreciate your assistance, Chaplain."

Margot stood and left the room. As she moved down the hallway, she felt the hairs on the nape of her neck bristle. She turned slowly and met Lieutenant Banks' gaze. He took a step toward her, but retreated when the MP appeared in the doorway, calling over his radio. "Get me Private Parnell."

Lieutenant Banks pivoted on his heel and disappeared out of view. His quick retreat didn't bode well. Still, if she wanted to know what, if any, involvement Banks had in what happened to Henry, she needed to speak with him. So, without appearing to chase after him, she followed in the direction he'd gone. She rounded the corner and spotted him in a tight huddle with two other officers she didn't recognize. A tall man with a deep tan spotted her first. The conversation ceased as she approached.

"Lieutenant, I was hoping I could speak with you," she said, keeping her tone calm and even.

Banks glanced at his compatriots before stepping up, so he was toe to toe with Margot. "I thought you found who you were looking for earlier, Chaplain, and didn't need my help."

"I think you're the only person who can help me. Please, I could use your help."

"Don't leave the little lady hanging," the tanned officer said, clapping Banks on the back.

"See you around, LT," the other officer said before they retreated.

"I didn't mean to disturb you, but I just thought you ought to know one of the soldiers that looks up to you was injured earlier."

"And who would that be?"

"Henry McPherson."

"What did the kid do? Get himself blown up by an IED or something?"

"I think he was shot. A pretty severe leg wound. They think he'll be laid up for a while. You wouldn't know how he got hurt would you?"

"Not a thing. Thought the kid had his head screwed on better than to go cavorting with the locals alone."

"I didn't say he was with the locals," Margot replied.

"You aren't insinuating he got shot by one of our boys, are you?" Banks leaned over her, a menacing scowl on his face.

"I wasn't there, so I can't say what happened. He did stop by to see me before it happened. Most soldiers only come to see me when they want to share something that's been weighing on their hearts. Henry wouldn't have anything to worry about, would he?"

"Nope," Banks answered, crossing his arms over his chest.

Margot took the signal for what it was and stopped asking questions. "Well, I just wanted you to know, seeing as you've been looking out for him."

"You've done your good deed for the day, Chaplain. Why don't you go back to your chapel and pray for him?"

Margot gritted her teeth and retreated to the chapel. Not because he'd banished her to her domain. She could use some prayer and quiet to sort her thoughts. She hadn't been sure that Banks could have shot Henry and gotten back to base, but that didn't mean one of his comrades hadn't pulled the trigger on his orders. She just needed to figure out the why.

The space was empty. She hadn't expected anyone else to be there, so she sat in front of the crucifix hanging on the wall and bowed her head. She wrapped both hands around the cross hanging between her dog tags and took in the silence, trying to sort through what she knew.

Henry had a wife and child back home. He'd known something that disturbed him enough to seek out Margot, although he'd retreated before confiding in her and that perceived betrayal had earned him a bullet in the chest. Banks seemed the type to want to keep things quiet, especially if he was doing anything illicit. A lot of things could motivate a man like him.

Thundering footsteps broke her contemplative silence, and Officer Bianca Forte, one of Margot's bunkmates, appeared, bending double to catch her breath. Her hazel eyes were wide. "Margot, come quick."

5

S he didn't ask where they were going or what had prompted Bianca's appearance. Margot simply followed the other woman until they reached the barracks. It was trashed. Margot's bed was overturned, the blankets crumpled on the floor.

"Who did this?" Margot demanded.

"No idea. I just came back and found it like this. Who'd you piss off?"

She had an idea, but it had been a quick job. It was entirely possible that Banks' buddies had stopped by while she was speaking to him. This incident only solidified her belief that Banks and his men were behind what happened to Henry. Margot knew that Bianca didn't need to get dragged into the mess. She'd already involved too many people for her comfort.

"Thanks for letting me know. I'll get this cleaned up."

"I can help."

"No, it's fine. I need to see if anything's missing, and it's easier if I do it myself."

"You should report it to the MPs."

Margot fixed Bianca, with a smile. "If anything's missing, I'll be sure to do that."

Bianca nodded and left Margot to organize her belongings. As she righted the mattress, her fingers brushed against something thin and papery. She withdrew her hand to find a wad of folded American bills. She didn't have money here since she didn't need it. *Is this what it's all about?* She set the money aside and remade the bed. She checked the journal she kept to help corral her thoughts and process her time overseas. Pages were crumpled, but none appeared to be missing. She hadn't had time to write about her encounter with Henry. Still, whoever had tossed her belongings didn't' know that. A thought occurred to Margot as she pocketed the money.

Margot traced the path to Henry's room and found his belongings similarly in disarray. The photo of his wife lay on the floor, a boot print marring the pretty young woman's face. The mattress sat askew on the bedframe. Moving towards it, she found what felt like an envelope secured to the bottom. Whoever had been searching hadn't looked very hard. She pulled the envelope free to find a letter to Carissa, presumably Henry's wife. Margot's palms grew clammy as she stowed it in her pocket, too. If someone had been in the room, they could still be nearby, and she couldn't risk them seeing what she'd found.

Blowing out a breath, Margot retreated to the chapel. It remained as empty as she'd left it when Bianca came to fetch her. She settled in one corner at the front of the space and angled her body so she could keep an eye on the door. The fact someone had gone into her space and violated her privacy unnerved her. Her heart beat a little faster and her nerves were that much more frayed at the sound of a passing voice or the beat of footfalls. She'd never had to seek solace in this sacred space before, but she let the peaceful atmosphere wrap around her like armor, fortifying her against whatever was to come next. She pulled Henry's letter out of her pocket and studied the neat penmanship.

"Forgive me," she whispered to the air around her. It was directed more to Henry than God. She wasn't about to violate God's privacy, after all.

Her finger slid beneath the envelope flap, and she pulled out a single sheet of paper with a stack of neatly organized bills. All crisp US currency, like the ones she'd found stuffed under her mattress. The weight of the forbidden money felt heavy in her pocket, but she didn't dare touch it. Instead, she focused on Henry's letter to his wife.

Carissa,

I know we barely had a chance to start our lives together before I got called away. And right when we found out we'd be parents! You have no idea how happy that day made me with our positive pregnancy test. It made me love you even more. It gave me the motivation to come home to you when all of this is over.

But being here has changed things. It's not like I thought it would be. If I'm being honest, I didn't know what I was expecting. We're not at war, not exactly, but we aren't here in peace, either. I look around at the soldiers who've been here for months, and I see the toll it's taken on them. I didn't want that to be me when I'm done, but I'm afraid it might be.

I've done something I knew I shouldn't have done. It felt wrong the minute it happened. I'm nobody here. My opinion doesn't matter. So, I went along with it. I told myself it would provide for you and the baby. Still ,I know it's wrong. So, if this letter gets to you, please know that this is all I'm ever going to send you. I don't know if I'll be seeing you again.

Please know how much I love you and our baby. Please forgive me.

Henry

Margot's eyes welled with unshed tears as she silently counted the money. Two thousand dollars, all in twenties. It was beginning to make sense now. Greed could make good men do terrible things, and morally questionable people do even worse. She had no doubt in her mind where Lieutenant Banks fell on that scale. Still, she had one man's letter with what amounted to a partial confession of his own wrongdoing. It didn't name any co-conspirators. She had no proof that Banks' men had ransacked her bunk or planted money there. She couldn't go to the MPs with what she suspected unless she had proof. After all, the minute they saw she had the money on her, it would appear as if she was trying to cover up her own involvement.

A plan began taking shape in Margot's mind. As she stowed the letter and its contents back in her pocket, the door opened. Her heart skipped a beat, and she took a step back, cornering herself when Private Parnell appeared.

"How'd it go with the MPs?"

He closed the distance between them and sunk onto a bench. "I don't think they've got McPherson's best interests at heart. Something just rubbed me the wrong way while they were questioning me. Did you notice Banks' boys were hanging around?"

"Did they approach you?" Margot settled down beside him.

"No, they aren't stupid. What is going on here, Chaplain?"

Margot reached into her pocket and showed him the envelope with the stack of money. "I don't have anything beyond this and some money that was planted in my room. Although I think Banks may be stealing money."

"Son-of-a …" Parnell trailed off, his hands balling into white-knuckled fists. "Sorry. I know I've got a mouth like a sailor."

"If you think the MPs can't be trusted, then we need to do something about this. We need to have ironclad proof of what's happening and take it higher up the chain of command."

"We, huh?" He quirked a brow at her.

She smiled at him. "You gave up that lone wolf act the minute you helped me drag a wounded soldier back to base. You're invested in this just like I am. Be honest you would still be watching over him if the MPs hadn't called you away."

Parnell closed his eyes and hung his head but didn't deny her statement. "After what happened with Abrams, I guess I'm just a little protective of the young guys."

"You aren't the only one. I know there was nothing anyone could have done for Peter, but I know there's something I can do for Henry. I'm not going to let him down."

"So what's the plan?" Parnell leaned back against the bench, eyeing her with an expectant expression.

"I need to have a discussion with my roommate, Bianca. I didn't think of it before, but part of her duties involve monitoring all the US funds coming in to help provide aid to villages in the region. If money's gone missing, she'd know about it. Or at the very least, be able to tell me if we're on the right track."

"Say we are. Then what? Banks is well-connected. If he's got an MP in his pocket like I think he does, how do we get around that kind of power?"

Margot's stomach dropped as the next words left her mouth. "I told him Henry was shot in the leg. Banks thinks that he's still able to share the details of their plan. If that's the case, I suspect he will try to silence Henry permanently."

"You're going to use a comatose patient who can't defend himself as bait?"

"I will not let anyone lay another hand on him. But it is the only thing I can think of to get Banks to confess: to catch him in another criminal act. They'll have to investigate him after that if he's caught attempting to murder a fellow soldier."

"It's ballsy. I'll give you that, Chaplain."

"I may be a woman of faith, Private, but I also have conviction. I believe the Lord put me on this Earth to do good and help people who cannot defend themselves. Right now, that means a young man lying in an infirmary bed who was trying to clear his conscience."

"Well, I'll keep an eye on Banks and his boys while you square away the motive. Be careful, though. If they ransacked your bunk, that was likely a warning."

"Too bad I don't scare that easily," Margot said with a determined smirk. Time to set the trap.

6

Margot found Bianca back in the barracks. She was sitting on her bed staring at Margot's belongings. The other woman looked up at Margot's entry.

"So, was anything missing?"

Margot shook her head. "No, but I found something that shouldn't be there." She took the bills she'd found under her mattress and handed them over. "I think this belongs in your care."

Bianca's brow furrowed as she stared at the wad of bills. "Why do I get the feeling I'm missing something here?"

"You're in charge of monitoring the disbursement of regional aid, aren't you?" Margot sat beside the other woman.

"Yes." Realization dawned on Bianca's face. "You think I'm doing something illegal?" Bianca's body language changed. She moved to the other end of the bed, putting distance between them. She tossed the money on the bed as if it would contaminate her just by being near it.

"No, I don't think that at all. But I was hoping you could help me figure out how much has gone missing and where it might have ended up," Margot answered, trying to make her tone as conciliatory as possible. She needed this woman on her side.

Bianca looked around the empty room. "I want to help, but …"

"You're worried about the repercussions of being a whistleblower," Margot finished, and Bianca nodded. She couldn't blame the woman for her fears after all, look where it had gotten Henry. "I just need you to check some numbers. I have an idea of where it might have ended up."

"Okay. I can do that."

Margot reached over and took Bianca's hand. "That's all. I just need you to do your job. Nothing else."

"I need to know when I should be looking. How far back do I go?"

Margot opened her mouth to answer, but closed it again. She wasn't entirely sure. "At least the last six months."

"I'll be in the infirmary. Come find me when you're done," Margot said and stood up. She pointed to the cash. "And please do me a favor: return that to where it belongs." She kept the envelope and money from Henry to his wife. She needed it as evidence.

Bianca stood, saluted, and left the room. Margot took a slow inhale and let it out just as slow. The proof she needed was coming, but she didn't have time to waste. Even if she did get the evidence that Banks and his men had been stealing money, she still needed to catch him in the act of trying to silence Henry. She just hoped that she wasn't wrong and wasn't too late.

THE TREK ACROSS THE BASE TO THE INFIRMARY WAS interminable. Everything felt as if it were working against Margot. The air seemed heavy, weighing her down. The sun above and the sand below were too hot, seeping through her clothing and making her sweat. She reached the exterior door to the building and paused, that sense of being watched returning. She glanced over her shoulder and spotted the deeply tanned officer she'd seen with Banks just dart out of view.

So he is watching me. She stepped inside, letting the cool air wash over her, sending shivers down her spine as she wound her way to the recovery rooms. Parnell sat outside Henry's room. He looked up at her, much like he had the last time she'd come by.

"Any word on his condition?" she asked in a hushed tone.

"Unchanged. I'm not letting the kid out of my sight."

"If what we're trying to do is going to work, they have to believe he's just been minorly injured. No one would be guarding him. I know you want to see justice done, but you can't be here."

"Do you have the proof we need to nail them for what they did to this kid?"

"I'm working on it. I'll have it before we bring them to the MPs. I promise."

Parnell glowered, but stood up and marched back in the direction Margot had come. She slipped into Henry's room and sat on the edge of the bed, pressing her right palm to his left hand. "I found the letter. I know what you were trying to tell me. I'm so sorry you didn't feel that you could tell me the truth. But I'm going to help you now. You won't have to go through this alone. Whatever it takes, I'm going to get you home to your wife and baby, Henry."

She slid the chain from around her neck and slipped the cross under his hand. "Hold on just a little longer, soldier."

7

Margot left Henry's room and retreated down the hall. She considered leaving and coming back in another entrance, especially knowing Banks' men were surveilling her. If they thought she'd left, they might feel emboldened to act. Deciding that was the best course of action, she left through the door she'd come in and clocked the same officer watching her as she made her way toward the mess hall. Just as she stepped through the door, she caught him reach for a radio on his shoulder.

She didn't wait for more confirmation. She wound her way through the empty mess hall, back out and around the side of the building, slipping into the infirmary through the side entrance. The usual sounds of the facility—beeping monitors and low voices of staff—fell away as she walked the halls. She pressed her body to the wall catty cornered to Henry's room. The tanned officer appeared in her line of sight, followed by Lieutenant Banks.

"You're sure you saw her leave?" Banks asked.

"She headed for the mess hall," he answered. After a beat, he leaned in. "I told you I should have handled this situation, LT."

"Maybe so, but I'm going to take care of it myself right now. Keep an eye out in case anyone comes looking for our little friend."

"I know you think you got the message across, but I don't think she's going to be scared off like that. She's tough," the tanned officer said.

Margot was disgusted with the topic of discussion. She certainly wasn't going to be scared away or bribed into silence. She was tough. Just because she wasn't here in the same capacity as them didn't mean she wasn't also a fighter. Her hands balled into fists as she watched them still standing in front of Henry's door.

"Well, if she didn't get the message, we'll just have to deal with her too," Banks muttered before shouldering his way into the room. Margot wanted to be there, to catch every word Banks said to Henry. It would be the confession she needed, but she couldn't get into the room with the other officer keeping watch. She didn't need to worry about his interference for long, because Parnell came barreling down the hallway.

"There you are!" He shouted and grabbed the officer by the lapels of his uniform jacket.

"What's wrong with you?" The other man shouted as Parnell slammed him against the wall.

"You didn't think I'd notice you messing with my stuff. No one touches my stuff," Parnell spat. He looked over in Margot's direction and gave a subtle nod toward the door.

"I didn't go near your stuff, psycho," the officer answered and shoved Parnell back.

"I know it was you," Parnell retorted.

"You better watch yourself, *Private*," the officer snarled. "I'll have you court martialed for assaulting a superior officer."

"Yeah? Maybe we should go sort this out with Flannery.

I'm sure he'd love to hear how you're stealing from your fellow soldiers," Parnell replied.

"If it will make you shut up, then fine," the other officer said. Parnell led the way down the hall, giving Margot her chance to peer into Henry's room.

Banks stood beside Henry's bed, leaning on the bedrail. "I really thought you were a good kid. Loyal even. All you had to do was keep your mouth shut, and your little family would have been set for life. But you had to go and blab about everything to that Chaplain. Well, joke's on you, kid ... because no one is going to find out what you told her."

Margot's body froze, keeping her rooted to the spot. She knew she needed to act, but the fight or flight response which she'd so finely honed in training was failing her now. Banks reached for a pillow and pressed it to Henry's face. Despite being in a coma, Henry's body reacted to the lack of oxygen, jerking slightly under the larger man's weight.

"No!" The words tore from Margot's lips and spurred her to action. She charged through the door and tackled the burly officer to the ground, ripping the pillow away from Henry's face in the process. For the moment, he was out of danger.

"I know what you've done, Lieutenant, and you are not going to get away with it," Margot said, doing her best to pin Banks to the ground. Parnell had led the other officer away to give her a chance to eavesdrop, but no one else knew what was happening here. No one was coming to help her if Banks got the upper hand.

Just as she felt Banks stop moving beneath her weight, a sharp pain hit her in the ribs, and she staggered backward, pressing a hand to her side. A short blade protruded from Banks' left hand, and it was now stained with her blood.

"You shouldn't have gotten involved," he grunted and pulled himself to his feet.

"A man needed help. That's my job," Margot panted, trying to staunch the wound.

"We had a good thing going. No one would have ever known."

"Is that why you joined the Army? To steal from people who need our help?" The edges of her vision were beginning to go hazy.

Banks laughed. "I saw an opportunity, and I took it. But you wouldn't understand that, would you? Bet you've never done a sinful thing in your life."

"You can't possibly believe you're going to get away with all of this now. There are too many witnesses for you to cover it up," she repeated, ignoring his verbal jab at her.

"I think I can handle two people," he scoffed.

Before Margot could respond, the door behind her slammed open and two pairs of footsteps thundered into the room. She looked to her left and her right to find Parnell and Commander Flannery aiming their weapons at Banks.

"You want to drop that knife, soldier?" Flannery's words may have been phrased as a question, but the firm tone signaled it as an order.

"If you think your boys have your back, you're mistaken. They're spilling their guts to the MPs right now. Something about a lesser sentence," Parnell said with a satisfied smirk.

More footsteps echoed in the hall as two MPs appeared. One twisted Banks' wrist until he dropped the blade before ushering him out of the room. The adrenaline left Margot's body in a rush, and she slumped against the foot of Henry's bed.

"Let me see," Parnell said, gently moving her hand away. "You'll need an X-ray, but I'd say you got pretty lucky."

"Don't feel so lucky," Margot said, her words slurring together as the walls closed in.

MARGOT AWOKE IN ONE OF THE INFIRMARY ROOMS WITH

Commander Flannery sitting vigil by her bedside. She sat up and winced at the pain in her side. He turned to face her at the sound of the blankets rustling.

"You know, I could court-martial you for disobeying a direct order," he said with none of his usual gruffness.

"I couldn't leave a man in need alone. I had to help the only way I know how," Margot said, situating herself against an array of pillows.

"Well, if you hadn't gone looking, Banks may have gotten away with murder."

"He and at least two other officers were skimming money. I don't know how much or for how long though, Henry was trying to blow the whistle," Margot said. She decided implicating the young soldier when he couldn't defend himself wasn't worth it.

"Parnell told me everything. Lucky he did, too. I'd hate to think what would have happened if we'd gotten to Henry's room a minute later."

"I would have handled it." Her hands drifted to the spot where her cross usually hung before remembering she'd left it with Henry. "I try not to judge people, Sir, but I can't fathom the level of greed Banks and his men showed. Was what they'd been given not enough?"

"You go down that rabbit hole, and you might not come back out. You did a good thing, Chaplain. You rest up. After all, you've only got eight days left before you're out of here. Try to avoid any more fun before then."

"I'll try."

"That's an order."

"Yes, Sir."

8

The medical staff discharged Margot five days before she was set to return home. She'd returned to the barracks to find Bianca waiting for her with a thick folder sitting on Margot's bed.

"I didn't want to disturb you while you were recovering, but I dug into things like you asked. You were right. Banks and his men were stealing money from aid for months. It looks like they took more than sixty thousand each over a course of nearly ten months," Bianca announced as soon as Margot sat down.

"Thank you for your help. I am sorry I had to bring you into it," Margot said and studied the documents in the file. It would be good evidence for the MPs.

"If anything, I owe you for putting me into it. We can now work to recover some of the funds and send it where it truly belongs."

"Glad I could help," Margot sighed and gently eased herself back on the bed.

"I'll let you get some more rest and bring this to the authorities myself."

No sooner had Bianca disappeared than a knock came at

the door. Margot struggled to a sitting position before calling, "Come in."

Private Parnell appeared with a small smile on his face. "Sorry if you just got settled, but a patient is asking for you."

Margot vaulted from the bed, ignoring the ache pulling at her stitches. "Henry woke up?"

Parnell nodded. "He's been asking for you for the last twenty minutes. Insisting that he talk to you privately."

Margot shouldered past him into the hallway. "Thank you for everything. For having my back and trusting me when I asked for a little leeway."

"We're family. Family always has each other's back. Now, you better get going before they send out a search party to find you just to shut him up."

Margot wound her way through the barracks and back to the infirmary. She found Henry propped up in bed. His cheeks were paler than when he'd first showed up in the chapel, but he was alive. His brow furrowed with concentration, and he lifted his arm holding out her cross. "I think these are yours, Ma'am," he said.

"Please, it's Margot," she said and accepted them.

"You saved my life. I owe you an explanation."

Margot held up a hand. "You don't owe me anything. I found the letter to your wife. I know what Banks roped you into and that you were trying to expose what was going on."

"I knew what I was doing was wrong. It felt dirty the entire time I was doing it, but I wanted to fit in here. Banks seemed like he cared about my family and me. He said he'd have my back, but he lied."

"He's going to be held accountable for what he's done. They'll take the fact you were trying to blow the whistle into account," Margot said, patting his hand. It was then that she really took in his appearance. His hands trembled.

"How bad is it?" She made a small gesture toward his body.

"The bullet hit my spine. It did a lot of damage. They don't think I'm ever going to walk again. Still, they said if they hadn't operated when they did, I'd be dead."

"I'm so sorry, Henry," Margot grasped his hand between both of hers.

"It's my penance for what I did. I'm still going to get to go home to my wife and see my baby born … and even grow up. This is just going to have to be my new normal."

"I applaud your courage, Henry. Not many in your position would be so optimistic about what lays ahead of them."

"Yeah, well, I don't really have a choice."

"Do you know who shot you?" Margot hated to ask, but that piece of the puzzle was still missing in her mind.

"One of Banks' guys. He saw me leave the chapel and figured I'd told you everything. He had told me to meet him by the transports going out into the village, but then there was no transport. I knew I shouldn't have gone with him. I thought that maybe if I went along with it, he'd think he could still trust me. And I hadn't told you anything."

"They're all going to go away for a long time. I promise," Margot repeated.

"Thanks. I know it doesn't make up for what I did, but I'm glad you figured out what happened."

"I saw a fellow human in need, and I did what any good person would do. Besides, true family, blood or not, we all have each other's backs. No matter what."

Margot left Henry's room. She made her way back to the chapel, sitting in the front row, her hands clasped around her cross. The last few days were not how she'd expected the end of her deployment to go. Somehow, she'd made it through, and in a few short days, she would be starting the next part of her journey of faith. She trusted that whatever lay ahead of her was what the Lord knew she could handle. She looked toward that future with hope, wondering if perhaps Banks and his men had done what they did out of fear. The fear of losing material wealth that made them feel important, not understanding that what awaited them was far more valuable.

~

Continue the *Reverend Margot Quade Cozy Mystery* Series in Book One, *Into the Lion's Den.*

Sarah Biglow is the USA Today Bestselling author of several urban fantasy, cozy mystery and paranormal romance series. She is a licensed attorney and spends her days combating discrimination as an Investigator with the Massachusetts Commission Against Discrimination. She lives in Boston with her husband and son.

Read More from Sarah Biglow

www.sarah-biglow.com

RING GONE 'ROUND THE ROSES

AUBREY ELLE

1

Somewhere in the neighborhood, the guitarist slid into a deeper rift and I envisioned skilled fingers on the instrument, strumming an almost perfect cover for a Hendrix tune. I bobbed my head to the beat, digging the wailing music—

"And then that time you and that senior on the baseball team hooked up." A derisive snort. "You *totally* stole him from me!"

I snagged my lower lip between my teeth, distracted from listening to the music.

Can't she...shut up?

I'd *just* managed to tune out Wanda Sanger's constant nagging. For the last half-hour, she'd been tanning on a lounger positioned in the worst possible spot on her patio—a place that put her right next to the garden bed I was currently weeding.

With my head lowered as I focused on removing dandelions from the faded mulch, I doubted she could see my reaction. Because that was all she'd been after. Ever since she realized I worked for Alton Landscaping, the company her husband hired to tend to their property, she'd made it her mission to "catch up." We hadn't seen each other since high school graduation. Heck, I hadn't seen much of Payton, Ohio, since I nabbed my diploma seventeen years ago. Coming back to the small town after a failed marriage and a detested career guaranteed I'd encounter other faces from my past.

However, she was one I'd particularly rather not deal with. Especially not while I was stuck working in her garden of neglected rose bushes, sweating my butt off under the unrelenting sun. It wasn't that I disliked my job. Working outside and dirtying my hands with plants and soil beat slaving away in an office all day. I was blessed to earn my pay in the fresh air, and when I'd realized a neighbor was offering music nearby, it seemed my afternoon would be downright enjoyable. Anywhere near this woman would be grating, though.

"I don't know what he saw in you," Wanda went on with a huffed laugh. "And he should see you now. On your hands and knees, working in lawn care."

Still, I ignored her. I didn't care one whit that she still held a grudge from when we were teenagers—and I did *not* steal any boy from her. He'd asked me to prom and then stood me up anyway. Nor did I care that she deemed landscaping a pathetic means of employment.

"*So* ironic," she taunted.

No. What was ironic was the fact she might have thought I was listening to her. Well, I *was* because we were merely three feet from each other and she'd never been able to speak without a loud braying tone. But I'd been paying attention to the pseudo-Jimi in the background.

"You never could stand it that I was better than you," she said.

I deadpanned at the pile of weeds I'd removed. Better than me? When was it ever a competition?

"You know?" she asked.

I exhaled a long breath and straightened from my crouch

in the baked garden bed. An errant stem brushed my arm, the thorn snagging my flesh. As I sat on my haunches and faced her, my long brown hair fell back from the messy ponytail I'd secured it in. Upright, I let the cords of my earbuds dangle forward, clear for her to see I hadn't been an audience for her unwelcomed tirade. I had been trapped, listening the whole time since my phone battery had died, but I'd left the earpieces in as a disguise so as not to have to speak with her.

I tugged an earbud out and blinked away the sweat that slid along my brow. "Did you say something?"

Her lips pursed and she jerked sitting up. Indignation blazed from her slitted gaze.

Holding back a grin at denying her the satisfaction of harping at me, I cleared my throat. "Dang, Wanda." I shook my head. "Maybe use *some* sunscreen. Your face is looking really red there."

She scowled and swung her legs off the lounger. "Like I'd listen to you."

Suit yourself.

Before she could speak further, men's raised voices sounded near the front of the yard. Craig and Jon Alton were at it again. My boss and coworker were constantly arguing, and I wasn't sure if it was because Craig was an overbearing father or if Jon was a rebellious teenager. Maybe both. Either way, the father-and-son duo failed to present a professional image. And despite what Wanda thought of landscaping as a career, I wanted to work for a decent company. Or at least one void of family drama.

As I turned from the direction of Craig and Jon sharing heated words near the road, Wanda's daughter Amy exited the house. She tromped out to the patio as a mess of long limbs, wavy hair, enormous shades, and a skimpy bikini. A younger version of what Wanda was likely trying for in a figure past its prime.

"Hey," Amy said, her face lacking any emotion as she

knocked her knuckles on Wanda's lounger. "My dad's looking for you in the house."

"Oh." Wanda grinned at the daughter who was probably in Jon's class. Amy didn't linger long enough to witness her new stepmom's smile, turning immediately for the sliding door into the house. A burst of chilled air escaped from inside, setting goosebumps to my arms.

"Always has to rub that in," Wanda whined with a smirk, her disgust at someone other than me evident as she peered at the door Amy had closed in her wake. "*My* dad. Like the man doesn't belong to *me* at all."

"Well, he *is* her dad. Not yours."

Wanda leveled an icy glare my way. "Never. Mind."

I shrugged, figuring it wasn't worth the space in my day to worry over Wanda's reception in the Sanger household. If I had to live with this spiteful woman who still cared about what happened years ago, I'd want to distance myself too. Obviously, Amy's dad had wanted Wanda there —they'd eloped not long ago. Craig had said she'd married Mr. Sanger just this past spring, but it seemed his daughter from his first marriage wasn't keen on her joining the family.

"Hey, Madis!" someone called from the front yard.

I took a few steps from the patio garden and peered around the house. Only one Alton stood near the pickup we'd parked. The trailer ramp was still down as we weren't done with the Sanger property yet. Craig was nowhere to be seen, his truck gone from the curb. "Yeah?" I hollered back.

The teen ran a hand through his long mop of sweaty hair. "Can you do me a favor?"

"Maybe."

"I need a hand with this trimmer. I think it's broken."

Rolling my eyes, I sighed. Jon asking for a favor, again. Needing help starting equipment, again. Broken, my butt. It didn't matter how many times I lectured and demonstrated how to properly prime a simple tool, he'd flood the engine. "Yeah."

A swoosh sounded and a breeze of air-conditioned air teased me. Wanda had gone inside. Go figure. As soon as I had a chance to work in peace, I was asked to be elsewhere.

I cracked my back and twisted side to side before heading to Jon. Honestly, walking around wouldn't be a bad idea after all that crouching over I'd done. It wasn't that I minded helping the kid. Anyone with even a moderate range of patience would get tired of showing someone how to do a simple task when they never showed any inclination to listen.

Before I walked off, I stooped to grab my water bottle. I tugged my gloves off, slapped the dirt free, and stuck them in my back pocket. As I weaved around the too-crisped and underwatered rose bushes, I glanced up to see someone intercepting me. Slowing, I took a sip.

From the next yard, a woman jogged toward me. I had to be her destination because she waved and smiled right at me. "Excuse me," she called, panting between breaths. She wasn't *that* out of shape, but it seemed rushing over the twenty-some feet separating us was a caliber of cardio she didn't care for.

I lowered my bottle too fast and sun-warmed water dribbled from my mouth. *Nasty.* I really needed to find a decent insulated container. Drinking tepid water in this heat was just as bad as going without. "Hi," I managed as I wiped at my chin. I tossed my useless water bottle back toward the garden bed I'd been weeding.

"Hi." She gushed it out in two syllables, a heave of a breath cutting in the middle. Leaning forward, she rested her hands on her knees. Brown curls curtained her sweaty face as she caught her breath.

"It's a hot one, huh?"

"You got that right," she said, standing now. Her face twisted into a wince but she immediately slid it into a bright smile. "Running's not my thing."

Since she was dressed in a yellow blouse and tight gray pencil skirt and sporting dozens of bangles and high-heeled pumps, I didn't see why she would be running. To me or anywhere. I nodded.

"I'm Doris. Live next door." She jerked a thumb toward her house.

"Kinda figured." I smiled to mask the sarcasm.

She chuckled with a nod. "Yeah. Well, I just wanted to catch you for a sec."

"Okay." For hiring us? Had to be. Alton Landscape gained the majority of its business through word of mouth and neighbors seeing us on the clock. Maybe once they saw how much Jon and I worked our butts off in the summer heat, they realized how nice it was to only watch the labor being done from inside. I glanced at the yard behind her only to find nothing was there. Sure, there was grass, but other than the slightly drying expanse of green-slash-brown, there was nothing that needed work. Trees, shrubs, flowers...they were all absent.

"Oh. Alton doesn't offer a mowing service. Landscaping only." I never could figure out why. Cutting grass was a job that would never go out of demand.

She shrugged. "No. No. I just wanted to see how much Wanda's paying for y'all to do her yard."

I tilted my head, maintaining my smile the best I could. Forget my grasp on my patience. I knew it only had a couple of threads left. "All...right..." What business was it of hers what Wanda paid for us to work in her yard? Not that Wanda likely paid for any of it—it seemed *she* had been paid to be there as the housewife.

"So what's she paying you?" Doris asked.

"What we charge."

Her too-bright smile waned a bit. That could have been her residual reaction to rushing toward me, or maybe she didn't appreciate my attitude. Either way, I saw no reason to share business details if she wasn't interested in our services. If she wanted to know how much it would cost for us to do anything, why not ask what we charge?

"Would you like a referral to a mowing company?" I tried instead. I had no reason to be standoffish with her, but I saw no point in this conversation either. She wouldn't be a client for a landscaper if she had no landscape.

"No. No." She set one hand to her pudgy waist and waved her free hand in an exaggerated arc of dismissal. Chuckling, she shook her head. "No. I can get my hubby to mow the lawn. All the exercise he gets, anyhow."

I nodded.

"I was just curious what she's paying. She'd been going on and on about having the *Payton Pages* come do an article on her"—she pulled a face and raised her fingers to air quote —"*award-winning* gardens. And you and I both know she doesn't do a lick of the work."

Now, I joined in her light laughter. That was true. It didn't surprise me for one second that Wanda would try to claim "fame" or recognition for a landscape she didn't personally create. "Ah," I said knowingly.

"Mmm-*hmm*." Doris crossed her arms. "You know what I mean?"

That Wanda lacked morals to fake her way into a small-town newspaper article? Sure. I didn't know why it was any of Doris's concern, though. Checking another glance at her desolate grass yard, I knew it wasn't out of competition. The *Payton Pages* was a tiny periodical that breathed fuel into gossip lines. Perhaps it made rumors seem more polite and legit being on printed paper than by whispers across fences. Regardless, Doris couldn't be nosy about this for the sake of *her* yard being bypassed for recognition.

"Ever since she moved in…" She groaned. "Always has to be the best at every little thing on this block."

And to think I'd left the big-city anonymity of Columbus

for this Podunk town. I held back the regret. I'd had my reasons. And I'd be sticking to them—catty neighbors or not.

"Madis?"

I scrunched my face at Jon's call. Doris had intrigued me for the half-minute long enough to forget about him. "Sorry. If you want to know the prices, maybe ask Craig Alton?" I suggested as I backpedaled from Doris. I'd left a career in marketing and now that I was free of it, I had no desire to do even the bare minimum of PR.

Continuing on my trek to Jon, I partly turned to her and added, "Or maybe he can contact the paper and tell them she's stealing his fame?"

Doris let out a bark of laughter. "Oh, I'd love to see that!" She waved at me, smiling charmingly once more. "Well, see you around, hun."

Facing forward once more, I hustled toward Jon. He stood at the end of the trailer, a hedge trimmer in his hand.

"I tried to do just as you said," he started, tugging his long locks back from his forehead. How he could stand that wavy mess of hot hair in his face… I shook my head. I could get the whole bad-boy rebel look he had to be going for, but come on. Comfort first?

Or maybe that's a sign I'm getting old…

"I pressed that thing three times and then started it," he explained as I approached.

"Uh-huh." I gestured with my hand for him to let me see the tool.

"I did!"

"Uh-huh." I raised my brows at him as he handed it over.

He groaned at my smirk. "I don't need you getting on my case too. Dad's been nagging me all morning."

I wouldn't admit to getting on his case. More like holding his hand through nearly everything. "What's he nagging you about now?" Jon could be a pain, but sometimes it was like an annoying younger brother irritation. I could remember being a teen and thinking the world was against me. What teenager didn't? There were plenty of times I'd butted heads with my mother. And Craig *was* kind of hard on the guy. Feeling sorry for the kid came naturally.

"I broke some limited-edition NASCAR beer mug that he liked. It was a gift or something, and he's making me buy a replacement."

I squinted at him as I began to let the air from the fuel line. "Beer mug? For…*your* beer?" Last time I checked, Jon was well under twenty-one.

He shrugged, looking anywhere but at me. "Yeah. For a… root beer float."

I laughed. "Come on, man. A root beer float?" I bumped my shoulder into his, still smiling. "At least learn how to lie better."

He playfully shoved me back. "Oh…don't poke fun at me." A blush spread up his cheeks and he frowned. "Hey, want some water?" With a thumb over his shoulder, he indicated a case of waters in a bag. "Even though Dad's a nag, he won't let us pass out from the heat. He just dropped those off."

"Yeah. Thanks. Can you dump one into my water bottle?"

He glanced down at my cargo pockets where I normally tucked the so-called chilling container.

"I left it by the bed I was working on. Back by the patio."

"I'll grab it." He took off toward the house and rounded the corner to the back. In the half-minute he'd been gone, I'd cleared the air from the fuel line. As he jogged back to the trailer, I shifted the trimmer at my waist and gave the starter cord a testing tug. One more pull and it revved up just fine.

"Well, that's the first 'broken' tool for the day."

"Oh… Don't start." He scowled as he dumped the water into my bottle.

"Need anything else?" I asked, holding the shear trimmers

out to the side. There wasn't any point in shutting it off and leaving him to screw up restarting it.

"Nah." He traded my supposedly high-tech water bottle for the trimmer. "Thanks."

"No problem," I drawled.

Before we could resume working, me heading toward the back yard and Jon aiming for the hedges lining the front sidewalk, Wanda stormed from the front door. Earlier, she'd been snippy. Now, she was livid. Her lips slashed an ugly snarl on her face and her hands curled into tight fists at her sides as she marched toward us.

She wasn't my favorite person in the world, but she *was* a customer.

"Hey," I called out to Jon over the roar of the trimmer. He didn't shut it off yet, even though it was obvious the woman wanted a word. I elbowed him. At his frown of confusion, I pointed at the trimmers. Somehow, I had a hunch we couldn't pretend to not hear whatever Wanda had to say.

He silenced the trimmer just as she stomped right up in front of me. With her face close enough that I could smell the alcohol on her breath, she seethed at me. "You stole it!"

I blinked, refusing to flinch at her invasion of my personal space. This couldn't be about something from high school again. "Excuse me?"

"You stole my ring!"

2

It was as hot as it had been when I'd been working in the garden bed that surrounded the patio Wanda had sunbathed on, but I felt an extra brand of heat searing my face now. For close to an hour, Jon and I had been speaking with a member of Payton's police department. An officer spoke to me and Jon, and once Craig showed up, he was questioned as well. Facing the officer and explaining where I'd been during the day wasn't the hard part. The older man speaking with Wanda and her husband was the one who had me fidgeting.

Tommy Walsh.

He was still exactly the same as I remembered him when I left town. Chief of our small town's police force, Tommy was still the lanky, white-haired, wrinkly-faced giant from years ago. He still had that slow smile when he was amused, that steely glint in his stare when he was intrigued. Most of all, that aura of cleverness was just as sharp. It didn't matter if I was a kid getting busted trespassing in the city's public pool or if I was an adult woman as a person of interest in the theft of Wanda's engagement ring—there was no way to get anything past this old coot.

He glanced at me again, breaking his attention from

Wanda on the patio, almost smirking at me. It was enough to break a frown on my face.

Person of interest? No. Wanda had declared me the suspect.

To avoid getting lotion on it, she'd left her engagement ring on the small table next to the lounger she'd been lazing on while I'd worked. Jewelry she deemed *I* wanted as soon as she'd left the patio earlier.

Jon and I both explained what we'd been doing on the job site and where we were during the hours of our work. Craig supported us with what we had to share, but still, Wanda's none-too-quiet tone would rise above the small crowd of us in the back yard, blaming *me*.

Only me. Never mind the fact I'd emptied my pockets and that we'd let the officer look in the work truck.

She blamed *me*.

As the officer spoke with Craig and Jon some more, I rubbed at the back of my neck and chanced another look at Tommy. He was busy writing in a small notepad as Wanda spoke, ticking her fingers off in the air as she complained.

Heck. I didn't have to stand here in the sun. I wasn't going anywhere, not that I felt they'd force us to stay after we'd cooperated and spoke with the cop. Still, I'd be present for whatever they needed from me, like, maybe the tenth repetition of what I'd seen and done that day.

I stepped further toward the shade of a dogwood and hunched lower to fit beneath the canopy. It was a tad cooler here, and I noticed it was a spot of the garden bed I hadn't worked my way to yet. Instead of another lounger sitting on the paver bricks, a small wrought-iron table and chair set waited. I wasn't about to assume I could claim a seat, but I wasn't expecting someone else to be sitting there already.

"Oh," I said, surprised to find Amy on a chair. She must have had the same idea as me, seeking refuge from the sunshine. Leaning forward with elbows on the tabletop, she posed as the ever-bored, sullen youngster. She lifted her face from its resting spot on her hands and nodded at me.

"Hey," she muttered. Then she leaned back even more and gestured at the vacant chair. "Wanna sit?"

I shook my head and stuck my hands in my pockets.

"It's not like you're some slave or something."

I tilted my head at her attitude. "Considering I receive paychecks, I'm well aware I'm the master of my free will."

She twisted her lips, perhaps appreciating a like-minded smart aleck. "I'm just saying you can sit down. I heard her complaining about you earlier. Just because she treats you like dirt doesn't mean you are."

"Yeah?"

I didn't see how she'd eavesdropped. She'd come out of the house for that one moment. I'd been the only person in the back yard with Wanda.

Nodding, she pointed up. "On the balcony." She brushed at her bare shoulder. "I like to catch a little sun too, but up there, I don't have to be near her."

"Ah." I glanced up at the railing that lined the edge of the second floor.

"The further from her, the better," she scoffed.

"Probably hard to do that when you live together."

"No kidding." She reclined from the table and crossed her arms. On a long exhale, she said, "She shouldn't even be here at all."

"Because married couples are supposed to live in different houses?" The heck with it. It was hot. She'd offered the seat. I sat down and sighed at the slight break of being off my feet. I was as spry as any other thirty-something, but boots were *hot*.

"No. Because Dad had no business marrying her. I mean, she's what? Pushing forty?"

I grinned at Amy. Wanda wouldn't care for that miscalculation, as close as it was to the truth. "Well, we graduated the same year, and I'm thirty-six."

Amy snorted. "Yeah. Dad's almost twice that. She's young enough to be my sister, not a replacement for my *mother*."

"Are your parents divorced?"

She shook her head. "Mom passed away just before Christmas. A car accident. And now *she's* here. Pretending to be my mom. Touching all of my mom's things. Rearranging artwork my mom made. Donating my mom's furniture. Selling off mementos my mom collected."

"I'm sorry."

"And now that ring is gone. My *mom's* ring. It's been in the family for years. Something Mom wanted *me* to have someday. I can't believe she lost it!"

"I'm sorry." Although losing a ring wasn't the same as having it taken. A loss or a theft. Funny how they could imply the same thing, and not. "Could she have misplaced it?"

She barked a bitter laugh. "Yeah. She's a ditz." After she glowered at the sky for a hard breath, she said, "I don't know why my dad ever married her. She's totally brainless enough to leave a ring somewhere and spaz out to call the cops."

Brainless. Well, she said it. Not me. Nor was I about to argue her assessment.

Amy leaned toward me as though sharing a secret. Maybe she was. "It came here on the Titanic. Mom always loved the history behind the jewels. My great-great-somebody. Yeah." She smiled a little now, enthused with this memory, perhaps. "There was some relative back then who'd gone on the Titanic and wore that ring on the trip—" She laughed once. "I mean, they survived, obviously, but it was such a cool thing about the ring."

"Family heirlooms usually do have a neat story to them."

The young brunette smiled wider and nodded. "Yeah, they do." Just as easily as she'd brightened up, speaking about the missing ring, she'd soured. Her smooth face crumpled into a scowl. "And now it's gone. Hope Dad will finally see how worthless she is in our so-called family."

"Because her ring was taken?"

"Um, yeah?" Smirking at me, she said, "What kind of an idiot leaves a priceless family heirloom on a table and walks away?"

A sharp gasp to our side cut off our chat. Wanda stood there with her husband and Tommy.

"Amy!" her father scolded. "That's no way to speak to your—"

"My *what*?" Amy snapped as she rushed to stand. "She's not my mother. And she shouldn't have even had that ring!"

Before anyone could argue, Amy barreled past them and entered the house. The sliding door swooshed shut gently, likely a disappointing parting call for the distraught young woman.

"Why were you speaking to her?" Wanda demanded.

I opened and closed my mouth, too long of a stall at her constant rudeness.

"And why hasn't *she* been arrested yet?" she insisted, pulling on Tommy's elbow. "Do something!"

Tommy twitched his lips and nodded. "Perhaps you should take a breather inside, Mrs. Sanger, while I speak with Ms. Harrah." He patted her hand and when she didn't release him, he pried her fingers off. "Please? I'd hate for the heat to bother you."

"He has a point, sweetcakes," Mr. Sanger said, urging Wanda toward the sliding door.

"They're gonna arrest her, right?" Wanda asked as she followed her spouse.

Tommy didn't answer as he took the seat Amy had stormed from.

"Sweetcakes?" I huffed. "Wanda *sweet*?"

Tommy peered at the closed sliding door before facing me. "To each their own…"

I frowned. "I guess…"

Folding his hands together, Tommy settled into his seat. "Madis Harrah. Welcome home."

There was no stopping the groan from my lips. "Home?" Payton was a far cry from the city where I'd lived for so long.

"Sure. You grew up here, didn't you?"

I studied the smart man who took no nonsense. He'd always had such a taunting tone when he spoke to me, but I'd never walked away feeling like he'd belittled me.

"Or did you forget?" He gave me half of a smile now. "Because *I* sure remember. Let's see. Graffiti—"

"I was eight. And it washed off."

He nodded. "Trespassing in the pool—"

"It was hot!"

"*Every* summer."

I crossed my arms. Well, so what? It was cruel to close the pool that early in the season and not even drain it…

He nodded once more. "Then the speeding."

I winced. "Only a couple times."

"And the complaints about loud music—"

"I—" I lowered the finger I'd raised to point at him. He had me there. I shrugged instead.

"You ever make it out there in the big bad world? You coming home as a famous rock star now?"

I kept a deadpanned stare as I said, "Try marketing analyst."

"That's what you've been doing all those years?" He chuckled. "I thought for sure you'd taken up with a band or something."

No. He'd assumed that because I'd gone through a phase of thinking I had musical talent and had been too taken by my high school boyfriend who actually had said talent. I couldn't play if my life depended on it. I loved it, but I never considered making a living from it. "More or less."

"Sounds like misery." His wince had me grinning. "And

now you're back with a green thumb, huh? Working with Alton."

I'd always had a green thumb. Gardening had been my hobby since my grandpa had me doing chores over summer breaks. Mom's yard had been listed in *Payton Pages* three times for my work there. It was only once I'd surrendered to a job I hated that I'd considered working with my passion. Alton Landscape was the only place that could cater to my interests locally. So there I was. "For now."

"And you didn't see the ring this afternoon."

"I tried to minimize my exposure to Wanda altogether. I hadn't looked at her long enough to see if she had a ring—on her or a table."

Tommy nodded and rubbed at his temple. The skin slid as he massaged the spot, proving his flesh was still as lined and leathery as before. His gesture hinted at fatigue, though, which contradicted his usually energetic self—despite his age.

"I didn't take her ring," I stated once again.

He sighed. "Someone did." Looking me straight in the eyes, he raised his brows. "It's a crime—"

"No. You don't say."

"It's a crime that I've gotta deal with this now."

Now? It was his job. But I could pity him for having to deal with Wanda.

"I've got three days until I'm done."

I gaped at him, hating the finality in his words. Done… how? He'd always been something of my nemesis, busting me for misbehaving. But he was…a staple to this town. Payton wouldn't be the same without him keeping order.

"I'm retiring Friday, and *this* is how I'll go out."

I sighed, relaxing into my seat. Old Tommy Walsh was the figure of authority in our little town, but he'd always…well, he'd always looked out for me. It didn't matter that we met up after my less-than-stellar decisions, with him making me explain myself to my mom as the true punishment. Despite my "rap" sheet, I thought I was a good kid. Tommy was never truly the bad guy in my books. Knowing he wasn't really going anywhere reassured me.

"Retiring, huh?"

He smiled, weaving his fingers together and setting his hands behind his head. "Can't wait."

"I bet everyone will be annoyed with whoever they consider for your replacement." No doubt it'd be a transplant from somewhere else. It took a while for outsiders to truly be welcomed as one of our own here.

"Nah, they've already got someone lined up. He's been shadowing me for a couple of weeks." He quirked a brow. "You know, he kind of reminds me of you."

I dropped my jaw. "Huh?" I couldn't imagine that Tommy thought much about me since I'd left town. Reuniting with him now, so to say, felt odd with that comment. "Reminds you of me? What about me?"

"Your…" He let go of his hands and gestured at me. "Your…attitude."

Sarcastic and slow to trust? Oh, I bet this new guy would last long here. I grunted for a reply. "Well, early congrats, then." I scooted forward in my seat and picked my stiff, sweat-dried shirt from my back. "In the meantime, am I free to go?"

"Of course." He stood. "You're staying at your mom's?"

"For the time being," I admitted as I stood as well.

He slanted me a look. "You're not planning to stick around for long?"

I narrowed my eyes. Did he believe Wanda after all? He could be so calm and cool, it was deceiving, but, really, I didn't take her stupid ring! "Are you implying I shouldn't leave town?"

He pouted his lips. "No. Not at all. Just curious."

Sure, because he kept tabs on *every*one in town. I smirked. "Uh-huh."

He shrugged. "Then we'll be in touch. You take it easy in this heat, huh?"

"You too." I stood there for a moment as he walked toward his officer.

I wasn't sure if it was because I was a tried and tested adult now, or something else, but this interaction with Tommy didn't leave me grumbling about his questions. I certainly appreciated him believing me when I said I hadn't taken Wanda's ring.

I didn't want to give Wanda a chance to return and repeat her accusation that I was a thief, so I stepped through the garden the same way I'd entered it. Out in the sunshine, I caught Craig walking away from Tommy's officer.

"Hey, Madis," my boss said brusquely as he met up with me. "What the heck is going on here?"

"For God's sake, I don't know!" It wasn't often that the guy could rile me up. He was my employer and I wasn't stupid. But sometimes that arrogant tone of his voice pushed the wrong buttons. "I was just doing my job."

"Yeah, well, you might not have one if this is what's going to happen on the site."

I pushed my palm at his chest as he made to move past me. He frowned at my gesture but I didn't drop my stern look for a breath. "Is that a threat?"

He stepped to the side, avoiding my block. "No. I don't need to threaten you with anything. If word gets out that my employee is stealing property, no one's gonna want to hire us."

I crossed my arms. "Are you firing me?"

He rubbed at his mouth and looked to the ground. Then he stepped closer and whispered, "Well, *did* you take that ring? I know you two never got along."

High school was years ago... I reined in my frustration. "No," I got out between clenched teeth. "I didn't take her ring."

He retreated and flung his hand to the side. "All right, so until somebody figures out where her jewelry is, you can assume you still have a job."

I huffed at his back. An ultimatum?

Yep. An ultimatum. That was what he left me with as he strode for his truck in the front yard, muttering and shaking his head the whole way there.

"Who the heck does he think he is?" I scoffed to myself, staring after him.

"Lord, he sure lacks some tact."

I whipped around to see who'd spoken.

Doris stood several feet away, still in her office gear. I watched as she fiddled with a bird feeder hanging from a tall free-standing hook. I was aware she'd been nearby since Tommy's officer had questioned her earlier, but I didn't realize she'd lingered. Or that she'd been close enough to eavesdrop on my chat with Craig.

"Is he always that mean?" she asked.

Considering this was the first time a theft happened on the clock, I didn't have much to compare. Craig had a right to be upset. One of his customers was accusing his worker of a crime—it *would* make for a horrible business reputation. But he didn't have to be so willing to threaten *my* job.

Besides, how could he know Jon hadn't taken the ring? He'd come back here to get my water bottle, after all.

No. He can't lie that well. When the officer questioned him, he hadn't stuttered or blushed that I could tell.

Doris didn't let me ponder it for long, asking, "Is he really going to fire you just because Wanda's blaming you?"

I blinked at her, surprised that she'd believe me. We'd spoken for less than a couple of minutes and she was automatically on my side? She barely knew me. Or perhaps, out of spite, she only wanted to go against anything her neighbor claimed.

"I…don't know." Until I had another job opportunity lined up, I didn't want to find out either.

"I sure hope you can find some other work then, hun." Doris smoothed her blouse as she turned away from the bird feeder. "I'd hate for that woman to cause you to lose your job."

"Thanks."

"She's got no idea of what it's like having to work." Doris scowled at the Sanger house. "Gets everything just handed to her like a spoiled princess over there. And she doesn't hesitate to flaunt it."

I watched her step closer to me, crossing an invisible line marking the boundaries of the adjacent yards.

"She showed off that ring every chance she could," Doris confided in me, stabbing a finger into her palm as an emphasis for each word she spoke. "For a good few weeks, all she talked about was the wedding, the honeymoon, and that old rock on her finger." She shuddered with a growl. "I was sick of it!"

Then why, I wondered, did she bother trying to be friends with her or hear her out?

"People like her don't know what us working women have to put up with." She gestured toward Craig as he entered his truck at the curb. "Like putting up with your boss."

I nodded, suddenly exhausted by the whole ordeal.

"You listen to me, hun. If that awful woman causes you to lose your job, I'll hire you. You hear?" She patted my shoulder and I winced at the start of a sunburn on my bare skin. I'd meant to reapply sunscreen but the afternoon had gotten away from me with the ring going missing.

She'd hire me? And who else? Yet as I bade her farewell and went toward the truck Jon and I had come here in, I couldn't shake her words.

Instead of dread hanging heavy on my mind with

Wanda's accusation and Craig's ultimatum, I held on to the possibilities of a different future.

I recalled Tommy's question about me staying in town. Honestly, I'd debated long and hard over my decision of coming back to Payton. I'd been looking forward to a simpler life in a simpler place. Being near Mom again. Enjoying the freedom of the countryside instead of skyscrapers. I didn't want to mooch off my only parent and live with her like a dependent, and to avoid that, I needed money. A job.

But maybe I *could* strike out on my own. Have my own company. I wouldn't have to take Craig's treatment. I wouldn't have to babysit Jon. And certainly, I could choose who I wanted to work for—and avoid the Wanda types in town.

Yet, as I flirted with the idea of a different job, I feared losing this one before I could clear my name.

3

J on drove the work truck and dropped me off at my mom's house.

"See you in the morning."

Would he, though? We had another day's work of work to complete on the Sanger property, but returning to the yard would be…awkward.

"Sure," I said as I headed inside. Until we were given word otherwise, I had to assume we'd be finishing the job.

Mom wasn't there, of course, already at the diner where she waitressed on Main Street. I made quick work of showering and removing the grime of the day so I could walk to the diner and grab a quick dinner with her before the rush. Being alone in the house I'd grown up in was the last thing I wanted this evening. Too many thoughts and questions swirled in this unusual loneliness.

Who'd nabbed Wanda's ring? Why? I wasn't taking Craig's ultimatum to heart, but I truly wanted to figure out what happened to that historic jewel.

Would I even want to continue working with the Altons after this? Craig getting so snappy with me seemed like the last straw, but I wasn't eager to make a big decision about my future.

So, naturally, I sought out my most reliable sounding board.

If not for her graying red hair and well-worn wrinkles around her green eyes, Patty Harrah would look like a woman half her age. She had a spring to her step and an easy smile for everyone, both of which she showed as she made her way around tables in Payton's only diner. At least, she seemed her usual easygoing self until she saw me at the front door.

"Hi, Mom."

"Madis." She pressed her lips together, nearly frowning, and shook her head. "What's going on?" With a tip of her head, she gestured at a booth in the far-back corner—the one we always shared whenever I visited her at work.

"Who told?" That the gossip had reached her here was no wonder. Wanda had called the police at least three hours ago now. Plenty of time for mouths to be yakking.

"Doris," she said with an eye roll as she walked parallel to me on the other side of empty two-seater tables. "She came in for a pie and told Bonnie at the register. That Wanda girl is blaming *you*?" In a whoosh of her light-blue dress and apron, she slid into her half of the booth and snorted.

"Yep," I admitted as I took my seat. I slouched back, resting the back of my head against the chilled hard vinyl of the backrest. Shivers took hold instantly and I winced.

"Oh, Madis. You're toasted. Don't you use sunscreen anymore?" Mom scolded.

Normally I did. I hadn't refreshed it with all the hoopla of the theft. "You know I do."

She harrumphed. "You want your regular?" Before I could even reply, she twisted to call back to the kitchen for my chicken BLT. "I've never liked that Wanda. She's so…" Her lips curled in a twist of disgust and I held my hand up.

"Yeah, I know. She's...a piece of work." I didn't need a reminder of how much I disliked Wanda at the moment. "We've never run in the same circles—"

"Circles *years* ago." Mom rolled her eyes again.

"And yet she still has it out for me."

She frowned. "More like the other way around if she has any say in it."

I deadpanned at her.

"Which is ridiculous." She fussed with straightening the sugars and glanced up at me. "Because you surely don't need the money."

I shrugged. Divorce hadn't left me filthy rich, but I wasn't hurting by any means. My comfortable savings account wasn't public knowledge. "What, you think someone took it for money?"

Mom laughed half of a breath. "A *lot* of money." She pulled her phone from her apron pocket and slid the screen to unlock. "Don't you know about that ring?"

"Mom, I've been back in town for a month. I haven't given Wanda a thought, much less her jewelry."

She tapped on the screen. "Mrs. Sanger—Amy's mother, not Wanda—spoke about it in a big piece written last fall. Some kind of special anniversary of something to do with the Titanic. It's a tiny piece of history, and hardly related to that boat if you ask me, but she let the Historical Society take pictures and such." Spinning her device around on the laminate tabletop, she showed me what she'd been recalling.

I slid the phone nearer and read the headline. A couple of swipes of my finger brought me toward the images. An enormous emerald with diamonds surrounding it. It was a bit gaudy for me, but I couldn't deny its exquisite design. "Wow."

"Wow's right."

"And...*wow*." I exhaled a low whistle at the digits

showing the estimated worth of the ring. Glancing up at Mom, I widened my eyes.

She nodded.

I returned to the dated article, reading on about other pieces of jewelry that were designed in a set with the ring. Wanda's piece was only one of a collection of rare gemstones artistically placed on various accessories. "If someone wanted a small fortune, pawning that ring would bring in a pretty penny."

"I'll bet old Tommy's been asking around the pawnshops," she said.

Could someone have taken the ring for money? It was certainly a motive. But…who?

"Now tell me exactly what happened," Mom said.

Before I could share the details, my plate of food arrived. In between bites, I explained all that I knew of what occurred in the Sangers' back yard. Once I was finished, Mom crossed her arms and relaxed back into her seat, like a judge considering the evidence.

"Jon," she said, nodding as though to emphasize her guess.

He had been back there, but he'd sworn he hadn't even stepped onto the patio when he retrieved my water bottle. "He's a lousy liar, though," I told her about him fessing up to drinking out of his dad's beer mug and breaking it, how he'd stammered and blushed.

"How's that a lie, though?" Mom raised her brows. "Maybe his behavior was more about being embarrassed at telling *you* what he'd done. Maybe he's got a little crush on you."

That couldn't explain how his pockets were empty. He'd been nothing but willing to show he didn't have a ring on him when the pair of cops showed up. I'd stood right next to him as he'd said he hadn't seen any jewelry lying around.

Then again, despite the largeness of the rock, the ring was small enough to slip somewhere…

I shrugged one shoulder, picking up another fry. "I guess it's possible." Still uneasy with the focus of her stare, I asked, "Who else, though?" The yard was fenced off on the other three sides of the back yard. I wasn't there when I'd been "fixing" Jon's trimmer. He'd only gone and come back.

"Maybe Wanda's just making it up."

I dropped the fry and scrunched my forehead. "Huh?"

Mom flapped the hand on top of her crossed arms. "I don't know. It's not impossible. Maybe she's hiding it and just accusing you for the heck of it, to get back at you for old grudges."

Clearly, Wanda had some issues with me, but to take it this far? "You think? To even go so far as to call the cops to frame me?"

"Why not? She's a vindictive, bitter girl with nothing better to do. I wouldn't put it past her to stir up trouble for no good reason."

"So you think she came back out of the house and hid it?"

Mom shrugged.

I'd finished with my dinner, full of food and frustration now. If Wanda was playing games, then so be it. I wasn't about to try to change the way she lived her life—I didn't care. But her accusations were interfering with *my* life.

"I'll catch you later," I said as I gathered my plates into a pile.

Mom stood, glancing at the first trickle of customers coming into the diner. "You're staying in tonight?"

"Don't worry," I drawled. "Tommy's implied I should stay put."

Smiling, she dismissed me with a wave. "Oh… I doubt he thinks you did it."

It was a small vote of confidence, but I'd take it. Of course, she had to be on my side since I was her daughter. Despite my rebellious youth, at least she—and Tommy—had a higher respect for how I'd turned out as an adult.

"Too bad he's got to deal with this mess just before he retires," she said, taking my plates toward the counter. I followed her as she went on. "Nothing much happens in town but now he has to put up with Wanda like this." She shook her head as she set the plates on the stainless-steel ledge for used dishes. "Too bad the new guy couldn't have taken this case for him."

"Oh?" I propped my hip to the counter and watched her turn back to me. "You've met him?"

"Met him? No."

Darn. I wondered what her opinion was of Tommy's replacement for chief. If this man would "remind her" of me as he did for Tommy. Besides, if I was going to stick around in Payton, it'd be nice to know who'd be in charge.

"But I've seen him around."

I didn't miss the twinkle in her eyes. She was positively giddy, holding something back from me. "And…?"

She fanned herself and winked. "He's a cute one."

I rolled my eyes yet chuckled at her. "Oh boy."

"Too young for me, though."

"Oh, sure." I exaggerated a nod, appeasing her humor. "Good night, Mom. Have a good shift."

We hugged quickly and I left as more customers entered the diner. A few tossed a *hello* or *welcome back* as I passed, and I hoped my wave and smile were sufficient. Small talk with everybody and anybody wasn't what I wanted at the moment. In a little locale like Payton, we all knew each other's business. Such was the way of small-town life. Yet I hadn't been back long enough to *want* to get in anyone else's business. Which, unfortunately, had me at a disadvantage for figuring out who could have taken Wanda's ring. I was out of the loop, not up-to-date with the goings-on to be able to speculate who the thief could be. While I wished to have answers, I simply wasn't in the mood to be this peopley and gossip.

So lost in my thoughts and worries about my job in this close-knit community, I wondered how many people might believe Wanda and how many might think I was a scapegoat. I hadn't been *that* unruly of a kid, and I liked to think I didn't have a long list of enemies by any fault of my own. Sure, I had my flaws, but I wasn't a thief. If Wanda's accusation spread and stuck, I doubted many locals would want to hire me for any landscaping near their personal properties.

"Oh!"

I slammed back from walking into someone, reaching out instinctively to steady whoever had been in such a hurry.

Amy stood in front of me, her face sporting a look of a surprise that must have mirrored mine. She held a phone in her outstretched hand as she reclaimed her footing. "Sorry!" She smiled sheepishly, showing me the screen of an addictive game. "Wasn't looking where I was going."

I nodded. "That's all right. Neither was I."

"Hey, I'm sorry Wanda's being so awful about what happened earlier." She glanced past me, as though spotting the diner—the hub of all gossip. "I know people must be talking…"

Shrugging, I stuck my hands in my pockets. "Nothing will ever stop tongues from wagging around here."

Amy smirked. "You got that right. But before today, all anyone talked about was the new chief."

Him again. This mystery man. I slanted my brows and tilted my head at her. "Yeah?"

Her grin was so suggestive I knew that my mom's appraisal of "cute" had to be a tame one.

"But, honestly, I'm sorry Wanda's being so nasty about all of this."

Which meant she figured I was innocent? I appreciated her words, but how much did they really matter? I bet, like Doris, anything that displeased Wanda would be a positive to this unhappy teen.

"What do you think happened to the ring? You were at the house…"

Amy rolled her eyes. "Simple. She lost the ring. Duh."

"Lost, as in it might show up at home? Like it was an accident?"

"No. She started bawling after the cops left, so Dad looked all over the house for it. Someone took it. Lost, as in it's no longer hers."

She sounded so sure. "Well, where do you think the ring is?"

Her arms folded over her chest and she shrugged. "All I know is that it's not on her anymore."

"Do you have any idea who could have taken it?" I rubbed the back of my neck, irked at the slight burn, and fell deeper into the intrigue about this conundrum. It wasn't as though that patio had a lot of traffic to warrant a lot of suspects. "It baffles my mind. I'd been in that garden working all morning, listening to her complain… No one else was there."

"If I had to guess…" Amy rocked back and forth on her feet. "I'd say, Doris?"

"Your neighbor?"

Amy nodded. "Sure."

Sure. Like tossing names around was a pastime.

"She can't stand Wanda. Always envious of what Wanda brags about." She scoffed. "Which was freaking everything. Wanda never hesitates to show off."

Doris envious of Wanda… It made sense. I could see it. As a neighbor, Doris was certainly exposed to Wanda's way of life. I couldn't help but pick at the pudgy woman's questions, asking about what Wanda was paying for landscaping, miffed that Wanda would try to claim recognition for work she hadn't personally done.

"But she wasn't there."

"Not there?" Amy laughed. "She lives, like, a few feet away. Doris is never far. And she's a nosy old lady."

True, they were neighbors. And the plots of land weren't spacious. The houses weren't situated wall-to-wall, though, and there was more than a few feet separating Doris's back door to the patio where Wanda had been lazing. Definitely more than a few yards. Doris had been huffing and puffing just to rush up to me, and after our chat, she'd gone back to her house. I couldn't see how she'd clear that distance in a rush to steal the ring on the patio and disappear into her yard again.

"Then it's a good thing Wanda only wore that one ring out of the set," I said.

"What do you mean?"

"My mom just told me about the jewelry. I didn't realize it was a whole set. The ring sure is beautiful, but at least the necklace and earrings are still safe at home. Right?"

Amy didn't meet my gaze as she nodded, seeming to concentrate on the storefront window of the bakery we stood in front of. "Yeah. Right. I mean, I wouldn't be surprised if Wanda wanted to bring out *all* of those pieces and flaunt them day in and out, but they're protected in the safe."

"So there's a silver lining," I suggested. Amy was clearly possessive of the family heirlooms, but still having some of the jewelry had to be an assurance—even if they weren't passed on to her yet.

"I guess," she said, still facing away before she began to move down the sidewalk, her phone off and seemingly forgotten in her hand. "See you around."

4

When Jon picked me up in the morning, he was more chipper than usual. By the looks of his tall coffee cup in the cupholder, it seemed he'd had plenty of the nectar to warrant a good mood. I'd had a lousy night of sleep, held up with worries about what to do. I'd gotten addicted to working with my hands and being outdoors, and if I wanted to continue, I'd either need to secure my employment for Craig or start my own business. Weighty ideas that countered every chance at restful sleep.

"Ready to go?" he asked as I climbed into the cab of the truck.

I had my own car, but it seemed pointless to drive separately. Today, I kind of wished I'd said I'd get to the Sangers' house myself, perhaps stopping by the café for a large dose of caffeine to go like he had.

"As much as ever I will be," I groused.

"Wake up on the wrong side of the bed?"

I shrugged, yawning as he pulled from the curb. "I guess." I glanced at him smirking at me and noticed the scrapes on his arms. "Why don't you wear gloves if the hedges are cutting you up?"

He lowered one arm to his lap. "I don't want tan lines from gloves."

"For God's sake…" I grumbled.

"Are you going to be a grouch all day? Or are you just still annoyed about Wanda saying you took that ring?"

Annoyed was putting it mildly. He was too young to understand the ramifications of being accused of a crime, in a small town or not. If he did anything wrong, Craig would be held responsible for his actions. Me, I was on my own and potentially out of a job.

"It'll pass. My mom says Wanda just likes attention and probably just forgot where she put the ring."

I straightened in my seat. "You didn't see the ring on the table when you got my water bottle?"

"Uh…no? I didn't really look that way."

Huh. Back to the stammering.

"I was distracted. That lady in the yellow shirt was out in her yard. It was a bright color and it distracted me. I watched her go into her house."

I twisted my lips, wondering just how long Doris might have been outside even remotely near the Sangers' rear patio.

"It'll all die down. Just watch. Dad's mad, but it's not like —" He cleared his throat.

I turned from yawning and watching the scenery pass through the passenger window. He was facing forward, his focus zeroed in on the vehicles parked in front of the Sanger residence.

Craig Alton and Tommy Walsh.

I tipped my lips down. So much for a normal day at work. Seeing Payton's law enforcement so soon again didn't bode well for any morning.

"Uh… It's nothing," Jon said, rubbing at his forehead. "I'm sure it's nothing to worry about."

Oh, sure. "You're not worried? What if we lose our jobs because of this?"

Jon snorted. "I'd say good riddance."

"What about the laptop you're saving up for? And this trip to Lake Tahoe you keep talking about wanting to take after you graduate?"

"Eh." He glanced at me. "I can…make money somewhere else, right?"

He could, I supposed. I was so used to thinking of the two Alton men as a team that it never occurred to me that Jon might seek a different job. A sort of implied mandatory nepotism. Plus, after witnessing how overbearing Craig was toward Jon, maybe it was something the teen had been planning for a while. I loved my mom, but I doubted our personalities would mesh well as coworkers.

Worrying about why Craig and Tommy were speaking in front of the police cruiser wouldn't answer any questions. I stayed as calm as possible and stubbornly shut off new guesses as to what developments might have cropped up over the night.

Jon parked behind his dad's Alton Landscape truck and turned off the engine. We exited, and Craig pushed from the cruiser's bumper and approached us.

"Are we finishing up the job here today?" Jon asked his dad.

"With supervision?" I added, peering around to meet Tommy's gaze. He almost smiled.

"No. He's got better things to do than babysit you two," Craig snarled. "But I'm here to warn you. If I hear the tiniest complaint from Mrs. Sanger about anything—"

"You'll what?" I snapped back, fisting my hands on my hips. His attitude had certainly woken me up and peeved me beyond imagination.

"I'll…" Craig frowned and pointed at me before lowering his finger, as though his retort seemed to wane. "I'll… Well, I won't have thieves ruining my reputation."

"Fine. Then I'm going to start my work, and let it slide that you think you can get all high and mighty on me. However, I won't for a second stand here and let you accuse me of something I didn't do." If he insinuated I'd taken that ring just one more time...

"We got it, Dad. Jeez," Jon said next to me.

Craig glowered at him and then headed toward his truck. "I want this job done *today*." As he left us, he muttered, "Bad enough I'm comping the whole dang project for that woman now anyway..."

"I'll... Um." Jon glanced at Tommy still leaning against the cruiser, watching us. "I'll get back to where I left off yesterday."

"Not so fast." I grabbed the trimmer before he could. As I started the tool, Jon blushed. Once it was running, he took it with a nod of thanks.

Jon brought the trimmer toward the hedges, and I gathered the tools from the trailer that I'd need to finish weeding in the back. May as well tackle pruning the rest of the roses while I was at it. If Tommy wanted to wait out the remaining minutes of his career until retirement watching me prepare for a day's work, so be it. I refused to face him after such blunt and rude words from my boss. The idea of being a...victim irked me. Nor did I want to face him after being so sassy standing up for myself. I didn't want Tommy to assume I was still the headstrong girl I was before, the kid who never failed to talk back. Regardless of how old I was, his opinion mattered, seeing that he was something of a fatherly figure in my life.

"You like working for Alton?" he asked finally, coming toward me as I shoved a pair of hand pruners into my cargo pocket.

"Not especially, but I do like having an income."

He nodded.

"Is Wanda pressing charges?" On the heels of Craig so clearly expressing his displeasure of having me as an employee, I was once again flooded with worry that I could be fired because of Wanda's blame.

"No." Tommy sighed as he came to stand next to me, watching Jon slide the trimmers over the hedges. Back and forth, back and forth. "She's green to have someone punished but I can't arrest someone for something they didn't do. And while I don't know who took her ring, I have proof you didn't."

I raised a brow at him. "Oh?"

He jerked a thumb over his shoulder, pointing to the other side of houses on the quiet street. "Livia Beans. She's the babysitter over at 2453. She was taking a selfie video with the kids and caught you in the background." He tapped a knuckle to the trailer's wall. "You were standing right here the time she said the ring was taken."

I exhaled a long breath at the news. Thank God. "Does Craig know that?"

"Told him just fifteen minutes ago." Tommy smirked and nodded. "You shouldn't put up with someone like him."

That jerk. He'd been informed of my innocence and still blamed me. "Unless I want to start my own gig, he's the only local landscaper."

"Afraid to be his competition?" he teased.

I wasn't, but starting a company seemed like an even bigger endeavor than I'd planned coming back home. "Nah. It's...something I'm considering, though. Especially after yesterday's events." If my options were to work for someone who wouldn't trust me or myself, then I'd pick me.

Jon throttled the trimmer too high and we both winced.

"Seems like we're both at a crossroads. Me leaving my career, you maybe starting your own."

I huffed. He made it sound like I was still a kid, someone just heading into the world of work. I supposed new beginnings could take off no matter how old one was. "What are you doing after you retire? Going to be a sunbird and head to Florida?"

"Nah. I like it here. Gotta make sure this new guy will do right by Payton." He sighed and tipped his chin toward the Sanger house. "But I can't leave without resolving this mess."

As I glanced at the well-maintained home, I spotted a curtain swishing back into place behind one of the front windows. Was Wanda spying, waiting to make up another lie about me?

"Wish I could help."

He crossed his arms and leaned one hip to the trailer. With raised brows, he said, "Maybe you can."

"How so?"

"By hearing me out? Maybe you know something I haven't considered." He straightened with a deep breath before saying, "There are only three people who could have taken that ring."

I nodded. "Amy, Jon, or Doris."

He grinned. "I always knew you were a smart one. What makes you think that?"

"They were the only ones near the patio when Wanda wasn't there." I wasn't sure about Doris's ease of dashing to the Sangers' patio and back to her own house so quickly, but if Jon had seen her outside when he'd gotten my water bottle, maybe she'd lingered longer than I'd assumed after our chat.

Tommy nodded. "What else?"

I chuckled. "What, are you egging me on to do your work for you now?"

"Try telling me you haven't been curious."

Had me there. While the tasks at my former job were mundane, I'd gotten some satisfaction from working behind the scenes for a company that produced a TV series centering a murder mystery. I'd always enjoyed riddling out a good puzzle, but I'd never imagined applying my scheming thoughts to events in my own life.

"Okay." As long as we were just tossing ideas about… "Amy wants that ring, probably thinking it should already be hers. It was her mother's and perhaps it was supposed to go to her, not her father's new wife."

A nod.

"Jon needs money. That ring would fetch a hefty chunk of money." He'd broken his father's mug and was constantly asking to borrow money for lunch. If Craig cut his check for grievances at home, it showed a good cause for needing money.

"And he's been spotted near the pawnshop in Horton," Tommy supplied. "But why Doris?"

I rubbed at my neck and then regretted the move. I'd smeared some of the sunscreen, darn it. "Envy?" I thought back to her chat with me before Wanda declared the ring missing. "She seems very concerned and bothered by Wanda's style of showing off. She could have taken the ring to hold one over her."

Tommy nodded. "I'd wondered at first if she was just making it up to cause you trouble."

I shrugged. "If she had, and the ring showed up at home, then she'd look like a liar." If her popularity mattered that much, it seemed too risky.

"Too bad they don't have any surveillance cameras outside," Tommy admitted.

I was surprised as well. "Maybe that's what those yipping dogs inside are for."

He guffawed with my laughs. "Some security system they'd be." His following sigh tugged at my conscience. I doubted he was severely put off by the end of his career with this little mystery being unsolved, but I could understand his pride. His desire to resolve this case. I wouldn't want to leave anything undone after decades on the job either.

"I…have an idea…" I admitted, still watching Jon as he worked on the hedges. It'd struck me during the late hours of the night when I wasn't able to rest. Maybe the police chief would be open to my suggestion since new clues were scarce. If he was willing to entertain my opinions, why not?

Tommy raised one brow. "Try me."

5

"I don't understand why you want me here, with *her*." Wanda looked down her nose at me as I waited with her and Tommy on the sidewalk.

"Just a moment, Mrs. Sanger. Please," Tommy said.

How he could muster that much patience was beyond me. Maybe it was a trait he'd developed over the years. There was plenty of small-town drama to practice with.

Wanda huffed, flinging her hands to her sides. "I just don't see the purpose—"

"Bait," I snapped out. "It's called a bait."

Wanda smirked at me. "I can't see how it will work. It might not work at all."

"But it might," Tommy argued.

We paced on the sidewalk, out of sight of the Sanger residence. I glanced back toward the property, waiting for Tommy's officer to wave us back.

Wanda was a simple-minded soul, but I couldn't comprehend how my plan was too hard to grasp. After I'd explained it to Tommy, he'd readily agreed. Convincing Wanda had taken a little effort, but we were here, and now all there was to do was wait.

Any minute now…

All three suspects were within close range of the patio once more. Jon was working on the hedges in the back now. Doris was puttering with her bird feeders in her yard. Amy had been watching Netflix in the family room.

Per Tommy's suggestion, Wanda made a big show of opening the safe in the library, making sure she expressed the need to reassure herself the rest of family jewelry was safe and secure. Instead of locking it back up, she said the earrings were too pretty to hide, and so she'd wear them as she lounged under the sun again. Just like yesterday, she left the jewelry on the table—to avoid the shadows interfering with an impeccable tan and protect the metal from her suntan lotion—and vacated the patio. She'd gone into the house, grabbed a cover-up, and told her husband she was heading to a friend's house down the block to take a dip in her pool. Instead, she'd come out to meet us at the corner and wait to see if anyone would nab the earrings.

"But—"

Tommy quieted her, still calmly but with a fraction less of patience. "Someone wanted that ring. Either for money, or envy, or greed. If more of the same set was left out, whoever took the ring wouldn't hesitate to grab the earrings as well."

"And I'll get them back?" she asked, pouting.

"Of course," he assured her. "That's why my officer is hiding around the corner, to catch the culprit red-handed."

"*If* the culprit is there." She eyed me with scorn. "*If* she's not standing here with us."

I licked my lips, fighting to rein in my temper. "Wanda. I never have and never will desire anything of yours."

"Oh!" She lowered her arms and set her hands on her hips, getting into my face as she retorted. "What about the senior on the base—"

"That. Was. Almost. Twenty. Years. Ago!"

Wanda reared back as though I'd slapped her. Maybe the

reminder that we were that old stabbed a little too harshly for her liking.

"Get over it already, will you?" I taunted.

Tommy chuckled for a moment until someone called for him down the sidewalk. "Chief? I caught her in the act."

I turned in unison with Wanda, spotting the officer with Amy trailing behind him.

"Why that little…" Wanda growled as Amy walked toward us, her face lowered as she refused to meet her stepmom's gaze.

"See?" Tommy said. "It was as simple as that." He gestured for Wanda to lead the way back and grinned at me.

In the distance, the guitarist played a few chords. I couldn't help but feel even lighter at his choice of a classic Stones' song. Satisfaction? Oh, I had plenty at the moment. I was clear of any involvement of this supposed crime. Since Amy was the one who'd taken the ring and now the earrings, I bet Tommy could share in the sense of satisfaction that his hands were wiped clean. This was no theft, but a domestic dispute.

"He better get his music in now while he has the chance," Tommy muttered good-naturedly, walking at my side.

I watched Wanda march up to Amy. "You know who that is playing?" Tommy likely knew everyone in our little town. Regardless, I glanced around the area, as though I might spot the neighborly musician.

He nodded. "He's new to town, but he's got a heck of a taste in music." Bumping his elbow to my side, he added, "Kind of like you." He tipped his chin at the logo of a tongue sticking out on my shirt.

I plucked my classic rock band t-shirt from my skin, already too hot under the fabric. Maybe I shouldn't have worn such a dark color again. Already the sun was heating up for another summer day. "I wouldn't say I'm *new* to town. I'm born and raised."

"But nothing is stopping you from starting something new while you're back."

I faced the kind officer next to me and nodded. My own company? It wasn't *that* bad of an idea.

If it meant I could pick and choose my customers, it could promise an absence of pesky people in my life. "You know what? I think I just might."

～

AUBREY ELLE IS AN AUTHOR OF COZY MYSTERIES. WHILE SHE also writes romantic suspense as Amabel Daniels, *Ring Gone 'Round the Roses* is her debut cozy mystery of a brand-new series. By day, Aubrey chases after her daughters and tries to keep up with her own landscaping, and by night, she writes until the midnight hour. Aubrey lives with her family and many pets in Ottawa Hills, Ohio.

Find more about Aubrey Elle
www.authoraubreyelle.com

THE MYSTERY OF THE STOLEN RING

BEATE BOEKER

CARLINA

~ 1 ~

M y mother took my arm as we ambled along the *canale* Burlamacca in Viareggio, Italy. "My dear, this was really an excellent idea of yours. Isn't it lovely to spend the weekend together?"

I suppressed a smile. Actually, my mother had come up with the concept of spending a relaxing summer mother-daughter weekend by the sea together. I didn't correct her, though. At the rare times when my mother complimented me, it was wise to accept it, no matter how undeserved the compliment.

At first, I had hesitated to agree to this trip. After all, I had more than enough to do with my lingerie store, Temptation, in the historic old town of Florence. Besides, I tried to spend every free minute with my husband, who wasn't home much due to his job as a *commissario* at the homicide department of Florence. But then, Stefano had been called into a big case, which meant he would rarely be at home for the next few weeks, so I told my mother she could go ahead and book three days of mother-daughter fun.

This morning, we'd boarded the train at the Santa Maria Novella Station in Florence, and in less than two hours, we'd arrived at the coast in Viareggio. My mother had chosen Viareggio because this was where the *crème de la crème* of Europe had gone on vacation – at a time when going on vacation had first become popular. I didn't spoil her joy by mentioning that the *crème de la crème* of Europe probably traveled to other coasts now, Viareggio being seriously overcrowded in summer.

Instead, I prepared myself for a relaxing weekend with my mother. Well, as relaxing as humanly possible when traveling with a member of my family. At least we'd left the rest of the clan at home. The Mantonis were famous for creating havoc wherever they went – or so my husband says.

So far, it had been unexpectedly lovely. We'd arrived early and had spent the whole morning at the beach, having had the presence of mind to book a parasol and *due lettini* – two sun loungers – in advance. The broad white beach at Viareggio is organized into parceled areas, which in turn are dotted with parasols and sun loungers that usually match in color. Depending on the club that manages the corresponding parcel of beach, the sun loungers/parasols follow different color schemes. One parcel was striped in red and white, the next was light blue, the third all black, and so on. This way, nobody would get lost, and everyone would know exactly where to return after a stroll along the coast.

I know that some people find it overcrowded and horrible, feeling like sardines in a can, but I always enjoy watching the bikini fashions and getting inspirations for new designs at my store.

Happy, sandy, and bronzed, my mother and I had a snack at one of the many small restaurants along the promenade for lunch, then retired to our room at the hotel to shower and take a loooong siesta. When dusk had fallen, we'd hit the streets and browsed through a few stores. Lovely little boutiques made me glad I'd overcome my reluctance for some time off. In fact, I felt stimulated and refreshed by seeing something else for a change.

Now, we were ready for dinner, strolling along the canal, looking for a restaurant that promised culinary delights, a tempting catch of the day, and a lovely homemade pasta.

I'd just opened my mouth to point out a restaurant with colorful red- and white-checkered tablecloths, candles that flickered in the light breeze, and a trailing vine canopy above, when a whooshing sound came from my right.

A black form raced past, grabbed my mother's handbag, pulled it from her grasp, and left at a run.

TONIA

~ 1 ~

I stepped onto the wrought-iron balcony in front of my bedroom and stretched while taking a deep breath. It was already dusk outside, but the air was warm and summery, and a lingering light shimmered on the water of the *canale* Burlamacca right in front of me.

Oopsy followed me and looked up with a hopeful expression in her eyes, her little rear-end wagging with delight. I bent down and patted her glossy black back. "We'll go out in a minute, darling. But we'll take the stairs this time."

I came up again and looked with infinite content along the street where a few tourists promenaded. How lucky I was to live right here, in such a beautiful spot. But even as I congratulated myself, I saw a young man jogging up from behind a pair of tourists. He was clad from top to toe in black. His face was impossible to see because he wore mirrored sunglasses, and the hood of his sweatshirt covered his head. I had just enough time to wonder why anyone would run around with the hood up on such a mellow evening when the man overtook the two women in front of him, grabbed the handbag of the older one, and took off at a run – coming right at me.

For an instant, I stood frozen. This couldn't be happening.

The two women started to run, shouting, "*Ladro!* Thief! Help! Catch the villain!"

They were no match for the thief, who was quickly pulling ahead. There were no other people around, certainly nobody close enough to stop the thief.

A crime right in front of my eyes, and I could do nothing but watch … but then again, no! I *could* do something.

Before I had finished the thought, my body had sprung into action. I bent, grabbed the ready thick coil that was already fixed securely to the railing, and threw it over.

Oopsy gave a delighted little woof. For once, I ignored her, swung myself over the railing, and reached the pavement in less than three seconds. The thief was right in front of me – and suddenly, I realized I had no chance to grab the bag from him or stop him in any other way. He was at least two heads taller than I was, and at least twice as broad. So I did the only thing that came to mind: I stretched out my foot, and he, probably stunned by a woman dropping from the sky, had too much impetus to stop or swerve. He stumbled headlong over it and fell with a full-body impact crash onto the pavement.

Up on the balcony, Oopsy woofed her little heart out.

With my pulse pounding in my throat, I jumped forward and pulled the handbag from the thief's weakened grasp.

By now, the younger of the two tourists had come up. "*Madonna!*" she shouted. "What on earth was that?"

We both threw ourselves forward to hold onto the thief, but he quickly came to his senses, jumped to his feet, and ran on.

Without losing a second, we raced after him, followed by Oopsy's now hysterical woofs.

But neither the tourist nor I was a match for the young man. He sped along the canal at incredible speed, then turned left and disappeared before we could blink.

We stopped, panting, our hands on our knees, while the

older tourist caught up with us, half-running, half-stumbling, waving her arms, still shouting.

CARLINA

~ 2 ~

The savior of the evening righted herself, wiped her brow, and held out *mamma*'s handbag with the other hand. "I'm sorry we didn't catch him," she said.

I stared at her in disbelief. She had short dark hair cut in a pixie style that suited her admirably. Long lashes fringed her huge brown eyes, and with her cheeks now reddened from the chase, she was beautiful. She was also about a head smaller than I was, and about a third of *mamma*'s size.

Mamma now came puffing up. "Holy Maria and Joseph, what was that?" She threw herself at our rescuer and enveloped her in a crushing hug until she all but disappeared in my mother's ample folds. "Thank you, *grazie, mille grazie!* You are an angel, a wonder, a miracle."

The woman laughed and handed my mother her bag. "It was nothing."

"Nothing!" My mother pointed at the rope still hanging from the balcony behind us. "You call it nothing to jump from a balcony three stories high to stop a thief? That is not nothing, young lady! That is incredible!"

I eyed my mother. She was as voluble as ever, but her face

had lost its summer glow and was now pale and wan, her hands shaking.

Spontaneously, I turned to the woman. "Would it be all right if we just sat down for a moment, until the shock abates a bit?"

"Of course!" The woman held out her hand. "I'm Tonia, by the way."

"My name is Carlina." I smiled at her. "And this is my mother, Fabbiola Mantoni-Ashley."

We returned to the small house with the wrought-iron balcony. A little dachshund was up there, barking like crazy.

"Shh, Oopsy, I'll be right up!" Tonia went to the glass door on the ground floor. The windows to the right and left were illuminated with spotlights that highlighted three mannequins in glittering evening gowns. She tried the door, then stopped with an exclamation of dismay. "Oh, drat, of course. I don't have my keys. Let me just get them, and I'll open the door from the inside. It won't take a minute." She grabbed the rope and shimmied up as if she were a monkey.

We stared after her, open-mouthed.

"Do you think this is normal behavior in Viareggio?" my mother asked with awe in her voice.

I swallowed. "I doubt it."

Tonia had, by now, reached her balcony. She pulled the rope up behind her, dropped it onto the balcony, soothed the dachshund, then disappeared inside the house.

A minute later, she was downstairs and came to the glass door, which she unlocked and held wide open. "Don't fall over Oopsy," she said, just in time.

The excited dachshund darted forward and was now busy sniffing our shoes while wagging his backside with enthusiasm. She had a tan nose, tan feet, two tan spots on the chest, and little tufts that looked like tan eyebrows, but was otherwise pitch black. I smiled and bent down so the little dog could sniff my hand. She did, then gave it a quick lick before investigating my mother.

Mamma dropped into a brocaded armchair with a tremendous sigh. "*Incredibile,*" she exclaimed. "Mugged in broad daylight. I would never have believed it!"

I threw a glance out of the door. The last lingering light of the summer evening had gone, and it was now pitch-black outside. "Hardly daylight," I murmured.

Tonia smiled but didn't say anything. She seemed to have instinctively grasped that discussions about details would lead nowhere when talking to my mother.

My respect for her rose.

She handed us two glasses of water. "Here you go," she said. "I'm so sorry about that bad experience. Normally, this is a safe area."

My mother blinked but was obviously not inclined to discuss the matter of safety in Viareggio for the moment, having more pressing things on her mind. "Why do you jump from the balcony like this? Is this how you do things in Viareggio?"

Tonia blushed. "No, no, that's just me. You see, I grew up in a circus, and when I had to leave, I missed it terribly. So I continued with my training. When I got this little lady here," she pointed at Oopsy, who woofed as if confirming her words, "I often had to take her out at night, but leaving the house via the front door is sort of awkward because of the security system. So I came up with the exit via the rope. We just swing down for a quick trip to the closest tree, and then, we swing up again." She made it sound like a walk in the park.

My mother stared at the dachshund. "And you taught this dog to climb the rope as well?"

Tonia laughed. "No. I created a sort of baby pouch that I can affix to my torso."

"I see." I really liked Tonia and her dog. What an unusual woman.

"You'd better check that nothing is missing." She pointed at the handbag.

For once, my mother just nodded and did as she was told.

I blinked. *She must have sustained a more severe shock than I thought.*

"It's all there," she said a moment later. "Thanks to you." Her hands were more stable now.

"And you say you don't get a lot of incidents like this in Viareggio?" I asked.

"Not at all." Tonia shook her head. "This is actually the first time that I've personally come in touch with theft –" She broke off, turned beet red, then corrected herself. "… with a mugging."

My mother pressed her lips together. "Well, I think someone must have cooked the statistics. They always say New York and Napoli are dangerous. They never mention Viareggio. How very negligent. In fact, it is a hotbed of crime, and nobody knows." She looked ahead, a frown gathering on her face. "That's probably due to the Ministry of Tourism. They suppress the data." She nodded, satisfied to have explained the inexplicably misleading statistics on international crime.

Tonia opened her mouth, but I managed to catch her gaze and slowly shook my head. With my family, it is best to avoid discussions that lead nowhere. You must reserve your strength for the battles that really matter. "We should call the police," I said, "and report the crime. To make sure the statistics are fine."

Tonia jumped. "Do you think that will do any good? After all, we can't describe the thief, can we?"

I eyed her, and for one crazy moment, I wondered if somehow, she'd been in league with the thief, and if all of this had been an elaborate hoax. I mean, swinging from a balcony really sounds a little far-fetched. Talk about *deus ex machina*. But with what aim?

Tonia caught my look and immediately got the message. "Oh, no, no!" She threw both hands out. "I had nothing to do with the mugging, I swear. I just happen to know the *commissario* here, and I really don't like him. If you want to report the crime, of course we can go ahead."

I couldn't tell why, but I believed her. At the same time, I wished Stefano were here. He had a lot more experience with judging people than I had, and he kept saying that the best criminals were super charming – which certainly applied to Tonia.

My mother stared at me. "Let me get this straight, Carlina," she said. "Are you seriously insinuating that Tonia here staged the mugging and the rescue? What on earth are you thinking?"

I lifted both hands. "Nothing. I apologize."

Tonia smiled. "Don't worry. It does seem crazy, but life sometimes is, isn't it?"

My mother, no doubt under the impression that she had to counteract the unsatisfactory mistrusting disposition of her daughter, looked around the store and said, "These are wonderful gowns, Tonia."

Tonia turned pink with pleasure. "Oh, do you think so? I designed and sewed them myself."

"Really?" My mother jumped up and went to a full-length evening gown in a magnificent green with a long slit along the leg. "I think this would look very good on you, Carlina."

I joined her. The material, a heavy silk, felt wonderful, and when I moved it, the sheer wide sleeves of the dress sparkled with sequins. Having studied fashion myself, I recognized the talent and craftsmanship right away. "It is stunning," I agreed. "But I really don't know when I would wear such a lovely dress. I don't often have the opportunity to go out to red carpet events."

My mother pressed her elbow into my ribs. "But surely you need something for Annalisa's wedding!"

I blinked. My cousin Annalisa didn't have a boyfriend at the moment, so the question of her marriage had not been under discussion. Even in a family as crazy as ours, there were some limits. So far, we hadn't bought dresses for weddings with non-existent fiancés.

My mother stepped onto my foot, and finally, I got the message. She wanted to thank Tonia for her rescue-act by buying one of her dresses. Good idea. "Oh, yes, Annalisa's wedding. Excellent thought, *mamma*."

I lifted the dress and held it to my body while turning to the mirror. "Do you think this dress would suit me, Tonia?"

Tonia took a step back, cocked her head to the side, and took me in. "Yes, the color goes very nicely with your brown curls and your green eyes. Would you like to try it on?"

"It's a bit late now, isn't it? Should we come back tomorrow, maybe?" I knew all about customers who appeared after opening hours and kept one for ages.

Tonia smiled. "That's no problem. I didn't have any plans for tonight." She pulled forward a heavy curtain made from brocade, creating a spacious dressing room all around the armchair my mother had just vacated.

"Oh, what a clever construction." I stepped inside.

Tonia laughed. "I had no other choice, as this location is way too small for a permanent changing room."

"It's cool." I continued talking while undressing. "I've got a small lingerie store myself in Florence, so I know how difficult it is to make the best of small spaces."

When I appeared from behind the curtain, my mother clapped her hands. "Oh, this is wonderful! We'll take it."

I gave a wry little smile. When my mother said, "We'll take it," it meant she approved, and I would pay. She kept telling me she was just a poor little widow while I was a store owner with money to spend. But in this case, I didn't mind. It did look stunning and made me appear taller, slimmer, elegant, and poised. I wondered what Stefano would say when he saw it … and I wondered if I would ever find an occasion to wear this dress. Maybe I would have to create my own red-carpet event.

At that instant, someone knocked on the glass door of the store. "Police! Open up!"

TONIA

~ 2 ~

I jumped. *Bernardo.* Just when I thought the evening would turn out nice. With a sigh, I went to the door and unlocked it. "*Buona sera,* Bernardo. What can I do for you?"

He came in without returning my greeting.

Powerfully built, with black hair smoothed back, he was an attractive man – or so people told me. I'd never been attracted to him and never would be. He was way too aggressive and pushy for my taste.

"I'm here to learn a bit more about a recent theft." His gaze raked me up and down, disdain in every line of his face.

Fabbiola clapped her hands and ran up to Bernardo like Oopsy when she sees her favorite people.

I looked around to see where my dachshund had gone. Oopsy had not taken to Bernardo – a mutual antipathy, I reckoned – so she kept in the background.

"*Commissario,*" Fabbiola gushed. "How amazing! We were just talking of you, and here you are already. I'd never have thought that the police could be so quick. We didn't even call you! Why, it's a miracle. This town seems to be full of miracles. Full of crime, too, so maybe you need the miracles."

She fell silent and frowned, obviously working out the logic in her mind.

Carlina stepped forward. "My name is Caroline Garini," she said. "And this is my mother, Fabbiola Mantoni-Ashley. We want to report a mugging."

I really liked Carlina. She had a warm, deep voice, and somehow, she radiated good sense combined with friendliness.

Bernardo stared at her. "A mugging?"

Fabbiola clapped her hands. "But yes, that's why you've come, isn't it?"

Bernardo blinked. "I came because of a theft."

"Yes, yes, that's what I'm saying!" Fabbiola beamed at him. "There was a horrible man who tried to steal my handbag, but due to Tonia's super cool reaction, we were able to stop him and –"

Bernardo held up a hand. "Excuse me, *signora*. Did you say that someone stole your handbag?"

Fabbiola eyed him, her good opinion of the Viareggio police obviously draining away. "Yes, that's what I'm saying, *commissario*."

"But isn't this your handbag?" Bernardo pointed at the handbag she'd left on the armchair.

"Yes, it is, but –"

"Well, if it's still here, it can't have been stolen." Bernardo turned to me.

I tried not to show it, but inwardly, I quailed.

"I'm here because of a missing ring." He glared at me.

I swallowed.

"But there was no ring in my handbag. In fact, nothing was taken." Fabbiola beamed at him. "Thanks to Tonia here, who jumped from the balcony just in time to stop the thief. She was amazing, really."

Reluctantly, Bernardo turned back to Fabbiola. "I'm afraid I didn't quite catch your name, *signora*."

"Fabbiola Mantoni-Ashley," Fabbiola stretched out her hand. "From Florence. We're here for the weekend, and an hour or two ago, no wait, maybe it was only forty minutes ago, hard to tell with all the things that are going on, because you see, it's so easy to lose all feeling of time when something extraordinary happens, as you might know." She cocked her head and frowned while sizing him up, but continued speaking without once taking a breath. "But then, you don't look as if you did know; anyway, it was just after sunset, I mean the sun was still setting because there was a bit of lingering light, so obviously it can't have been after sunset, because in that case, it would already have been very dark, wouldn't it, though it's funny how long the light lingers on the sea, amazing really, I've often wondered if it's physics or something else, someone has to write a paper about it, I think, though I doubt I would be able to make heads nor tails of it because these scientists have never learned to express themselves sensibly, and–" She broke off. "Where was I?"

"At the sunset, *mamma*." Carlina moved forward, her silk dress rustling. "About an hour ago, my mother and I walked along the canal, when a young man overtook us, grabbed my mother's handbag, and ran off with it."

Bernardo stared at her. "But … have you reported it?"

"Not yet," Carlina stated with admirable charm. She looked like a queen in my dress, and whenever she moved, the light blinked on the sequins of her wide sleeves. Her eyes were a bit slanted, like those of a cat, and the fabric really did match their color. "We tried to run after him, and –"

"In that dress?" Bernardo blinked.

"No, I only tried this on a minute ago." Carlina kept on smiling, but I could tell it was an effort. "We tried to follow him, but he was too fast for us, and –"

"You're saying you were mugged, and instead of reporting the crime right away, you started to try on evening gowns?"

"Well, we had to use the opportunity, didn't we?" Fabbiola

cut in, obviously thinking that things were not moving as fast as they could. "Besides, it's not as bad as it could be because I got my handbag back, and all due to Tonia who jumped from the balcony with the help of a rope, which she apparently does quite often, only with her cute little dachshund, where is she, oh, yes, over there, anyway, she jumps from the balcony with the dog, though she puts her into a carry-thing, I forgot the name, surely you know, a sort of baby carrier that you can attach to your shoulders and your hip."

Bernardo stared at her as if she had lost her mind.

I couldn't suppress a giggle. That was a mistake. Bernardo gave up on trying to make sense of Fabbiola's tale and turned to me. "I'm looking for a lost ring in a spectacular design, formed like a flower. It's extra-large, easily covers at least three fingers, and it's studded with diamonds. In the middle, there's a huge emerald."

"Oh, that would look nice with Carlina's new dress," Fabbiola cut in.

Bernardo pressed his lips together, then turned his back to her and focused on me. "Have you, by any chance, seen this ring, Tonia?"

I swallowed. "No. No, I don't think so."

"Funny." Bernardo narrowed his eyes. "Because Camilla Tatti swears she still had it when she came to your store this afternoon."

"I … I can't remember," I said. "She tried on plenty of different dresses, and it was quite exhausting. I really can't tell you anything else."

Fabbiola frowned. "Who's Camilla Tatti?"

"She's the wife of the biggest yacht builder here in Viareggio," I said.

Bernardo wasn't distracted. He kept staring at me. "So you know nothing about the ring and didn't see it?"

"I'm afraid not."

"Smooth answer," Bernardo said. "Way too smooth."

Help came from an unexpected corner. "I see nothing smooth about it," Fabbiola said. "Besides, I fail to see how this will help to catch the thief who tried to take my handbag."

"I'm not here to investigate the almost-theft of your handbag," Bernardo snapped. "I'm here to investigate the loss of an extremely valuable piece of jewelry. It just happens to have disappeared in the vicinity of this store, and, if I may say so, this is not the first time!"

"Not the first time of what, young man? You should endeavor to speak clearly and unequivocally, or you'll go nowhere in your career."

Bernardo turned so red, I wondered if steam would come out of his ears in a minute. "Would you please hold your peace, *signora*. I've got to get some answers from Tonia here."

I saw Carlina grin and realized that Bernardo had just made an enemy. You didn't tell Fabbiola Mantoni to hold her peace … not if you cherished your life, you didn't. I let out my breath and leaned against the counter. Maybe I could just relax and let Fabbiola lead the warfare.

"*Commissario!*" Fabbiola went up to Bernardo until she had crowded his personal space in such a way he had to take a step back. "Will you please remember the manners your *mamma* taught you? You don't tell a lady to hold her peace. You listen politely until she has finished, then you commit everything into a report, and only when this is done, you may continue with whatever you were doing before. Have I made myself clear?"

This time, I was careful to suppress the chuckle in my throat. Instead, I turned to Carlina. "Should I help you to undress, Carlina?"

"Yes, please." She turned her back to me, so I could open the zipper, then disappeared again behind the brocade curtain.

Fabbiola, in the meantime, had badgered Bernardo into

taking out a notebook and was dictating the evening's events to him.

Bernardo's face was puce, and great drops of sweat were rolling from his forehead.

I felt almost sorry for him.

"Here we are." Carlina had returned and put the dress onto the counter. "I'd like to buy it, please."

I looked at her. "You really don't have to take it, you know. I'm happy I could help to avoid the theft of the handbag, and you don't need to return the favor at all." *Besides, it might even out some things in the universe for me. Reverse karma, so to say.*

Carlina smiled. "Don't worry. I really would like to have it. Here's my card."

I gave in, rang up the purchase, and packed the dress into a garment bag with the name of my brand, Toniella, printed onto it. "You know, I'm really glad you bought this dress. Not only because of the turnover, but because you look so nice in it. Sometimes I have to sell my dresses to ladies who don't really belong to them. I'm not sure if you can understand. But in your case, it just fits." I looked into her cat-like eyes. The green dress was perfect for her.

Carlina nodded. "I know exactly how you feel. I mean, most of the underwear I sell is not designed by me, but I still feel bad to hand it over to some women who I know don't take good care of their clothes."

"So you do know!" A glow spread throughout me. I'd never discussed this before, and it was so good to see I wasn't the only one with such curious ideas.

Carlina grinned. "I've often been grateful I don't have to sell livestock."

I shuddered. "Gosh, yes, that must be a hundred times worse." I glanced at Oopsy, who was busy chewing up an old shoe of mine. Impossible to think of selling her anywhere.

Fabbiola came up to the counter with Bernardo in tow.

"Tonia, can you add anything to the description of the mugger?"

"Black sneakers, black jeans, hoodie, mirrored sunglasses. That's all I saw, I'm afraid. I only had a very fleeting glance at him."

"He was slim and fit," Carlina added. "I tried to remember the way he ran because Stefano always says the most difficult thing to dissemble is a person's gait, but I'm afraid it looked just like ordinary running to me."

"Stefano is my son-in-law," Fabbiola explained. "He's a *commissario* at the Florentine Homicide Department, a very able man."

I saw Carlina blink. Apparently, that was the first time Fabbiola had paid her husband a compliment – well, maybe it was only in relation to Bernardo, which turned it into a non-compliment after all.

But Bernardo was obviously past caring to being compared – which said a lot about his mental situation – and even more about Fabbiola's destructive powers. "Right. I'll file this, and you'll hear from us in due time." He turned to me. "And now, Tonia, I'd like to hear some more about your afternoon with Camilla Tatti."

I'd had enough time to collect myself, so I told him in detail about all the dresses Camilla had tried on. His eyes glazed over, but a side glance at Fabbiola told him she was still watching like a hawk, so he didn't dare to treat me with anything but respect. I enjoyed myself and drew out the description of the dresses.

Carlina was watching us, a smile hovering on her mouth. I bet she knew exactly what I was doing.

Finally, when I thought he'd had as much as he could take, I came to the end. "And as I said before, I really can't remember her wearing that ring at all. Where was she before she came here? Did she tell you?"

"She came straight from the golf course, where she played at a tournament," Bernardo replied. "And that's also why she was so positive she still had the ring when she left there. She usually takes it off when she plays golf because her glove doesn't fit on top of it. She says she put it on as she left the building."

"Well, she probably had a lapse of memory," Fabbiola said with an impatient shrug. "Has she searched her car?"

"She searched everywhere," Bernardo replied with dignity.

"That's what they always say." Fabbiola nodded with grim satisfaction, as if she'd spent a lifetime discussing possible thefts, "but they're always wrong."

I could tell Bernardo was fed up to the gills with us. "I'd like to search your store," he said with a belligerent thrust of his lower lip to me.

Carlina leaned against my desk and inspected her fingernails in a casual way. "Do you have a search warrant?" Her voice was gentle.

Really, I loved these two. They were better than an army.

Bernardo pressed his lips together. "Not yet."

"In that case, I suggest you get one and return afterwards." She smiled at him.

Bernardo finally realized he would get nowhere with these two sentries at my side. He took a curt leave.

When the door had closed behind him, the three of us looked at each other.

"Well," Fabbiola said. "It seems there's not only more crime in Viareggio than in Florence, but the police are also a lot less competent. I pity you."

I couldn't help it; I had to laugh. "I admit you didn't have a good introduction to my city today, but I assure you, it's really nice. Usually."

Fabbiola crossed her arms before her chest. "Not as nice as Florence."

I grinned and couldn't resist the opportunity to rile her up a little. "But don't forget – we've got the sea."

"They have the sea." Carlina smiled. "And that's such a big plus, we'll be hard pushed to compete."

"Bah." Fabbiola made a swiping move with her hands. "We've got Davide."

"Davide?" I frowned. Hadn't she said that her son-in-law was called Stefano?

"Davide, you know him! The statue by Michelangelo. And the Dome. And the Uffizi Galleries. And –"

Carlina took her mother by the shoulder and gently propelled her to the door. "Undoubtedly, there are a good many points to be said for both cities. But I'm famished now, and I think we should call it a day." She held out her hand to me. "Thank you for everything, Tonia: for the amazing rescue of the handbag, and the lovely dress. It was a pleasure getting to know you. I hope we'll stay in touch." Then she bent down and tickled Oopsy, who rolled over onto her back and stretched all four short legs into the air in delight. "*Arrivederci*, Oopsy."

Fabbiola hugged me again, almost stifling me.

I recommended my favorite pizzeria around the corner, telling them to mention my name so they would get a seat.

Carlina nodded, grabbed her clothes bag with one hand, her mother's elbow with the other, and then, my rescuing angels left.

I closed the door behind them and sank with my back against it. My legs felt weak, and my head was empty.

Oopsy nudged my foot.

I sighed. "Oh, Oopsy, I'm such an idiot. What have I done?"

CARLINA

~ 3~

For once, we didn't linger over our dinner. I had chosen a pizza *bianca*, a white pizza without tomatoes, while my mother had gone for a pizza *quattro formaggi*, four different kinds of cheese. The pizza had a thin crust and was delicious, just as I loved it, but I sensed that my mother was exhausted, and to be honest, I was ready for bed as well. A day out on the beach has that effect, not to mention a near-mugging.

We returned to our hotel. It was a small house not far from the beach, with the typical green shutters of Tuscany, the walls painted in a faded orange. We had been given keys so we could come and go as we wanted, and as we came into the lobby, the faint smell of the roses that stood in a thick bunch on the reception desk welcomed us.

We shared a room, and in no time at all, my mother was in bed, gently snoring. I lay down and tried to fall asleep, but somehow, the events of the day kept me awake. From outside, the light of a lantern fell in a wide ray of yellowish light into the room, illuminating the shapes. I stayed in bed, my eyes wide open. After twenty minutes, I realized I was still too keyed up to drop off, so I got up and opened the window wide.

Viareggio was still awake. The occasional Vespa roared past, a group of laughing girls went by, and cars honked. In between, when all was silent, I could hear the regular swishing of the ocean. The wind must be coming from the sea. I looked over my shoulder. My mother slept like a log.

I turned back to the window and breathed the mild salty air, so different from the air in Florence. I sent a text message to Stefano, hoping he would reply, but there was no answer. He was probably still busy with his project. I missed him and wondered what he would say about today's happenings.

Restless, I prowled around the room, trying not to wake my mother, but unable to sit still or lie down. Finally, I stopped in front of the garment bag that held my new dress. I switched on the small light next to the long mirror, then took out the dress and held it in front of me as I had done at the store. It really was a lovely dress, and it didn't really matter that I had no occasion to wear it. It would come. I smiled and flattened the material against my body when I sensed something hard and knobby underneath my fingers. *What on earth is that?*

I fingered the material and discovered that my elegant dress had wide pockets. *What fun.* But one of the pockets wasn't empty. My fingers dived into the pocket and pulled out … a ring. A huge ring formed like a flower. It glittered like a million Arabian nights, even in the uncertain light of the small hotel room.

My knees gave in. I sank onto the bed, clutching the dress and the ring, too stunned to think.

Could the VIP woman … what was her name again? Yes, Camilla. Could Camilla have lost the ring while trying on my dress earlier that day? In front of my inner eye, I saw Tonia again, explaining all about the dresses Camilla had tried on, talking in unnecessary length, driving the *commissario* nuts. She hadn't mentioned the green dress, not even in passing, though it had been right in front of her eyes.

Tonia must have smuggled the ring into my dress. My mind balked at the idea. *No, no. I can't believe it.* I had sensed an instant connection to her, had felt she might even become a friend. Besides, she'd stopped the theft of the handbag. Could she steal a ring with one hand and foil the theft of a handbag with the other? It didn't make sense. But I couldn't see any other explanation. Was Tonia a thief? I recalled how she'd stumbled over the words when she'd said she'd never seen a theft. She'd quickly changed that to mugging. But would an experienced and hardened thief be so transparent? I couldn't wrap my mind around the whole thing. And why had she hidden the ring in the pocket of my dress?

Well, at least it was easy to guess an answer to this one: the *commissario* had rattled her. She couldn't be sure if he would search the premises, so she'd grabbed the opportunity and smuggled the ring out of the store right in front of his eyes.

I hadn't taken to the *commissario*. He was a boar. But he mentioned that things had disappeared from her store before – and *mamma* and I had jumped right into the fray, defending Tonia. Had we been right in doing that?

I shook my head, thoroughly confused. The facts spoke one language, but my experience and feelings said something else. I forced myself to think this through. What if Tonia had really stolen the ring and smuggled it into the pocket of my dress? How did she plan to retrieve it? She hadn't asked where we would be staying. I swallowed. She didn't need to. After all, she had my name because I'd paid with my credit card, and she knew I had a lingerie store in the old town of Florence. So she could easily find me again … stalk me until she found out where I lived, so she could break into my house and get the ring back. But what a risk. Chances were far too high that I would find the ring in the meantime. And then … did she think I wouldn't react? Did she think she could involve me in her crime, me, the wife of a policeman?

Hot anger rose inside me. She'd have another thought coming.

I threw the dress to the side, slipped on my jeans, stuffed the ring into the pocket, and finished dressing. Then I dug out a receipt – I couldn't find any other paper – and wrote: "Have returned to Tonia's store. Back soon." If my mother should wake and ask me later, I could always say I'd forgotten my credit card.

I activated the GPS-system on my phone and gave Stefano access. In case anything should happen, he would be able to trace me as long as I had my phone with me. He would be surprised because I usually didn't hold with being supervised 24/7, but I was not going to dive into this adventure without some sort of safety net.

Thus prepared, I slipped out of my room and walked back to Tonia's shop. It only took me ten minutes. Amazing how close some places were if you didn't linger anywhere. When I arrived, I stopped a moment, leaning against the trunk of a palm tree, gathering my thoughts and my courage. It was by now almost eleven p.m. At least, Tonia hadn't yet gone to bed: Light fell through the glass door behind the balcony. While I watched, I saw Tonia coming out, the dog carrier fixed around her torso.

She threw the rope over the railing and started to climb down.

I stepped forward.

TONIA

~ 3 ~

J ust as I helped Oopsy out of the carrier, a shadow detached itself from the trunk of the palm tree and came toward me. I almost jumped out of my skin.

Oopsy barked, then yelped and ran forward with a happy woof.

I relaxed. Someone we knew, not another mugger. The events of the day had made me nervous.

However, when I recognized the woman in front of me, I quailed. *Oh, no.*

"Tonia." Carlina's voice was calm. "I think we've got to talk."

I swallowed hard, then cleared my throat. I knew it wouldn't do to feign innocence. She hadn't deserved that. "You … you found it?"

"I found it."

At her quiet confirmation, my heart sank to the tips of my toes and stayed there. *It's all over.* Because I'd been so stupid, stupid, stupid. Because I had no control over me. My arms hung limply at my sides, and I stayed motionless.

"Tonia?" Carlina came closer and put a hand on my arm. "Shall we take a walk along the canal and you'll explain?"

Hot tears came to my eyes. She was way too friendly. Too fair to someone like me. "Okay." My voice sounded scratchy.

"But first – put the rope away?"

I nodded, padded my pocket where I'd put my keys, then made a knot into the end of the rope and threw it up onto the balcony. Without another word, I turned toward the harbor.

Oopsy looked at me in surprise. She knew that we usually just made a brief stop and didn't go exploring , at this time of night. But when she realized that tonight was different, she skipped in happiness and raced ahead as far as the leash would go, her long ears flapping behind her. *My little Oopsy.* My heart contracted. I had a responsibility for her. What would happen to her if I had to go to prison?

We walked on in silence, the sound of our feet on the pavement loud in the stillness of the night. I realized Carlina was waiting. I took a deep breath, but no oxygen seemed to get into my lungs. "I stole that ring." My voice sounded flat. I had to force myself to get out the words. There. I'd said it.

Carlina didn't reply. She just went on walking, looking at me from the side.

I didn't know what she felt. Was she repelled? Shocked? Disgusted? She was such a nice woman. I'd felt an instant connection to her, had hoped we might become friends. All over now, because of my stupid weakness, my inability to control myself. A sob gathered in my throat, but I forced it down. This was not the time to wallow in self-pity. I had to explain. But I felt oh so exhausted. The admission hadn't helped. I didn't feel relieved. I had created too much havoc.

"Tell me," she now said. "What happened?"

"Oh, just the usual." I kicked at a stone, and it flew with a splash into the canal. "I see something glittery, beautiful, and then, it comes over me like a flash. I simply can't resist, and I find no rest until I've taken it."

She didn't say anything.

This time, I knew what she was thinking. I'd shocked her.

How I hated myself for my weakness. "And then," I continued in a low voice, "then I can't find any rest until I've given it back."

Carlina stopped and stared at me. "Until you've given it back?"

I swallowed. "Yes. At least, I try to. But it's not easy, and … Bernardo, I mean the *commissario*, … you see, we went to school together, and he fell in love with me, but I never liked him. Subtle hints were lost on him. In the end, I had to tell him in a rather brutal way that I didn't want to be with him – and he's never forgiven me for that. He also suspects something."

"But he doesn't know for certain?"

I took a shuddering breath. "No. Not yet. But if I continue in this manner, one day … I'll end up in prison."

"How often do you … steal something?"

I hung my head. "Not often. I … I try to fight it as much as I can. And I never plan it. It's only when something is right in front of my eyes that I can't resist. Twice in the last three years."

Carlina didn't say anything.

On and on we walked, with Oopsy always in front of us. Happy little Oopsy, investigating the smells of Viareggio at night. When she ran, her ears flapped, and the lighter underside of her ears showed like little flashes in the dark.

"But this time, you didn't give it back." Carlina's voice sounded neutral. "You foisted it onto me."

"I know, and I feel horrible. When Bernardo showed up, I panicked. I didn't know if he had a search warrant, and I didn't know how much Camilla had noticed. I only wanted to get rid of the horrible thing."

Carlina stopped and turned to me. "How on earth did you manage to steal a ring from her finger?"

"She forgot it next to the bathroom sink."

"Oh, but that's not stealing!" Carlina sounded relieved.

I hugged myself. "I'm afraid it is. I saw it while she was still in the store and didn't return it to her."

"I see." We had reached the harbor by now. The sea murmured against the stone walls of the canal, and the wind had freshened up. It smelled of tang and salt. It also smelled of loneliness. Out at the horizon, the moon had started to rise. Its silvery light trembled on the waves.

Carlina took a deep breath. "Have you tried to get help?"

"My father booked me into a special course when I was a teenager."

"And?"

"Nothing. I went there for three years. Three miserable, expensive years. And it didn't get better. Not one bit."

Oopsy raced ahead and was on the beach now. She started to dig a hole with enthusiasm, the sand flying up in a cloud.

Carlina put a hand onto my arm. "I still have one question, and I hope you won't be offended. Please answer me honestly."

I braced myself. "Go ahead."

"Did you stage the mugging and the rescue earlier tonight?"

I was shocked. "No! Oh, no, I didn't! I swear I had nothing to do with it! In fact, I'd never witnessed anything like that before."

"So you don't know the thief?"

"I don't know the thief from Adam."

"Your reaction was incredibly smooth. I thought a female Tarzan had dropped from the sky."

I swallowed. "That's because I've trained myself to do it with my eyes blindfolded. I thought it would be fun because I don't have much time to train on the trapeze. I … I like to do it to remember my childhood at the circus."

"So it was a coincidence?"

"Yes. I was so grateful when I realized I really did help

you. It … it sort of seemed to even out things, put some weight onto the other side of the scale."

Carlina stopped and turned to me. Her cat-like eyes stared into mine with a strange glimmer. "What do you want to do now?"

I sighed. "I guess I've got to take the ring back and return it to Camilla."

"How?"

"I don't know. If Camilla sees me in connection with the ring, she'll be able to put two and two together."

"Then we'll do it together."

I blinked. "What?"

"We'll do it together."

"We-we'll do it together?" I stuttered.

"Yes." Carlina took my arm and turned me around. "Let's go back. We need a plan of attack."

I hung back. "Carlina, you don't have to do this. I'm in your debt already, and I don't want to embroil you in my messy affairs."

"I don't see that at all," she replied. "I'm in *your* debt because you saved my mother from being mugged. So we'll get rid of that ring, and that will be it."

I took a deep breath – the first since I'd taken the ring from the sink. "Thank you." Then I whistled for Oopsy. "Oopsy! Let's go home!" Oopsy came running, her tongue lolling out of her mouth, her ears fluttering behind her. "We've got work to do."

It didn't take us long to return to my house. I made some tea, figuring that we had enough adrenaline going without the added stimulus of coffee.

"*Grazie*," Carlina said as she took the steaming mug. "It was starting to get a bit cold outside. Now let's see. I think it might be easiest if I ran into Camilla somewhere."

"And drop the ring into her handbag?"

"Yes. She'll find the ring eventually, then she can

apologize to the police, and that will be the end of the story. Do you have any idea how we can contrive a meeting?"

I sat down on the sofa, next to Carlina. "The opening night at the theater would be perfect, but that's only next week." I frowned. "Let's see if the Internet can help us." I pulled my tablet closer and tapped in Camilla Tatti's name.

Carlina looked over my shoulder. "She's been in an awful lot of golf tournaments," she said.

"Yup, I know. Let me see ..." I tapped in the name of Giorgio Tatti. "That's her husband. I believe ... Yes, it's just as I thought. See, he's a director at the Massaciuccoli Golf Club. That's outside of Viareggio."

We both stared at the website that showed a sweeping expanse of green dotted with lakes and bunkers.

"Doesn't it get on your nerves that it's always the men who are the directors?" I shook my head. "See here: she's even got a better handicap than he does. She should be a director too."

"I couldn't agree more." Carlina nodded. "But that's Italy for you. The men are parading at the front, and the women are still kept in the background. Thank God, my husband is different."

I wished I had someone willing to tackle life with me. But that meant I would have to open up to him, confess all my weaknesses, and that was something I'd never been able to do. For some reason, Rick's face rose in my mind's inner eye. With an effort, I pushed it away and concentrated on the screen again. "*Signor* Tatti is a pretty big fish, you know. His company even finances an international golf tournament. It's called the Tatti Open." I bent forward, checking the dates. "But this is amazing! We're lucky, Carlina! Guess when the Tatti Open is taking place?"

She looked at me, her green eyes narrowed. "This weekend?"

"Yep. And on Sunday, the prizes will be handed out by

signor and *signora* Tatti personally! So all you have to do is go there and play a bit of golf. Easy."

"Yes, but –"

"She will probably also join in the tournament, and golfers always leave their bags standing around. You can just drop it into the bag when walking past."

"Yes, but –"

I frowned. "Though no, on second thought, that won't work. If you do that, the clubs might smash the ring. They're quite heavy, and if they end up on top of the ring in the bottom of the golf bag, the ring will break." I scratched my head. "But maybe you can sneak it into one of the club covers. Some are really funny, in the shape of teddy bears or Mickey Mouse. Though I think Camilla only has serious tops."

"Tonia, I –"

"It might be difficult to sneak the ring inside, though. These covers are a bit tight. Let me think –"

"Tonia!"

Oopsy whined.

I stared at Carlina, astonished. She had kept admirably calm all the time during our walk, when she had had more than enough reason to shout at me, so why was she raising her voice now?

"I'm sorry to shout," Carlina said with a twisted smile, "but you didn't hear me, and I've got to tell you something before you plan the whole thing: I don't play golf."

I stared at her. "You … you don't play golf?"

"No. I've never done it. And I don't think it would be wise to start with an international tournament if I've never even had a club in my hands in my whole life."

I swallowed. "I didn't think you'd be part of the international tournament. I just thought you'd be around to play a bit on the driving range."

"I'm sorry, but I don't have the equipment and no idea at

all how this whole golf thing works." She looked at me. "How come you do?"

"Oh, I've been playing golf since I was a kid. My father owns a music & theater hall here in Viareggio, and he started to play golf when he founded the theater, to get to know some people with influence. He took me along, and I liked it. It's a great way to find new customers for my boutique, so I play from time to time."

Carlina blinked. "Your father owns a theater? Is that what you meant about opening night?"

"Yes. And he always throws a party for the opening night of a new show. All the important people of Viareggio come, and that includes Camilla and Giorgio Tatti. They are great theater fans and rarely miss a show. Here, let me show you the theater." I opened the page on my tablet while talking. "It's such a shame opening night is *next* week. I'd –" I broke off and stared at the page.

Carlina looked at me. "What's up?"

I stared at the announcement I'd found: the opening night was scheduled for tomorrow. I blinked and grabbed my phone, scrolling through my messages. "*Madonna*, I've mixed up the dates!" I beamed at her. "But this is perfect! You'll have your chance to wear your new dress tomorrow night."

"Excuse me?"

"Let me just make sure." I grabbed my phone and sent a text message to my father. "I've asked my father to confirm. The Tattis will have told him if they're coming."

Carlina looked at me, incredulous. "Do you think your father will reply in the middle of the night?"

"Oh, yes. During the day would be another matter, but this should be fine." I was right.

Within one minute, my father had confirmed that the Tattis were planning to come to the theater tomorrow night. "Why do you wish to know?" he texted.

I hesitated. I didn't want to lie to my father; he had

suffered enough from my weakness. I decided to answer with half the truth. "She bought one of my dresses yesterday. I hope she'll wear it." Then I looked at Carlina. "Are you in? We'll have a good chance of smuggling the ring back to Camilla during opening night."

Carlina nodded. "Sure. But we'd have to bring my mother, too."

"No problem." I grabbed my phone and texted, "Can I bring two friends?"

The answer came right away. "Sure."

I grinned. "That's settled."

Carlina looked a bit perplexed. "There's still availability for the grand opening?"

"Theoretically, it's been sold out for months. But we've got our own VIP gallery space, and we can always squeeze in some extra chairs on short notice."

Carlina frowned. "But if we return the ring to her during opening night, and if she should find it right afterwards, won't she add two and two together, knowing you were there? Particularly if she doesn't usually use that handbag? I mean, you don't take your everyday handbag to a grand opening."

"That's right." My joy deflated. "It would be too obvious. Yes, of course she would immediately link it with me. *Maledizione.*"

Carlina rubbed her forehead. "Does her dress have pockets, too?"

"Yes. They all do. It's one of my trademarks."

"Well, in that case, we just have to place the ring onto her seat. She'll think it somehow got caught when she tried it on at your store, and then, it might have fallen out during the show. What do you think?"

I took a deep breath. "That should work. I think."

Carlina grimaced. "It's not a perfect plan."

"I know." I bit my lip. "If you … if you'd rather not have

anything to do with it, that's fine. I can return the ring myself."

Carlina looked at me for a long moment. I'm not sure what she saw, but suddenly she smiled. "Nonsense. We're in this together."

CARLINA

~ 4 ~

My mother – rigged out in a splendid black dress Tonia had lent her for the night – clutched my arm as we walked up the red carpet. "How very generous of Tonia to invite us to this special night." She patted her freshly styled henna-red hair. "She seems to be very rich and well-connected."

"Yes." The ring was burning a hole into the pocket of my gown.

"And friendly." My mother beamed as she looked around her.

"Absolutely." Everything *mamma* said was correct. But suddenly, a wave of doubts overwhelmed me. Stefano had called me today and asked why I had given him tracking access on my phone. He knew me too well, so of course he'd heard alarm bells ring. I'd not told him everything. I would do it later because keeping secrets from Stefano made me unhappy. But it was something I wanted to discuss in person rather than on the phone. Nevertheless, I'd left on the tracking.

"Hey there! Smile, gorgeous!"

A light flashed as I looked up.

The reporter winked at me.

This was unreal. The red carpet beneath my feet, the whiff of perfume from the sculptured woman in front of me, the swish of my gorgeous green dress as it swung around my legs … unreal. Why had I agreed to this? What if someone found the ring in my pocket? I'd be arrested straight away. I swallowed. But then, Tonia would speak out. I knew she would. I felt I could trust her. But could I? Had I walked into a trap? A glittering trap, letting all this glamour seduce me? Yesterday, at her apartment, with little Oopsy snoozing at our feet, it had seemed so clear. I was sorry for her weakness, and I wanted to help Tonia to correct the wrong she had done. Today, I realized that Tonia moved in another world, a world of money and power. A world where ruthlessness reigned. Had she used me like a pawn in her game?

We entered the building through a wide hall paved in marble. Well, the Carrara marble works weren't far. Tonia had told me that the first harbor here in Viareggio had been built to transport the blocks of marble to all the world. I looked over the milling throng. There she was.

I sighed in relief.

Tonia wore a short dress in a warm cream tone that looked great with her dark skin and black hair, which shimmered like a glossy cap. It vaguely reminded me of the twenties, straight and deceptively simple, with a long glittering fringe at the knees and sheer lace sleeves. It was the perfect choice for her boyish figure. She turned to the side, showing the back of the dress, which was cut into a deep V. But the detail that knocked the outfit out of the water was her choice of shoes. She'd combined this ultra-elegant dress with a pair of sparkling cream-colored sneakers. The outfit said clear and loud: "I'm elegant, I've got my style, and I don't give a damn about your conventions."

My mother gasped. "What a great dress. But those shoes! Does she want to go running tonight?"

I froze. Maybe that was the reason for Tonia's unusual choice of footwear – so she could escape at top speed. But no, this was her town, her world. Everybody knew where she lived. If she wanted to run, she had to run pretty far … and *not* in that dress.

At that moment, Tonia saw us and came straight toward us with outstretched hands. "I'm so glad you came!" She hugged my mother and me. "I was waiting for you. Let me take you to the gallery." She flagged down a waiter, pressed two glasses of sparkling *Prosecco* into our hands, then led us to the side where a wide staircase swung up to the next floor.

At the top, she opened the door to the gallery loge. My mother clapped her hands. "How beautiful!"

The theater box was wide and surrounded by an ornamental stone balcony. It offered a grand view of the stage below and the sparkling chandelier in the middle of the theater. The loge was filled with wide seats in a dark red cover. They had gilt bowed legs and plush armrests. Tonia presented us to a handful of people already there, laughing, drinking, chatting. In my agitation, I forgot all their names right away, but my mother was immediately drawn into a conversation with a silver-maned gentleman.

Suddenly, I knew I couldn't do this. I grabbed Tonia's lace sleeve. "We've got to talk. Now."

She gave me a worried glance. "Let's go outside."

We went back to the aisle. With care, I closed the door behind us and took a deep breath. "I'm not sure I can go through with this, Tonia. It's way out of my class."

"What is?" Tonia opened her dark eyes wide.

I made a vague motion with my hands. "Everything here. You're part of the rich and famous. I'm not sure I … I can trust you." There. I had admitted it.

She stared at me, then she swallowed. "I see. Yesterday, you trusted me."

"Yesterday, I hadn't realized in what kind of set you move."

Her face crumbled. "It's funny that one's environment can mean so much. When I was five years old, I had to leave the circus and came to Viareggio. Nobody trusted me then. They all said I was a circus child, wild, unpredictable. It seems now I belong to a different class that can't be trusted either." She visibly fought with herself, then she smiled. "But I understand, and I can't expect to embroil you in my troubles." She stretched out her hand. "Would you give me the ring? Thank you for your help so far. It... it was wonderful to talk last night."

I had my hand in my pocket, clutching the ring, but I felt I couldn't move. If I gave her the ring now, I would lose a friend. Irrational, I know, but there it was. I opened my mouth, not even sure what to say when a voice interrupted us.

"Tonia! *Carissima*, you look wonderful."

We both jumped.

A tall woman bore down on us. She wore a dress in sparkling blue, all covered with sequins. I recognized Tonia's brand immediately.

"Camilla." Tonia's smile was forced. "This is my friend –"

Camilla interrupted her, the sentences gushing out of her. She didn't even glance at me. "My dear, you can't believe what I've been through since I was at your store! I lost my wonderful ring, the one formed like a flower. Have the police been to see you? They said they would retrace my steps that day. I don't trust them at all; they even had the audacity to say they had too much to do, but my husband soon made them see sense. What is the world coming to if the police are not looking into our things? Apparently, they got a *commissario* to do the job, even though he's supposed to be doing different things. I just hope he knows what he's doing. I mean, finding a murderer is not the same as finding a thief, is it?"

"Er. No." Tonia flushed. "I'm sorry to hear about your misfortune, Camilla."

The sharp edges of the ring were pressing into my palm. I stretched my lips into a commiserating smile, or so I hoped. The drat woman wasn't even carrying a handbag. Maybe I could trip her up somehow, then throw down the ring next to her?

"The show will soon start," Tonia now said. "Let me accompany you back to your box."

Camilla turned, and together, we walked down the gallery. Camilla's wide skirt swung out as she walked. I could just make out the slits of the pockets in the material.

Tonia was on Camilla's left side, one step behind her, and I was trailing along yet another step behind. Invisible to Camilla, Tonia stretched out her hand behind her back so I could put the ring into her hand.

I stared at her open palm, waiting for the ring, accepting my refusal to help her. With a dry mouth, I clenched my teeth, clutched the ring even harder, and sidled up to Camilla's other side. "I'm very much looking forward to the show tonight." I smiled at Camilla.

She gave me a surprised look. "I'm sorry, I didn't quite catch your name."

"Caroline Garini," I said. "I own a luxury lingerie store called Temptation." I offered her my right hand while my left was still clutching the ring.

Her eyes lit up as she shook my hand. "Oh, that sounds nice. Where is it?"

We resumed walking, the three of us now abreast, with Camilla between us.

"It's in the old town of Florence."

"What a shame it's not in Viareggio."

"I'm here for a short vacation," I continued. "With my –" I

pretended to stumble and fell heavily against Camilla, turning to her as if for help. My right arm clutched hers, while with my left, I slipped the ring into her pocket. "*Santi numi!*" I struggled upright again. "I'm so sorry!"

"Are you hurt?" Camilla looked at me in surprise.

My face flamed, and my hands trembled. "No, no, I'm fine. I'm so sorry. I think something snagged my heel …" I lifted my long skirt and looked at my high heels. "But it's all right now."

A gong sounded. "Oh, we've got to take our seats." Camilla started forward. "My husband hates it when I'm late. I'll see you later, Tonia and – em. I'll look up your store in Florence." She gave me a perfunctory smile and hurried away.

Tonia and I stared at each other.

"Did you just do what I think you did?" Tonia asked in a low voice.

I nodded.

TONIA

~ 4 ~

I sagged against the wall, closed my eyes, and took a deep breath.

A hand grabbed mine, then I heard Carlina's voice close to my ear. "This is not the moment to faint, Tonia."

I pulled myself together and opened my eyes.

She looked back at me, and slowly, a smile started in her eyes and spread over her face.

It drew an answering smile from me. And at that instant, I knew I had found a friend. A friend who knew my weakness and liked me in spite of it. A friend who'd helped me out of the hole I'd dug myself in. I felt giddy with relief.

Carlina's smile grew even wider. "Tonia, I think this is the beginning of a beautiful friendship."

EPILOGUE

CARLINA

"So you're now friends with a kleptomaniac?" Stefano asked while handing me a mug of coffee. He had finally found some time, and we were enjoying a precious lazy hour on the sofa. I'd just told him our Viareggio adventure in every detail.

"*Grazie*." I took the coffee and smiled at him. "Yeah, I guess you could call Tonia a kleptomaniac. Sort of. But she's really sweet. You should get to know her."

"I admit I'm curious." He grinned and sat on the sofa next to me while sipping his own coffee. "And how did the story end?"

"We were lucky. Apparently, Camilla Tatti found the ring the following Monday when she handed the dress over to the cleaner. She thought she'd put it in there while she was trying it on and then completely forgot about it."

Stefano shook his head. "You really ran a great risk when you put that ring into her pocket. You know that, don't you?"

I inhaled the aroma of the coffee. "Yeah, I do. I sometimes even dream of that moment. I could never have chosen a life of crime. Way too exciting for me. Tonia called me yesterday and thanked me once again." I chuckled. "Apparently, she met Bernardo while taking Oopsy for a walk, and he told her the whole story. He was fuming."

"I can understand his irritation. After all, a *commissario* is not usually employed to catch thieves. Talking about thieves, what about the mugger who tried to snatch your mother's handbag?"

"No trace of him, but that was to be expected. We had too little to go on."

My husband grinned. "I admit I enjoy listening to Fabbiola when she insists on describing Viareggio as a hotbed of crime."

I stared at him. "You do? Why?"

He leaned back and put his arm around my shoulders, then drew me closer. "Because in comparison, Florence looks a lot better. As your mother believes I'm single-handedly responsible for the crime rate here, it takes the pressure off me."

"Brilliant." I snuggled up to him. "Let's go to Viareggio next weekend and help Tonia create a little havoc."

He drew back and looked at me. "You're kidding."

I laughed. "Of course I'm kidding. I'm the honorable wife of a *commissario*, remember?"

CARLINA AND HER ZANY FAMILY HAVE BEEN INVOLVED IN QUITE A few murders, and you can read all about them in the cozy mystery series series **Temptation in Florence**. The first book in the series is called **Delayed Death**. Tonia will have her own series one day, and if you sign up for Beate's newsletter via her website, you'll be the first to hear about it.

GET YOUR COPY OF *DELAYED DEATH NOW!*

• • •

BEATE BOEKER IS A USA TODAY BESTSELLING AUTHOR WITH A passion for books that brim over with mischief & humor. She writes cozy mysteries and romantic fiction, many of them set in beautiful Italy. While "Boeker" means "books" in a German dialect, her first name Beate can be translated as "Happy" . . . and with a name that reads "Happy Books," what else could she do but write novels with a happy ending.

Read More from Beate Boeker:
www.happybooks.de

WHEN THE CLOCK CHIMES TWO

ADRIANA LICIO

1

MISS ZERBINO

"Good morning," Miss Zoe Zerbino said, entering Agnese's perfumery.

"Good morning," Agnese answered, closing the drawer she had been trying to sort out. The small lipstick boxes, arranged in numerical order by colour, tended to topple over and get mixed in with other shades. She was going to add her customary "Can I help you?" when she noticed the sturdy, thickset woman was gulping…

Was she sobbing?

"Is there something wrong?" Agnese asked, approaching Zoe. The woman had been coming into her shop frequently in the past few days, asking advice on everyday make-up, a good cream for her face and eyes, a clay mask for her skin.

"There is." As tears filled Zoe's eyes, misting up her thick glasses, she could no longer contain her emotions and loud sobs broke free.

"Oh, you poor love, come over here," and Agnese gently invited her to take a seat in the only armchair in the shop, just in front of a white cupboard containing a library of perfume books. She handed the woman a pack of tissues and patted her gently on the back without saying any more, waiting for Zoe to recover from her outburst.

When the sobs finally diminished into gulps, the gulps into sniffles, Zoe blew her red nose loudly. Agnese wondered if the moment of revelation had arrived.

"Do you feel like telling me what has happened, dear?"

"I'm so sorry, Agnese, I shouldn't have caused you all this trouble. I shouldn't have come here…"

"Nonsense," Agnese interrupted her gently, but with her typical touch of sweet determination. "What's happened?"

"You know my father can be really hard to deal with at times…"

Agnese nodded. Mr Zerbino was well-known to each of the 5,000 inhabitants of Maratea, the beautiful coastal town Agnese called home, perched above the stunning Policastro Gulf of Southern Italy and watched over by the massive statue of Christ the Redeemer from the top of the mountains that plunged down into the sea from a great height all around. He was renowned for being an obnoxious man, stubborn as a mule; he was also believed to be the reason why his daughter Zoe had never married as he had scared away all her suitors. Although to tell the truth, there had never been too many of them to begin with.

"I imagine he's not an easy man to live with," Agnese said tactfully.

"And if it was only him, it wouldn't be so bad," said Zoe, again blowing her bulbous nose. "But there's my brother too. I do love him, and his family; I'm always buying them presents, running errands for them. As my sister-in-law keeps telling me, I don't have a family of my own so I don't know how hectic family life can be. And of course, it's true; I don't have children of my own, so I dote on my niece. But it seems the nicer I am to them, the more awfully they treat me. I invite them for lunch every single Sunday, but they have never returned the invitation. If only they did a little something for me every now and then... I know I'm not as busy as they are, but still..."

"You're not as busy? Nonsense! As a matter of fact, it's you who works full-time, and you attend to your father's needs all by yourself. Your sister-in-law is a housewife, and she's got a husband to help her bring up one 14-year-old girl. I don't think they've got any reason to believe your life is less busy than theirs."

For once, Agnese was grateful to live in a town full of gossips. In Maratea, the chatter was so reliable and precise that she had built up a clear picture of Zoe Zerbino's situation, and she knew for a fact that the woman had a distorted view of her own worth.

"And finally there's my boss. I've been working as his secretary for almost two decades, but he's never been appreciative. He's never suggested I deserve a pay rise, or even given me a simple compliment... I'm such a failure in my professional and private life!"

Zoe's eyes were watery again.

Thanks once more to the Maratea gossips, Agnese knew that by hiring the woman in front of her, Mr Eugenio Scalzacane had actually hired the equivalent of two, maybe even three people for the price of one. Zoe Zerbino was never off sick, and she worked at all times, weekends included if need be. Her skills went well beyond the secretarial duties she was paid for; she dealt with all his administrative, marketing and customer-service needs too.

"I don't know why people are so mean to me. I try to do my best – I understand I'm no good, but I really can't be better than this."

"Can I be brutally honest?" Agnese asked. Zoe sniffed pitifully.

"Are you turning against me too?"

"No, not at all. I'm on your side, but I do feel you might be a part of the problem."

"But they're the ones being nasty, not respecting my feelings. What more can I do for them?"

"I don't think you should do more, rather the opposite. Please come along with me." As she spoke, Agnese led the other woman outside, only to re-enter the shop immediately, stopping for a moment so they could both clean their shoes on the doormat.

"Did you notice what we just did?" Agnese asked.

"No, what?" By now, Zoe was feeling more puzzled than desperate.

"There was a doormat, and we used it."

Zoe looked at Agnese through her large black-framed glasses, still not understanding.

"What I'm trying to say is that it's not necessarily other people being mean. They might be a little selfish and careless, but the main fault, I'm afraid, lies within you. If you act like a doormat, people will assume they can use you as a doormat. It doesn't make them bad, it's just human nature."

The thought seemed to hit Zoe like lightning. "You mean the way people treat me might be my fault?"

Agnese nodded, flashing the woman a sympathetic smile. "More than likely."

Zoe stood in the middle of the shop, a confused ugly duckling confronted by a totally different perspective on her own life and behaviour for the first time in 44 years.

"You know what you need?" Agnese said cheerfully.

"I need to change my character?"

Agnese shook her head. "No, you need a perfume."

As Zoe stood rooted to the spot, unable to move, Agnese fetched her 'Back Soon' sign, closed the shop door, and invited Zoe to a little alcove in the inner part of the perfumery. Zoe sat at the ebony desk that rested in the alcove. Opposite her, Agnese, looking thoughtful, selected eight different scented candles from a nearby drawer. Pulling out her choices, she placed them on the table and invited Zoe to smell them one by one.

"Don't think too much, and when you're ready, tell me which you prefer."

Zoe did as she was asked, inhaling the scent of each candle.

"This one!" she said after having excluded all the others.

She's chosen a beautiful, bright frankincense, Agnese thought. *That's good, it will help to clear her mind.* She put the candles back in the drawer, extracted eight dark bottles, and dipped in each one a thin paper strip – Agnese called them *touches* – again asking Zoe to make her choice.

"This is easy," Zoe said when she had finished smelling the *touches*. "I love this flower."

Agnese nodded in approval "White lilium? I find it enchanting too, and very appropriate for you. Now you have one more choice to make."

She withdrew eight more essence bottles from the drawer, placed them on the table and repeated the process. This time, almost to Agnese's surprise, Zoe selected a dry woody accord. Very refined.

"Well done!" Agnese concluded. "So far, it's been your choices leading you here, but now we need to interrogate Chance and see where it will bring you."

Agnese felt Zoe's eyes on her. The woman was clearly devoured by curiosity as Agnese flicked through a collection of cardboard charts beside her desk.

"These charts, or tables, represent perfume families. Your choices seem to indicate a preference for a light oriental," Agnese explained, picking out the appropriate table and turning it face down so neither woman could read the perfume names on it. She then handed Zoe a wooden spinning-top in vibrant colours and invited her to launch it across the table.

When it stopped spinning, Agnese pinned its position on

the table, turned the card over and cried, "Passage d'Enfer!" Zoe started at the provocative name, but Agnese carried on as if she hadn't noticed. "I don't think you could have chosen anything better," she said as she moved towards a cabinet on the other side of the shop. Taking out a hexagonal bottle, she brought it back, asking Zoe to hold out her wrists. Agnese sprayed them with a couple of squirts, then formed a little cloud of essence high over Zoe's head to envelope her. Zoe's nostrils were twitching, on high alert.

"Such a good smell. I couldn't ever have imagined frankincense being this bright."

"To my mind," said Agnese, "this is Olivia Giacobetti – the French perfumer who created this scent – at her best."

"Then I would like to buy a bottle," Zoe said, flashing the first shy smile she'd managed since entering the shop.

"I'm happy you like the fragrance. Tonight, before you go to sleep, spray a few drops on your pillow and bed linen. I'm sure it will reinforce your determination not to act like a doormat any longer. Learn to say no when need be."

"I promise I'll do that, especially now I know it's my fault that people treat me the way they do." Taking the turquoise bag Agnese handed to her, Zoe thanked and left.

"Let's hope it helps," murmured Agnese to herself, but in her heart of hearts, she wasn't convinced.

2

A DIFFERENT DAY

The next morning, Zoe woke up feeling she'd had the best night's sleep ever. She hadn't worried about the things she had to do; she hadn't cried herself to sleep, thinking how mean people had been to her; she hadn't dreamed of people teasing her.

Her hand reached for the perfume bottle on her bedside table. Passage d'Enfer. Well, she had been through hell, trying to please everyone in her life. Now it was time to change the state of things.

"Zoe!" a harsh voice called from the other side of the corridor. She sighed, put on her slippers and walked over to her father's room. "Zoe, where's my breakfast? It's 7am."

"Good morning," she said, her voice determined. There was a pause.

"Good morning," replied her father, a note of surprise in his voice.

"I forgot to tell you last night," she continued, "that if you want your breakfast, you'll have to come downstairs."

"What the heck is going on?" His thick eyebrows met over his aquiline nose as he frowned.

"Nothing much, apart from the fact slavery was abolished a couple of centuries ago."

"I'm not moving from my bed until I get my breakfast tray," he grumbled. "You should be ashamed, treating an old man like this."

"If your legs are strong enough for you to enjoy playing bowls with your friends, they're strong enough to carry you downstairs for your breakfast."

"I won't do it!"

"Suit yourself. I don't mind – it means I'll get two croissants instead of one."

And with that, she shut her father's bedroom door behind her back.

Once she was downstairs, her old guilt returned. Feeling mean and ungrateful, she poured two glasses of orange juice, laid the table for two and waited with a sinking heart. As the Moka-pot gurgled, announcing that the coffee was ready, Zoe relented and started preparing a tray for her father; she simply couldn't be this cruel to the poor man. She had just put his coffee and croissant on it when she heard the bedroom door open from above, then footsteps sounded on the stairs. The tray disappeared in seconds, and when her father's bulky figure entered the kitchen, Zoe pretended to be absorbed in reading a magazine.

The man, grumbling something about respect for one's elders, cut his own bread and poured his coffee. As they ate their meal, not a word was spoken.

When she'd finished eating, Zoe put her dish, cup and bowl in the dishwasher. Before she knew what was happening, she heard herself saying something quite extraordinary.

"Dad, I'm going to get ready for work. Please clear the table once you're done."

Dad, of course, had never done such a thing in his life.

"That's women's work. If you don't clear the table, you'll find it exactly as it is when you come home for lunch."

Typical of my dad, spoiled and expecting to be waited on hand and foot! thought Zoe, feeling rebellious for the first time in her life.

"That's another thing I forgot to tell you: I'm not coming home for lunch, so you'll have to clear the table now, then prepare yourself something to eat later. I'm going to get the delivery boy from the market to call round, so you'll have plenty of fresh veg. Remember to put all the shopping in the fridge, each item separately."

And with that, she walked out of the kitchen, leaving her father speechless and flabbergasted.

As she'd promised, Zoe made her way to the market before going to the office, and there she encountered Antonella, her sister-in-law.

"Zoe, just the person. Would you call at the butcher's shop on your way home for lunch and pick up the order I left earlier over the phone?"

Zoe was ready to say "Of course" when three things struck her simultaneously. First, the butcher's shop was on the opposite side of town to her route home from the office. Second, she had already decided not to go home for lunch. Third, Antonella, with her perfect make-up, immaculately styled hair and smart clothing, looked as though she was ready for a morning of taking it easy, window-shopping and enjoying her free time.

"Why don't you do it yourself right now?"

"There's bound to be a long queue. At one o'clock there won't be so many people."

"No, I can assure you there'll be a queue at one o'clock

too. And in any case, I'm afraid I don't have the time. It's going to be rather a busy day for me."

"Fine! I just thought that as you'd be passing the butcher's, it would make sense for you…"

Zoe interrupted, flashing her sweetest smile. "As you know, I don't ever pass the butcher's on my way home. Instead, I have to go out of my way, so no, it doesn't make sense."

"Oh, OK, I didn't think. I suppose I'll have to go myself."

"What a splendid idea."

"Thanks in any case, Zoe."

How weird. It was the first time Antonella had ever thanked her, and she had actually said no. Agnese had been dead right – it had been her own fault entirely that everyone had treated her like a doormat and walked all over her. Now she was determined to say no at every opportunity if it meant it'd gain her more respect than years of compliance, goodwill and hard work.

She had at least one more chance to test it out today. Once she'd finished placing her order at the market, she walked towards the office of Mr Eugenio Scalzacane.

Mr Scalzacane was drumming his bony fingers on his desk as Zoe arrived, a sure sign he had something for which to reproach her.

"Good morning, Miss Zerbino," he said, picking up a wad of papers. "May I draw your attention to the fact it's quarter to nine? Wouldn't it be better to get our work started a little earlier in the morning?"

She immediately felt as intimidated as a school kid. After 20 years of working for this man, she was still bottom of the class. But as she brought her wrist close to her face to adjust the enormous glasses on her nose, a whiff of perfume entered her nostrils.

Passage d'Enfer. I need to work my way through hell if I want my freedom. A flash of inspiration crossed her brain. Her neurons were startled, her synapses connected and a whole new chain of chemical reactions occurred.

"Mr Scalzacane, may I remind you that my contract says I start work at nine o'clock and I get paid for an eight-hour working day, five days a week? While in actual fact, I tend to work an average of at least ten extra hours per week, if not more."

He dropped the papers and his lanky figure rose stiffly from the chair as if he had received an electric shock.

"Miss Zerbino!" he shouted, "I won't accept threats of any kind from my staff."

"I'm not threatening you," she explained, her voice shriller than she wished. All noise had stopped in the back office; the other employees must be listening to what was going on in the boss's room. "I'm simply informing you that from now on, I will only work my contracted hours."

"How dare you!" He started to list all the meagre privileges she had received from him; how work duties could not be confined to the small print of a contract; how employees should be grateful to have a job at all, especially in such uncertain times. He was so red in the face that she feared he might go into cardiac arrest at any moment, but she waited patiently for the storm to pass before delivering her final blow.

"From now on, if you need me to work extra hours, you'll have to pay me overtime. That includes Saturdays and Sundays. And while I accept that I may need to be available evenings and weekends on some occasions when there's work that needs finishing urgently, I will say no if you try to make it a general practice again."

"Have you gone completely mad?" But now he wasn't

shouting. It was as if the reality was finally getting through to him that there was something very different about his most reliable employee today.

"Give some thought to what I said, and then get back to me." Zoe walked all the way to the open door, and then stopped to add, "And I forgot, if it doesn't work for you, then let me know as soon as possible. I've just received an interesting offer from Mr Lisciagatto."

MUCH AS ZOE HAD SUSPECTED, SHE FOUND THE OTHER employees eavesdropping behind the door. As soon as she walked into the back office, they burst into silent applause, clapping their hands without making any actual contact, grinning and whispering congratulations to her. They were still too afraid of Mr Scalzacane's temper to give vent to their approval noisily.

But, Zoe thought, *haven't these very people completely ignored me for years?* Now, even the snooty Mrs Limone was inviting her for lunch. The world was much more bizarre than she had ever thought, she told herself as she walked to her desk and started work. Her heart thumping, she wondered when her boss would call her back into his office. Would she manage to keep her cool a second time?

Lunchtime arrived, but her boss still hadn't called for her. Zoe thought better than to go back on her word and return to her father's house, but she didn't fancy joining Mrs Limone and her other four female colleagues for lunch either. Instead, she bought herself a croissant stuffed with Parma ham, rocket salad and stracchino soft cheese, and walked to the Villa Comunale. There, she sat on a bench and took in the beautiful view of the mountains all around, the glittering Mediterranean Sea below, the first few sails of spring in the distance. Maratea, perched on the mountainside, afforded the most spectacular views, and she felt a new euphoria running through her as she gazed at them. At the noble age of 44, she'd discovered the power of no.

She drank some fresh water from a little fountain in the shade of a plane tree and checked her mobile. No calls from her boss. Had she been too harsh on him?

She decided she'd go back to the office five minutes early, just to clarify things and let Mr Scalzacane know she wasn't waging a personal vendetta against him, but he couldn't take her for granted anymore, either. Should she also tell him she hadn't actually received an offer from his business competitor, Mr Lisciagatto? No, maybe she'd stick to that little white lie.

No one else was yet back in the office, but through the window she had seen the boss's desk lamp on. It was always lit if he was in, even during the day. She knocked at his door.

"Can I come in?"

No answer. She knocked again. Nothing. Had he seen her coming and was hiding from her like a sulky child? In her bold, excited mood, that thought made her blood boil.

She opened the door, saying, "Mr Scalzacane, I don't think that's a very adult way to behave at all…" but the rest of her speech stuck in her throat. Mr Scalzacane was fast asleep on his desk, his arms sprawled around his head. The chair was pushed back, as if his body weight had slid it across the floor.

"Mr Scalzacane?" she called again. But there was no reply. Was there something wrong with him? She went closer and noticed a dark purplish stain on the paper under the thick hair of his head.

"Mr Scalzacane, are you OK?"

Of course he wasn't. She took in the unnatural position of his legs underneath the ebony table. Standing next to him, she saw… was it a gun? Was it real or a toy?

Her hand reached for the weapon to check.

"This is just a stupid joke," she said, but her hands were

shaking. The metallic feel of the gun, its weight – it was all far too real.

The door opened and her colleague Mrs Limone walked in.

"Mr Scalzacane, this is the report you asked me…"

The woman stopped in shock, taking in the scene in front of her rapidly: the figure of her boss sprawled across the desk; Zoe holding a gun, then dropping it on the floor. Stepping forward, Mrs Limone saw the rivulet of blood staining the papers under Mr Scalzacane's head.

"What have you done, Zoe Zerbino? What have you done?" And then she ran back into the main office, shouting for help.

3

DINNER WITH THE BRANDO WOMEN

That evening, Agnese closed her shop with a heavy heart. Her husband Nando and two children were away for the weekend, visiting her mother-in-law. Despite every now and then wishing desperately for a little time to herself, not to be so pressured to get things done at home, she had found it quite surreal to be alone at lunchtime. The longed-for silence had been a bit too silent, although she had managed a rare catnap on her sofa while pretending to read a novel.

Luckily this evening, Granny had invited both her and her sister, Giò, for dinner, and Agnese's spirits lifted at the thought of that. Giò had returned from the UK in September after her fiancé had let her down and their wedding had been called off, and while she decided what to do with her life and her career as a travel writer, she had been living in the panoramic attic of the same building that Granny, Agnese and her family also occupied. Granny had the ground floor, while Agnese lived on the first floor.

It was Giò who opened Granny's door to let her sister in, hugging her as if they lived miles apart and hadn't seen each other for months.

"You're in a good mood," Agnese observed.

"An excellent mood. I've just finished writing up my five itineraries for unusual things to do in Prague. It's such an atmospheric, mysterious city."

"That's why I haven't seen you since you came back last week."

"I had to work while my memories were still fresh," Giò apologised. She could turn into quite a hermit when she had a good writing spell.

"You look skinnier than ever, have you eaten at all during the past seven days?" Agnese looked critically at her sister's tall, thin figure, and the dark circles under her green eyes.

"Of course I have. Granny has been feeding me all day long, but I'll never be as curvy as you are," sighed Giò, looking enviously at her sister's womanly figure, generous bosom, round face – all features very much appreciated in that part of Italy.

Agnese gave a laugh, as she usually did when the sisters compared their appearances. She wished she was slightly taller and thinner, admiring Giò's boyish figure. What she didn't envy was when Giò emerged from a spate of writing, both physically and mentally exhausted.

Agnese sniffed the air, her nostrils twitching like a cat's whiskers. "Timballo di patate?"

"Indeed," a shrill voice confirmed from the kitchen. "Wash your hands." Granny still tended to address them as if they were children, even though Giò, the younger sister, was in her late thirties. "Dinner will be served in less than five minutes."

The soft timballo with its crunchy breadcrumb crust was made with mashed potatoes, a couple of fresh eggs, slices of mozzarella and local salami; the aroma of parsley contrasting nicely with a touch of nutmeg was simply irresistible. It was accompanied by a fresh salad that included apple slices and pomegranates, and fresh onions chopped very thinly, dressed in olive oil and lemon, and mixed with minuscule pieces of anchovy, which were delicious spread on the local brown bread lightly toasted. Pears in mint chocolate for dessert completed the menu.

During dinner, Giò and Agnese chatted about anything and everything, while Granny was uncharacteristically quiet.

"The dinner was simply Pantagruelian, but how come my favourite Granny is so silent?" Giò asked.

"I'm amazed. Not so much by you, Giò – when you lock yourself away, you wouldn't notice if the town was attacked by bombs and cannon – but I wonder how it's possible that Agnese hasn't heard of it in her shop."

"Heard what? It was a disappointingly quiet afternoon at the perfumery, I was expecting more clients."

"They were probably all at Mr Scalzacane's office, hoping to catch a glimpse of the killer."

"What killer?" Agnese and Giò asked in unison. And Granny, her white bangs quivering with the excitement of being the first to share the latest gossip with her granddaughters, told them what had happened to Mr Scalzacane that afternoon, and that Zoe Zerbino stood accused of murder. Agnese went pale, her eyes wide open and horror compressing her lungs.

"My goodness, what have I done?"

Shocked, Giò, who had been enjoying Granny's tale as she lazily scraped the last remnants of chocolate from her dish, dropped her spoon and stared at her sister.

"What do you mean, what have you done?"

"It's terrible! I believe I may have instigated the change in Zoe, so I'm a party to the murder."

Granny and Giò looked at each other, baffled. When Agnese finally calmed down a bit, she told them what had happened in the perfumery the previous day.

Granny nodded meditatively. "That explains a few things."

"What things?" asked Giò.

"From what I've seen and heard, it seems that Miss Zerbino hasn't been herself at all today. When I met her in the market early this morning, she was unusually picky. Generally, stallholders manage to palm off all their old withered stuff on her, but this morning, she was so choosy, nothing seemed to be good enough for her. She then demanded that the shopping be taken to her father's home, more assertive than I've ever seen her."

"That doesn't sound that bad…"

"Not at all," Granny agreed. "But apparently there was a pattern of uncharacteristic behaviour from her today, and that's what worries me. You see, her sister-in-law, Antonella, said she'd asked Zoe to do her a favour and Zoe refused quite harshly."

"How do you know?" asked Giò.

"Antonella's sister told the butcher as she had to go in Zoe's place."

"Were you at the butcher's today?" asked Agnese.

"I wasn't, but Mrs Parasole was…"

"And you ambushed her from the window?" Giò asked, exasperated. Granny was known to lurk behind her living-room shutters and prey on the occasional passers-by for news.

"I did not ambush anybody. She happened to go by as I was weeding the geraniums."

"Anything else?"

"Yes, as Mrs Parasole left, I saw Mr Zerbino. I could see from his face that he was in one of his tantrums."

"You didn't dare ambush him too, surely?"

"Of course not, I merely greeted him! He used to be one of my students, and he was quite happy to speak to me." Granny, once a schoolteacher in Maratea, still commanded respect from her former pupils, even though some of them were getting on in age themselves now.

Giò chuckled. "I'm not sure *happy* is the right word for someone you've obliged to endure an interrogation."

Granny waved her words away as if they were an annoying insect. "Piffle! Anyway, he too complained that his meek daughter had turned into an insolent rebel."

"Do you think," Agnese asked, getting more worried by the moment, "her brain was somehow impaired by the perfume I gave her?"

"Personally," mumbled Giò, "I have no doubt."

"It's never happened before, and Passage d'Enfer, despite its name, is such a soothing fragrance."

Giò couldn't help her eyebrows shooting up in dismay each time she heard the perfume's name.

"Well, that's as may be," she said. "It doesn't alter the fact that Zoe has been arrested and is now in a prison cell. I can hardly imagine a more hellish place than that."

Agnese felt her heart sink. She'd been running her perfumery and helping customers find the right scent for them with her fragrance game for 15 years, and nothing of this kind had ever happened before.

"Nonsense, Giò," said Granny emphatically. "You're scaring your sister. And after all, don't you remember Aesop's tale of the *Wolf and the Lamb*?"

"A wolf is always a wolf," said Giò, "and cannot be turned into a lamb. It is a rather brutal tale, but I can't see what it's got to do with us now."

"I'm actually more interested in the lamb than the wolf on this occasion."

Granny, her lips curved in a mischievous grin, her eyes twinkling, enjoyed creating a bit of suspense for her listeners with her sibylline way of speaking. Unfortunately, patience wasn't Giò's best virtue and the two quite often ended up squabbling. This time, though, Giò, happy from her day's writing, fell into the trap.

"What do you mean?"

"A wolf cannot turn into a lamb, but the opposite is just as true: a lamb cannot be turned into a wolf," Gran explained. "I frankly do not believe in the slightest – even more so after what Agnese has just told us about Zoe – that she killed her boss."

"Really, Granny?" Agnese felt relieved for the first time since she'd learned about the murder. She had total faith in the old lady's opinion – Granny had seen so much in her 82 years of life, she hardly ever misjudged people.

Granny nodded. "I think you, Giò, should get in touch with that friend of yours, Paolo the brigadiere, and see what the carabinieri are up to. We know Maresciallo Mangiaboschi likes to take the easy route, but that rarely leads to the truth. Someone needs to do something to make sure no one is wrongly accused while the real murderer gets away scot-free."

For once, Giò was only too happy to obey her gran and called Paolo. She and the young carabiniere had collaborated on a couple of occasions to solve murders in both Maratea and nearby Trecchina, and a good friendship had sprung up between them. On this occasion, Paolo wasn't happy to speak on the phone, but as soon as he heard Granny was worried that something in the story of Mr Scalzacane's murder didn't add up, he agreed to meet Giò at Leonardo's bar early the next morning.

4

HARSH EVIDENCE

When Giò awoke the next morning, the sun was shining on her terrace. From there, she had a perfect view of the Policastro Gulf in the distance, its waters glittering and rippling under the morning light, the huge rocky mountains framing it. It had been a rather harsh winter by Maratea's standards and Giò almost regretted missing the opportunity for her first breakfast of the year on her terrace.

Nonetheless, she made her way to Piazza Buraglia, the town's lively and colourful main square, and spotted the carabiniere in his uniform already sitting at one of the round tables outside. He was chatting with Leonardo, the bar owner. A plump man with a velvety voice, Leo was a talented storyteller, as well as an expert on the real lives and secrets of most of his fellow citizens.

"Hello, Giò," said Paolo, standing up to greet her.

"Morning, Giò," said Leonardo, looking her over from head to toe. "No computer? I take it you're not writing today, so you must be here for some serious sleuthing," and he nodded towards Paolo. Giò, despite having been back in Maratea for six months, was still flabbergasted that people seemed to know her every move and read her every thought.

"Cornetto and cappuccino, I guess?" Leo continued.

Giò nodded, and Paolo asked for the same. Then he smiled at her.

"It won't be a secret meeting, I'm afraid."

"I wonder if the word 'secret' is even in Maratea's dictionary."

"So let me guess. For some tenuous reason, you're involved in Miss Zerbino's case." His frank hazel eyes twinkled at her with a hint of irony.

"To tell you the truth, this time it's not me who's involved, but Agnese."

Paolo gulped in surprise. He had conducted some thorough interviews the day before at Mr Scalzacane's office and with his family, but Agnese's name hadn't been mentioned once.

After the waitress had left two foamy cappuccinos and golden-brown croissants on the table, Giò told Paolo what had happened in the perfumery, and the uncharacteristic behaviour people had observed in Zoe the following day.

"I was hoping you'd come up with something in her favour. She doesn't look evil like other criminals, but maybe she's been bottling up her rage for years."

"But I contacted you for exactly this reason. Is there any way she might not be the guilty party?"

"No. All the evidence is against her," said Paolo, biting into his chocolate cornetto. "She refused to go to lunch with her colleagues so she could get back to the office before the others and do him in. As if that wasn't enough, Mrs Limone found her at the crime scene still holding the gun, and now you're telling me she hadn't been herself all morning."

"Did she confess to the crime?"

"She says she doesn't think she killed him."

"She doesn't *think*?" asked Giò.

"It happens, especially when people kill in a fit of rage,

that the logical part of their brain refuses to accept they've really done it. But there was no one else at the crime scene."

"How do you know?"

"Giò, we always check facts. All facts."

"And what are the facts?"

Paolo explained that the weapon was Mr Scalzacane's own gun. He kept it locked in the office safe and stored the key with his house keys, so it was easily accessible.

"When he left his office to run a couple of quick errands yesterday morning, he didn't take his large black bag with him, only the pouch containing the office keys. So any of the office staff could have got the gun, but there were only two people, Miss Zerbino and Mr Cambiale, who had keys to get into Mr Scalzacane's office while he was out."

"How many people work for him?" asked Giò, not satisfied by the quick summary.

"Besides Miss Zerbino and Mr Cambiale, there are five women who went for lunch and came back soon after the murder. They were together the whole time, so they all have watertight alibis. When they returned to the office, they found it closed and had to wait for Mr Cambiale to open the door for them just before a quarter past two. Mrs Limone went to her desk to pick up some papers, entered her boss's office, and then raised the alarm."

"Anyone else on the staff?"

"There's Mr Luigi Montagna, who is young and brilliant. The five female employees believed he would end up as a partner in the business."

"That's interesting. An ambitious young man – could he have been embezzling money from the company and was discovered by his boss, so he killed him before…"

"He's got an alibi." Paolo cut her short with a cheeky smile. "He was having lunch with a client at the White Horse pub in Marina di Maratea."

"Have you checked his timing?"

"That's what I'm supposed to be doing now, but he knew we would check with both the pub and his client, so frankly I don't expect to uncover too many surprises."

"Anyone else at the office?"

"Mr Riccardo Cambiale is the accountant. He's the old, methodical type. Said he came here to Leonardo's bar for lunch, returned to work just before 2.15 and found the five women waiting for him outside…"

"Any reason for him to want to kill Mr Scalzacane?"

"None, apparently."

"And Leonardo confirmed his alibi?"

"Definitely. He said the man left in a hurry at ten past two; he was a bit later than usual and Mr Scalzacane was a rather pedantic man. Mind you, Mr Cambiale still got back on time, but the boss liked his staff to get in early."

"Who else might have had an interest in killing Mr Scalzacane?"

"His wife, maybe? They've got no children and I expect all her husband's wealth will go to her, but again, she's got a perfect alibi."

"And what's that?"

"Her hairdresser. She arrived for a colour and perm at 1pm and left just after 2.15, and the hairdresser's in Sapri."

"Have you checked her alibi?"

"Yes, she gave me her hairdresser's contact details – she's someone I happen to know, and she confirmed Mrs Scalzacane's statement exactly, almost word for word."

Giò thought about the 30 minutes it takes to reach Sapri from Maratea and mentally crossed Mrs Scalzacane's name from the list of suspects.

"Maybe a client or a disgruntled employee?"

"No, the office door was locked. According to the pathologist, the killer shot the victim from behind. She walked in from the small photocopier room, which has two doors – one into the back office and one into Mr Scalzacane's – and shot him."

"What time?"

"Between ten to two and twenty past."

"So you really think it was Miss Zerbino?"

"I do, but I'll check everything there is to check, Giò, you can be reassured on that."

"Is Maresciallo Mangiaboschi pressuring you to hand him a murderer as soon as possible?"

"Sorry to disappoint you, but he's away on holiday in Sicily. I'm in charge."

"At last! A piece of good news." Giò and Mangiaboschi hadn't hit it off six months ago, when a woman had been crushed to death in her car by a falling rock and Giò had been among the suspects, and it had been anything but smooth sailing when he was around ever since. "Is that why you're telling me about your investigations so openly rather than advising me to keep out of it?"

"No, that's not the reason. Since we've already arrested the killer, the investigation is in its final phases, so I feel safe as there's not much room for you to stick your nose in this time."

Paolo paid the bill – they tended to take it in turns, depending on who was quicker to get their money out. Splitting a bill is not an acceptable practice in the Southern part of Italy.

"Where have you parked your car?" asked Giò.

"In Piazza Europa."

"I'll walk back with you, I need to stretch my legs."

They took one of the tiny cobbled alleys leading off Maratea's main piazza and walked downwards, catching tantalising glimpses of the sea every now and then between the houses and the balconies.

"Not been kayaking yet?" asked Paolo, concerned by Giò's silence.

"No, Romolo hasn't opened yet, but he said he might do so before Easter, especially if the weather improves."

They had reached Paolo's car, Giò lapsing into silence again. As if guessing her thoughts, Paolo tried to reassure her.

"Please tell Agnese she's got nothing to do with what happened. Zoe Zerbino has been stressed out for years, and her accumulated rage and frustration finally exploded out of her. There's no way a perfume could turn anybody into a killer. It would have happened, with or without Agnese's advice."

Giò shook her head, unconvinced, and whispered, more to herself than to Paolo, "A lamb is always a lamb."

CHIMING BELLS AND CHARMING WILLS

T aking a different alley to the one she had just walked with Paolo, Giò slowly returned to the upper part of the town. She'd intended to visit the public gardens of the Villa Comunale, but she thought she might as well make a strategic stop on her way there.

She entered the newsagent's shop, and Nennella, the owner, welcomed her in. Nennella had thick curly hair and a round face typical of Maratea, with equally round eyes, and she was a whirlwind of energy and dynamism. But mostly, she was renowned for being the most informed person in town. Some even referred to her as the walking newspaper, a title that complemented her job nicely.

Giò bent down to caress Annina, Nennella's Jack Russell, who had inadvertently saved her life during the first case she'd solved as Maratea's amateur sleuth. She did feel gratitude towards the little dog, but stroking her also gave Giò an excuse to take the time to consider how to bring up the subject of the murder without sounding too involved in it.

In the end, it was Nennella who broke the ice with her usual directness.

"So, are you investigating this case too? Will you be sleuthing?"

"What case?" Giò pretended ignorance, but Nennella didn't buy it.

"Come on, Giò, I'm talking about poor Miss Zerbino. Mr Scalzacane was really mean to her; she's worked like a slave for him for years, going over and above what should be asked of an employee, and he never once thanked her. If he had only behaved differently – the poor woman must have suffered so much."

"Do you think she's innocent?"

"Well, in a way, yes. She's been pushed beyond the limits of human endurance."

"But still you think she committed the murder."

"Of course. How could she not have done? She had the opportunity, she had a motive, and she was found with the weapon in her hand. That's what I'd call irrefutable evidence."

"And you think frustration is enough of a motive?"

"No, of course not. I believe frustration was the fuse, but the will was the reason for the crime."

"The will? What will?"

"Don't you know?"

"Nope."

"I see," said Nennella with sparkling eyes. Nothing was as good as knowing more than her companion, especially if the companion was supposed to be the town's official… or rather, *unofficial* sleuth.

Giò sighed. Nennella fell back on to her chair behind the counter and broke the news with as much satisfaction as she could muster.

"This morning, Mr Delizia, the local solicitor, came in to get all his newspapers. I asked him if he knew about poor Mr Scalzacane…"

"Wasn't Zoe the poor one a few minutes ago?" Giò

couldn't help interrupting, her sense of justice pricking despite how curious she was to hear the rest.

Nennella waved her hand to dismiss Giò's objections as utterly irrelevant. "The *poor* man has set off for the afterlife, while Zoe is *poor* for altogether different reasons."

"Never mind, carry on," said Giò.

"In short," said Nennella, seeing from the window that three women from the local crochet club were coming over, "Mr Delizia told me plainly, as he had already spoken to the family that morning and the news was no longer private, that Mr Scalzacane had left all he could leave to Miss Zerbino."

"All he could leave?"

"Yes. Maybe the solicitor used a different term, but he explained to me that our law doesn't allow you to cut a close relative out of your will unless you have a very good reason, so you can only freely bequeath part of your fortune. And that part, large or small as it may be, Mr Scalzacane left to Miss Zoe Zerbino."

Giò was bewildered.

"So is it a large sum?"

"It's not a small one, the solicitor said."

"And did Zoe know?"

"That's the very question I asked the solicitor, and he said presumably not. But in truth, who knows?"

"So why did you say Scalzacane was awful to Zoe if you knew he had left her his fortune?"

"Don't you see? For her, a word of appreciation would have been much more important than money…"

"Maybe," said Giò meditatively. "Can you tell me anything about the other five women who work in the office besides Zoe?"

"They're just five gossips. They always have a tall tale on the tips of their tongues – they said Mrs Scalzacane had an affair with Mr Montagna, then they changed their minds and instead it was with Mr Cambiale. A second later, they said that Mr Montagna is a dangerous man with a passion for women and sports cars, neither of which are low maintenance. In any case, as you know, the dog who barks is not the one who's going to bite."

At that moment, the crochet club women, who had stopped outside Nennella's shop to discuss every single magazine cover that was on display, finally came in, laughing loudly and browsing through everything. Giò decided it was about the right time to leave, as much as she would have liked to ask Nennella who exactly the barking and biting dogs were.

I JUST NEED TO CHECK IT OUT FOR MYSELF, OR I'LL NEVER FEEL happy about it, thought Giò as she pushed open the door of the Le Margherite restaurant.

"Good morning," a waiter greeted her, uncertain what to say next as the restaurant wasn't yet serving food.

"Sorry to disturb you…" What was she supposed to tell him? A lie? Lies do help when the truth fails you. "I'm the private investigator helping the local carabinieri with their enquiries into Mr Scalzacane's murder. Brigadiere Rossi tells me you've been a great help so far." While she was speaking, Giò opened her wallet and showed her Friends of Friendless Museums Association card from her days in the UK, hoping the large crown displayed on it would have the effect she hoped for on the uncomplicated man in front of her.

"A British investigator?"

"The two countries are collaborating closely on certain cases."

"I didn't think this was an international affair…"

"There are certain ramifications, but as you can imagine, I'm not allowed to disclose any information at this stage. Everything needs to be kept confidential."

"Sure, sure. Please take a seat."

As Giò sat, accepting the coffee that the waiter offered to her, she asked him to cast his mind back to the previous day.

"Almost every Friday, they come here together for lunch."

"I see. Did you notice anything unusual in the way they were acting?"

"Not really. They were laughing a lot, but they always do. They're a merry party, except when Mr Scalzacane has one of his bad days… Maybe I shouldn't say that."

"Please, be as blunt as you like," Giò encouraged him. "Did any of the five women leave during their meal for, let's say, ten minutes or so?"

"For business lunches, we serve food quickly. I would have noticed if one of them had been absent for that long."

"And they all arrived and left together?"

"Exactly."

"What time did they leave?"

"A couple of minutes past two."

"How can you be so sure?"

"When I was collecting the payment, the church bells chimed. I remember it well as I had to show Mrs Limone the exact amount on the bill; she couldn't hear me."

"That's very helpful," said Giò, shaking his hand positively even though she left feeling a little down. She had actually hoped one of the women might have been involved, but the restaurant was in the other part of Maratea from Mr Scalzacane's office. There was no way any of them could have covered the distance without the others noticing she'd gone.

And then there were the bells chiming, an objective signpost. People could lie about some details, but hearing the bells was something definite.

She continued her walk towards Piazza Buraglia, feeling rather low, but with the weird feeling she had just thought something significant. What was it? The bells… so reliable.

But maybe a person's watch wasn't as reliable. Maybe it was just one of her dumb ideas, but it was worth a try.

With her enthusiasm reanimated, she stopped in front of Leo's bar. It was quiet; only a few tables were occupied, but it seemed the clients were mostly there to pass the time lazily.

"Hello, Giò, still gathering clues?"

She flushed. "Indeed I am. In fact, I wanted to ask you something."

"Fire away," Leo said with an amiable smile.

"You told Paolo, I mean the brigadiere, that Mr Cambiale left here at ten minutes past two, didn't you?"

"That's exactly what happened."

"Lunchtime is such a busy time for you, how did you notice the exact time when you were dancing between the tables?"

"You're right, Giò, at lunchtime, I don't have time to look at my watch. Customers come first."

"So?"

"When Mr Cambiale called me to the table – he was sitting inside that day – he was flustered and agitated because he was late. He showed me his watch – it was ten past two, so I hurried to get him his bill."

"I see," said Giò coolly. "Now, Leo, forget that watch and concentrate on the bells. The church bells. Did they sound before or after Mr Cambiale left?"

"Of course it was before. They chime at two o'clock…" He stopped, his expression aghast. "Oh my goodness!"

"What's the matter?"

"Actually, I was clearing Mr Cambiale's table when I heard the chimes." Leo was stuttering. "I… I… remember stopping with the tray… as if my brain was registering there was something amiss, but I was too busy to make the connection."

"You mean the bells rang *after* Mr Cambiale had left?" Giò repeated to make sure.

"That's correct!"

"How long an interval passed between Mr Cambiale leaving and you cleaning his table?"

"A good ten minutes, I believe." Leo was obviously shaken. "I had customers waiting to pay their bills so they could get back to work. As there were quite a few free tables for new clients, and most of them prefer to sit outside anyway, I finished with the bills and payments before cleaning Mr Cambiale's table."

"So he actually left at least ten minutes before two o'clock?"

"I'd say so, a good ten minutes. Do you think his watch was ahead of time?"

Giò didn't reply. She leapt up and ran from the piazza, leaving a puzzled Leo behind.

6

GRANNY'S HUMBLE OPINION

Giò's phone rang; it was Paolo. He was leaving the White Horse pub and the owner had confirmed what Mr Montagna had told the carabinieri. He had been there with three other people for lunch; they had arrived around 1.15pm and left a good hour later. In fact, it had to have been almost half past two by the time they'd paid the bill and got in to their cars.

"And," Giò ran a few calculations in her mind, "because of the distance between Maratea and the White Horse, it would have been impossible for him to have sneaked out for 20 minutes without the others noticing."

"Correct," Paolo confirmed.

So Luigi Montagna, the man the five women in the office thought was after Mr Scalzacane's position, was in the clear.

"While Mr Montagna has left the suspects list," announced Giò, "Mr Cambiale has just gone back on to it." She told Paolo what she had discovered at Leonardo's.

"How do you do that?"

"What?"

"Prove us wrong," said Paolo, more sheepishly than he had hoped.

"A born scepticism when it comes to men in uniform." Giò chuckled, but what she had to say next was serious. "But why would he lie? Why draw Leo's attention to his watch, other than to provide himself with a good alibi?"

"I'm not convinced it is such a good alibi. I mean, Giò, it only holds if no one suspects him. If we did, even we – the carabinieri – would have double checked with Leonardo and found out the truth."

"I'm not so sure," she said, shrugging her shoulders. "I think it was quite ingenious. But don't tell me you still suspect Zoe Zerbino?"

"Giò, she has motive. Cambiale, as far as we know, doesn't."

"You mean her alleged grudge against her mean boss?"

"There's more to it than that," Paolo said. "The solicitor informed us that…"

"She has inherited Mr Scalzacane's fortune," Giò finished for him.

"How did you know?"

"It's a long story, but it's not his entire fortune. It's only a fraction."

"A big fraction. She's inherited half of it."

"Half? I thought the greater part had to go to his wife."

"No, Italian law says that if you're married with no children and no living parents, you have to reserve at least half of your legacy for your wife, but you're free to dispose of your other half as you wish. Now, except for modest bequests to a couple of nephews, all the other half goes to Miss Zerbino, and I can assure you it's a small fortune."

"And did Mrs Scalzacane know?"

"Yes, she did."

"Wasn't she mad at him?"

"No, she mentioned her husband was free to dispose of his legacy as he wished, and she was aware that during her working life, Miss Zerbino had received much less payment than she deserved."

"How about Zoe Zerbino, did she know about the will?"

"Mrs Scalzacane says she did, that her husband had informed her. They had agreed that she should know, never suspecting this information could turn into a death sentence."

"But when you told Zoe about the will, how did she react?"

"She promptly denied knowing anything about it. She's a good actress, too, pretending to be shocked by the discovery. Luckily enough, she was found beside his dead body, still holding a gun on which there were no fingerprints other than hers."

GIÒ CLOSED THE CALL WITH PAOLO AND KEPT WALKING, TRYING to clear her mind, but her way to the Villa Comunale was long, winding and full of unexpected meetings. At the top of Mandarini street, Giò bumped into Granny just coming out of the Immacolata Church.

"Have you become a practising Catholic all of a sudden?"

Gran shook her head, as if not understanding what her granddaughter was saying.

"The church brings peace and joy in this life of hardships."

"Yes – peace, joy and plenty of gossip," Giò commented.

"At least I don't look like a miserable wraith," remarked Granny caustically.

"Are you going back home?"

"I was, but I believe we'd better take a cup of barley coffee and cappuccino together first."

Granny pointed towards La Merenda, a little bar down a nearby alley. Five minutes later, they had ordered their drinks and were biting into fragrant bocconotti, a Maratea speciality filled with custard and wild cherries.

"So what did you find out?" Granny asked when she saw the tension in Giò relaxing a little bit. Giò told her about the church bells chiming and the will – all the findings the busy morning had brought, and her frustration at being unable to make any sense of them.

"You know, Giò, I think you should go back to the beginning and work from there, according to your best hypotheses."

"Well, we know exactly how things have worked. Zoe Zerbino was found with the gun and is assumed to be the villain. But let's imagine no one had found her holding the gun. Where would our suspicions have gone then?"

"We'd probably still have ruled out the Famous Five," said Gran, referring to the other women who worked for Mr Scalzacane. "They had no opportunity and they had no motive. Gossipy as they are, something would have come out – one of them would have betrayed the others."

"The same goes for Mr Montagna," confirmed Giò. "From what we know, he had no motive, and certainly no opportunity."

"The only other person with a motive is the victim's wife…"

"But she's got a cast-iron alibi. I'm left with only Mr Cambiale, and the case against him is strong. Why would he make sure Leo saw his watch if not to establish an alibi?"

"What if his watch really was fast?" asked Gran.

"OK, let's assume he acted in all innocence. What did he do in the 20 minutes it took him to join the Famous Five outside the office? It only takes five minutes to get there from Leo's bar, but the Famous Five said he turned up at quarter past two and opened the door for them. He's never explained that. Also, Nennella mentioned some rumours that Cambiale and Mrs Scalzacane might have had an affair…" Giò left a meaningful pause. "Maybe this is an important piece of evidence."

"I could believe that Mr Cambiale fell for Mrs Scalzacane, but there's no way that I'm ever going to believe she would have had a crush on him."

"Why not?"

"Have you seen Mr Cambiale? He's not only charmless, but he also belongs under the heading of small-time bully: meek and mellow with the powerful, but hideously menacing towards his subordinates."

"Maybe what you call meek and mellow was just him being a faithful lover to Mrs Scalzacane. If they are together in this, it explains a lot of things," Giò said, her enthusiasm growing as she latched on to a new theory.

"Like what?"

"Don't you see? The motive! If he were to marry Mrs Scalzacane, they'd get to share her significant inheritance. Maybe they just disregarded that Zoe would take a large chunk of it – we have only Mrs Scalzacane's word for it that anyone knew the terms of the will. Maybe the husband didn't even tell his wife."

Gran intervened rather brusquely, despite her soothing premise. "In my humble opinion, I still can't believe a woman like Mrs Scalzacane would look twice at a man like Mr Cambiale, especially when he's so overshadowed by Luigi Montagna."

"Granny, you're confusing my thoughts just as I'm getting to grips with how things might have played out. I need a few minutes of peace to think it over. I feel it in my bones – I'm almost there."

With that, Giò got up and left. Granny sighed.

RESUMING HER WALK ALONG MANDARINI STREET, GIÒ PASSED Mr Scalzacane's elegant home. There were no people around; Mrs Scalzacane had asked to be left alone until her husband's body had been returned. That very afternoon, it had been announced that the funeral would be on Monday as the post-mortem was complete and the judge had signed the papers necessary to return the corpse to his family.

From the Scalzacane residence, it was just a stone's throw to the Villa Comunale. Maratea's public gardens lay just outside the town, and Giò loved to visit for some peace and quiet to do a little thinking. The plane trees already had their first leaves of tender spring green, their stripy cream trunks creating a pleasant contrast to the darker evergreens. Calmed by the serene beauty around her, she sat on one of the stone benches to collect her numerous and scattered thoughts.

Giò had been sitting for fewer than ten minutes when she heard voices coming towards her – a woman's and a man's. The couple were strolling along the path, and the green barrier must have offered her protection as they didn't seem to notice her. She recognised the smart figure of Mrs Scalzacane; she had met the woman once at her sister's shop. With her was a nice-looking man: tall, slender, dark hair and confident manners.

They came so close that Giò could hear their conversation. Mrs Scalzacane was sobbing, trying and failing to remain dignified.

"Oh Luigi, I can't stop thinking how much my husband trusted her. Eugenio thought the will was the right compensation for all she had done. And now I can't bear it – if only he hadn't told her about the will, he'd still be alive."

The man, who Giò decided had to be Luigi Montagna, was trying to soothe Mrs Scalzacane.

"You mustn't dwell on that. The carabinieri have no doubt she would have committed the murder one way or another…"

She stopped him. "I'm certain it was a plan she and Cambiale hatched together. They are both involved in this. I believe they were going to run away and build a new life. If

Mrs Limone hadn't surprised Zerbino just after she had committed the crime, they would have got away with it. Cambiale always hated my husband, and I'm sure he is the mastermind behind it all. Zerbino might have killed Eugenio, but he's as involved as she is…"

"How do you know?"

"That vile man, while my husband was still alive, made a pass at me, and I was too ashamed to tell Eugenio. I was wrong, I can see that now…"

The couple walked past her, leaving Giò appalled. Half hidden, she remained still, sitting on her bench behind the plane tree. She had called it correctly: there were two people behind the murder, but she'd got the wrong couple. Well, one of them at least. As Granny had said, there was no way Mrs Scalzacane would have fallen for her husband's accountant, but poor, lonely Zoe Zerbino must have been easy prey for the loathsome man. He'd convinced her, probably promising her they would enjoy eternal love and who knew what else, and the woman had fallen into the trap. Now, the least Giò could do was to prove Mr Cambiale was involved. Zoe would have to pay for her crime, but so would he.

Then Granny's words sprang to mind – "A wolf is always a wolf, a lamb is always a lamb" – and with them came sudden inspiration.

7

IN THE DARK OF THE NIGHT

S hocking news had reached the gossips of Maratea. The accountant Mr Cambiale had been arrested early Saturday evening, charged with being Miss Zerbino's accomplice in the murder of Mr Scalzacane.

It was the middle of the night. Paolo and Giò, in the carabiniere's private car, had been following a sports car that was now parked below Mr Cambiale's house. A dark silhouette left the car, furtively entering the accountant's home a few moments later carrying a bag. Paolo and Giò got out of Paolo's car and followed closely behind. The door to the house had been left ajar, the intruder clearly wishing to make as little noise as possible, so they slid into the darkness inside. Not daring to switch on so much as a small torch, they waited while their eyes became accustomed to the feeble light filtering in from the street lamps outside.

Out of the silence, they heard a low crumpling noise and caught the flickering of a torch coming from the same direction along the corridor. Hardly breathing, they crept towards the torchlight, fearing that any moment something as banal as a creaky floorboard or gurgling stomach would give them away.

Looking into the room at the end of the corridor, they could barely make out the mysterious silhouette placing something on a piece of furniture. Maybe a chest of drawers? They were clearly in a bedroom. The figure searched around and closed a wardrobe, bending over something on the floor. Perhaps it was the bag they had seen him or her carrying.

Giò and Paolo were still holding their breath when all of a sudden, to their utmost surprise, a powerful and uncontainable sneeze broke the *tenebrae* and stillness of the night.

"Damn," the figure murmured as he blew his nose into a tissue.

The lights went on and Paolo pointed his gun at the man.

"Good evening, Mr Montagna. Do you want to give me Mr Cambiale's jacket?"

The man hesitated, taken by surprise.

"Come on, Mr Montagna, I'm here to help, after all. You were trying to get rid of it, weren't you?"

The man looked at him in shock.

Giò pointed to the portrait of Zoe Zerbino, which was standing on the chest of drawers.

"When you visited this flat soon after the arrest, that portrait wasn't there, was it, Brigadiere?"

Paolo shook his head. "It wasn't. How very nice of Mr Montagna, he is a fair man. He was taking something away while making sure he left something behind."

Montagna was still holding the jacket, uncertain of what to do.

"It's generous of you to take Mr Cambiale's jacket away, with all its incriminating evidence. How come you're so concerned about him all of a sudden?" Silence. "He's not replying, Giò, so maybe you could suggest an explanation."

"Well, if I had to hazard a guess as to why Mr Montagna would go to all the risk of breaking into this house, it would

be because he wanted to make sure nothing could incriminate
Mr Cambiale of anything… illegal."

Montagna started while Paolo shook his head, a roguish
smile on his face.

"I'm afraid I'm lost, Giò, why would he do that?"

"How much do you know of inheritance law?"

"A little."

"Good, then maybe you can answer this question: what
would happen if someone – Miss Zerbino, for example – were
to be a beneficiary of a will, but was subsequently found to be
guilty of murder?"

"Well, in that case, she would lose all rights to her share of
the inheritance."

"Really?"

"Yes, our Civil Code is very clear. In the case of you
committing criminal actions against the person you would
have inherited from, you lose all your rights, which I guess is
a good way to prevent foul play…"

"Then who'd get her share of the money?"

"In this case, it would go to the only legitimate heiress."

"You mean Mrs Scalzacane would inherit the whole lot?"

Montagna's eyes were flitting from Giò to Paolo and back.
His apprehension was clear – were the two of them playing
cat and mouse with him?

"Exactly," Paolo nodded.

Giò shook her head. "On the other hand, what would
happen if we were to find something – shall we say, useful? –
on Mr Cambiale's jacket?"

"What, such as traces of gunpowder on both his jacket and
shirtsleeves that match the gun used for the murder?"

"Good golly!" cried Giò, feigning surprise. "Are you
telling me it was Mr Cambiale who killed Mr Scalzacane?"

"I have no doubt."

"Why are you arresting me, then?" Montagna finally

found his voice, pointing to Paolo's gun. Paolo glanced out of the window.

"You'll be happy to know you're not alone." He nodded his head towards a team of carabinieri outside, his eyes firmly on Montagna again. "My colleagues are arresting Mrs Scalzacane who was waiting in your car."

"On what charge?" The man had gone pale, but he tried to smile boldly. "A stolen jacket?"

"No, tampering with evidence is considered a worse charge than a simple robbery. Besides that, you're being arrested for being the masterminds behind Mr Scalzacane's murder. You do not have to say anything..."

"You've no proof!" Montagna interrupted in a sudden burst of rage.

"Mr Montagna, you still don't understand. We've been following you all evening, from when you broke into Zoe Zerbino's house while her father was out and planted evidence against her." He turned to Giò. "What was that?"

"A few photos of Mr Cambiale in Zoe's bedside cabinet, as if she was in love with him, and a fake message, printed in the main office of Mr Scalzacane's premises, with the details of the getaway plan."

"Unfortunately for you, Mr Montagna, we also ran an inventory of Miss Zerbino's belongings in her house soon after her arrest and found no such evidence then. Bad mistake. Greed has condemned you."

"And I guess when Mr Cambiale gets to know that the woman he loved – the woman who persuaded him to carry out the brutal murder – was having an affair with you, and that you were both trying to frame him as Miss Zerbino's accomplice... well, I bet he will be more than willing to collaborate with us. After all, he's got nothing to lose."

As Paolo was taking the man away, Montagna's wrists handcuffed, Giò followed on his heels.

"But Paolo, if Mrs Scalzacane is responsible for her

husband's murder, who will be receiving her part of the inheritance?"

"I asked Mr Delizia the same question. He said the will states Mr Scalzacane's intentions clearly: 'I leave everything I can to Miss Zoe Zerbino', and since his wife has forfeited her rights, the whole lot now goes to Zoe."

"So even if these two don't get a life sentence, as they didn't actually pull the trigger..."

Paolo continued her train of thought. "They will not benefit from a single penny."

EPILOGUE

On Sunday evening, Nando and their children arrived home. Agnese had prepared a special welcome dinner, and chatter, laughter and stories filled the living room until much later than usual. Both Lilia and Luca had plenty of adventures to share with their mother. But when they asked her how her weekend had gone, fearing the truth would excite them too much to sleep when they'd got school the next day, Agnese simply shook her head.

"Quiet, ordinary. Nothing happened, nothing at all."

But once she was in her bedroom, Agnese opened her diary. Nando was still watching TV on the sofa, so she'd have a little time to herself. Using her favourite bullet points, she listed the main happenings of the actually very eventful weekend.

- I asked Giò to tell me the whole story; I couldn't get to grips with how she'd realised the conversation between Mr Montagna and Mrs Scalzacane in the public gardens was a red herring. She believes they saw her going into the Villa Comunale from Mrs Scalzacane's house, which she passed on the way, and decided to follow her and perform their little charade. She remembers thinking at the time how unlikely it was that they didn't notice her sitting there, and once they were gone, she was left with the feeling they had both been acting out roles. After all, a lamb is always a lamb, but Mrs Scalzacane is a wolf. And so, it seems, is Luigi Montagna. That set her on a series of "What if?" questions until she realised she could explain everything that had happened.

- When Giò shared her thoughts with Paolo, he suggested they arrest Mr Cambiale, and then follow the other two to see if they panicked. And they did – they walked straight into the trap.

- The stupid Cambiale didn't realise there was no way Mrs Scalzacane would ever love him, and that she was just using him so she could free herself up to be with her true love, Luigi Montagna. And when Zoe got involved just by chance, they realised it couldn't have been better – with her accused of murder, they'd not only get away with their crime, they would have the whole of the inheritance to themselves. Cambiale would never give Mrs Scalzacane away as that would mean he'd have to admit he had killed her husband.

- But what if Zoe had not inadvertently come into the picture? What if Mr Cambiale had confessed the truth, but said he had committed the murder at Mrs Scalzacane's request? Well, he'd have had no proof. The staff would have backed her up, saying that if Mrs Scalzacane had feelings for anyone in the office, they were certainly not for Cambiale. The plan was so well-conceived, almost the perfect murder.

- Mr Scalzacane himself turned out to be a lamb in

wolf's clothing. Maybe he realised his wife was cheating on him, or maybe he simply felt Miss Zerbino deserved more than he had ever acknowledged. I don't know if he ever suspected his wife would go to the extreme of killing him. Maybe he had a hunch, hence the words in his will: 'All I can leave goes to Miss Zoe Zerbino'.

- Zoe has announced that she will soon be leaving for a three-month tour of Europe, which has left her father dumbfounded. But I think he will have to put up with much more independence from her upon her return. The most amazing thing is that she's thinking of continuing her boss's business, which will save the jobs of the Famous Five whose gossip inadvertently proved useful in helping Giò find the truth.

- All this proves that a wolf will always be a wolf, a gossip is always a gossip, but… a doormat can turn into something better.

- Once more, I have to acknowledge that Giò has a real talent for sleuthing. But she's in an altogether different frame of mind now. Annika, her Swedish friend and fellow author, is organising a writers' retreat here in Maratea shortly. They will stay at the panoramic Pellicano Hotel – I can already imagine the beginning of a new adventure. Just think – a group of wordsmiths, a remote hotel. Outside, the winds howl and the seas rage. ~~But the real danger lurks~~…oh no, enough of the drama!

Continue reading about Giò Brando and her family in the *An Italian Village Mystery* series with Book One, **Murder on the Road**.

Adriana Licio lives not far from Maratea, the Mediterranean setting for her first series *An Italian Village Mystery*. She loves loads of things: travelling, reading, walking, good food, small villages, and home swapping. She runs her family perfumery, and between a dark patchouli and a musky rose, she reads and writes cosy mysteries.

Read More from Adriana Licio

And get the free Prequel to the An Italian Village series.

www.adrianalicio.com/Murderclub

HIJINKS IN AJIJIC

VIKKI WALTON

1

I'd expected my daughter's response, but maybe not as dramatic. "Listen, sweetie. It's no big deal; people travel solo all the time."

"But Mom," my daughter pushed her curly blond hair behind her ears, "You're—"

Here it comes. "Old?"

"I don't mean you're old, but... um, have you looked in a mirror lately?"

Boy howdy, had I! It occurred around six months after my dear Bryce had passed. I had stared at the pale, drained, elderly woman and wondered who the hell was that person? When had I become an invisible shell of a woman? Certainly my body bore the scars of childbirth and many accidents, my face bore the wrinkles and laugh lines of a life well-lived, and even my hair's pigment had fled, leaving my hair a term I prefer to call antique blond, thank you very much. Even worse, while the hair on my head had thinned, fresh ones popped up, moving south to my chin and upper lip. Yes, I had seen that woman.

"Just because I'm about to turn sixty doesn't mean I'm decrepit. Just wait; if you're lucky, you'll get old too."

Anne reached over and clasped my hand in hers. "Mom, I'm worried, that's all."

I patted her hand. "I'm not going to Antarctica." I didn't tell her it was on my new travel wish list. After plodding through day after day doing the same thing, I'd sat down and written out sixty things I wanted to do when I turned sixty. Things I'd put off over the years, because of children, work transfers, and the inevitable "tomorrow." Nothing was stopping me now, but I still dragged my feet.

Over brunch with my old friend, Cheryl, I'd told her about my bucket list, with travel being one of the major themes. She pulled a card from her purse. "You need to connect with this lady. Monica does house and pet-sitting all around the world. She spoke to our ladies' lunch group just last week."

"Pet sitting?" I waved to the waiter for another Mimosa. "Sounds interesting. Tell me more."

"Well, it's probably best to talk to her, but you stay at a person's home and care for their animals while they're away on vacation. No money's exchanged. It's a barter system. Obviously, there's responsibility for the animals and things like watering plants, but other than that, you can often go out and explore."

I didn't hesitate to call Monica when I returned home, and we went over everything. I took courses on animal care, updated my passport, and gathered recommendations from people in town. I'd signed up on a house-sitting platform, not unlike the new-fangled dating sites people use. I'd chosen not to start the dating route after finding that most men wanted someone younger or that older men were often looking for a nurse or a purse. As a married woman most of my life, it was now time for me. I sought, and wanted, freedom, so I signed up on a house-sitting platform. The next thing I knew, I'd been accepted to do my first sit in Mexico.

"Mom, people are getting killed there. The cartels, the—"

I shook my head and tried not to roll my eyes. "People are

dying every minute all around the world. I don't plan on seeking out the cartels for drug deals." I spied the disapproval and frustration on her face. "Don't look at me in that way and use that tone. I've traveled before."

"Yes, but always with dad or your friends. Why don't you wait until the kids are out for school this summer, and we all can take a trip together?"

"That would be nice. However I want to travel off-season when it's less expensive and not so hot. Plus, fewer tourists around." I gave her my mom look so she would know it was the end-of-discussion.

She crossed her arms. "Okay, but if you get killed, don't come crying to me."

"Don't be stealing my lines." I smiled and held up two fingers, "I promise to be safe."

The next month flew by, and before I knew it, I sat in an airport lounge awaiting my flight to Guadalajara, Mexico.

I pulled out my book and became engrossed in a story about a mysterious English manor house. Hmmm, maybe a trip to the United Kingdom next. I pulled out my ever-growing list of things I wanted to do and added it. I closed my book and surveyed the crowd of travelers. Where were they all going? I spent the rest of the time people-watching and making up stories about them until my phone vibrated, alerting me to line up. Gathering my carry-on, I made my way to the gate.

One perk I'd discovered over the years had been easily accruing bonus miles, and I'd snagged a business class seat for the brief trip. After they'd called a thousand other areas, they finally called those of us in Group One to board. I found my seat next to the window and settled in for a comfortable flight.

A young woman glanced from her ticket to the seat numbers. She stowed her backpack overhead and plopped down in the adjacent seat. "Hi! I'm Suzanne, but most people call me Suzy."

"I'm Viviane, but most people call me Viviane."

She threw back her head, laughing. Shifting in her seat, she remarked, "That's great. Where you headed?"

"Well, since this plane is going to Guadalajara, I'm hoping there."

"You're funny. I mean, are you on vacation, going home… wait, let me guess." She acted like she was conjuring up a thought, "Ajijic."

"How in the world do you know that I'm going to—I struggled with the pronunciation—Ah-he-hek?"

"It's a big expat place for, um…"

"Old people?"

She pursed her lips and zipped them. "I never said that." She adjusted her seat belt. "This is serendipitous, though. Since that's where I'm going too!"

"You are? To see someone old?"

She chuckled, "You really are funny. No, I'm a pet-sitter."

"Me too."

"Get out! This is cray-cray. Of all the people to sit next to each other. Two pet-sitters. Have you sat there before?"

"No. Actually, this is my first ever sit."

Suzy beamed at me, "You're going to love it. You meet such pleasant people—well, most of the time—and you get to love on all kinds of animals too. You can't beat it." She accepted water from the steward while I chose orange juice.

"Where do you live, if you don't mind me asking?" I took a sip of my juice. Ugh, canned is not a suitable substitute.

"Well, for the next three months I'll be living in Ajijic."

"But where's your actual home?"

"Wherever I lay my head, actually. I've been doing this full time for, um, let's see," she counted on her fingers, "Four years now."

Four years, really? Had she started when she was ten? I reflected on how to word my next question.

She grinned broader than the Cheshire cat showing sparkling white teeth, "I can see the wheels turning. I turn twenty-eight next week. Started this right after high school, and now I've been traveling the world. No rent. No worries."

"But how do you make money?"

"My channel and some writing. It's enough for me."

I handed the glass to the steward as they prepared to take off. "My birthday's next week, too. On the fifth."

"Seriously?" Suzy sang the *Twilight Zone* theme. "We're both going to Ajijic, both pet-sitters, and have the same birthday. Is that weird or what?"

"I have to agree with you there. It is a bit strange we're going to Ajijic at the same time."

"Listen, let's trade numbers so we can meet for dinner on our birthday."

"That would be nice." I gave Suzy my info and where I'd be staying.

"This is where I'll be staying."

Suzy stifled a chuckle, "Of course."

"What?"

"Nothing. I'm in that same part of town, that's all." She yawned. "I need to get some shut-eye. I caught the red-eye to catch this flight, and all the time changes are catching up with me. Later." She closed her eyes, falling asleep instantly. Our brief chat left me feeling like I'd just emerged from walking through a tornado.

2

———————

Arriving at the airport, I waved goodbye to Suzy and took my place in line. After seeing the button turn green, I proceeded on toward the arrivals area. On the plane, I'd worn a smart pantsuit with a jacket to allow my ride to find me easily. A smiling tan woman waved to me, so I headed over to her, and the woman enveloped me in a hug.

"Welcome to Mexico." She pointed at my jacket. "Trust me, you're not going to need that here!" As soon as we exited the airport, I shucked out of the jacket. Margaret walked ahead, and I followed her to the parking garage, pulling my carry-on bag behind me. As I looked at everyone in casual clothing, I wondered if I had brought the right items with me. The drive passed quickly as we made our way to the lakeside town. We pulled off the primary artery or namely, the Carretera, as Margaret had told me. In no time at all, I found myself ensconced in a delightful upstairs guest bedroom.

Walking over to the French doors—or should I consider them Mexican doors?—I opened them onto a covered patio with a pair of chairs and a table. The view over the back walled garden was impressive with a kidney-shaped pool and an abundance of greenery and flowers in every direction. I sighed when a knock sounded on the door. Why hadn't I looked into this pet sitting thing sooner?

"Okay to come in?" I responded with a yes while crossing the room. Margaret opened the door, and I saw she held a stack of towels. "These were still in the dryer when I left earlier." She entered the adjoining bathroom and placed them on the counter. "Let me know if there's anything else you need. We can always go to Super Lake later, for any groceries or toiletries. Also, you're more than welcome to stay in the master bedroom once I've left."

"I think this room is perfect for me."

"Great. The view over the gardens pretty much sold me on this house. Still, should you decide to change rooms, you're more than welcome. Once you're rested, we'll go over everything, and then head out for dinner. I have the taxi driver picking me up early evening tomorrow, so that should allow plenty of time for me to show you around the area and where I walk Scooter."

Scooter was the dog I'd be watching while Margaret was on her trip to Italy. "Sounds good." On arrival, Scooter had wagged her tail at me, and we'd become quick friends.

I unpacked before taking a nice cool shower and putting on a slip dress in a vibrant turquoise. Moisturizing my face, I stared at the woman in the mirror and pointed, "Now listen up, you. This is an adventure, so enjoy every minute." The woman in the reflection had the audacity to stick her tongue out at me. "Old, shmold."

Mindful of the cobblestones on the street, we crossed over to the main road before making our way to the restaurant through a simple door in the side of a stucco building. Inside, though, it revealed a sizeable building that opened into a courtyard. A young man escorted us out to an area where an enormous wall twinkled with lights and greenery abounded. A group of men sat eating at a table nearby, and as I looked toward them, one of them raised his glass and smiled. I nodded and smiled back, feeling a bit strange at the moment, but the harmless flirtation changed to surprise when another of the men in the group sprung to his feet. A tall, fit man with a head full of romantic, swoon-worthy silver hair and a silly what's-the-point soul patch beard had arrived. The shorter man from the table clenched his fists and fired off words to the man as he approached, "Who do you think you are? Coming in here and—" I struggled to hear the rest as his friends admonished him to lower his voice. Finally, another man from the table pulled the man back toward them, but not before the man said to the silver fox, "Leave her alone."

Silver Fox laughed. "Or what? She's a grown woman."

"I'm telling you, back off. Or you'll regret it."

SF, as I'd now designated him, shrugged his shoulders, and hurried over to a group of women who fluttered about him like a troupe of high school fangirls with the popular football team captain. I guess the shock of it all was apparent on my face as Margaret said, "That's one thing you'll have to get used to here, lots of retirees. Many of them are out on the prowl too. Lots more women to men, so they think they're God's gift, if you know what I mean. So too many egos in a room, you need a shovel to move through all the you-know-what." She signaled to our waiter before turning back to me. "White or red?"

I smiled before responding, "I'll have what you're having."

3

The next morning I pulled on a pair of sneakers along with denim capris and a magenta tee-shirt. I gathered up my travel hat and sunglasses before heading downstairs. Margaret showed me where she kept Scooter's leash and treats before we headed toward the Malecón for our walk. As we strolled along the esplanade next to Lake Chapala, Margaret shared about her decision to move to Mexico, and I shared about my venture in pet sitting. We both agreed it was a marvelous way to travel and meet people. We passed an older Mexican gentleman sitting on a bench, and he tipped his white hat while I replied with a rudimentary, "Buenos Dias."

"Hola!" A familiar voice caused me to search out its owner. I waved as Suzy sprinted towards us with two happy hounds in tow. "Hey there. Good to see ya again." She noticed Margaret, and a knowing look passed over her face. "Hi. I'm Suzy." Margaret responded in kind. Suzy knelt down and patted the spaniel's head. "Hi, Scooter." The hounds began pulling at the leash. "I better get going. These two love their walks. Hasta Luego!" She set off at a jog, the dogs happily moving beside her.

I looked down at Scooter, who had sprawled out on the pavement. "Scooter, I'm glad we're a suitable match. Not really sure I could jog at all." He wagged his tail, and we set off down the path, the sounds of brooms sweeping the nearby sidewalk the only distraction. On the way back, we exited half-way down the Malecón so Margaret could take me to Edith's hair salon to set up an appointment. We turned onto Ocampo, and on the way, Margaret pointed out a day spa that I might want to visit later.

At Edith's, I followed Margaret into the tiny beauty salon. Two women sat in each of the stylist's chairs. One woman looked to be about my age with a short bob as the technician worked quickly with her scissors to trim the back. In the mirror, I saw her staring intently at the woman in the other chair.

The other woman was of an indeterminate age due mainly to the layer of make-up she wore. She was blowing lightly on manicured nails as the hairstylist applied a deep scarlet color to the hair not already in foil. Margaret spoke to the stylist, who stepped over to the counter. I made an appointment for the following week, and we were soon back outside in the warm sunshine.

After we'd crossed the street onto Colón, we decided to grab coffee at Café Grano. I ordered my café con leche and sipped the soothing brew. Margaret placed her cup on the table. She leaned toward me and spoke softly, even though there were no other people at the surrounding tables. "Did you see that woman getting her hair done in the salon?"

"Umm—"

"The one with the bright red nails and lipstick."

There was no denying who she meant now. "Yes."

"She's the one those two men were fighting about."

"Really?" I guess men were more easily fooled than I thought. I'd seen less makeup on a Hollywood actress.

Margaret nodded. A strange look crossed over her face as she reached for her cup. "Women are so gullible."

"Who was the other woman?"

"That's Marva."

"Marva? That's an uncommon name."

"Different is definitely one way to put it. She's a tarot card reader. Are you into the cards?"

I scrambled for my response. "Never considered it. Not sure I want to know what's going to happen in the future."

She nodded and ran her finger over the cup's rim. "Done? We can take Scooter home, and then I can drive you to get anything you need. Along the way, I'll show you where the bank and grocery stores are, and where they hold the Wednesday market. It's worth checking out." The rest of the day went quickly, and by late afternoon Margaret had pulled her luggage out into the front hallway. Her suitcase showcased a raised monogram of three letters. M, R, and an S. "So I know it's Margaret Ridge. What's the S stand for?"

She replied, "Suzanne."

"Funny, that's Suzy's name too. Lots of coincidences here."

"Yes, lots." Her phone beeped. "Ah, the taxi's here."

"Let me help you." I took one case, and together we pulled the rest of the luggage out to the waiting vehicle. As the driver put her bags inside, she hugged me. "Take care. I'll see you in a few weeks."

That night I'd gone out to my balcony with a wonderful glass of Prosecco picked up at the store earlier. We'd eaten a fairly substantial lunch, so I'd made a simple tray of veggies, fruit, hummus, and crackers along with olives that I picked at while enjoying the coolness of the evening. The phone rang, jarring me from my thoughts.

I rushed over and picked it up. "Hello?"

A rush of Spanish filled the phone line. I paused, trying to remember *No habla Espanol* when laughter came through the line. "It's me, Suzy! I'm just playing with you."

"Hi Suzy. What's up?"

"Want to go to the hot springs with me tomorrow? It's not far down the road from here, and it's quite nice."

"That sounds great, but I can't leave Scooter on his own until Thursday when Margaret's housekeeper is here."

"I can do that. Spread out our birthday week, right?"

"Sure." I popped an olive in my mouth and waited.

"Doing anything tomorrow?"

"I'm planning on checking out the Lake Chapala Society. We drove by it, but it was closed."

"Hold on." I heard Suzy call, "Boys, get in here." I thought I heard a female voice in the background and then a door slamming closed. "These two. There's a cat that comes over and sits high on the wall, taunting them. They go nuts, and the cat just stares at them. During the day, I let them have at it, but the neighbors won't take kindly to all that barking going on in the evening. How about after you walk Scooter tomorrow, I take you to the writers' group at the hotel and then we can walk down to the LCS? Maybe grab some lunch too."

"I could do that. What time should we meet?"

"I'll stop by after I take these two on a good long run in the morning. The group starts at ten, so we could go early and grab a coffee too."

"Okay, thanks. See you tomorrow." I rang off. A wave of exhaustion came over me, and I packed everything into the fridge before calling it a night.

I was sleeping peacefully when a strange noise jolted me awake. I felt movement on the bed. Startled, I saw two beady brown eyes staring back at me. Scooter must have joined me on the bed at some point. I whispered, "You heard it too, huh?" I swept the bedcovers back and warily crept over to the drapes. I could see light peeking around the edges, which meant that the security lights had come on. I slid the curtain back, and a face turned toward me. A tabby cat sat on the iron railing of my balcony. After determining I was of no consequence, it licked its paw and then strode over to the edge where it dropped out of sight. I threw open the curtains and went out on the balcony. The rest of the yard was deep in shadow. I followed along where the cat had disappeared and spied a small ledge. It must have climbed down that way. However, instead of making me feel more at ease, I realized how easy it would be for someone to climb up that way. I went inside and made sure I locked the doors. After a quick bathroom stop, I was back in bed, where Scooter snuggled up against me. I fell into a dreamless, deep sleep.

4

In the bright light of the morning, I realized how I'd overreacted. I knew that, like any unknown place, it would take some time getting used to it. Suddenly, a series of fireworks shattered the quiet. I'd been told about those and doubted that I'd get used to them. The sound of the man's voice selling gas from his truck came through the window as I made coffee in the kitchen. Not wanting to be too late, I dressed and set out on my walk with Scooter. By the time I returned, Suzy was already waiting for me on my step.

I glanced at my watch. "Am I late?"

"No. You're fine. I took the dogs out at six this morning so I could do a couple of miles with them, wanted them to be happy and ready for a nap."

I made a face. "That means you got up before six to go do that. Ugh, no thanks."

"I love it. I've always been a morning person, so it helps when I have dogs that get up early to sit."

"I'll have to remember that. No early morning dogs. I think Scooter would have kept on sleeping if I hadn't woken him." I unlocked the gate in the wall, and we entered the front courtyard area where a fountain splashed water. After giving

Scooter a treat, I went upstairs to change while Suzy sunned herself up on the mirador. I hadn't spent any time up there in the open-air rooftop terrace, but I'd planned on reading there in the afternoon. "The view up here is wonderful."

"Yes, you've got a glorious view of the lake and the mountains. Where I'm sitting is a bit more compact and has more views of the town. Ready?" She hopped up, her legs and arms tinted pink from the sun.

"Yes, let's go." We walked over to La Nueva Posada, a hotel where the writers' group met. As we entered, it surprised me to see many of the men from the other evening as well as the two ladies from the beauty salon. Others sat around at various tables.

"Come on. Let's sit over here." Suzy motioned for me to follow her to a table. We joined the women from the beauty salon. After we'd ordered coffee, a man I hadn't seen before approached the table. "May I join you lovely ladies?" I almost thought Ms. Makeup purred when she told him yes and patted the seat next to her.

After the presentations were over, we ordered lunch, which came with buy one-get one beer free. Not normally a beer drinker, I chose the tostado plate, which was a generous portion. After no breakfast, it was a welcome meal.

Ms. Makeup bent toward the unfamiliar man at our table, exposing her cleavage with what had to have been implants. I have to say no matter what age or stage, the flagrant move had always grossed me out. The man, thankfully, didn't take the bait. Instead, he simply turned to us. "Did I hear that you two are pet-sitters?" Ms. Makeup pouted and crossed her arms across her ample surgically enhanced breasts, searching the scene for an easier prey.

Suzy replied yes, when Ms. Makeup pushed back her chair, almost knocking it to the ground. "I hate to have to leave you, but I have a prior engagement." She smiled down at us as though we would be heartbroken at her leaving but dismissing us peons all the same. "Oh, Freddie!" She waved her multi-ringed hand, "I'm over here." It was Silver Fox.

He walked over to the table, and I wondered how quickly I could count all the women's mouths hanging open ogling. I have to admit, he was a fine male specimen, but really, come on ladies, have some self-respect. I patted my hair in place.

To Ms. Makeup's dismay, he greeted me first. "Hello, I don't think we've met before. I'm Freddie." He stuck out his hand. I raised mine to shake his hand, but he took it and brushed his lips across the top of my hand. "Mucho gusto." I could drown in those baby blues that held mine. Okay, maybe I understood the other women's responses now as butterflies danced in my stomach. What in the world, Viv? I jerked my hand from his, but not quick enough as I spied the look of pure hatred that Ms. Makeup shot my way.

She turned to him and pushed out her lower lip. "Freddie, I hated that we didn't get to have our date last night."

His tone took on a healthy dose of disgust. "Mildred—"

"You know, I prefer Millie." She tapped her foot.

"Look, if you're going to cause a scene—"

"No, no. Can we still go into Guadalajara? Does that work for you?" Her high-tone begging grated.

"Sure. Meet me in the car."

Without another word, Mildred gathered her things and left, although as she moved past another table further on the patio, I noticed her exchange looks with another woman. I almost laughed aloud at what I was seeing. The unknown woman, the woman scorned, the man who played to every woman's fantasy of romance—the entire scene was all there in full color. It took me a minute to realize he was speaking to me again.

"I'm sorry. My mind was wandering. What?"

"I was asking you to dinner. Tonight."

I fumbled for words, "I… uh, well… um." Jeez. Get it together, Viv.

"I'll go." Suzy jumped in, helping ease my sudden lack of a brain.

He turned to her. "That's great. The more, the merrier."

The other man interjected, "Does that apply to men too, or only lovely ladies?"

Freddie smiled, but it didn't reach his eyes, "Of course."

That left the other lady from the salon. She and Freddie locked eyes. "I have plans for dinner, but I'd be happy to read your cards. I'm sure you have a most interesting future ahead."

"Thanks. I prefer to let the future surprise me."

"Oh, it's going to surprise you all right." She rose from the table, and with a nod at us, walked toward the exit.

Very strange. I felt like everyone was in on a joke I wasn't privy to knowing. I turned back toward Freddie, whom I realized was still awaiting my answer. "I guess that's fine. Where should we meet?"

Suzy piped up, "Cocinart?"

We all agreed to meet there at seven. Freddie left, probably to meet up with an angry Mildred. I paid my bill and made ready to leave. The man at the end of the table rose at the same time. "I need to get going too. By the way, my name's Perry." He shook my hand, and then Suzy's. "See you this evening."

So much for a relaxing, quiet first sit. I felt like someone had dropped me into a reality show episode.

5

On the way back to Margaret's, I stopped at the consignment store to see if I could find another dress. While I'd noticed most people wearing capris and sleeveless tops, I preferred a dress for going out. I found a light cotton skirt with a belt to accessorize it along with a couple of fun tops. I enjoyed the casual stroll back to the house. Any tension I'd felt from the day dissolved.

As I made my way around the corner, I noticed a piece of paper wedged into the gate. I pulled it out. In bold words written with a Sharpie, it said, "STAY AWAY!" I turned and looked in both directions on the street. I don't know what I expected to see—as if the person who'd written this would wait in full view for me to acknowledge them. Stay away from what?

I stuck the paper in my bag and unlocked the gate to the courtyard oasis. Inside, I turned the lock on the gate. While it had taken a bit of getting used to, the extra protection gave me a sense of security in this unfamiliar environment. Inside the house, I set the bag down on the table and spied the phone's answering machine blinking. One of Margaret's friends had left a message. I looked up the number on a list she'd left me and rang her back.

"Olivia, hi. This is Viviane, Margaret's pet sitter."

"Oh hello. Is Margaret there? I wanted to ask her something." The voice seemed on the edge of some emotion which I couldn't quite place.

"She's left for her trip already."

"Um, okay. I guess I misunderstood. I thought that she said she was leaving tomorrow, or was it next week? Maybe I got the days mixed up. Oh well. I'll connect with her when she returns." The line went dead.

"And goodbye to you too." I furrowed my brow. It was evident by the woman's voice and demeanor that something was going on that I wasn't privy too.

I poured myself a tall glass of iced tea and made my way outside to the stairs leading to the mirador. On the way, I passed the pool and decided to take a late-night dip before bed. Up on the mirador, the combination of sun and light breeze lulled me to sleep. I awoke with a start at hearing two male voices from beyond the wall that divided the property from the street below. "What's your angle?"

A deep chuckle from a familiar voice, and I realized it was Freddie. "You really think I'd tell you?"

They moved on down the road, and I popped my head above the mirador's edge to see the other person. From my vantage point, I spied the short man who'd yelled at Freddie in the restaurant. Although now the tone had changed to almost buddy-buddy. I guess since everyone knew everyone in this small town, you had to make peace with each other rather quickly.

I was more confused than ever. I made my way back down to the house as the phone rang. It was Margaret. "Hello!" She chirped. "Just wanted to call and see how everything's going."

I glanced toward Scooter, who hadn't moved a muscle since I'd gone. "All's well."

"So nothing exciting then?"

The note I'd found in the gate flashed in my mind. Had it been intended for Margaret? There was no point in telling her as she certainly couldn't do anything about it now. Besides, I didn't want to cause her angst on her trip. "No, all good."

Her affirmative reply held a discouraging tone to it. "Okay, well, call me if anything… and I mean if anything should happen."

"I will." I set the glass in the sink.

"Well, bye then. Have fun at dinner tonight."

We rang off, and I stared at the phone for a minute. How did she know about the dinner? Could someone had told her, or was she simply making a statement to enjoy going out for dinner? I shrugged my shoulders, and my thoughts returned to the message in the gate as I pulled the paper from the bag. Did someone want Margaret to stay away? But did that mean from there or from someone? Something else niggled at my mind, but I couldn't grasp it yet.

That night we enjoyed a meal with lots of conversation and laughter, but I could tell Suzy wasn't quite herself. "Are you all right?"

She looked at me. "Yes, sorry." She glanced around the table and lowered her voice, "I just have something on my mind. I recently found out that I've come into a small inheritance. I won't receive it for a few weeks, though. In the meantime, they have asked me to join in a fund that would see double that money. It's pretty much guaranteed." She shrugged her shoulders. "Unfortunately, since I don't have the funds now, I'll have to pass on it. It's been weighing on me, that's all."

Perry sipped his drink. "It happens. Opportunity sometimes knocks at the wrong time."

"How much is the buy-in?" Freddie asked.

"Five hundred thousand."

"Five hundred thousand!" I've never been known for my tact. If she considered that a small inheritance, I wonder what she'd think of a big one. "So you're saying that this investment could double your money to a million dollars?" So much for my pitiful retirement fund. I wanted to know how I could double my money too.

Suzy sighed. "Crazy, right? I've gone from pretty much living month-to-month to suddenly having quite a nice nest egg in a short time."

Reality kicked in, and I responded, "I don't know. That sounds almost too good to be true. You don't want to put all your funds into something that could be a bust."

Suzy shook her head, "Nope. I've even contacted my lawyer from the trust about it. He says it's legit. Still not much I can do about it. I won't have access to those funds for a while." She signaled to the waiter for the check. "It's been nice, but I have to get back to the pups."

We paid our bills. After the giving and receiving of friendly hugs, all of us went our separate ways. I looked back and saw that Perry had caught up with Freddie. They were in deep conversation, but their demeanor left me with the impression of anger.

6

I arrived back at the gate, and in the crack, found another piece of paper. I pulled it out, tearing it in the process. With shaking hands, I put the two pieces together. **LEAVE HIM ALONE.**

I unlocked the gate and made my way inside the house. After letting Scooter out in the back garden, I put the two pages side by side. They matched with the same paper and the same capital letters. I made my way up to my room and looked out over the back-lit garden. A dip in the pool would be nice, so I changed into my suit and made my way down to the backyard. The pool was cool, and I floated on my back. My mind raced as I thought over the last few days.

Who had written those notes to Margaret? Leave who alone? To be honest, that answer came pretty easily. However, the more I thought about it, maybe the message had been for me. But who had sent it? Mildred, the overly made-up matron, Marva, or possibly even someone else? I flipped over and did strokes across the pool as Scooter lounged nearby on a low chaise.

I was drying off when the mirador light came on. My heart quickened, but I realized it was most likely the cat coming to visit again. Grabbing my robe, I started toward the house when I heard my phone ding.

Margaret: If you're up, call me.

I sat down on the chaise, and Scooter moved from his spot to my lap. I petted him as he laid his head on my legs. "Hi, Margaret. Everything okay?"

"Yes. You know how it is. I forgot something. I mean, I forgot to tell you where the money is for the housekeeper and the gardener. It's in the drawer in the credenza in the dining room."

"Thanks." I didn't say that she'd already shown me where she'd put those funds.

"How's Scooter doing?"

"Well, we're out in the back. I took a dip in the pool. Now we're enjoying the chaise and the cool breeze."

"Perfect." There was a moment of silence. "Could you look in the back right corner of the yard and see if I left my kitchen shears over there? I realized that I'd cut flowers for the house the other day. I'd hate for it to rain, and they get rusted while I'm away."

"Sure, I can check. Is it okay to look tomorrow? It's pretty dark out here."

"Would you mind looking now? The rains often come in the middle of the night at this time of year."

"Okay." Were all homeowners this needy? I picked Scooter up and moved toward the area in question. I looked in the area Margaret instructed. "I don't see anything here."

"Just a minute." She muffled her voice, "We're all good now. Night!" She ended the call.

I stared at the phone. Strange, very strange indeed. I walked into the house and crossed over to the front. Something had triggered the light in the courtyard. I went outdoors, and the silence of the night surrounded me. It took me a minute before I realized the gate wasn't closed fully. I could have sworn I had locked that gate when I came in. I shoved the gate in place and turned the lock.

After reading more of my current book, I fell asleep to the sounds of rain. I guess Margaret had been right. I awoke to a thunder crash. Reaching for my light, it didn't turn on. I grabbed the flashlight by the bed, now realizing how its convenient position. Lightning must have knocked out the transformer. I'd been told that could happen. I went around the house, and everything was in order. Not much I could do in the dark, so I climbed back into bed. After finally finding the right position, Scooter and I fell back asleep.

Bright sunlight flooded my face from the window where I'd neglected to pull the curtains back. I yawned and stretched. Scooter opened his eyes but didn't move as I padded into the bathroom and shucked into my robe. Downstairs, I glanced at the clock over the stove and realized it was ten in the morning already. Wow, I couldn't believe I slept this late. Scooter had joined me and danced around my legs. "Here, I'll let you go out in the back. Once I wake up a bit, we'll head out for our walk." Leaves and debris littered the ground in the backyard, and I spied a branch that had broken next to the wall. Good thing the gardener came soon. If nothing else, I could point it out and have him take it down.

The sound of chainsaws broke the silence. I climbed up on the mirador and saw a group of men beside a gigantic tree with storm damage, possibly from lightning last night. It must have been that large crack I'd heard. They had laid the electrical wires on the cobbled street while workers cut at the broken section of the tree. I drank my coffee as I watched them work. As the sun's heat penetrated that side, I moved to the west portion of the mirador. I looked down the street, and I could see Suzy. She was with another woman I hadn't seen before. This woman reminded me of Mildred, though, with lots of lip color, jewelry, a large hat, and sunglasses. They hugged, and the woman took off in a taxi that had been waiting at the curb.

Maybe that was the homeowner from where Suzy was staying. But why would she still be here? My stomach rumbled. As much as you've eaten here and you're still hungry? I admonished myself. The phone rang as I made my way inside.

"Hi!" It was Suzy. "I'm in your neighborhood."

"Yes, I saw you." I shifted my phone between my ear and shoulder so I could rinse out my coffee cup.

"What?"

"This morning. You were talking to a lady. Is that the homeowner?"

The phone had gone silent.

"Hello? Are you still there?" I transferred the phone to my hand.

"Sorry, no. It's someone that may be able to help me with the money issue."

"Listen, Suzy, it's none of my business, and you can tell me to butt out, but I'd be very careful about giving your money to people you don't know."

Laughter came across the line. "Isn't that the truth? Thanks for the tip, but I'm not the one who needs to worry."

What did she mean by that? "Um, we had a tree get hit by lightning last night. I'm going to take Scooter out for a brief walk now and then do a longer one later. Are you going to the market?"

"Already been this morning, but you have to go. Take a bag for your goodies. Bye." She ended the call.

7

_____

After Scooter's walk, I made my way down to the busy market on Revolution. Margaret had told me about this market on Wednesdays. I walked down in the center of the village to grab some molletos for lunch. As I approached the restaurant, I saw the woman who'd been with Suzy earlier speaking to Freddie. They turned toward me, and I saw the woman tell him something before she strode rapidly in the opposite direction. So much for saying hello. I made it down to where Freddie waited.

"Hello."

"Hello to you. You going in?" He nodded toward the restaurant.

"Yes, late start to the day after the crazy weather last night."

"Pretty much every day is a late start here, as you'll find out. Unfortunately, I have an appointment, or I would have liked to stay and enjoy your lovely company."

My 'bull-meter' went off, and I saw Freddie for what he was—a skirt-chaser. He'd probably say anything to get what he wanted. Well, this old broad had learned a thing or two on my many turns around the planet. "That's okay. Have a good day." That was a much nicer response than what I really wanted to say.

After enjoying the molletos, I spent some time visiting the various shops in town. I made it home in time to let Scooter out. I had never felt so relaxed, and I allowed the warmth of the day to lull me into a much-desired siesta. I awoke to Scooter's barking. I went up a few steps on the mirador and saw the gardener working in the yard next door. A man stood on the porch. I realized it was Perry, and he waved. "Do you live there?" He pointed toward me. Then realizing we'd be yelling across the fence, he gestured toward the front. I met him at the gate after checking myself in the hall mirror. Thankfully, I didn't have any fabric crush lines on my face from the nap.

"Hi. No, I'm only house-sitting for the owner. I live in the states."

"Ah, a shame. I would have loved to have you as my neighbor."

I pointed toward the gate. "That's your place?"

"Yep. I visited last year, and when this place became available, I snapped it up."

"You're retired?"

He leaned up against the wall, "Some people might think that. I'm an author."

"Really? I don't think I've ever met an author before... other than like at book signings, that type of thing."

"I know. We're like normal people, right?" He winked, and I laughed.

"Do you mind me asking? What are you writing?"

"It's a historical novel. Do you like that genre?"

"Sometimes." I smiled at him. "Well, I better let you get back to it."

"Want to join me for dinner this evening?"

"That would be nice."

"I'm still at a hotel for now while they finish the

remodeling. Want to meet at Alex's Pasta Bar? When it gets hot, I love their watermelon gazpacho."

"That sounds yummy. Seven-ish?"

We agreed on the time, and I spent the rest of the day catching up with friends and family on social media.

In the evening, I dressed in my new multi-colored skirt and donned a white top. I added the new necklace I'd purchased earlier that day. Slipping on my woven flats, I headed to the restaurant. Walking in front of Gossip's, I spied Suzy sitting with Freddie on the patio. They were deep in conversation. Sitting back from them at the table in the corner was the woman I'd seen with Suzy earlier. On seeing me, she raised the menu in front of her face. She didn't seem to be a friendly person, unlike everyone else I'd encountered.

Suzy spied me, and a range of emotions passed over her face. "Hi."

Freddie looked at me. It was evident I'd interrupted their discussion and would not be asked to join them.

"I think I took a wrong turn. I'm trying to get to Alex's Pasta Bar."

"Did you ever!" Suzy rose and pointed down the road. It's that direction and quite a ways down from here. Do you know where Marisa's Pastry Shop is?"

"Who doesn't? I picked up some yummy cake there."

"Alex's is on that street just past that. Have fun." Freddie spoke to her again, and I could tell they had dismissed me.

I waved goodbye, but my mind raced. I sure hope that Suzy wasn't falling for fake Freddie. He was old enough to be her father. No, make that grandfather instead. Gross. Maybe I was reading more into it. Also, what was up with that woman? She didn't even know me, so I felt her responses to seeing me were a bit rude. Oh well, I'd learned over the years you can't please everyone.

I arrived at the restaurant, and Perry, wearing a crisp white shirt and khakis, waved to me from inside. "I made a reservation as it can get packed. This time of year isn't as bad since they're fewer tourists. No problem in finding it?" He motioned to the waiter who brought menus. I ordered a glass of Chardonnay.

"I goofed and went in the other direction, but I saw Suzy and Freddie, who steered me back the right way. Still getting my bearings."

"You'll get it. It's fairly simple. What's your thoughts on ol' Freddie?"

"My mama told me if you can't say something nice—"

He laid his hand on his chest in mock shock, "What, a woman who's seen through Freddie's charms?"

"Guilty." I thanked the waiter who'd brought my drink. We ordered the gazpacho and our entrees.

Perry took a sip of his wine. "So, why do I see a look of consternation on your face? Penny for your…"

I sighed. "I'm worried about Suzy. She is coming into some money, and now Freddie is on her like white on rice."

"Say it ain't so." His smile exposed less than perfect teeth making him more charming.

I sat back as the waiter set the bowl in front of me containing herbs and croutons. He poured the gazpacho on top. I took a bite. "Delicious. Thanks for letting me know about it."

"Certainly. As you were saying… you think Freddie is after Suzy or her money?"

"I know it sounds crazy. But he's way too old for her." I sipped the wonderful cold soup.

"Older man, younger woman. Stranger things have happened."

I wiped my mouth with the napkin. "Yes, but I think Mildred has her tenterhooks in him."

"No. That's done and over. I heard them yelling at each other. Well, she was mainly yelling. 'How could he do that to her? What kind of man was he?' And so on."

"Wow. When did that happen?"

"Yesterday, I think. She even threatened to call the police on him. Can you imagine?"

I shifted in my seat as our entrees arrived. "That is strange." I swirled the pasta on my fork and took a bite.

"Enough of that. Let's change our conversation to something more fun. Why don't you tell me about you?"

We spent the rest of the evening laughing and sharing about our lives. I allowed him to pay for the meal only if he'd let me reciprocate next time. He agreed, and we made our way back to my house. Perry wanted to check on the renovation and what they'd finished that day before heading back to his hotel. Thankfully, no paper stuck out from the gate this time. I bid him goodnight and ensuring the gate was locked, shut myself in for the night.

8

Even though our walk the day before was shorter, Scooter and I woke early for our walk. We walked along the Malecón, stopping to visit with other dogs and their owners. Farther down, I heard familiar laughter. It was Freddie, and he was with that same woman from the other night. She had her arms wrapped around him and was practically falling all over him. Even in the shade, she wore big sunglasses, reminding me of another diva. They were completely engrossed in each other, so I crossed over to the grassy area to access the street. I wasn't in the mood to chat with him or be rebuffed by her yet again. Maybe she thought I was encroaching on her territory. As I made my way on the street, I saw Suzy jogging with the two dogs. My head swiveled back to the pair who were oblivious to others. I apologized for cutting through a group of people playing some kind of game with balls and met up with Suzy.

I took deep breaths. "Suzy, I wanted to catch up with you. How are you?" I tried blocking her view, but she saw the pair anyway.

"Excuse me." She sidestepped me easily, and I trotted behind her, feeling a bit like a mother hen. I wouldn't let

Freddie humiliate her in public. "Freddie! I wanted to let you know everything's taken care of with the money. I don't need your help anymore." She pointed toward the woman. "Rose will put up the funds for me on the investment."

"What?" He sputtered. "I thought we had an agreement."

The woman turned her back to me and cooed at him. "Freddie, I must help this young lady. It's the least I can do. In return, she's offered me twenty percent to use my money. How sweet is that?"

I tried to get closer to the group, but Scooter kept barking and pulling on the leash. "What's the matter with you?" I bent down and tried to calm him.

Freddie dropped Rose's arm. He turned to Suzy. "That's nuts. I'll do it for nothing!"

Suzy touched his arm, "You're so thoughtful, Freddie. I could never ask you to do that."

"Okay, ten percent. Happy?"

Suzy lowered her head in thought. "I don't know. I'd need the money today."

"I'll go right now. You can send me the transfer information." He moved closer to her. "I only want to help. You know that, don't you?"

"Freddie, you're such a gift. Rose has already agreed, though."

He turned to Rose. "When are you able to get the funds, because I can access them in a few minutes as soon as I get back to my house?"

Rose turned to Suzy, "Well, it could take me at least a day—"

Freddie puffed up his chest, "See, we can do this a lot quicker."

"Well, I don't have the contract paperwork with me. So we'd have to get that done. We certainly want everything on the up and up. Wait—" She rummaged through her bag. "I have this, and it's basically what I had planned to take to the notary."

Rose said, "Can I see that, please? I used to be a legal assistant."

Suzy handed her the paper, and Rose spoke, "Let's see, this says you'll provide Freddie with the return of his funds plus a bonus of ten percent or the amount of $100,000 of the proceeds for—"

"Sounds good to me." He smiled. "Should I sign it now?"

Suzy signed the document, as did Freddie. I started to speak, but Suzy gave me a strange look, so I remained silent. No way that would hold up in a court of law. It stunned me. Had Suzy been a con artist all along, and I'd failed to see it? My mind raced as I tried to figure out what to do. In the states, I could have contacted the police, but here in Mexico, I was at a loss.

Suzy put the paper back in her bag. "Thank you, Freddie. For everything."

Without another word, Freddie sprinted away. The woman followed swiftly behind him before I could speak to her. Only Suzy remained, a big smile on her face. "Have to run, Viviane. Let's talk later." Without another word, she jogged off with the dogs, leaving me wondering what had just happened.

9

————

Sixty years old. Even though today was my birthday, I felt no different. Shouldn't I feel wiser? Something? The only thing I felt was I needed to pee. After making coffee, I checked messages of cheer and happy wishes from my family and friends. After taking Scooter for his morning walk, I treated myself to donuts from Dona's. Perry walked up to where I sat on a curb. "Good morning. If I recall correctly, today's your birthday. Feliz cumpleaños!"

"Gracias. Are you getting donuts too? Want to join me?"

"Sounds like a plan. Back in a jiff."

I took a bite of the sugary twist. Good thing I didn't have a donut store this close to my place back home. I'd be as big as a house. We ate our donuts and drank our coffee in silence before I bid him goodbye. I had made an appointment at the spa where I would pamper myself with a facial, manicure, and pedicure. As I waited for my esthetician, Marva arrived. She spotted me but went to the desk to check in.

Returning, she sat down next to me on the red sofa. "Hello, I believe you were at the last writers' group meeting?"

"Yes, I'm Viviane." I folded my hands in my lap.

She nodded. "You should let me read for you sometime."

"Thanks, I—"

"Don't believe in it." She smiled, but it disappeared quickly. Freddie was walking outside, and Marva immediately sprung up. "Freddie. You should have let me read for you. Your surprise is at hand."

He shook his head and swatted his hand toward her in dismissal.

"Senora, senora?" I glanced up at her. "Oh yes, sorry." I nodded at Marva and followed the woman to a room. On the way, she asked me to pick out a color for my nails. The various hues brought to mind how easily you could change your appearance simply by picking a soft peach or a dramatic red. I went with a bright orange for my toes and the peach for my fingernails. A while later, I emerged from the salon and made my way home. I'd be meeting Suzy to celebrate our birthdays together. After applying mascara, a touch of eyeliner and shadow, along with a new coral lipstick, I gazed at the woman in the mirror. I pointed, "You and I have been through a lot, haven't we? Sixty years now, can you believe it? I don't know about you, but I feel like I'm still in my forties." The woman continued to stare at me. Ugh, you know you've officially rounded the bend when you speak to your reflection like they're another person. I turned left and then right. With my new, updated hairstyle from Edith, a fun outfit, new makeup, and accessories, I felt like a new woman. And that's when it hit me.

Arriving at the restaurant, Suzy waved to me. Although I responded with a wave, I walked over to where the woman from yesterday sat at a corner table with her sunglasses on, even though the sun was now setting. I sat down. "Hello, Margaret."

She took off her sunglasses. "Viviane."

"What are you playing—" My question went unanswered as Suzy laid a hand on my shoulder and Rose, I mean,

Margaret slipped her sunglasses back on her face as Freddie stormed towards us.

His demeanor was menacing as he spat at Suzy. "Where is it? Where's my money?"

"I have no idea what you're talking about."

He shook his finger at her, "Don't lie to me. You took my money. Where is it?" His voice cracked with evident desperation.

Suzy crossed her hands in front of her. With measured words, she replied, "I'm sorry. I didn't take anything. You gave money to a very needy charity in Chapala. It's for battered women. You know, women who've been taken advantage of by men." She sat back and crossed her arms.

His mouth dropped open. "You're not going to get away with this!"

"Really?"

He turned to Rose; I mean Margaret, maybe her actual name was Rose… whoever she was. He yelled, "Are you in on this?"

"Whatever do you mean, Freddie? Suzy told me about a women's shelter in need, and I told her I'd be happy to contribute."

He shoved his hands through his hair. "I'll… I'll get you for this."

"Get me for what? You transferred funds into a charity's bank account. What are you going to "get me" for, huh?" She waved to the waiter. "Senor, please, this man is bothering us." Two waiters came over and escorted Freddie to the door. He shucked them off and sat down on a bench, his head in his hands.

I turned to Suzy. "What is going on?"

She looked at Margaret, who'd removed the glasses, but not the wig and hat. "Gran?"

"Gran?" I pointed to Margaret, and just like that, pieces fell into place. How Suzy had known Scooter's name. They'd named Suzy after her grandmother, Suzanne. The pieces of paper stuck in the gate to warn me to stay away from Freddie. Why Scooter had gone crazy the other day when next to Margaret. She looked different, but he could still tell it was her.

"Drink?" Margaret waved to a waiter and ordered margaritas for the table. "I have a dear friend named Olivia. She fell for him, and he proposed marriage. Of course, that's what he always does. Then he needs to borrow some money. Of course, it starts out small. He repays it, and then he goes for more. He got her entire life savings. She's moving back to Texas to live with her daughter now."

"That's horrible! I feel terrible for your friend."

"It wasn't just my friend, though. He sees this area as his hunting ground. I was visiting her in Chapala, and she saw him. Though he had been calling himself something else then. He changes his name and his appearance a bit, and then he's on to the next prey. The problem is the women, his targets, were ashamed. They didn't want to tell anyone that they'd been a fool. That's why he's been getting away with it for so long."

I thought back to the writers' group. I realized the woman's expression I'd seen aimed at Mildred hadn't been anger; it had been pity. "You told me Marva had also dated him?"

"Yes, but she caught on right away. She tried to warn Mildred, but she just thought Marva was jealous since he'd dumped her. After we got talking to other ladies, more admitted that he'd taken money from them too. Some negligible amounts and others, like my friend, a lot more. We knew we had to stop him. When Suzy said she was coming here, we started working on our plan."

I turned to Suzy. "Did you come in the house one night?"

She shrugged her shoulders. "Sorry about that, but Gran

forgot the wig. We'd worked too hard on her appearance, and we couldn't find anything, so I had to get it."

Margaret said, "I didn't want to draw you into this, but then you met Freddie. Also, I saw you all having dinner. It worried me that you'd be sucked in by his charms or throw off our plans. Sorry about that."

I glanced over at the bench where Freddie had sat, but he was no longer there.

"I couldn't leave Suzy to fend him off by herself either. I had to keep an eye on her, and we were going to back off if it got too dangerous."

Laughter spilled from my lips. "So that was the reason for the garden shears hunt!"

Margaret shrugged, "I had to keep you out of the house while Suzy was in my room, grabbing the wig."

I took a swig of my drink. "I have to say, for my first house sit, this has been a lot more exciting than I thought it would be. But what about Italy?"

"I'm still going to Italy, but next week. This way, all my friends would say I had gone to Italy. I tried to stay away from any place that might recognize me and only venture out when I needed to be seen. I was Plan B in case the original plan with Suzy didn't work out. To be honest, it surprised me that he fell for it so easily since he's done so much of the same thing himself. Compared to him, we're amateurs. However, we had something better." She patted Suzy's hand. "A young woman. He simply thought she was just another gullible female. He never even considered that women could steal from him."

"Where are you staying?"

"In the same place Suzy's staying. I've just been careful not to let anyone see me go in or out."

"I feel sorry for those women." I shook my head at how easy it was to be fooled by someone like Freddie.

"Yes, but hopefully, this will stop him. There's not much

we can do here. Most of the women won't come forward, but this will be a good lesson. We had to figure out the amount that would be enough bait, but not more than he had. Believe it or not, we've been working on this for quite a while."

I lifted my glass. "I offer a toast to you. Well done!"

We clinked glasses. Over dinner, they explained that they'd gone to the women, and all had agreed that the money should go to women in need. Even Olivia, who'd pretty much lost everything, wanted the money to go to a women's charity. She knew it would be the safest thing for Suzy as no money ever came to her. We left the building and were walking up the road when Freddie appeared again. He moved toward Suzy, who gasped as he grabbed her arm. "You *will* give me back my money."

"Sounds like it's not your money at all. You're a thief." I regretted the words as soon as I spoke.

"Are you in on this too?" He pulled Suzy along as he strode over to me.

"I, I…"

"Let her go." A male voice spoke.

Freddie turned toward the sound. As he did Suzy pulled away from his grasp and ran to Margaret.

Perry stepped from the darkness, and with one solid punch, Freddie lay sprawled on the ground.

Marva walked to where he lay sprawled on the cobblestones. "Surprise!"

A FEW WEEKS LATER, I BID GOODBYE TO MARGARET, SUZY, AND Scooter. Freddie had been ostracized as word spread of what he'd been doing, and everyone avoided him everywhere he went. With no money, he'd put his house on the market and left without a word. I hoped he'd learned his lesson, but I feared that he would only go somewhere else and start over with his scheming ways. For now, though, the women had won. The charity had helped twenty more women in their shelter that had expanded, and others had begun work training. I hugged Margaret and Suzy, and we agreed to keep in touch. Perry had extended another donut date should I return, and I'd replied with, "I may take you up on that offer."

As I reached the airport, I received a message of confirmation on another housesit. Just wait until I told my daughter. This time I'd be going to England. What could go wrong there?

~

CONTINUE READING THE *VIVIANE'S ADVENTURES MYSTERIES* series with Book One, *Deception in Dartmoor*.

VIKKI WALTON HATES WRITING SHORT BIO BLURBS, BUT IN A nutshell, loves living in Colorado, gardening, walking, travel, and Dona's donuts. You can check out her books at **www. vikkiwalton.com** or purchase her books wherever fun, light-hearted mysteries are sold.

VENDORS AND VILLAINS

ANGELA K. RYAN

1

"Thank you for shopping at *Just Jewelry*. We hope to see you again soon!" twelve-year-old Emma Miller said to a woman after ringing up her purchase of a Fair Trade bracelet.

The customer winked at Emma, then smiled at Connie Petretta, who was the owner of the shop that featured Fair Trade jewelry and Connie's handcrafted creations. The customer left the store with a smile on her face. Emma's enthusiasm was *definitely* good for business.

"Are you sure you don't mind having Emma help you in the store after school next week?" Elyse asked Connie. Elyse was Emma's mother and one of Connie's close friends. "When Emma found out her babysitter had to take the next ten days off for a family emergency, she begged me to allow her to come here after school. But if it's too much for you, just let me know. She is old enough to stay alone for a couple of hours after school, especially since she doesn't need to be driven to any extracurriculars this week."

"It's no problem at all," Connie said, putting her arm around Emma's shoulders. "It will be the perfect week for her to be here. I'm organizing a raffle, and I can use the extra help."

Emma's eyes widened. "Really? What's the raffle for?"

"It's a fundraising raffle for the expansion of an orphanage in Kenya. I've told you about my good friend, Dura…"

"The one who taught you how to make jewelry when you lived in Africa?" Emma asked. Connie had done a two-year term of volunteer service after college in Kenya.

"That's the one. Not only is she a dear friend, but she is also one of my best Fair Trade artisans. She and her team created a beautiful necklace to be raffled off. As a result of an earthquake, there were ten children orphaned in Dura's village, and the orphanage doesn't have enough beds to take in the children. If we can raise five thousand dollars, we could fund a small expansion."

"It's settled then," Grace, Connie's neighbor and a part-time employee, said. "I am happy to pick Emma up after school next week and bring her to the shop."

"That's very generous of you," Elyse said.

Emma was practically walking on air. "I can't wait to get to work selling raffle tickets."

"We certainly have our work cut out for us if we want to raise five thousand dollars as quickly as possible," Connie said. "I'd like to do the drawing a week from Saturday so they can start construction ASAP, but to do that, I'll need another plan besides just selling tickets in the shop. Business is slow in September in Sapphire Beach, since most of the snowbirds and tourists are still up north."

"Emma and I can sell some tickets to people we know," Elyse suggested.

"And I'm sure the jewelry-making class will do the same," Grace said.

"That's a good start. But if we charge $5 per ticket, which I think is a fair price, we will need to sell one thousand tickets.

And if we can raise a little extra, we can also fund a ribbon-cutting party for the children."

"Is that the necklace?" Elyse asked, pointing to a handcrafted necklace with multiple strands of colorful beads interspersed with metallic beads, which Connie displayed on the circular checkout counter in the middle of the store. "It's exquisite."

"It really is," Connie said. "Dura and the other women on her team worked tirelessly on this necklace, giving up lunch breaks and evenings to get it to us in record time. I don't want to let them or the children down."

"I will say a prayer that we find a way to sell one thousand tickets this week," Emma said.

Grace clasped her hands together in an exaggerated motion. "From your lips to God's ears, sweetie."

Ginger, the chestnut and white Cavalier King Charles Spaniel who unofficially came with the Gulf-front condo Connie inherited from her Aunt Concetta last year, came trotting out from the back of the store where her doggie bed was located. She looked up at Connie with pleading brown eyes.

Connie had to laugh. "I think this sweet girl is reminding me that it's time for her walk."

Elyse stooped down and scratched the top of Ginger's head. "On that note, we'll head out. I'm showing a house to a very high-maintenance client at 3:30, and Emma has homework. Dealing with impossible-to-please clients is my least favorite part of being a realtor."

"Will Emma be okay at home alone today and tomorrow?" Connie asked. "She is welcome to stay here if she'd prefer."

"She'll be fine," Elyse said as they were leaving. "I'm picking up Victoria at daycare at 5:00, so she won't be alone for long." Victoria was a little girl the Millers hoped to adopt.

When Connie returned from walking Ginger, Grace left for the day. Soon after, her other employee, Abby Burns, who was a student at nearby Florida Sands University, arrived for her evening shift. Connie spent the rest of the afternoon creating jewelry to build up her inventory for the busy season, while Abby served the occasional customer. The store had only been open since April, so Connie wasn't sure how much merchandise she'd need come January. But once the snowbirds returned and tourist season hit in southwest Florida, she didn't anticipate having much time for replenishing her stock.

At 7:00, she taught her Thursday evening jewelry-making class, and her students enthusiastically agreed to sell as many raffle tickets as they could over the next week.

The following morning, Connie and Ginger headed into the shop a little early. Connie relished mornings in downtown Sapphire Beach. She took advantage of the tranquility and brought Ginger for a leisurely walk before a long day in the store. As they strolled along the nearly empty downtown streets, the relaxing sound of waves rhythmically crashing on the beach just a couple of blocks away soothed her soul.

After returning to *Just Jewelry*, Connie settled in behind the large oak table, which she used for jewelry making and teaching her classes. She continued working on a gold and brown multi-strand necklace. Grace arrived shortly after and took care of the occasional customer, while Connie worked diligently.

At 3:00, Emma came bounding into the store, with Elyse trailing a few steps behind, as she struggled to catch up with her daughter's speedy pace.

Connie stood to greet Emma, who impatiently looked over her shoulder. Once they were both in the store, Emma finally delivered her news. "Mom and I just stopped by Our Lady, Star of the Sea Church so I could sign up for a field trip, and I told Fr. Paul all about our fundraising project. He told me that the parish is having a craft fair tomorrow on the church grounds, and he said he would donate a booth so that we could sell raffle tickets. He said to tell you that you could sell your Fair Trade jewelry, too, since it's for a good cause. All you have to do is call the church office by the end of the day to reserve a booth."

"The fair is a parish fundraiser," Elyse interjected. "Usually, there is a charge for the vendor booth, and vendors donate a percentage of their sales to the parish, but Fr. Paul said that since the proceeds from your tickets are going to such a worthy cause, and your Fair Trade jewelry supports workers in impoverished communities, he would donate the booth and waive the church's percentage. I tried to tell Emma not to get too excited, because I didn't know if you'd be able to be away from the store until 4:00 on a Saturday."

"Of course she can," Grace said. "Connie, this is a wonderful opportunity. I'll cover the store until you return."

"Then it's settled," Connie said. "Emma, you're a genius. I don't know why I didn't think of that myself."

2

_____

After swinging by the Millers' home on Saturday morning to pick up Emma, Connie stopped at *Just Jewelry* to gather the prize necklace, raffle supplies, and an assortment of jewelry from the store's Fair Trade section to sell at the fair and to bring Ginger to the store so she could stay with Grace. Shortly after, they arrived at the expansive parking lot behind Our Lady, Star of the Sea Church and checked in at the registration table.

"Welcome," came a friendly voice from behind the table. "May I have your name?"

"My name is Connie Petretta, and this is my assistant, Emma. We're from *Just Jewelry*."

The woman consulted the list in front of her. "Yes, here we are," she said, putting a check mark next to Connie's name. "Your booth is number twenty-two. It's about halfway down that row right there," she said, pointing to the second of two long rows of booths.

"I'm heading that way," a man standing behind the check-in lady said.

"Just follow Ken. He's the man."

Ken shook his head and laughed. He took one of the cases

Connie was carrying and walked Connie and Emma to booth number twenty-two.

"I'm in charge of grounds and maintenance for the church. If you have any questions or concerns, just look for me," he said, placing the case behind their booth.

After setting up a selection of Fair Trade merchandise, Connie proudly placed the prize necklace on a rosewood display and featured it prominently. If she was to meet her goal of selling one thousand tickets this week, she would need to put a serious dent in that goal today.

Connie and Emma stepped back to admire their display and gave each other a high five. Then Connie glanced around at the other booths, which held crafts of every kind – quilts, body scrubs, soaps, lotions, candles, and even Christmas ornaments. The craft fair was such a wonderful idea for a fundraiser. Local crafters could get some business during a slow season while the parish raised funds for its various programs.

"Ethan! Harry! Someone is going to trip over these backpacks."

Connie jerked her head toward a woman with wavy, dark hair, which fell just above her shoulders. She was reprimanding two boys.

"I'm sorry. I didn't mean to startle you," the woman said. "My name is Janet, and these are my nephews, Ethan and Harry. I'm sorry that their backpacks found their way behind your booth. We are in the booth next to yours, and it appears our stuff is spilling over."

Connie scanned Janet's booth, which was filled with handmade candles. It would be a challenge to not purchase something from every table.

"No problem," Connie said, introducing herself and Emma.

"Hi Ethan," Emma said to the older boy, who looked to be about Emma's age. The two explained that they went to school together and had been on the same beach volleyball team the previous spring.

"And how old are you, Harry?" Connie asked.

"Eight," he said with a broad smile that revealed a missing front tooth.

"Well, I'm sure the two of you will be a great help to your aunt," Connie said.

"Ethan and Harry are staying with me this week, because their older sister, Mia, got a concussion playing Lacrosse with a friend and needs some peace and quiet to recover. Staying still and keeping silent are not exactly Ethan's and Harry's strengths." Janet handed the boys some cash. "Why don't you two try to find a get-well gift for Mia while I finish setting up."

The boys accepted their aunt's money with a quick *thank you* and ran off.

As they were talking, a few of the other vendors browsed Connie's jewelry, admiring the necklace to be raffled off. Before the craft fair even opened at 10:00 AM, Connie and Emma had already sold a handful of tickets. Emma confidently took the lead and informed customers about the fundraising project. She was a natural. Connie snapped a picture of her young friend in action and texted it to Elyse. The day was off to a good start.

A steady stream of customers kept Connie and Emma busy all morning. Nearly everyone who attended the craft fair stopped by their booth to admire the prize necklace, and nobody could resist Emma's sales pitch. In the early afternoon, Connie counted the tickets sold. She was thrilled to learn they had already sold just over four hundred tickets. They were well on their way to meeting their goal of one thousand tickets sold. Until her tense shoulders began to relax, Connie hadn't realized how much pressure she had been feeling.

With renewed enthusiasm, Connie tucked away the cash

and credit card receipts in a money belt fastened around her waist for safekeeping. She wasn't taking any chances.

At 1:00, Elyse came with some sandwiches for Connie and Emma.

"You are a lifesaver," Connie said. "I completely forgot to bring lunch and was just contemplating whether I should run out or not."

"I'll watch the booth while you two eat," Elyse said. "You've earned a break."

Connie and Emma pulled their grey folding chairs back from the booth so they could eat in peace, while Elyse sold raffle tickets and the occasional piece of jewelry. As Connie was finishing her sandwich, a man with light brown hair that was graying around the temples wandered over to the booth. He and Elyse talked for a moment, then Elyse motioned for Connie to come over.

"Connie, this gentleman would like to purchase the prize necklace. I told him it wasn't for sale, but he insisted on speaking with the owner."

The man extended his hand to Connie, who shook it politely. "My name is Stanley. My wife and I will be celebrating our twenty-fifth wedding anniversary, and I would love to buy her this necklace as a gift. She would absolutely love it."

"I'm sorry," Connie said. "I can't sell it to you. We are raffling it off to raise money for an orphanage."

"Well, that's perfect. You just name the price," he said, pulling out his wallet. "I love donating to a worthy cause."

Connie shot Elyse a frustrated glance, then returned her attention to Stanley. "Unfortunately, I really can't. We have already sold more than four hundred tickets, and the winner will be expecting to win this particular necklace." Connie handed him her business card. "If you don't see anything else you like here, we have a much larger selection at my shop. I would be more than happy to help you choose another piece of jewelry for your wife."

Anger flashed in Stanley's eyes as he hastily stuffed the card into his wallet. "You're making a big mistake. I think you're going to regret that decision."

After he left, Connie rolled her eyes at Elyse and Emma, who came over after finishing her lunch.

"That was strange," Emma said.

"Very strange," Elyse agreed.

Connie wolfed down the rest of her sandwich, while Elyse and Emma ran the booth. When she finished, Elyse gave Connie the cash and receipts she had collected. "Here, put this in your belt right away," she said, discreetly motioning toward Ken, who was talking to one of the other vendors. "Keep a close eye on your money. I'm not sure everyone here can be trusted."

Connie glanced over at Ken. "Why would you say that? Ken seems really nice."

"Just between you and me, I happen to know that Ken has a police record. He served time for breaking and entering. You can't take any chances with those funds, not matter how remote. They are slated for an important cause."

"Even if that's true, I doubt Ken would steal from a church fair," Connie said. "Besides, Fr. Paul is a good judge of character. He wouldn't have hired him if he couldn't be trusted."

"You're probably right, but just the same, you can't be too careful."

Connie tightened the money belt around her waist. Normally, she wouldn't pay much attention to such remarks, but Elyse's husband, Josh, was a detective with the Sapphire Beach Police Department.

Tickets continued to sell consistently all afternoon, so as the fair drew to a close, Connie again counted the tickets sold. They just surpassed nine hundred. Between the tickets sold in the store and those her jewelry-making class had promised to sell, they should easily surpass one thousand tickets.

Connie broke the good news to Emma. "I couldn't have done this without you," Connie said to Emma, who was beaming with satisfaction.

"Since the drawing isn't until next Saturday, that will give us a chance to sell even *more* tickets in the shop this week. I can't wait to tell Dura that it looks like we will have enough money for the orphanage expansion."

"And don't forget the ribbon-cutting party for the children," Emma enthusiastically reminded her.

Their conversation was interrupted by a tapping sound, followed by the words, "testing, testing, testing." Connie turned to find Fr. Paul Fulton, who was standing between the two rows of booths with a microphone in hand and attempting to get everyone's attention.

"I would like to thank each and every one of you for participating in the parish's annual craft fair." He specifically thanked all those who organized the fair, especially Ken and his volunteers, as well as the vendors and attendees. Then Fr. Paul then added, "I'd also like to highlight a very special project that Connie Petretta and her young assistant, Emma Miller, are spearheading. Connie, would you like to tell everyone about it?"

Connie headed toward Fr. Paul, taking Emma's hand, and pulled her along. "How would you like to talk about our project?" Connie whispered into Emma's ear as they stood next to the priest.

Emma hesitated.

"You can do this. Just tell everyone what you've been telling the people who come by the booth."

Emma timidly took the microphone from Fr. Paul. Her first few words were shaky, but once she started talking, her initial shyness vanished. Like a pro, she told her listeners about the orphanage project and the raffle. She invited those who hadn't yet visited their table to stop by.

Emma's listeners smiled as young Emma spoke her heart out about the orphanage and the importance of the expansion.

Out of the corner of Connie's eye, she noticed a woman nervously pacing in front of *Just Jewelry's* booth. A few seconds later, another woman tapped her on the shoulder and ushered the first woman around the church and out of site. Apparently, Janet had noticed the woman's peculiar behavior as well, because when Connie and Janet made eye contact, she shrugged.

When Emma finished talking, they returned to the booth to greet a last-minute rush of customers due to Emma's speech. It wasn't until after they sold a few tickets that someone asked to see the necklace being raffled off. Connie gestured to the spot in front of her, where the necklace should have been.

No!

She frantically searched the display, in case it had become hidden behind another jewelry display, then hunted all around the booth. The necklace was nowhere to be found.

3

—————

"Connie, where's the necklace?" Emma asked, her mouth hanging open as she watched Connie desperately search.

Connie swallowed hard. "I don't know, honey. It's missing."

After realizing the necklace was gone, some of Connie's remaining customers assumed the raffle would be canceled and gave Connie a small donation anyway before departing.

Janet shifted her attention from a customer to the activity around Connie's booth. "What's all the commotion?" she asked from behind her table.

"The prize necklace is missing," Emma cried. "What are we going to do?"

Janet joined Connie and Emma as they continued their panic-stricken search. They searched everything, including their personal possessions, in case it had been knocked into someone's bag. Janet even insisted on looking in her nephews' backpacks, since they kept finding their way to Connie's booth, but there was still no sign of the necklace.

As Connie and Emma stood looking at one another in

shock, Elyse returned. It was after 4:00, and the craft fair had officially ended.

They quickly apprised Elyse of the situation.

Connie ran a hand through her hair. "What am I going to do? I have sold nearly a thousand raffle tickets for a necklace I no longer have."

"What kind of person would steal from orphans?" Janet asked, shaking her head.

"Couldn't you raffle off another necklace that Dura made in place of the one that was stolen?" Elyse asked.

"I suppose I could, but everyone who purchased a ticket did so to win that particular necklace. Dura and her artisans worked their hearts out to create it. Plus, I'd lose credibility if I ever decided to do another raffle. No," Connie said with a resolute shake of her head. "I have to figure out who stole this necklace."

"You can stop by the police station and fill out a report," Elyse said. "But, unfortunately, the likelihood of recovering it is low."

Connie let out a deep sigh. "I was so fixated on keeping the money safe," she said, patting the money belt around her waist, "that I guess I took my eyes off the necklace."

"When was the last time you saw it?" Elyse asked.

"I had just shown it to a customer when Fr. Paul called us up to say a few words, so it had to have been taken while we were up there with Fr. Paul." Connie pointed to where she and Emma had stood.

"While Emma was speaking, everyone's eyes were on her, including mine," Janet said. "Whoever stole it must have taken advantage of the distraction."

"I agree," Connie said with confidence. "I don't recall seeing it when we returned to the booth."

"Did you notice anything unusual while you were up there?" Elyse asked. "You had a unique vantage point."

Connie looked at Janet. "There were those two women

who made a mad dash for their car while Emma was speaking."

"Yes, I remember," Janet said. "That *was* really odd. I know one of the women. Her name is Rebecca Tyson. I said 'hello,' but she barely acknowledged me. She's not usually rude, so she must have had something on her mind."

"Do you know how I can find her?" Connie asked. "I'd like to talk to her. Even if she didn't take it, she may have seen something."

She works at a high-end boutique in downtown Sapphire Beach. Let me think.... Oh, yes, it's called *Butterfly Boutique*."

Connie searched her mind. "Yes, I know the one. It's a few streets over from *Just Jewelry*."

"I hate to bring it up, but given his police record, you should also talk to Ken, the church maintenance guy," Elyse suggested. "It will have to wait, though. I saw him pulling out of the front parking lot as I was arriving."

"That would have been right after the necklace was stolen," Connie said. "Why would he have left before the fair ended? He was in charge of logistics and there's still a lot of clean-up work to do."

"Let's find out," Elyse said. She called out to a volunteer wearing a blue staff t-shirt who was passing by. "Excuse me. Did Ken leave already?" she asked.

"Yes. He had a prior engagement, so we volunteers are handling clean-up. My name is Kelly. Is there something I can help you with?"

"Unfortunately, an expensive necklace was stolen from my booth, and I wanted to see if he saw anything suspicious," Connie said.

"Oh my, I'm so sorry. What a shame. If you give me a description of the necklace, I can call you if it turns up."

Connie gave her a description and left her phone number, but she was not optimistic.

"Janet, is there anyone else besides Rebecca you noticed by my booth while Emma and I were up front?"

"No, I was watching Emma."

"I saw that man who came by the table earlier," Emma said. "The one who wanted to buy the necklace."

"That's right," Connie said. "Good memory, Emma. I saw him, too. He hung around the table for a few minutes, but then he was gone before we got back."

With a heavy heart, Connie packed her remaining merchandise, while Elyse and Emma assisted.

"I'm so sorry, Connie," Elyse said. "Are you going to tell Dura right away?"

Connie let out a deep sigh. "The raffle drawing isn't scheduled for another week. Maybe I can figure out who stole it by then. But if I can't find it by the end of the week, I'll have to inform her."

"Too bad Zach is on vacation," Elyse said. "Otherwise, I'm sure he'd do his best to help you." Zach was the only other detective, besides Josh, at the Sapphire Beach Police Department. He and Connie had gone out in March and were planning another date as soon as their schedules permitted.

"He picked a fine time to visit his family," Connie said.

Connie and Janet also exchanged phone numbers, in case Janet remembered anything later that could help.

When they finished packing, Connie headed straight back to *Just Jewelry* to relieve Grace and catch her up on the day's happenings. Abby was also just arriving for her evening shift.

"I can't believe someone would steal from orphans," Grace said. "That's a new low. If there's anything I can do to help you find the necklace, let me know."

"Me, too," Abby said. "If anyone has the sleuthing skills to get to the bottom of this, it's you."

On Sunday morning, Connie went to the 7:00 Mass, so she would be on time to open the store at 9:00. Grace arrived at

10:30, with two coffees in hand, as was her Sunday morning habit.

"I'm going to stop by *Butterfly Boutique* to see if I can catch Rebecca and ask her a few questions," Connie said when they had finished their coffee.

There weren't many customers in the store yet, so Connie easily spotted Rebecca organizing a clothing rack and talking to a co-worker. She pretended to be browsing until Rebecca was alone.

Then Connie approached the woman. "Hi, my name is Connie Petretta. I own *Just Jewelry*, a few streets over.

Rebecca smiled. "Yes, you have a beautiful store."

"I stopped by, because I had a booth at Our Lady, Star of the Sea's craft fair yesterday. We were selling raffle tickets for a handmade necklace to raise funds for an orphanage and, unfortunately, it was stolen around 4:00."

Rebecca furrowed her brow. "Oh, yes, I remember seeing the necklace. I'm so sorry to hear it was stolen, but I don't know what that has to do with me."

Connie took a deep breath. "There's no easy way to say this. I noticed you and another woman hastily leaving the fair around the time the necklace was stolen."

The woman placed her hand on her chest. "I certainly hope you're not accusing me or my friend of stealing it. We would never do such a thing!"

Since being direct wasn't working, Connie backpedaled. "Of course not. I was just wondering if you saw anything unusual. Whoever stole it might have been exiting the parking lot around the same time as you. Or perhaps you saw something while you were standing near my booth."

Rebecca relaxed a little. "I'm sorry that this happened, but I'm sure I didn't notice anything unusual. I had to be at work at 4:00 yesterday, and when my friend alerted me to the time, I rushed out to avoid being late."

It sounded like a logical excuse, but that didn't change the fact that Rebecca was one of the last people to be seen near Connie's booth before the necklace disappeared. Since she didn't think she could garner any more information, Connie thanked Rebecca for her time and left.

When Connie got back to *Just Jewelry*, she filled Grace in on her fruitless conversation and took Ginger for a walk by the pier. When she returned, Grace was talking with a woman on the red couch in the shop's seating area.

"Connie, I'd like you to meet someone," Grace said.

"My name is Tess, and I work with Rebecca at *Butterfly Boutique*," the woman said, standing to greet Connie. "I couldn't help but overhear your conversation about the necklace. I have some information that might be useful to you. Rebecca has been acting strangely lately and, despite what she told you, she did not work last night."

4

"What makes you say that Rebecca has been acting strangely?" Connie asked.

Tess hesitated. "I'm only telling you this because I overheard you say that your stolen necklace was for a fundraiser, and I wouldn't be able to live with myself if I didn't pass along what I've observed. I don't know why Rebecca lied to you about working last night, but I've seen her on the phone several times over the past couple of weeks, when she thinks nobody is watching. Each time, as soon as she's seen me, she's stopped talking and abruptly ended the conversation. Rebecca has always been like an open book, so her behavior lately concerns me. She's also been working as many extra shifts as she can get over the past few months."

"Do you think she may be hurting for money?"

"That could be a motive for stealing the necklace," Grace added.

Tess shrugged her shoulders. "I can't say for sure, but there's definitely something strange going on with her."

"If she were having financial difficulties, do you think she would resort to stealing?" Connie asked.

"I wouldn't have thought so, but she hasn't been herself lately. When I overheard her lying about being at work yesterday, I thought you should know." Tess glanced at her watch. "I need to get back to work. I was actually in here last week and bought a raffle ticket, so I know about your project. I'm so sorry that this happened. I certainly hope it's not Rebecca."

Connie smiled. "Thank you. I do, too."

After walking Tess to the door, Connie and Grace returned to the sofa, and Ginger, who had been resting by Connie's feet, hopped onto her lap. Connie stroked her silky fur.

"What are you going to do now?" Grace asked.

"There are a couple of other people I'd like to talk to. There was a customer named Stanley who wanted to purchase the necklace. He was indignant when I told him it was not for sale and told me that I'd regret it if I didn't sell it to him. Janet mentioned that he was hanging out around my table when the necklace disappeared."

"Do you have any way to contact him?" Grace asked.

"He gave me his card in case I changed my mind. I also want to talk to the maintenance guy at Star of the Sea."

"Ken?" Grace asked, surprised. "Do you think he may have seen something?"

"Elyse mentioned that he served time for breaking and entering, but more importantly, she also saw him leaving the church parking lot around the time the necklace was stolen."

"I had no idea about his record," Grace said. "I'm sure Fr. Paul wouldn't have hired him if he was dangerous. He's usually a good judge of character."

Grace was right. But Fr. Paul also had a huge heart. Perhaps he wanted to give Ken a second chance and it backfired. "Still, it's worth a conversation with him. I don't have many leads and we're supposed to draw the winning raffle ticket on Saturday. I have to start somewhere."

When Connie awoke early Monday morning, after a night of tossing and turning, her first thought was of the missing necklace. She dragged herself out of bed, wishing it had all been a bad dream. What could she do to clear her head? She suddenly found herself changing into her bathing suit and heading for her storage closet in the garage to fetch her paddleboard. The Gulf of Mexico was calling her name.

Fastening her paddleboard to its dolly, she wheeled it around the fourteen-story high rise building that she had called home since March, launched it into the crystal-clear water, and paddled along the coastline. When the sunshine and salty air had worked their magic like faithful friends, Connie paddled back to where she had started, feeling completely rejuvenated by her mini-excursion.

Until she arrived at *Just Jewelry* and saw the basket filled to the brim with raffle tickets.

Grace arrived shortly after. "Why don't you try to lose yourself in jewelry-making?" she suggested.

Grace's advice proved to be solid. Connie became absorbed in her work, while Grace handled the occasional customer, and before she knew it, it was 2:30 and time for Grace to pick up Emma.

Less than fifteen minutes later, Grace returned with Emma. Emma had decided she wanted to make a necklace as a get-well gift for Mia, so Connie got her set up at the table. Then she said, "I need a little break. If you ladies can handle the store for a while, I have an errand I'd like to run."

Emma eyed Connie thoughtfully. "Does this have anything to do with the necklace that was stolen?"

Connie had to smile at the girl's perceptiveness. "You caught me. I want to talk to Ken, the maintenance guy from Star of the Sea, since Janet saw him near our booth just before the necklace was stolen."

"Can I come?" Emma asked.

Connie laughed. "I don't think that's a good idea. Your parents would be furious with me."

"Come on," she pleaded. "Even Sherlock Holmes had a sidekick."

"I'll tell you what. If you stay here and help Grace, I will tell you both everything that happened."

Emma looked disappointed but accepted Connie's deal.

Connie drove her silver Jetta to the church and pulled around back, keeping an eye out for Ken along the way. But she didn't see him. After parking behind the church, she walked over a covered bridge that led to a spacious courtyard lined in palm trees, which was between the church and the parish center. She was hoping she wouldn't run into Fr. Paul. He had enough on his plate running such a large parish, and she preferred to get to the bottom of this without involving him.

"Excuse me," she said, waving to capture the attention of a man riding a lawn mower.

The young man, wearing faded blue jeans and a white polo shirt embroidered with a logo containing the name 'Victor and Sons' Landscaping,' stopped and turned off the mower.

"Do you know where I can find Ken?" she asked.

"If he's smart, he's in his air-conditioned office." He pointed to a walkway that led along the side of the parish center. "His office is that way."

Connie entered the building through a glass door and proceeded down a long corridor that was surprisingly dark for such a sunny day. At least the landscaper knew she was looking for Ken. Connie scanned the plaques, which identified the various offices. She finally came across a door that said 'Maintenance,' and knocked.

"Come in."

She opened the door to find Ken leaning back in his chair, staring at the wall.

"Hi, Ken, I'm Connie Petretta. We met at the parish craft fair on Saturday."

His penetrating gaze shifted to Connie. "I figured I'd see you sometime today."

Connie hesitated at his odd greeting, but she pressed on. "I had a vendor booth at the parish craft fair on Saturday, and I noticed you were there."

He eyed her suspiciously. "Yes. One of my volunteers informed me that you lost a necklace."

"I didn't exactly *lose* it," Connie corrected. "It was stolen. Do you know anything about that?"

Ken sneered and clenched his fist.

Connie stepped back, wondering how quick an exit she could make if Ken's temper escalated. "You mean you heard about my incarceration and you wondered if *I* stole it."

Connie felt her cheeks grow warm. "It was a very important necklace," Connie said. "I'm following up every lead and simply wondered if you saw something suspicious while you were working. It was stolen right before you left the fair."

"So, you're thinking I took it, then made a quick getaway."

Connie was at a loss for words.

Ken rolled his eyes. "I don't know anything about your precious necklace. I left the fair early to attend my niece's birthday party. I wasn't anywhere near your booth while you and the little girl were standing with Fr. Paul. In fact, I was tending to the sound system that the microphone was connected to, in plain view of most of the attendees. If I had seen anything suspicious, I would have followed up on it. Fr. Paul even walked me to my car after his announcement to thank me for a successful event. He certainly would have noticed if I swiped any merchandise on my way out." Ken shook his head and let out a sharp breath. "Feel free to verify my alibi."

"That won't be necessary. Thank you for your time."

Connie departed feeling crestfallen and ashamed. She wasn't any closer to discovering who stole the necklace, and she had managed to insult a respected employee of the church.

5

When Connie returned to *Just Jewelry*, she relayed her conversation with Ken to Grace and Emma, as promised.

"At least it wasn't a total waste of time," Grace said. "Now you know it wasn't Ken."

"I'm glad he didn't steal the necklace," Emma said. "He does a lot for us kids at the church. He even set up an obstacle course for us at Bible camp."

Hearing that made Connie feel even worse. She would have to think of a way to apologize to Ken.

"Unfortunately, we still don't know who the thief is," Connie said. "It could be Rebecca or Stanley or someone we're not even thinking of."

"I think you need to get your mind off this so you can return to it with a fresh perspective. Why don't you and Emma go for an ice cream and I'll watch the store," Grace suggested. "There hasn't been much traffic today, anyway."

Connie and Emma looked at each other with broad smiles.

"Works for me. Why don't we get some ice cream cones and bring them to the beach?" Connie suggested. The temperature had climbed into the high eighties, so a cool ice cream and waves crashing on her feet sounded like the perfect way to beat the heat.

Connie and Emma strolled down the street toward *Friendly Scoops*, an ice cream shop by the pier. Connie ordered a mint chocolate chip cone, and Emma opted for bubble gum. They said a quick hello to Emily, the shop's owner, then strolled along the beach at the water's edge.

"I'm so sorry that our fundraiser has turned into such a disaster, Emma," Connie said to her young sidekick. "You worked so hard to make it a success."

Emma shrugged her shoulders. "We should still be able to raise the money that the orphanage needs." Emma had been trying hard since Saturday to mask her disappointment, but Elyse had told Connie that she hadn't been herself since the necklace was stolen. Connie noticed it, too. Her youthful exuberance seemed to have faded a notch. The last thing Connie wanted was for her young friend to become jaded.

However, Emma did make a fair point. They had sold more than nine hundred raffle tickets at the craft fair, in addition to what Connie's jewelry-making students were selling, and the ones that had been sold in the shop. Since Saturday, Connie had been telling customers that the prize would be a handcrafted necklace of their choosing from Kenya, so they were still selling tickets in the shop.

"That's true," Connie said. "But, after all the hard work Dura and her team put into creating it, and for the sake of my credibility for future fundraisers, I'd still feel a lot better if we could find the necklace."

As they were finishing their ice cream cones, Emma's eyes gravitated toward a beach volleyball game taking place a short distance away.

Connie smiled. "Would you like to watch for a few minutes?"

"I'd love to check it out."

"Hey, isn't that Ethan watching from the sidelines?" Connie asked as they got closer to the beach volleyball court.

"Yes, that's definitely him," Emma said. "Let's say hello."

They greeted Ethan and joined him as he watched the game. "Are you here by yourself?" Connie asked.

Ethan nodded. "Harry wanted to stay home. I think he's homesick and worried about Mia. Aunt Janet let me stay here and watch the game while she runs some errands."

Just then, a blue Ford pulled up. The window opened to reveal Janet waving at the three of them. Connie waved back, then Ethan disappeared into the passenger seat.

After a few minutes, Connie and Emma left to return to *Just Jewelry*. Grace was tidying a display while a couple browsed the Fair Trade section. The man looked familiar. It took Connie a minute to realize where she had seen him. It was Stanley, the man who had insisted on purchasing the prize necklace for his wife.

The couple must have felt Connie's stare. Stanley turned around and smiled when he saw her, then brought the woman over. "Connie, this is Kay, my wife. We are on our way to a restaurant to celebrate our anniversary, and we stopped by so she could choose a gift."

"Happy Anniversary," Connie said, with a warm smile.

The woman extended her hand. "I'd like to apologize for my husband's behavior. He told me he tried to purchase a necklace that was meant to be a raffle prize. My Stanley means well, but he doesn't always use the sense that God gave him. When he told me the story, I insisted we come to the store so I could pick out my own gift from your Fair Trade collection. He was right about one thing. I am thrilled that *my* gift will also be a gift to others."

"I personally choose all our artisans," Connie said. "The money they earn from their jewelry allows them to help support their families."

A broad smile spread across Kay's face.

Since opening *Just Jewelry*, Connie was more convinced than ever that most people really did want to make a difference in others' lives. They just didn't always know how. One of the things she loved about carrying Fair Trade products was that she helped provide that opportunity.

"My wife is right. I was out of line," Stanley said as Kay resumed her shopping. It seemed to be his way of apologizing.

"No harm done," Connie said. "Unfortunately, we ran into a problem. Somebody stole the necklace, and if we can't find it by Saturday, we'll have to substitute a different one as the raffle prize." Every time Connie explained the situation, she became nauseous.

Kay rejoined them, holding a necklace from one of Connie's Ecuadorian artisans. "I couldn't help but overhear what you just told my husband. That's horrible."

"Stanley, the necklace was stolen about 4:00," Connie said. "I saw you near our vendor booth about that time. Did you happen to see anything suspicious?" At this point, it seemed unlikely that Stanley stole the jewelry for his wife. It wouldn't make sense to then come to the store to purchase another necklace.

Stanley furrowed his brow. "While you and the little girl were up at the front of the room, I went back to snap a picture of the necklace to show my wife." He pulled out his phone and showed it to Connie. "I'm positive that the necklace was still there when I left, about halfway through her announcement."

Stanley showed Connie the picture. Janet was standing in front of her booth, apparently listening to Emma speak, and her nephews appeared to be playing a game on a tablet behind Janet's booth. Their backpacks were tossed in front of Connie's. Connie suppressed a smile. Janet would be furious at those boys if she knew they left their backpacks at Connie's booth again.

But wait, who was that woman approaching Connie's booth? Only her profile was visible.

"Can I see your phone for a minute, Stanley?"

He handed her the phone, and Connie enlarged the photo. Then she called Emma over to show her. "Who does this look like to you, Emma?"

"I think it's Rebecca," Emma replied.

"So do I," Connie said. "Thank you for showing me this, Stanley. It's very helpful."

After Connie rang up Kay's anniversary gift, the happy couple left arm in arm.

6

Between Rebecca lying about going to work after the craft fair and Stanley's photo of Rebecca poking around Connie's vendor booth just before the necklace was stolen, Connie was determined to find a way to talk to her again. She was now Connie's primary person of interest.

Connie dumped the basket of raffle ticket stubs onto the large oak table, and she and Emma searched them to see if by chance Rebecca had purchased a ticket. If she had, Connie would have her contact information.

But no such luck. So, Connie dove into Plan B. Through some comments and posts that Rebecca had made on the Facebook page of *Butterfly Boutique*, Connie was able to find her profile, which had her last name. Then a quick internet search revealed her home address and phone number. She decided to try calling first, since she didn't want to leave Grace and Emma alone in the shop again.

"Hello." It was Rebecca's voice.

"Hi Rebecca, it's Connie Petretta. We spoke a few days ago."

"Oh, yes, how are you, Connie?" Rebecca sounded less than enthusiastic.

"To be honest, not so well. We still haven't found the necklace that we were raffling off at the fair to raise money for the orphans."

"I'm very sorry to hear that," Rebecca said. "I wish I could help, but I don't know anything about that."

Connie hesitated. Once again, there was no gentle way to say this. "I've been asking around for information, and I was wondering if you could clarify something. I happen to know that you didn't go to work on Saturday night after the fair. I'm wondering why you told me that you did."

An annoyed sigh came through the phone. Connie heard a man's voice in the background, but it was muffled, and she couldn't understand what he said.

"It's okay. I've got this," Rebecca said, apparently to the man.

"Look, Connie, I really don't owe you an explanation of what I do with my time. I'm truly sorry about your fundraiser, but please don't call me again."

Click. Rebecca had hung up on her.

If she was innocent, why was she so short-tempered? Connie was beyond annoyed.

Grace was about to leave, so there was nothing Connie could do about it at the moment. She pushed her conversation with Rebecca out of her mind and focused on making a couple of pairs of earrings, while Emma worked diligently on Mia's necklace.

But once Emma left, she struggled to keep her mind on anything else. This was her most substantial lead. She simply had to pursue it.

Neither Grace nor Abby worked on Tuesdays, so the following day, Connie was alone in the store until Grace dropped Emma off at 2:45. Any more sleuthing would have to wait until the following day, so she tried to put the whole fiasco out of her mind. But, once again, it kept creeping back in.

On Wednesday morning, as soon as Grace arrived for her shift, Connie announced her plan to revisit Rebecca and practically ran out the door. Rebecca could avoid her over the telephone, but it would be much harder to do in person.

After tapping in Rebecca's address, Connie's GPS application led her to a single family home across town. Fortunately, Rebecca didn't live in a gated community, or access to her home would have been a lot trickier. She walked resolutely up a cement walkway that led to the front door. A dog barked aggressively as she approached.

"Quiet now, you big phony," a male voice said good-naturedly, and the dog stopped barking.

The door opened to reveal a kind-looking man wearing khaki pants and a black golf shirt. "May I help you?"

The brown mutt, who sounded ferocious when she approached, stood behind the man, wagging his tail.

"Yes, my name is Connie Petretta. I was hoping to speak with Rebecca."

The man grew annoyed, but Connie had the feeling his annoyance wasn't directed at her. It was more of a general irritation.

He closed the door halfway and turned around. "Rebecca, Connie Petretta is here to talk with you."

"You know I can't come to the door right now," she said.

"Honey, this is beyond ridiculous," he protested. "Just come over here and tell her what happened."

"Rebecca, I just want to know where my necklace is. If you took it, please give it back to me. I promise not to press charges. I just need the necklace back for my fundraiser."

"I won't come to the door," Rebecca insisted.

"Rebecca, please. You're making things worse. There is nothing for you to be ashamed of."

Rebecca's shuffled her way to the door and stood timidly behind her husband. Then she slowly peeked out, revealing her face, bruised, swollen, and wearing a compression bandage.

Connie gasped. "Are you okay? I don't understand. Why didn't you tell me you were in an accident?"

Rebecca looked at the floor and spoke softly. "Because I wasn't. I, um, had a little procedure."

"What Rebecca is trying to tell you is that she had a facelift on Monday. That is why she has been so secretive about her two weeks off from work. My wife may be vain, but I assure you, she is no thief, and she certainly would never steal from orphans. She rushed out of the craft fair on Saturday, because she was late for an appointment with her plastic surgeon. That is why she took two weeks off from work and didn't tell anyone the reason. She was trying to be discreet."

"It's true," Rebecca said. "I didn't want anyone to know what I was doing, so I didn't tell a soul, except my best friend and my husband. I truly am sorry about the necklace, but I would never do such a thing. I was just embarrassed to tell you why I rushed out of the craft fair."

That certainly explained Rebecca's odd behavior and her need to pick up extra shifts at work over the past couple of months. She wasn't hurting for money. She was saving for a facelift.

With great effort, Connie managed to suppress any hint of the laughter that threatened to burst from her mouth. "I apologize for putting you through that, Rebecca," she managed to say. "Your secret is safe with me. I wish you a speedy recovery."

As she drove back to the shop, she burst out laughing at the situation. But her laughter quickly turned to sadness when she realized that, with no remaining leads, the necklace was likely lost forever.

7

On Thursday morning, Connie mentally prepared herself for the likelihood that she would soon have to tell Dura the bad news. She crafted an email, explaining the situation, but instead of sending it, she saved it as a draft. She wouldn't hit the send button until she absolutely had to. There was still a part of her that held out hope that the thief might be discovered. However, it seemed like that would take a miracle, since all her suspects had been cleared – Rebecca, Stanley and Ken – and she was out of leads.

Connie was alone in the store until Grace arrived with Emma after school. Emma placed her backpack on the table and got right to work completing Mia's necklace. Grace wasn't working that day, but she brewed some iced tea for the three of them and sat down to keep them company for a few minutes.

"I'm almost done," Emma said. "I just have to attach the clasp."

As if she were a nurse assisting Dr. Emma in surgery, Connie dutifully handed her the wire cutters and pliers, as needed.

When the necklace was complete, Emma held it up. It was

strung with aqua glass beads, surrounding a shiny silver-plated seahorse pendant in the center.

Connie examined the necklace. "You did a fantastic job. I'm sure Mia will love it."

"I love the beads and pendant you chose," Grace added. "You are becoming quite the artist."

"Ethan and Harry are going home tomorrow, so Mom said she would take me to drop off the necklace tonight. That way Janet can give it to Mia when she brings the boys home."

"It's only Thursday," Connie said. "I thought Ethan and Harry were staying until Saturday."

"Ethan said that Harry is homesick. He hasn't wanted to do anything all week, and his parents are worried about him."

"He's only eight years old," Grace said. "That makes sense."

"True," Connie said, "but he seemed fine at the craft fair."

"Ethan doesn't know what's gotten into him. He told me at school that they've slept away from home before, and he's usually not like that. Ever since they left the fair on Saturday, he's been quiet."

Connie was moving Emma's backpack out of the way when a thought suddenly occurred to her. "Emma, I've never seen a backpack with so many compartments. Can I take a look?"

"Of course," Emma said.

"This reminds me of Ethan's and Harry's backpacks."

"That's because it's the same one. Mine is just a different color," Emma said, carefully wrapping Mia's necklace in tissue paper, then slipping it into a zippered pocket in her backpack.

As soon as Emma did that, Connie had a flash of understanding. Could it be that simple?

"Grace, would you be able to watch the store for a few

minutes, while I bring Emma to Janet's so she can drop off the necklace?"

"It's okay, Connie. You don't have to leave the store. Mom said she'd take me tonight."

"It's not just for that. I have to talk to Janet about something else. I think I might know what happened to the necklace. I'll tell you as soon as I know if I'm right."

"Go," Grace said. "I'll cover the store."

Connie shot off a quick text to Janet to ask if they could stop by. As soon as Janet texted back her address, Emma grabbed the necklace from her backpack, and they were on their way.

Janet lived in a high rise, a short distance from Palm Paradise, which was the condominium building where Connie lived. Janet buzzed them into the lobby, and Connie and Emma took the elevator to the fifth floor. Connie knocked on the door to Janet's apartment, and Janet greeted them with a warm smile.

"Come on in," she said.

Connie nearly tripped over the boys' backpacks, which had been left haphazardly in the foyer.

"I'm so sorry about that," Janet said, throwing the backpacks into the corner. "I've told the boys a million times to keep these out of the way."

Ethan and Harry came out from their room and greeted Connie and Emma.

"That's quite all right," Connie said. "Emma has a gift for Mia that she was hoping you could pass along."

Emma pulled out the necklace and gave it to Janet.

"Emma made it herself in my store," Connie said, bursting with pride for her youngest student. "She chose the beads and pendant herself."

Harry stared at the necklace. "But Mia already *has* a necklace," he protested.

"Honey, a girl needs more than *one* necklace," Janet said. "Mia will love it. It's just her taste."

Harry's reaction further confirmed Connie's suspicion. "Harry, did also you get your sister a necklace as a get-well gift?"

"I don't think so," Janet said. "He would have shown me. He tried to find a gift for Mia at the craft fair, he but didn't see anything he thought she'd like."

"Harry, do you mind if I look in your backpack?" Connie asked.

She didn't wait for Harry to reply. "Yours is the red one, right?"

Harry nodded timidly.

Connie opened the backpack and searched all the hidden pockets. Sure enough, in the last pocket she unzipped, was the prize necklace.

Janet, Ethan, and Emma stood with their mouths open.

Harry ran into the guest bedroom and locked the door.

Janet yelled after him, "Harry, you get out here right now and explain yourself!"

Sobbing came from inside the room.

"Let me try," Connie whispered.

"Harry, it's Connie. I'm not mad at you. I'm just happy to have the necklace back. Can you come out so we can talk?"

"It's okay, Harry," Ethan said. "She's really not mad. Just come out and tell us why you took the necklace."

The doorknob slowly turned and out came Harry with a tear-stained face. Connie gave him a tissue from her purse and led everyone to the living room, where they all took a seat.

As Connie thought back to the past few days, it all made sense. Harry wasn't homesick, his conscience was eating away at him.

"You wanted to get your sister something special as a gift," Connie said. "Is that why you stole the necklace?"

Harry nodded. "Mia looked so sick and scared that I wanted to give her something special to make her feel better. When I heard the necklace was for the children, I didn't think they'd mind."

"Do you understand now why that was wrong?" Connie asked.

"Yes," Harry said. "Because it was to raise money for the orphans. They need it more than my sister. By the time I realized that, it was too late, and I didn't know what to do."

Apparently, confession really *was* good for the soul. Harry looked as though a giant weight had been lifted from his shoulders.

And Connie was elated to have the necklace back.

8
_____

On Saturday morning, Connie arrived at *Just Jewelry*, with Ginger in tow, excited for the raffle drawing scheduled for noon. Connie and Emma had planned a little party for the occasion, so Emma and Elyse arrived at 11:00 to help Connie and Grace set up. Once the finger sandwiches, cookies, and pastries were set out on the table and the iced tea and fresh coffee were brewed, there was nothing left to do but wait for their guests to arrive.

The first to come through the door was Ken. After discovering on Thursday that Harry was the culprit, Connie's top priority the next morning was to pay Ken a visit with a box of pastries and a humble apology. Since the craft fair was one of the major factors in making the raffle a success, and Ken organized the logistics of the fair, she had personally invited him to the raffle drawing.

"Fr. Paul regrets not being able to attend, but he had a wedding this afternoon," Ken said upon arriving. Connie happily took Ken's presence as a sign that all was forgiven.

Janet and her nephews were the next to arrive, along with Mia, who appeared to have recovered from her concussion. She thanked Emma for the necklace, which she was wearing, and apologized for the trouble Harry caused. "I'm sorry for what my little brother did," she said, playfully tousling Harry's hair. "But he's definitely learned his lesson."

Harry nodded vigorously.

"After everything that's happened, we wanted to be here to see this raffle to completion," Janet said. "We are so excited to see who the winner will be."

"It's wonderful to have you all," Connie said. "Mia, I'm so glad you're feeling better."

Next, Connie set up her computer on the table for her final guest, Dura, who was calling in via Skype to attend the drawing.

Amidst all the activity, Emma hopped up when needed to help the occasional customer. After a week of being in the store after school, Emma handled customers like a pro – from greeting them and answering questions to ringing up their purchase. She only occasionally needed Connie's help. Between her retail skills and her growing knowledge of jewelry making, Emma would be running the show in no time.

By noon, everyone was present who was supposed to be, including Dura. The others stood behind Connie so they could see Dura and she could see them.

"It's lovely to meet you, Dura. I'm Grace. Your work is exquisite. It is an honor to sell it here in *Just Jewelry* and to wear it, as well." Grace pointed to a bracelet she had purchased, which Dura had made.

"Thanks to you Grace for all your hard work in selling our creations. It keeps many lovely people employed." Then she added, "Where's the little boy who made such a fine donation?"

"That would be Harry," Connie said, bringing him to the front, where Dura could easily see him. After the necklace was safe and sound, Connie had filled Dura in on what had happened. Connie had also informed Dura that yesterday she received a call from young Harry saying how truly sorry he was for what he had done, and, to make it up to the children, he wanted to donate his birthday money to the orphanage. Harry and Connie hatched a plan where Harry's money would be used for something fun – namely to purchase an array of athletic equipment for the orphanage, as well as candy for each child.

Harry beamed with pride as Dura told him he was the most popular boy at the orphanage. Dura also personally thanked Emma and Ken for all that they did.

"Okay, let's get down to business," Connie said.

Grace had placed all the raffle tickets in a basket and shook them up, before bringing it to Connie.

"Emma, would you do the honors?" Connie asked.

Emma dug her hand deep into the sea of tickets and pulled one out. "Katherine O'Callahan," she read, in a loud, clear voice.

Everyone applauded.

"Let's give Katherine O'Callahan the good news," Connie said. She put her phone on speaker and tapped Katherine's phone number onto her keypad.

"Hello," came a deep, soothing voice through Connie's speakerphone.

"Is this Katherine?" Connie asked.

"Yes, this is Katherine. How can I help you?"

"Hello, Katherine, my name is Connie Petretta. I'm the owner of *Just Jewelry*. My assistant, Emma, has some news for you."

Connie handed the phone to Emma. "Hello, this is Emma, and I'm happy to tell you that you won the raffle for the handcrafted necklace."

"Is this the same young girl who sold me a raffle ticket at the craft fair last Saturday?"

Emma smiled. "Yes, it is."

Connie chimed in. "You can come by the store anytime to pick up your necklace."

"Well, I'm just thrilled. I was admiring that necklace all day last week and hoping that I would win it. Thank you for giving me the good news. I'm in the neighborhood now. I could come by in a few minutes to pick it up if that works for you."

"Perfect. We'll look forward to meeting you. And have we got a story to tell you when you arrive," Connie said, winking at Emma.

$\sim$

DO YOU WANT TO READ MORE OF THE SAPPHIRE BEACH COZY MYSTERY SERIES? Jump right into Book One, **Condos and Corpses**.

ANGELA K. RYAN, AUTHOR OF THE SAPPHIRE BEACH COZY MYSTERY SERIES, writes clean, feel-good stories that uplift and inspire, with mysteries that will keep you guessing.

Read More from Angela K. Ryan
If you enjoyed *Vendors and Villains*, you can download
Vacations and Victims, the free prequel to the **Sapphire Beach Cozy Mystery Series.**
https://landing.mailerlite.com/webforms/landing/c6q6e7

THE AUTHORS

Dianne Ascroft
   www.dianneascroft.com

Ellen Jacobson
   www.ellenjacobsonauthor.com

Tamara Woods
   www.tamarawoodsauthor.com

Sarah Biglow
   www.sarah-biglow.com

Aubrey Elle
   www.authoraubreyelle.com

Beate Boeker
   www.happybooks.de

Adriana Licio
   www.adrianalicio.com

Vikki Walton
    www.vikkiwalton.com

Angela K. Ryan
    https://landing.mailerlite.com/webforms/
landing/c6q6e7

Made in the USA
Coppell, TX
18 November 2020

41605858R00256